The Letter

Ruth Saberton

Createspace First Edition

COPYRIGHT

All characters, organisations and events in this publication, other than those clearly in the public domain, are fictitious and any resemblance to real persons, living or dead, is purely coincidental.

The opinions expressed in this book are solely the opinions of the author and do not represent the opinions or thoughts of the publisher. The author has represented and warranted full ownership and / or legal right to publish all materials in this book.

ISBN: 1983623466
ISBN-13: 978-1983623462

ANTHEM FOR DOOMED YOUTH

What passing-bells for these who die as cattle?
Only the monstrous anger of the guns.
Only the stuttering rifles' rapid rattle
Can patter out their hasty orisons.
No mockeries for them now; no prayers nor bells;
Nor any voice of mourning save the choirs, –
The shrill, demented choirs of wailing shells;
And bugles calling for them from sad shires.
What candles may be held to speed them all?
Not in the hands of boys but in their eyes
Shall shine the holy glimmers of goodbyes.
The pallor of girls' brows shall be their pall;
Their flowers the tenderness of patient minds,
And each slow dusk a drawing-down of blinds.

Wilfred Owen 1917

The War Poems of Wilfred Owen: edited and introduced by Jon
Stallworthy
Chatto & Windus

DEDICATION

This book is dedicated to the memory of my Great-Aunt Ella and her fiancé, Arthur Sidney Bacon. Their sacrifices, and those of an entire generation, will never be forgotten.

PROLOGUE

MAY 1914

On her first night at the Rectory the old dream came again. It began, as it always did, with a moon the colour of honey slanting shadows across the counterpane while the night breeze enticed her out of bed. Somehow, she'd reach the window without her feet touching the floorboards, while her white nightgown billowed behind her like the sail of a stately galleon and bore her into the shadowscape.

In the mysterious way of dreamers, she'd find herself transported to a quiet cove where the waves knew all her secrets, each breaker sighing when the water retreated over rock pools and sucked time-smoothed stones into the depths. The sand was wet and cool beneath her bare feet, yet her footsteps never made prints.

She scarcely saw the cove. Her dreamer's eyes were frantically searching for him – although who he was she didn't know. She only knew that he had to be found and had to be kept safe. Nothing else mattered or would ever matter again. Sometimes she thought she glimpsed him just ahead, in a shimmer of moon-silvered hair and flash of pale limbs wading through the shallows, but no matter how fast she ran she could never catch up – and when she tried to cry out, her words were sewn up tightly inside her throat. It was always the same: no matter how hard she tried to call, he grew further and further out of reach.

She knew that danger lay ahead, not in the greedy currents or the sharp-toothed rocks, but somewhere deeper and unknown. Dread dragged her to her knees and the waves lapped her nightdress, weighing the cotton down.

It was always then that the strange purple clouds drifted across the moon, blotting out light and hope. The woods high on the hill grew as dark as grudges and the water dulled to pewter. She'd fly upwards, high over the cove until the cliff path was just a pale ribbon threaded through the gorse and the heather. The world dipped and span and now there would be heat and a dreadful stench of burnt earth. The sky was ripped with fire and flashes of light; shouting and screaming

i

drowned out the rhythmic crashing of waves, and mud now covered her bare feet. All was wet and cold and cloying. Grave dirt threatened to suck her under, to seal her nose and fill her mouth. It was hard to know what would drown her sooner – the choking clay or the suffocating terror. She was afraid she couldn't reach the person she sought, couldn't pull him back and couldn't save him from the gathering horror.

In the dream she stood paralysed. What she saw she didn't understand, but in her sleep her heart hammered as she stared into the abyss. The limbs of the burnt forest were charred skeletons against the bleeding sky. Sobs were torn from her throat as she pulled her way out of the sucking mud, her hands outstretched as she tried to reach him. But it was pointless: he always remained ahead of her and, every time, she could only watch as the smoke erased him.

The wind blew, cold and spiteful, whipping her away with the ashes. She saw a village cowering beneath a hill, and at the crest of the hill a large mansion house with ivy-blinded windows. Its manicured gardens had become choked with creepers and its smooth lawns had been scraped by rough plough. A ghost, she passed unseen. Time and space expanded and then compressed, and she was aware of everything being present and yet hidden. What had been and what was still to come began unravelling before her.

With the dreamer's magic she found herself high on the cliffs with the grass frost sharp beneath her bare feet. Gulls wheeled above and the whole world was bathed in light. She had no sensation of walking but instead glided over the chilled grass, drawn to the summit of a path she felt she had climbed a hundred times before. Every twist and turn was as familiar as her own breath, each knotted root and exposed fist of granite an old friend marking the climb to the headland. In her dream the known and the unknown began to blur, twisting together like barley-sugar sticks until it was hard to tell each strand apart. Her feet carried her forwards but fear made her reluctant; in front of her loomed a granite cross, stark against the sky and casting a long shadow across the path. She tried to turn and flee but Morpheus planted his hands in the small of her back and drove her up the final incline.

She couldn't read them but she knew there were names written here. Somewhere was the name of the person she'd been searching for, someone she didn't yet know but ached to find. Her hands stretched out to touch the rough stone, only for it to dissolve beneath her fingertips. Once again he was out of reach, as insubstantial as the sea fret swirling in across the water. And yet, even as she thought this, the fog began to thicken. Like a cold shroud it wrapped itself around her, smothering and blinding her, until her screams hurled her into gasping wakefulness.

At least here nobody would come running.

Sitting upright in a tangle of sweat-drenched sheets, bewildered and afraid, she drew the eiderdown around her shoulders and hugged her knees against her chest. The dream told of something she didn't understand. Now that dawn was breaking, the nightmare was fading as it always did, until she could only recall that she'd been searching in the wrong place and had let somebody down. He was lost forever and it was all her fault.

He was forgotten.

She shivered, certain that this dream was a warning. Whoever he was, when she found him she must never let him go.

.

PART 1

CHAPTER 1

CHLOE

The Old Rectory overlooks the graveyard and I'm having trouble getting past this fact. I know I'm being ridiculous. This is a rectory, so it stands to reason that the house is near a church and, by association, a graveyard. These weathered tombstones with their time-blurred inscriptions and crumbly lichen coats are hardly new arrivals. They were here when I viewed the property in August and they'll still be here when I'm long forgotten, so opening the curtains and seeing them again shouldn't have come as a shock.

I suppose I just hadn't realised the churchyard was quite so *close*.

I know this sounds crazy. Of course I *knew* that Rosecraddick's Old Rectory is next to St Nonna's, but in high summer, with the clifftop house brimming with light and the leafy garden tumbling away to deep blue sea, the sight of the tombstones didn't jar quite as much as it does now in the November gloom. I barely noticed them because I was so enchanted by the sparkling water and dramatic cliffs beyond them. From the sitting room I could see all the way to the headland war memorial; sailing boats were stitched along the horizon and when I raised the sash window warm air trembled with birdsong and the scent of honeysuckle. This was such a world away from rumbling lorries and main roads that I fell instantly in love. This was the place, I'd decided. It was a healing spot. A haven. A space filled with peace.

1

Maybe I'd be happy again if I lived here?

In November the Rectory's still peaceful. There's no place quieter than a graveyard and I had longed for quiet. It's just that there's a certain irony in having positioned myself next door to such stark visual reminders of mortality. It's going to be tricky not to think about loss when its markers stand metres from my front door.

I take a deep breath and try my best to turn this negative into a positive – something my counsellor, Perky Pippa, is very keen on. *There's always good to be found in a situation, Chloe!* I'm not convinced about this. It's pretty hard to find a bright side to losing your husband. I guess I can give up shaving my legs and eat toast in bed and never watch football again, but these things hardly compensate, do they?

Anyway. What kind of positives would Perky Pippa draw from having to look at a graveyard every day? Well, I suppose at least the headstones don't have the same potential to floor me as unexpectedly coming across something of Neil's or finding myself idly thinking I must ask him to fix the catch on the kitchen window. These gravestones aren't personal. They don't record my tragedy. They didn't end my world.

Losing my husband ended my world.

It's the little things that make grief so utterly unbearable. It's standing in the supermarket aisle frozen with the realisation that you'll never buy him another birthday card because there'll never be another birthday, or finding a stray football sock curled up with the dust bunnies under the bed. How long I sat on the bedroom floor clutching that sock to my chest I couldn't say, but I do know that the daylight bled away, shadows filled the room and the marching stripes of passing headlights swept the wall before my tears stopped.

How could something so real as the love we'd shared just vanish? It doesn't make sense.

Some people might find the familiarity of home comforting, but for me every memory was another loss, every recollection another death. The rawness would never heal if I stayed in our home. Being faced with reminders of the life I'd chosen and hoped for was too painful. The sofa we'd picked up from Gumtree. The hideous lime paint in the hall, which Neil thought was beautiful. The spare bedroom we'd tentatively earmarked as *The Nursery*. Memories, dreams and a future snatched away from me filled that flat. I couldn't think there. I couldn't breathe. I couldn't even paint anymore.

And this was when I knew I had to leave. If I can't paint, I don't know who I am.

To everyone else I'm still Chloe Pencarrow, but there's a nervousness about the way they talk to me, as though they're afraid the wrong comment will cause me to shatter. I've become someone who makes them feel awkward and a little bit guilty-smug that my bad fortune isn't theirs. Some avoid me as though death might be contagious and others find it tricky now that I'm no longer in a neat couple. I've thrown their dinner-party planning into chaos, that's for sure.

I'm not being paranoid. Neil and I had a busy social life and I thought we had lots of close friends, but more than two years on most of them have drifted away and the invitations have dried up. I don't blame them. Our friends' lives have moved forwards while mine stopped on a May night in an airless hospital ward. They have babies now and school runs and play dates to organise, exciting new worlds to explore with similar-minded people who can share their experiences. I don't fit in anymore and probably never will, because my life swerved and took a different path.

After Neil's funeral, life returned to normal for everyone else and there was a new version of normal for me too. Gradually people stopped asking how I was or calling by to check that I didn't have my head in the oven (no chance, as it was an electric one and not much good for suicide). Everyone assumed I was coping. Which I was, of course – outwardly, at least. Inside I was rocking and screaming at Fate that it was unfair, and hurling myself against imaginary walls. I couldn't sleep, I couldn't eat and whenever I picked up a sketchbook my fingers felt as though they were made of rubber. I lasted for ten months by going through the motions, until one day something in me broke. The doctor signed me off work and said that I was under too much stress.

I've never been signed off work in my life, but then again I've never been a widow before either. It seems I'm in for new experiences whether I like them or not.

A widow. I still have trouble getting my head around the fact that I'm officially a widow. Widows don't drive convertibles or go running – and they won't have been thinking only recently that it's time to add a folic acid supplement to their diet. When I think about widows, I picture elderly women clad in black, with crêpe-paper skin and scores of grandchildren they stuff full of sweets. They've lived long, happy lives with their husbands and managed to achieve all the things they dreamed about. Widows have thousands of memories to comfort them when they wake with a start in the small hours. Widows aren't thirty-two years old with less than three years of marriage to sustain them through the decades that yawn ahead. So how on earth can I possibly be one?

But I am.

I'm a widow.

That's a fact. Neil's gone and taken with him the life I thought I'd be leading. Everything that came before his death now seems like time spent living in a foreign land. Some fragments of the language still float through the memory, and the landscape's familiar, but it isn't home anymore. No matter how much you might ache to go back, you can never return. You can never recapture the past.

So a new beginning's what I need. A new place for this new version of me. A place to start over on my own. Never mind the gravestones. They're the least of my problems.

"Is everything all right with the property, Mrs Pencarrow?"

The letting agent stands in the doorway regarding me with a

worried expression. I smile at her apologetically.

"Sorry, I was miles away. The place isn't quite as I remembered it."

She bites her lip and nods. "I know it's a little unloved, but the last tenant left several months ago and houses in Cornwall don't do well when they're empty."

There's a ladder in her tights and her suit is cheap and shiny. The clipboard stuffed with particulars quivers in her hands. I feel sorry for her, a junior member of the team, sent down from Truro to hand the keys over and make sure the new tenant signs the paperwork before coming to her senses and running a mile. I'm surprised they didn't make me sign the contract the minute I said I was interested. If I hadn't sold my flat, meaning that living with my parents is my only other option, I'd be running too.

It's no surprise the Rectory hasn't let easily. It's in a beautiful spot with gorgeous views, but it's completely dilapidated. Apparently it belongs to an elderly man who's gone into a nursing home and who clearly hasn't touched the place since the eighties. It's too far gone to attract holidaymakers, although I should imagine the minute he passes away it'll be snapped up by somebody from London; whoever buys it will doubtless paint the front door sage and do up the interior with driftwood sculptures and twee sailing boats on every available surface. Still, even with the graveyard's proximity, there's something about it I like. I want to be here. That hasn't changed.

"The property's great," I say, and relief chases across her face like sunshine over the sea. I'm not fibbing: it is fine for me. If I'd wanted comfort, power showers and central heating, I wouldn't have sold our flat in Pinner. An avocado bathroom suite and flock wallpaper are a fair exchange for losing heart-twisting memories and endless echoes of happier times.

"I know Mr Sargent hasn't done much with the place for a while and it needs a little modernisation – but the views are wonderful, aren't they?" The letting agent is looking happier now. "The New

Rectory isn't nearly as nice. They really knew how to build houses in the old days, didn't they?"

She reminds me of my A-level students: hopeful, keen and eager to please the teacher. Nearly a decade of teaching kicks in like a reflex and I find I want to encourage her.

"They did. The views are exactly what I wanted," I agree. There's a pause while I think about what to say next, if anything at all.

"Once you've got your own things moved in it'll be lovely," says the letting agent optimistically. "The chimney's been swept and it'll be nice and cosy once the wood burner's lit."

Cosy isn't the first word that springs to mind. The house smells old, of rooms kept shut and of empty spaces that can't be reinvigorated by the opening of curtains or the pulling up of sash windows. Long-forgotten furniture shrouded in dust sheets slumbers in dim corners; the curtains are drawn in all the other windows and the room shivers with shadows. When our conversation falters, the house is as quiet as the graveyard. If I strain my ears I can hear the waves dashing on the rocks in the cove below and the mournful calls of a lone seagull. Waves and gulls and larks were the soundtrack I'd listened to when I first viewed the Rectory, but in high summer the windows were flung open, salty air blew through the rooms and sunshine spilled in honeyed pools across the floorboards. In my haste to outrun my grief I hadn't paused to consider how it would be in the winter.

"And it's all right for me to move things around and have a bit of a clear-out?" I ask. The place is full of junk and I have my own belongings packed and ready.

"Absolutely. Please, help yourself. Mr Sargent has even said in writing that we can clear the place if we want to and throw things away. He's taken all his personal effects to the care home. To be honest, empty houses are generally easier for us to let, but this place would take a lot of work and a house-clearance team. Mr Sargent's more than happy for carpets and furniture to go if you'd rather change them. He knows he won't be returning." She pauses, suddenly struck by a thought. "That's a shame, isn't it? It must be very sad for him."

"Very sad," I agree, and my heart aches for this unknown elderly man who shut his front door and walked away, knowing he would never come home again. I've done something similar and it hurts to know that life will never be the same.

"It's getting cold. Shall we do the paperwork at the pub where we can warm up? If you still want to take the Rectory, of course," says the letting agent. She knows as well as I do that this place is one thing in August and another altogether in the winter.

For a moment I teeter on the precipice. Do I jump? Am I brave enough?

It's only early afternoon but already the light's starting to die. The long sunlit evenings of late summer could belong to a different world. They certainly belong to a different life – the one I'm about to leave. The air thrums with possibilities, infinite parallel lives poised to go spinning off into creation. This is the moment where I pause on the brink of the unknown and the new.

Which is what I wanted and why I'm here.

I take a deep breath.

"I still want to take it," I say.

CHAPTER 2

CHLOE

"No, Mum, seriously. You really don't have anything to worry about. I love it here and the house is wonderful. This place is exactly what I need."

I tuck my phone between my chin and my shoulder and hope that fibbing in a rectory isn't an invitation to be struck down by holy lightning. To be doubly sure, I cross my fingers. I should be safe, since these are just a few white lies to soothe my anxious mother. Over two hundred miles away, and clearly thinking I've finally lost it after two and a half years of clinging on by my fingernails, she's finding it hard to understand why I've chosen to bury myself in Cornwall.

She's wondering? This makes two of us. I only moved in yesterday afternoon, but already I'm starting to think I might have made a mistake. If the unloved Rectory felt vast when I met the letting agent, it seems twice as big now that I'm here alone. When I turned the brass key in the lock after returning from signing all the paperwork yesterday, I hovered on the doorstep for a few seconds, feeling I should wait to be invited inside by a wise old vicar.

Telling myself I was being ridiculous, I'd stepped inside, abandoning my two cases at the foot of the imposing staircase, and decided to explore. As I'd drifted through the Rectory I'd felt as lost and as insubstantial as anything that might haunt the graveyard. I'd pushed open doors, drawn curtains apart and claimed the spaces, telling myself that once my own belongings arrived it would feel less abandoned. I'd found a study, a dining room and a games room with a listing ping-pong table and moth-nibbled net. The sitting room was at the far end of a panelled corridor whose dark woodwork had somehow escaped the eighties makeover inflicted on the rest of the house. The room itself was pleasant and airy, and I knew that once I'd moved my few pieces in this would be where I'd spend my time. There was a deep window seat too, which would be the perfect spot to watch the waves. I was struck by the notion that I'd be the latest in a long chain of people to do so. There was something soothing about this sense of continuity.

"What about the kitchen?" worries my mother, who's obsessed by the fear that I'll fade away without Tesco Express on the corner or her weekly food parcels. We both know that most of what she brings ends up mouldering in the fridge for weeks anyway, but we choose to pretend otherwise. Enjoying food, like being a wife, is something from another life. There's no fun in cooking huge curries or hearty stews without Neil to tuck into them or friends to come over for supper. The magic of tossing ingredients into a pan is no longer a pleasure either. These days everything tastes like ashes and I generally make do with toast.

"Is the cooker any good?" my mother continues. "I know how it can be in these rented houses. I've read some terrible things on the Internet. You have to be so careful when you rent a house."

I smile at this. My parents have inhabited the same house in Enfield since they were married over thirty-five years ago and know as much about renting as I do about particle physics. Mum's been busy Googling horrific stories about unscrupulous landlords, hot bunking and TB. She'll have been up all night fretting, convinced I'm about to fry myself on faulty wiring.

"Do the appliances comply with modern standards?" she asks now, with a note of anxiety. "Have you checked for PAT testing?"

"That sounds like something I should do with a dog." I attempt a joke but she isn't amused.

"I'm being serious, Chloe! I've read some dreadful stories. There has to be a reason a house like that's so cheap to rent. It's probably a

9

death trap and you'll be electrocuted."

"I'd take a quick electric shock over cancer any time," I say flippantly and before I can stop myself. There's a sharp intake of breath on the end of the line, which makes me feel terrible. Mum's only trying to show she cares. What does Perky Pippa say? *I must be patient. I must stop bringing up the past. I must stop making bitter comments. I must move on.*

I must. I must. I must. Maybe I should write these commandments out like punishment lines or repeat them as mantras?

"The cooker's solid fuel so please don't worry about anything there." I pinch the bridge of my nose with my thumb and forefinger and breathe deeply to steady my racing heart. I'm now two and a half years and a whole life away, sitting beside a hospital bed and holding a frail hand that was once so strong. "Anyway, I'm sure the agent wouldn't have rented the house out without making sure everything was safe. There are laws about that sort of thing."

"So I should think," says Mum huffily. Relieved to be back on firm ground, she's soon regaling me with some of the awful stories she's read. I make the right noises in hopefully the right places and let my mind drift.

Actually, my mother may have a point. I'm sure the letting agents know their job, but the Rectory must be several centuries old – and judging by the way the lights flicker, it was probably first wired when Queen Victoria was on the throne. Nothing I've seen since I arrived has convinced me that it's been updated since. There's an enormous range slumbering in the corner of the kitchen like a cast-iron dragon, and close inspection suggests I'll need to feed it with wood to have it breathing fire and running the massive radiators. It certainly won't go ping and serve me a ready meal in two minutes. Then there's a butler's sink so vast I could fit the butler in it, a refectory table big enough to seat a football team, and a larder the size of my old sitting room. Empty shelves stretch from floor to ceiling and there's a huge fridge marooned at the far end. Slight overkill for a loaf of bread and a jar of Marmite.

Once I've convinced Mum I'm not about to starve or electrocute myself, I think I'll make a start on unpacking. I couldn't face doing this last night. I haven't chosen to bring a great deal with me, for obvious reasons – but even so, the thought of seeing items from our home appearing out of context is reason enough to leave the sealed boxes where they are for now, piled in the hallway.

Last night, once the removal men had finally left and the boxes were stacked, it took all my strength to climb the stairs before I fell into bed. It didn't matter that the sheets were damp or the bed a little lumpy, because I wanted nothing more than to close my eyes and shut everything out. I feel like this sometimes, not as much as I did at first, but last night wasn't good. I lay in the big brass bed, with the covers pulled up to my chin and my eyes tightly shut. I tried to pretend I was at home with Neil sleeping beside me, and that all was as it should be. I used to be good at this – so good that when I opened my eyes and found his side of the bed empty it was a shock all over again – but in this Cornish house my old skills evaded me. I couldn't summon the familiar room and the soft breathing of my husband, no matter how hard I tried. Instead I shivered in the deep darkness while the house creaked and settled around me like an old ship. I didn't fall asleep until the moon sank and the gulls started to shriek.

Consequently, I'm gritty-eyed and tired this morning. What if I've left Neil behind and can never find him again? I wanted a new start but I didn't want to lose him totally or erase the memories of what we once had. I'm so afraid I've done the wrong thing. I'm terrified I've betrayed Neil by selling our home and moving away. It felt right at the time, but now I'm here I'm not so sure...

"Chloe?" My mother can tell I've tuned out. "Darling, have you heard a word I've said? Is everything really all right? You are feeling yourself, aren't you? You're not feeling unwell again?"

Feeling unwell is my mother's euphemism for *having a breakdown.*

She's always awkward about mentioning anything to do with what she would term "mental health", and I know she was embarrassed about having a daughter who needed counselling and antidepressants. That wasn't something to boast about to her friends at the tennis club. Well, she's got nothing to worry about now. Mum might think I'm crazy leaving London and moving to Cornwall, but it was the only way to hang onto my sanity. The dark days of pills and despair are behind me and this move is the next step on my journey. It's the opposite of crazy, not that I'm going to try to explain this to her.

"It's all good," I say vaguely.

"Are you sure the house isn't too lonely? You're not feeling too isolated there? It's such a long way away. I know Neil loved Cornwall but…"

Her words fade and there's an awkward lull in the conversation. This happens to me a lot. One of the hardest things about losing Neil is that almost overnight people stopped mentioning his name and avoided any conversations that might include him. I suppose they were trying to be kind and spare my feelings and, as is the British way, steer well clear of emotional minefields. If I want to talk about my husband, I'll have to do a Shirley Valentine and chat to the wall.

"You are coping, aren't you, sweetheart?"

Coping is one of those funny words I heard a lot when Neil was ill. People would ask me how I was coping with taking care of him, how he was coping with the treatment (badly as it turned out; Neil was an appalling patient) and how I was coping once I was alone. The fact is, no one really wants to hear the truth. The questions are a formality and you find yourself taking part in a ballet of evasions and acceptable answers. I know the steps off by heart.

"I'm fine," I say. "Just a bit tired."

This answer seems to satisfy her. My grief has been circumnavigated and now we're discussing how the sea air makes you sleepy. As we talk about nothing at all, skating on the thin ice of polite conversation, I contemplate the strange nature of grief. Some people hide from it, others devote their entire lives to mourning, and the bravest get on with living. I'm not sure what category I fall into yet.

"Cornwall is very pretty," my mother says brightly. "Dad and I love *Poldark* and *Doc Martin*. Lovely scenery."

I refrain from pointing out that these shows are filmed in the height of summer when the skies are duck-egg blue and the air's mild, and that "pretty" isn't the adjective I would have picked to describe this wild coastline. Dramatic, maybe? Bleak certainly.

"You'd love it, Mum," I say. "The house has lots of space and the views are beautiful. I think I'll be able to paint here."

I do want to paint again. I'm longing to capture this salty wilderness with its shifting skies and rough grassy cliffs. I'm scared and I'm nervous, but as I chat to my mother I'm wondering where the nearest art-supply shop might be. If I do paint again, I'll need to restock.

See? This is the right place. Trust your own instincts. Don't listen to your mum! She'd have you living back with them!

Neil's lounging in the window seat and beaming at me with his old confidence. His blue eyes sparkle, his tanned feet are bare and he looks as youthful as he did when we first started dating. Startled, I blink and he's gone. He was never there, of course, but for a moment he might have been – and this could have been a normal day on our holiday, in a tatty eighties time-warp house we'd laugh about for years and daydream about buying and doing up ourselves. We used to love spinning dreams and weaving plans for the future.

Sometimes I think it's just as well nobody knows what lies ahead.

"Well, that is good news!" Mum says, with such delight that it's apparent just how worried she's been by my lack of artistic output. I've been drawing and painting since I was old enough to hold a brush. Although I taught art until recently, I was on the brink of working full time on commissions. I'd enjoyed several relatively successful exhibitions, sold two big landscapes to a private collector and been signed by a top agent, but when I lost Neil I stopped painting altogether. I didn't care if I never picked up a brush again. My creativity had died.

At least, that was what I'd thought in those dark times – but now I'm wondering if it is time to paint again. The Rectory might be cavernous and cold, but knowing that my instinct to come here was right warms me more than any wood burner ever could. And I saw Neil too. I did see him! I'm closer to my husband here than I was in our own home, which proves I haven't made a mistake coming here after all.

Yesterday I wasn't so certain. While the removal men were unpacking their van, I'd continued exploring my new home, making mental maps and opening doors into rooms I knew I wouldn't use. Having wandered around upstairs, I'd decided I would sleep in the back bedroom, where the views out across the sea made up for the faded floral decor. There were five bedrooms in all, plus the avocado bathroom; then there was another flight of steps, albeit little more than a glorified ladder, which led up to the attic. The light had all but gone by then, but I remembered from my summer visit how the space had the potential to become a wonderful studio. Maybe…

"So what's the plan for today?" my mother's asking brightly, in the tone of voice you'd use with an invalid. "A nice walk on the cliffs and a pub lunch?"

I smile. That sounds like luxury compared to what I'll be up to.

"Not today. I'm going to sort out finding some logs and getting the fire going. It's pretty cold in here."

Cold is an understatement. I wouldn't be surprised if a glacier slid through the room. This morning's seen the dawn of a sharp and frosty day and I can see my breath clouding as I speak. The tip of my nose is numb, my fingers are turning blue and I need to see if I can have the wood burner working before I get frostbite. With her new-found obsession with faulty wiring, Mum's worrying about the wrong thing entirely; I'm far more likely to freeze to death than fry. Thank

God she hasn't discovered the wonders of FaceTime and can't see that I'm wearing a coat and scarf indoors. My parents have their central heating cranked up to subtropical and she'd be horrified. I'm convinced it's colder inside the Rectory than it is outside. I've never seen ice on the inside of windows before, and I have the troubling feeling that the whole place will freeze over if I don't get sorted.

I've been frozen for far too long, I decide once I've finished the call. It's time to head into the sunshine. I'll feel the warmth on my face and then discover whether there's any chance of a thaw.

CHAPTER 3

CHLOE

I was right about it being warmer outside the Rectory; I suppose the thick walls retain cold as well as heat. As I stomp around the garden with the sunlight brushing my upturned face, it isn't long before I feel slightly less like an ice lolly. While I search for the log store, I start to enjoy the wintery morning. Waves glitter in the bay, seagulls perform aeronautical displays high above and several keen walkers are already striding along the cliff path.

There's something soothing about being outdoors. The phone call with my mother has left me, if not unsettled exactly, then a little adrift. There were too many reminders of before – old hurts and worries that are the bedrock upon which our conversations are built, layer by layer. It's hard to leave the broken and signed-off-work version of myself behind when, with each anxious question and implied concern, my mother keeps resurrecting her. My London life's been cast off. With every mile journeyed further west in my little red Peugeot, the past dropped away and I felt increasingly relieved. Chloe the wife, widow and teacher has been left behind, and (hopefully) so too have *Poor Chloe, Mad Chloe* and *Have you heard about Chloe?* In Rosecraddick I'm free to rediscover myself without the past and pity dragging me under.

This doesn't mean I love Neil any the less or that I want to forget him. The opposite feels true: here I can find a side to him I hadn't always known. I decided on Rosecraddick because Neil loved Cornwall. In this seaside village where he spent childhood holidays and where he learnt to sail and kayak and climb and all the other active and outdoorsy things he loved to do, a new Chloe is going to take shape. I don't know her yet but it's time I made her acquaintance. In a small way she'll keep Neil alive by being here. A branch of his family came from Rosecraddick and it seems circular and right that I've returned to their roots. My mother thinks this is weird but she's never really understood me and, besides, her idea of making a change is deciding not to watch *EastEnders*.

So now I can walk on the beach and picture Neil as a small child scrabbling over rocks, armed with a bucket and fishing net. I'd loved the teenager and the man, but I'd not known the boy. Here I'll catch glimpses of him, scrapbook images of another time and half-memories as shifting and dreamy as the sky reflected in the rock pools. I'll see him again, I'm certain of it, but in Cornwall this feels like a comfort rather than a curse.

Anyway. Logs. Where might they be? A narrow path winds past the gravestones and weeping angels to the edge of the headland and the South West Coast Path. I could be wrong but I don't think there's a log store in that direction. To the left of the house is the church, dreaming in the sunlight today, and beyond this is the lane to Rosecraddick village. The latter is tucked into a valley hemmed by hills, all deeply wooded and still. In the summer I'd been struck by how green and leafy it all was, but today the trees are a tangle of bare branches; looking through them from one of the bedroom windows, I spotted the roof of Rosecraddick Manor, as vulnerable as a scalp when the hair has fallen away.

I push this idea out of my mind. I must stop thinking like this. Worm-cast beaches and fishing trips. Barnacle-embossed rocks. Sandy picnics. Skinny brown limbs sticking out of shortie wetsuits. These are the images I want to focus on. The happy times, not the last painful days.

"Hello there! Can I help you?"

I spin round. A red-haired woman in her late thirties and wearing a dog collar and ecclesiastical shirt smiles at me over the gate.

"Sorry, I didn't mean to make you jump. I'm Sue Perry, the vicar here – and at several other churches in the parish too, for my sins! You look a little lost?"

"No, no. I'm fine. Thank you." I hold out my hand, not wanting to appear rude. "I'm Chloe Pencarrow. I'm renting the Rectory."

As I say this I'm struck by an irrational arrow of guilt. By rights it's the round-faced Sue Perry with her twinkling Mrs Tiggy-winkle eyes and mop of auburn curls who should be living here. I think the letting agent said that the New Rectory's a modern house on the far side of the village, which seems a shame. This is a romantic, if exposed, spot.

But the Reverend Sue Perry doesn't appear put out in the least. Instead her smile grows even warmer and my hand, clasped in both of hers, is given a vigorous shake.

"Aha! I did hear on the village grapevine that a glamorous London artist had taken the place. You look surprised I know this?"

"How do they know I'm an artist?" I ask. The *glamorous* bit takes me aback too. I don't think I've worn make-up since Neil died (constantly removing tear-smudged mascara soon became tiresome), and my hair hasn't been cut since I had enough of it tumbling into my eyes and took the kitchen scissors to it. Let's just say I'm a better artist than I am hairdresser. Glamorous I am not.

Sue Perry laughs. "Believe me, MI5 has nothing on local intelligence – although I suspect the truth of the matter is far more mundane. The postmistress's son works for your removal company and saw your easel! The rest they'll have made up in the pub and the local shop. You'll be painting nudes and chopping your ears off by teatime!"

"They'll be very disappointed when they realise how boring I am. And anyway, I paint landscapes and buildings mostly."

The vicar grins. "Never let the truth get in the way of a good story! Welcome to Rosecraddick and village life. Seriously, though, if there's anything you need or would like to know, then please feel free to ask me. I'm up at the church all the time and you're very welcome there."

"Thanks," I say, although I can't imagine I'll be popping in to worship. Where did all my hours of praying and bargaining get me when Neil was ill? If God exists, He wasn't listening to me. It's hard not to feel bitter.

"So how are you settling in at the Old Rectory?" Sue asks, tactfully changing the subject. "Is there anything you need?"

"There is actually. I'm hunting for the log store because I need to get the range lit before I freeze."

She nods sympathetically. "I bet it's Baltic in that old house. Thank goodness the C of E had the sense to put me in something modern with central heating! It's bad enough trying to heat the church. The log store should be around the back but don't get your hopes up. I can't imagine anyone's filled it in recent months. The last tenants left at the end of the spring."

My heart plummets. Hot-water bottles and chilblains here I come. Or maybe I'll have to start burning the furniture?

"No time like the present to have a look though," says Sue. "I'll show you where it is if you like?"

I nod gratefully and she lets herself in through the gate and threads her way around the back of the house, towards a shed tucked away at the bottom of the garden. I have to carry logs from there? Seriously?

I'll have arms like The Rock.

"It's empty, I'm afraid," says Sue, after poking her head inside. "Hardly surprising but not much fun for you. I'll give you the number of Larry the Log."

"Larry the Log?"

"The local lumber merchant. You can order a load now – or if it helps, I'll call him for you? He might even deliver today if the vicar asks him nicely." She touches her dog collar and winks. "There are some advantages to this job, you know!"

"I'd really appreciate that," I say. "I don't think I'll last long without heating."

"You look as though you could do with a hot drink, if you don't mind me saying so. Your lips are practically blue. I've got a kettle and a fan heater in the vestry, and my mobile's there too. Why don't we have a coffee and I'll call Larry?"

I'm dying for some caffeine and the thought of thawing out is also very welcome, so I follow Sue back through the garden and across the graveyard to the church, listening to her chat away about the village and the people who live there. By the time I'm sitting in the vestry, with my hands wrapped around a mug of coffee and a pile of chocolate biscuits in front of me, my head's spinning with it all. While Sue makes a call on my behalf, I glance around with interest. A cassock hangs on the back of the door, the desk is piled high with books and papers, and the little heater Sue mentioned coughs out dusty puffs of hot air. The room is small and cosy and there's a cork board on the wall bursting with bright snapshots of Sue, together with a smiley man wearing wire-framed glasses, a chubby-faced little boy and their adorable curly-haired dog. The pictures make a striking collage of a happy life.

I surf a wave of grief. Neil and I will never have pictures like this. There will never be a cute toddler with Neil's dimples and my wild curls, and there will never be a family shot of us out walking with our dog. There will never be first days at school. University graduations. Weddings and christenings. These dreams are dead.

"Right. That's sorted. Larry will deliver a load of logs this afternoon," Sue says, ending the call and looking pleased. "Is that all right with you?"

I suppose I ought to check the price, but right now it could be a million pounds and I wouldn't quibble. Grief's viper strike has robbed me of any coherent words and I can only nod.

"That's Tim, my husband, and the cheeky monkey's Caspar, our son," Sue explains proudly as she follows my gaze. "The dog's called Molly and she's a poppet. Much easier to live with than the other two and far better behaved. You'll have to come over for dinner and meet them."

"Thanks," I say. "I'd like that."

"I can't cook to save my life," she warns. "We'll have to get pizzas in. They're all Cas will eat at the moment anyway, although by the time I get my act together and invite you properly he'll probably be onto the next fad! You know how kids are."

I might have been a teacher but my students were in their teens. I haven't a clue about toddlers and probably never will have now. The viper strikes again and I flinch. Luckily, Sue's too busy flipping through her desk diary to notice.

"Drat. I'm booked solid this week. Can I let you know when I have a window?"

"Of course." Is it wrong of me to be a little relieved? I'm not sure I'm up to other people's happiness yet.

"I'll pop your number into my phone," she continues, pulling it from her pocket with a flourish. She taps at it, a frown deepening between her brows. "This thing is so complicated! I can hardly work it. So, what's your number?"

I reel off my mobile number, which isn't nearly as impressive a feat as people seem to think it is. I had to give it out so often when Neil was ill that the digits are seared into my memory.

"Chloe—" Sue looks up from the screen. "Sorry, I have a brain like a sieve today. What did you say your surname was again?"

"It's Pencarrow."

"That's a local name, isn't it?" Sue enters the name into her phone. "Are your folks from here?"

"Pencarrow's my married name. I think a branch of my husband's family lived here a long time ago. Distant cousins, maybe?"

If Sue wonders where my husband is, she's far too professional to ask. She doesn't even check my left hand, where my wedding band and engagement ring still have pride of place.

"We're all cousins here! And Pencarrow's definitely a local name.

I've seen it on the war memorial and I think it's on the stained-glass window in the south transept too. Quite a few of the family's lads were lost in both wars. The Pencarrows didn't have a good time of it back then, that's for certain. They were very unlucky with their sons."

The Pencarrows haven't had a great time since either. Neil was the last of his family to bear the name and there won't be any sons to follow him now.

"That's so sad," is all I say.

"You should check the war memorial out. Family history and all that," says Sue. "It's a good walk and the view's stunning."

"The war memorial on the headland, you mean?" I can see the granite cross from the Rectory; grey and unyielding, it's as much a part of the landscape as the rock it's hewn from. The sight of it makes me feel unbearably sad. It's as though the losses of all those who looked out over the sea and prayed for their loved ones' safe return have seeped into the landscape with the rain and the years. The memorial serves as an eternal reminder that grief isn't exclusive.

"That's right. They'll be laying a wreath there for the Armistice and we're having a service of remembrance in the church this weekend as well. It's always very moving." Sue drains her coffee and places the mug on the summit of a paperwork mountain. "Did you want to see the window? I'm sure your surname's there somewhere."

St Nonna's is a small church with a sense of quiet watchfulness and peace. Although I'm still angry with God, its atmosphere makes me think, with some surprise, that I could spend time in here. The prayers of centuries hang in the stillness, and the light pouring through its stained-glass windows warms the flagstone floor. The hairs on my forearms stir.

"Here we are." Sue pauses at the furthest end of the south transept. Above us is a beautiful window depicting a scroll edged with poppies. The simple white war graves stretch into infinity and above these a yellow sun beams from an azure sky. Upon each gilded ray, the name of a local man has been lovingly inlaid in black glass.

"To the glory of God and the memory of the men of Rosecraddick who gave their lives in the Great War 1914–1918," I read out loud.

My goodness. There must be over thirty names here, a huge amount of young men culled from a small village. Of course, I know about the First World War from things I learned in school, and from bits and pieces I happen to have read or seen since then: Wilfred Owen, trenches, mud, *War Horse*. Yet seeing such blunt evidence of an entire generation being wiped out is shocking. These young men were sons, husbands, sweethearts and brothers. They laughed and cried and trembled and were alive. People loved them and mourned them and they were real, as real as Neil had been, but now they're just names on a pretty window in an obscure Cornish church.

My eyes flicker over the names until I spot the one I'm searching for. There he is, halfway down the rays listing the fallen: Gem Pencarrow. Poor Gem. He was still only a teenager. He wasn't much older than my A-level students, those awkward almost-adults who straddle a confusing hinterland of childhood and their shadowy future selves. At that age they glow with a potential they won't understand or even know they possess until it's gone and too late. As teenagers they still looked to me for guidance and reassurance. Some of them could barely complete their coursework to deadline or make it to school on time, yet Gem Pencarrow, this young man with my husband's blood in his veins and maybe even with the same blue eyes and deep dimples, went to war, faced unimaginable horror and lay down his life for King and country.

I'm so moved I can't speak. Seeing my own surname – my husband's name – on the roll call of the dead is a jolt. It strikes me that Neil was proof that life does go on after death, which is ironic really. But time's sands shift and raw losses do heal. I must hold onto this thought because there's comfort in it. I send a silent *thank you* to Gem Pencarrow.

"It makes you think, doesn't it?" says Sue quietly. "I know it's decades since the Great War ended, and all these young men would have been dead by now anyway, but that fact doesn't hide the ugly truth that they were robbed of their lives way before their time."

"No, it doesn't," I agree. Nothing soothes the wrongness of a life snatched away too soon.

"And, of course, here's Kit's memorial." Sue points to the next window. "That's the one all the visitors want to see. You'll probably meet quite a few of them over the summer months. They tend to come on something of a pilgrimage, armed with their poetry books!"

I turn my attention to the adjacent stained-glass artwork. This one's different, in that it depicts a single young man in uniform, as golden-haired as any saint and standing in a field of poppies and lambs. With his rifle laid down amongst the flowers beside him, he holds an open Bible loosely in his hands. His eyes are fixed upon the skies and a glorious sunset flames around him like a halo. Angels reach out to raise him up to heaven, where a solitary daisy – plain white and out of place against the explosion of crimson and gold – floats all alone in the top left-hand corner.

"It's stunning," I say, and Sue looks pleased.

"I think so too, even if others find it a bit OTT," she says, stepping back and narrowing her eyes critically. "Then again, that was what the family wanted. I'm not convinced it's a true representation of Kit. Most young lads I know aren't thinking about angels and heaven!"

As an artist I'm struck by the flamboyance and the hints of budding art deco in the gold and crimson rays of the sun. My teacher's eye picks out the homage to the Pre-Raphaelites in the angelic figure of the young soldier, as well as the hints of apotheosis as he ascends to the angels. The imagery of lambs, blood-red poppies and a Christ-like figure whose life is laid down for the good of Man is pretty much what I'd expect for this period. I'm perplexed by the daisy though. I can't recall daisies being significant to First World War iconography. Apart from that, the lead work around this one seems rather clumsy, as though it was added in haste as an afterthought. But why? What would it signify?

Now, this is the sort of mystery that intrigues me. I'm always interested in the symbols and messages one finds in artwork.

"Should I have heard of him?" I ask, having the feeling I'm missing something. This window is as large as the first one and far more ornate, yet it's dedicated to just one man, Captain Christopher Rivers, rather than the fallen of the parish. Swirling writing at the foot of the stained glass reveals that Captain Rivers was lost in 1916. I rack my brains but I still have no idea who he was or why visitors might make a pilgrimage to see this window.

"It depends how keen you are on English literature," Sue says. "Kit Rivers was a war poet and Rosecraddick's most famous son. Don't feel bad if you haven't heard of him though. I think he's quite minor in comparison to Wilfred Owen and co. I certainly hadn't come across Kit until I arrived here – but then again I'm a terrible philistine. I read the Bible and celebrity magazines, but that's about it!"

I trawl through my foggy A-level literature knowledge but draw a total blank. The English teachers at school would be bound to know, but apart from the usual trio of Owen, Sassoon and Brooke I can't recall any other war poets. That's actually quite a shocking admission.

"*Drum Flares? Smothered?*" Sue offers. "I think those are the best known. I've got a book somewhere; I'll see if I can dig it out for you. There's stuff on Wiki too, I'm sure, and the village shop sells pamphlets. We're pretty proud of Kit Rivers here."

I study the window. The winter sunlight catches it and turns Kit's hair to pure gold.

"A window like this one must have been very expensive," I remark, and Sue nods.

"I should imagine so, yes. I wouldn't like to pay for it today! Still, his family weren't short of money. They owned Rosecraddick Manor and were the major landowners in the area back then. Real *Downton Abbey* stuff with servants and horses and all that jazz. Kit was the only son and heir, so the line died out with him. From what little I know, the place fell into disrepair during the last century."

The viper's fangs take hold once again. I carry Neil's name and still wear his rings, but I won't be passing his name on now. I push the rising misery down into the deep place where the dark things hide and focus all my attention on the window. It's a remarkable piece of art but there's something impersonal and idealised about it. Kit Rivers looks like a saint rather than a young man. And Sue's right: in my experience, young men don't tend to have their noses buried in Bibles and spend their time contemplating heaven. They're too busy pulling girls, getting drunk or having fights – and I can't believe that Kit Rivers, war-hero poet or not, would have been any different.

"So his family commissioned the window?"

"I think Kit's mother did in the 1920s, although you'd be better off asking one of the local Kit Rivers Society bods about all that. You could try Matt Enys up at the Manor. He's with the Kernow Heritage Foundation, who've recently acquired the place. He's bound to know about the family history. The Foundation are planning an exhibition about the Great War; Kit's going to feature and Matt's the history expert on the team. *Profile raising* was how they put it at the last parish council meeting. What they actually mean is they want to get the tourists flocking here – and good on 'em."

"Are tourists interested in poetry?" I would have thought the beach, ice creams and pasties were bigger draws.

Sue shrugs her plump shoulders. "No idea. I think the Kernow Heritage Foundation are hoping to have a tea room and do tours, tie it in with the war and the whole *Downton Abbey* end-of-an-era thing. Anything that encourages tourism can only be good for the village. You can see how dead it is here in the winter, and the more money locals make in the summer the better."

Sue has a point. When I visited Rosecraddick in August, the village was so busy that my car could only get through it at a crawl. The narrow street had been thick with holidaymakers meandering along carrying beach paraphernalia or stopping abruptly to peer into shop windows or buy pasties. Every business had been open, the cafés had been bulging at the seams and the pub's beer garden had bristled with drinkers enjoying the sunshine. This week I drove through in minutes without seeing a soul and most of the shops were shuttered up for the winter. Making a living from seasonal work must be tough.

"So what's the daisy all about?" I ask, pointing at the brave white flower floating amid flames and seraphim. "It's a bit out of place, isn't it?"

The vicar frowns. "I hadn't really noticed that before, but now you've pointed it out I can't believe I ever missed it. It sticks out like a sore thumb."

"It looks as though it's been added at a later date," I say thoughtfully. "The style's different, cruder almost. It really jolts against the colour scheme and the design. Poppies make sense, but a daisy? I wouldn't have expected that. Certainly not in the sky."

"I can tell you're an artist. What an eye for detail," says Sue, with such admiration that I feel rather embarrassed. I'm only looking at a stained-glass window; I'm not splitting an atom.

I shrug. "It's a bit of a puzzle and I enjoy those."

"In that case you should definitely ask the history bods at the Foundation. They'll probably be able to tell you straight away and, if not, you'll have a mystery to solve just like in *The Da Vinci Code*!" she grins.

Channelling my inner Dan Brown wasn't on the top of my list when I arrived in the village, but as we make our way through the nave and back into the churchyard I'm turning the riddle of the daisy around and around. No matter which direction my mind takes, I can't make sense of it. I'm intrigued now. Maybe I will do some research – or at the very least read some of Kit Rivers' poetry.

I think you should! High time you dragged yourself away from celebrity magazines and read something challenging!

It's Neil, laughing and teasing me as he leans against the churchyard gate. He's wearing his favourite blue fisherman's sweater, together with faded fraying jeans with scuffed Timberland boots. Wrapped loosely around his neck is the Hugo Boss scarf I bought him when we visited New York one magical Christmas. I threw those dreadful jeans out long ago, but I guess you can wear whatever you want in the afterlife. The sun behind him dazzles me, so I blink. Of course, he's gone when my eyes adjust once again, but that's OK. Neil's in Rosecraddick: that's the main thing. I haven't made a mistake coming here. He was waiting for me and he wants me to put my brain to use.

And if I'm only imagining things? Maybe that doesn't matter. Either way, perhaps I was supposed to come here and discover more about Kit Rivers. For the first time in longer than I care to remember, it feels like I have a purpose.

CHAPTER 4

CHLOE

Although the morning sun's streaming into the Rectory, my return finds the old house no warmer and I'm grateful to Sue for managing to arrange a swift log delivery. My trusty fan heater's all very well in a small flat, but it can't heat a place this size. Short of holing up in the bedroom with my electric blanket cranked up and my hat and coat on, I can't imagine how I'd manage to stay warm otherwise. It's something that didn't cross my mind in the summer. I wasn't thinking very far ahead then; I was still chunking time into sections and ticking off the minutes, hours and days that had passed since Neil died.

If I'm honest, I'd very nearly got to the stage of chalking tally marks on my wall – what I was counting down to I daren't contemplate. I longed for oblivion, but I dreaded falling asleep because waking up meant losing Neil all over again. For a moment everything would feel normal, before the realisation hit me with the force of a wrecking ball and my world splintered once more. I'd wondered how long the loss would shock me anew before it felt real, and how long it would take for coffee and pills to seem like a normal diet. I got through those long, colourless days by barricading myself in my bedroom, burrowing beneath the duvet and only surfacing when I absolutely had no choice. I've got no desire to revisit those days spent languishing in bed, even if I'm only trying to avoid frostbite. I need to move and do something.

I have to keep busy.

It's late morning now and my log delivery's still a few hours away. I head for the kitchen but I can't boil the kettle until the range is lit. I should have brought my electric one with me; in the turmoil of the move I've forgotten it. I'm not hungry enough to make anything to eat either. There never feels like there's much point cooking without Neil to hoover it up and wolf down my leftovers too. If he was here now, he'd be sitting at the table shovelling in a sandwich. I can see him vividly, munching through a doorstep of cheese and pickle and scattering crumbs everywhere. It drove me crazy at the time, but now I'd do anything to fetch my dustpan and brush and sweep them up. I'd sweep all day if I could only have five more minutes with him.

My eyes blur and the room trembles. Funny how it's the little things that hurt the most.

Feeling rather lost and dangerously close to crumpling, I sit down at the refectory table and fish out my phone. I'll Google Kit Rivers and distract myself that way. I have to focus on something; drifting with the tide is dangerous. At times, the Internet can become a lifebelt.

The brief Wikipedia entry doesn't really tell me any more than I'd already gleaned from chatting to Sue. I compare it to the entries for Brooke and Owen and feel saddened that in contrast Kit's entry feels bald. An upper-class young man from a military family enlisted, went to France and died. If it wasn't for his poems there'd be little to set Kit apart from thousands of others like him. I sigh and close the page. There must be so much about Kit Rivers – and all the men who died, for that matter – that we'll never know. Details lost in time and that will never be unearthed. What was Kit's favourite food? Did he want to fight, or did he enlist under the weight of duty and family expectation? Was he light-hearted or serious? Did he want to be a poet? Who were his friends? Did he have a sweetheart? Was he afraid? I could ask endless questions but there are no answers to be found online except these few lines and the poems, which are all that remain of his brief life.

Will it be the same for Neil? Or myself, come to that? Who will remember us once I've gone? The nursery remained empty and neither of us have written poems – unless I count a rude Valentine's limerick he once scribbled into a card. I wouldn't want that published!

I rub my eyes until I see a burst of stars. Everything feels transient and terrifyingly meaningless. Knowing where these spirals of negative thinking can take me, I shake my head as though physical movement can scatter my thoughts, but no matter how hard I try my mind insists on drifting back to the sad story of the young poet and the heartbreaking loss of young life. The faces of those whose names feature on the stained-glass window might be long forgotten, but I can feel the despair of the people they left behind. Their grief wasn't any different from my own.

Dwelling on this won't do me any favours, I know that much from bitter experience, so I tug my thoughts back to the mystery of the daisy in the window. My Internet trawl hasn't unearthed anything about it, but I can't believe the flower was placed there at random or as a quirky repair. It has to mean something, surely?

I dig out my wellington boots, grab my bag and venture outside. A good walk will clear my head and keep me warm. I'll stomp up to the war memorial and then follow the path back across the fields to Rosecraddick. This route should take me onto the cliffs and then up across the headland, past Rosecraddick Manor and back into the village. I've been surfing the Net for long enough as it is, and I don't want to waste an entire day in front of a screen. I've even forgotten about lunch.

You can't keep skipping meals, Chloe! You need to eat healthily and look after yourself. Don't think you can live on toast or the odd biscuit either!

Neil's standing in the hall, his backside perched on one of the ancient cast-iron radiators, and shaking his head at me. He shimmers in the sunlight streaming through the big window halfway up the stairs. Then, as the light makes my eyes water, he fades away.

He might have vanished but his words make me smile. An exercise junkie who lived for his running and cycling, Neil would always tell me off for my poor diet, although I know for a fact that if he was with me now he would have been looking forward to loading up on pie and chips at the local pub, and promising to start healthy living tomorrow. As it turned out, I'm glad he enjoyed every carb-filled mouthful. All the grilled fish and salad in the world couldn't have made any difference to his diagnosis.

It's a beautiful day. The sun's tickling the waves and the sky is ink blue. I start off feeling cold but by the time I've climbed to the headland I'm sweating and doing my best to tie my coat around my waist so that I don't cook. The path to the war memorial's far steeper than it looks but the ascent is worth the effort. Endless water stretches out before me, domed by a vast arc of sky. Distance and freedom merge and as I crest the final twist of the cliff path I understand why a memorial would be placed here. Under these shifting skies and racing clouds, and with the water crashing relentlessly below, there's a sense of timelessness and of my own insignificance. I realise that what seems to matter so much to us in the here and now is nothing in comparison to the sea and the rocks and the turning of the tides; we're just tiny grains in the sands of time. Rather than filling me with despair, I find that there's peace in this thought.

There's a simple bench opposite the memorial and I sit on it to catch my breath and drink in the view. Then I turn my attention to the names listed in neat columns. I read them all, struck by how the same surnames are repeated among the fallen of the next generation. There's my surname again, with Gem Pencarrow in the First World War followed by three other Pencarrows lost in World War Two. Sue wasn't kidding when she said they weren't a lucky bunch. It seems that another seventy or so years hasn't improved our fortunes either. Maybe it's just as well Neil and I never had a family.

Not wanting to dwell on this thought, I turn inland and follow the well-worn route back to Rosecraddick. The coastal path's a popular choice on a sunny Saturday afternoon, and I pass serious walkers armed with poles and kitted out in gaiters, plus families with dogs and red-wellied children, as well as several runners. They're all heading in the opposite direction to me, so by the time the path drops into the woods I'm alone again with just my rasping breath for company.

It's cooler under the trees and the earth is dank. As I walk, I wonder whether Kit Rivers ever came this way. It's odd to think that he could have trodden the same track and seen the same views. Give or take some National Trust steps on the path and gangly trees that must have sprung up over the past century, I can't imagine much has changed.

The footpath wiggles through the woods, shaves through fields of bristly stubble and then ends abruptly with a stile into a sunken lane. Even in midwinter the limbs of trees embracing overhead plunge the narrow byway into shade, and I find myself enclosed in a tunnel of branches and knotty roots. Deep ruts either side suggest this is a popular route with green-laners, keen to test their four-by-fours somewhere other than on the school run, but apart from these and the occasional horse I don't suppose much traffic passes. This half-forgotten byway is as silent now as it must have been in Kit's day, a time before growling engines and the throb of traffic were commonplace. When I emerge onto the road leading into the village, it's a shock to see a car pass by.

I laugh out loud. What was I expecting? A pony and trap? Honestly, Chloe Pencarrow! You've been following the South West Coast Path – not passing through some magical time tunnel. Still, I can't help wishing this was a time-slip movie, rather than real life. If only I could bump into a villager from the turn of the last century, or even Kit Rivers himself. I'd ask him about the daisy in the window and I have a feeling he'd be able to tell me exactly what it means.

I really would love to know why the window was altered to incorporate it. My mother would worry that this is one of my strange obsessions to deflect the agony of losing Neil. (It isn't and nothing could do that anyway.) She'd mutter about seeing my doctor again (no thanks) and then ask if I should start the pills again too (absolutely not; things might hurt now, but at least I can *feel*). Anyway, none of this really matters. I'm relieved to feel a fizz of interest in anything other than making it through another twenty-four hours. Since I lost Neil, it's as though time's been wearing concrete boots; I'd forgotten what it feels like for a day to fly by like this.

It's been a long time since life felt like a joy rather than a feat of endurance.

As I turn a corner, the gates of Rosecraddick Manor stop me in my tracks. I've driven past before, of course, but only on the way to the Rectory and without having taken the time to stop. Now though, knowing this is the childhood home of the young man honoured in the window, I pause for a proper look.

Two weathered pillars topped by balls of stone and velveted with moss flank a pair of ornate wrought-iron gates. Once upon a time these would have been glossy and imposing, but today one lists drunkenly on its hinges, clinging to its twin with a piece of rusty chain. I allow myself to step right up to the gates, and my fingers curl around the metal. I hardly notice the flakes of paint that flutter down to the sparse gravel drive. Despite its dilapidated state, the sight of the Manor surrounded by specimen trees and lawns takes my breath away. The house is set at the end of a short drive, with a green turning circle just before the crumbling steps to the front door. Shuttered windows give the impression that the place is slumbering in the pallid winter sunshine, waiting for the spring to arrive in a haze of bluebells and bright splashes of rhododendrons and kiss it awake. As I gaze through the gate, I can imagine moonlit nights with carriages rumbling up the drive to deposit bare-shouldered beauties in ballgowns. I picture their white-gloved hands resting upon the suited arms of handsome gentlemen. Music plays, torches throw leaping shadows and voices rise and fall. Or maybe the hunt meets outside, hoofs stamping and hounds waiting for the command as side-saddle ladies and men in pink coats sip from stirrup cups? All this is long-gone now, of course.

I shiver even though the low sun spills onto the road. My imagination's running away with me. My artist's eye is suddenly painting pictures that my hand longs to trace. That's a good thing, I think? Not something to fear or shy away from.

Is my need to paint, once as essential as my need to breathe, returning?

I'd like to wander down the weed-pocked drive and explore, but the gates are padlocked with a heavy chain. Sue Perry mentioned that the Manor had been purchased by the Kernow Heritage Foundation, but maybe they don't open at the weekend? I make a mental note to find out more the next time I see her. Then, with one last look over my shoulder, I continue on my way back. The sun's starting to slip lower in the sky; soon twilight will fall, and I'd like to be back at the Rectory before it's dark. My logs should have arrived too. I suppose I'll need to figure out how to light the range. I've no idea how long it will take the house to heat up, but it would be nice to think that by bedtime I could take my coat off.

The village is deserted, the light spilling from cottage windows being the only evidence that anyone lives here at all, and by the time I arrive at the Rectory the first stars are freckling the sky. After a lifetime lived in London, it's a shock how dark the world still is away from streetlamps and permanently lit offices. Graveyards and bats and pools of darkness bring all kinds of fears to mind. Remind me again why I thought a house next to a graveyard was a good idea?

I'm rooting through my jacket pocket for my keys, which seem to have vanished beneath the detritus of tissues and Chapstick, when a tall figure looms out of the darkness and lurches towards me. Instinct makes me gasp, my hand flies out of my pocket and the keys clatter onto the ground.

"Sorry! Sorry! I didn't mean to make you jump!"

Thankfully the moon chooses this moment to stop being bashful and reveal the person making the apology. It isn't a zombie as I'd feared. Instead, standing in front of me is a tall man with long raven hair and a friendly face that must smile a lot, judging by the crinkles that star out around his eyes. He's not wearing bloodstained rags either, but instead is clad in overalls tucked into country boots. In any case, his arms are too full of logs to reach out and grab me.

I pause with my hand pressed over my galloping heart, feeling like an idiot. The lumber man. Of course. There's a truck pulled up by the gate, which I would have noticed if I hadn't been so lost in thought.

"You must be Larry the Log," I say.

The man smiles. In the moonlight his teeth are white and even.

"I'm afraid I'm just the lowly stand-in. Larry's my uncle, and I know he'd have made a much better job of stacking the logs than I have, but the vicar said this was an emergency delivery, so I lent a hand. I was just about to leave these in the porch to save you a trip to the woodshed."

"You've carried them all up and stacked them?" I'm thrilled to hear this. I'd thought I was about to become very fit courtesy of *The Log Workout*. Picking splinters out of my palms might have passed a few hours too.

The stranger looks shocked. "Of course I have. You didn't think you'd have to do it on your own?"

I do a lot of things on my own these days and I'm getting used to it. Neil would be amazed how good I am at putting bins out and catching spiders.

"It's called girl power," I say, and the log man laughs.

"That dates you! And me too, I think!"

I look at him with interest, trying to place his age. He's got to be mid-thirties at least and has dark grey eyes, a full mouth and wide high cheekbones crying out to be sketched or painted. For the second time today, my fingers itch to hold a paintbrush.

"So, can I put these down?" he asks when I don't reply. "Only, my arms are killing me and I'm running a bit late."

I'm glad it's dark so that he can't see my face turn red. Lost in thoughts of light and angles, I've been staring at him. Goodness knows what he thinks. That I fancy him, probably. After all, I'm a cliché aren't I? The young widow turning up to grieve in a clifftop Cornish house and being swept off her feet by a local tradesman who mends her broken heart. It's classic Mills and Boon stuff.

"Sorry, yes of course," I tell him quickly, stepping back to allow him to stack his armful of logs. I don't comment while he does so, simply because I don't have a clue what to say. I'm so used to being on my own that making conversation feels like an effort; it's as though my vocal cords have silted up from lack of use. Maybe I should get a cat to talk to?

I wasn't always so useless when it came to chatting to men, of course. It used to come easily and one of the things I loved about being married was feeling protected from all the misunderstandings and silly games that occurred to friends who were single. I belonged to Neil and he belonged to me; nothing and nobody else mattered. Nobody else ever will matter. We were each other's best friend. *Are* each other's best friend. Neil might not be here but that doesn't mean I love him any less. I touch my wedding ring for reassurance and instantly my pulse begins to slow. I can do this. I can lead a normal life. By the time the logs are neatly stacked I have control of myself again.

"How much do I owe you?" I ask.

The log man smiles and, just as I suspected, the smile crinkles his eyes. "Call it a moving-in gift. Welcome to Rosecraddick."

I can't accept charity. It doesn't feel right. Especially not when it's offered by an attractive man.

"Absolutely not. I have to pay for them."

"Then you'll need to take that up with my uncle and the vicar, but maybe once you've carried a few inside and lit the fire? It's getting cold."

He's right. I can see our breath as we speak.

I nod, not wanting to keep him a second longer. "OK, I'll do that. Thanks for dropping them off at such short notice."

"No problem," he says. "Besides, I couldn't have you freezing to death on my conscience, could I? That wouldn't be a good start to your time here."

I open my mouth to quip that this would be a happy release, but stop myself just in time. One thing I've learned is that people don't know how to handle my dark comments. They either laugh awkwardly or wonder if I actually mean it, and the trouble is I'm not always sure myself.

Anyway. I need to stop thinking like this. It worries Mum and sent my GP into a tailspin. I have to focus on practical things like lighting my range and settling in. Gallows humour is a delicate art when you're a widow. It's probably best left well alone.

"Thanks," I say again. Then, with another crinkly smile, he's walking away down the path. Moments later the truck's engine coughs into life and the vehicle drives away, its headlamps sweeping beams of light through the gathering darkness. Once the truck rounds the corner and the only light comes from the fat moon rising above the Rectory's roof, I stand alone in the porch with just my log pile and the odd screech owl for company. The log man was nice, and the quiet that falls now he's left feels deeper and lonelier than before. I sigh and scoop up some wood. Solitude was what I wanted and I'd better get used to it.

It's only when I've laid and lit the fire, coaxed the range into life and made tea that I realise I never even asked his name.

CHAPTER 5

CHLOE

I've never been religious – at least, not in the sense of going to church regularly – and after Neil died any faint hope I might have had in a benign universe or a kindly deity perished with him. I couldn't make sense of a being who'd let the children he supposedly loved suffer, who could step aside and watch as needles pierced veins and hair drifted to the floor, and I certainly couldn't countenance a God who'd close his ears to my pleas and prayers or let my tears fall and have no compassion to dry them. None of it made sense to me.

I railed against what was happening. I begged for it to be different. I read books. I chanted. Prayed to angels. Burned incense. Talked to priests. I did all of it and the outcome was still the same. As a result, I've come to only one conclusion, albeit a depressing one: we really are on our own and there is no rhyme or reason to anything that happens. We look for sense and we search for patterns or a grand design in the desperate attempt to make meaning out of what frightens us the most – the possibility that there is no meaning. Bad things happen to good people. Evil prospers. Young fit men get sick and die. Children starve. Teenagers are murdered in bomb blasts at music concerts. There is no reason or divine plan. Crap things happen. End of.

That's been my reasoning over the past two and a half years, although I'm not sure whether it's a comfort or not. Sometimes the loss of my constant, if faint, belief that there was something more, something greater than we can see, is as painful as losing my husband. Those are the days when it all feels especially bleak, days when I might not go far from the house, and it's even an effort to haul myself out of bed. If there's no meaning to it all then what's the purpose of anything? I said as much once to my counsellor, which was tantamount to pressing a big red alarm button, and I've been very careful to censor expressing such sentiments since. Now I keep my nihilistic thoughts to myself and if I don't want to get up or eat anything then it's my business. Whoever wrote that *Stop all the clocks* poem was bang on the money.

But since I arrived in Rosecraddick something's shifted. Try as I might to keep hold of my new faith in the certainty of nothingness, it's starting to slip away from me. Maybe it's something to do with living next door to an ancient church; perhaps the peace and the faith of generations have crept into me as though through osmosis. Or perhaps it's the ceaseless sound of the waves breaking onto the rocks below, as they have done for centuries. Or maybe it's seeing those names on the stained-glass window, recorded in the firm belief that their sacrifice was for a greater good and would be remembered long after their faces faded from memory. I can't say for sure, but I do know that when I wake up in a house a little less arctic than before (if not exactly warm), something's changed deep down inside of me. It's something I can't explain or rationalise, but while I sip coffee in the kitchen and watch the day break I have the strangest feeling that there is meaning after all. Maybe I just haven't known quite where to look. The daisy in the window has raised a thousand questions and I want to examine it again. Maybe I'll even sketch it.

That's more like it! Neil's nodding approvingly at me from the doorway. *Get outside and do something! Get drawing!*

Sunlight spills from the landing window and he trembles for a moment in the dust motes before vanishing. Not that he was ever really here, but the fact that my mind can still conjure him again makes my heart lift. For months I've struggled to picture his face and this has terrified me. I've closed my eyes and tried over and over again to dream him back into being: the startlingly blue eyes, the funny little scar that bisected his left eyebrow, the chicken-pox dent on his opposite cheekbone, the lock of hair that always fell over his face and that grew back as fast as he cut it. No matter how much I wished for them, these images wouldn't come. I tortured myself by looking at photographs but when I put them away again there was nothing but a blank. I'd had the feeling that coming to Rosecraddick was the answer to finding Neil again and it turns out that I'm right.

Does that mean that there is more to life? Am I any closer to finding the answers?

Anyway, Neil always was one for getting up at the crack of dawn and beginning the day. I've lost count of the times I wanted to burrow under the duvet or just turn the electric blanket on, drink tea and read a book but was chivvied into an early morning walk or a 4 a.m. spin to the coast. I might have complained then but now I'm so glad I didn't waste the short time we did have together. I finish my coffee, rinse the mug in the kitchen sink, throw a couple more logs into the range's firebox and wander upstairs to get dressed. By the time I let myself out of the Rectory, swaddled in my coat and with my feet scoring dark green prints in the white grass, the sun is higher and busy turning the frost to diamonds. Iced spider webs sparkle on bushes, the path crunches under my spotty city wellies and a blackbird trills alarm at my approach. The notes, loud and jarring against the morning quiet, make me jump.

It might be early but as I enter the church a rush of dusty warmth tells me that the heaters have been busy for some time. The neatly stacked hymn books and flickering candles hint that an early morning Eucharist has already been celebrated. Lights suspended on chains lashed to ancient beams throw puddles of brightness into the shadows, and somebody's arranged displays of poppies on the windowsills. The petals are vivid splashes glowing with life and colour against the sober stonework.

I find Kit's window and study it. There's no mistaking the exquisite skill of the craftsman who pieced together the design in such intricate fashion. I paint with acrylics and watercolours, but this

41

craftsman painted with glass and lead; I'm in awe of his talent. The longer I look, though, the more the daisy seems out of place, even though I suppose it's intended to be seen and acknowledged. The style of it's different and I'm certain it's been added later than the rest of the window. But why would that be?

It's a total mystery. No matter how long I stand and stare at the window, I can't make any sense of it. My eyes are dazzled by a kaleidoscope of jade and gold and vermillion, and my head spins with questions.

"What a lovely surprise to see you here, Chloe!"

Sue Perry's beaming at me. She moves in front of me and the window forms a halo of primary colours behind her. For a moment I imagine I'm talking to a frizzy-haired angel.

"You've come for the Remembrance Sunday service?" Sue continues. It isn't really a question though; she's already passing over a hymn book while gently shepherding me along to a pew. Glancing at my watch, I'm stunned to see that it's almost ten thirty. People are walking into the church and the organ's playing in the background. I must have been studying the window for well over an hour. No wonder my cramped feet tingle when I move them. Over sixty minutes have flown by. How on earth did that happen?

I have noticed that time's been weird recently. It drags or it gallops but it's never constant. Since Neil died, days can seem like years – but in the bitterest of ironies, the time we spent together feels as though it tore past in a blur. There were never enough minutes to tell him all the things I needed to say. In the early days I devoted a lot of effort to pleading for more time and making ludicrous bargains that of course I would never be able to fulfil. Perky Pippa tried to explain that this was all part of a process, but it didn't feel nearly that organised to me.

I'm about to tell Sue that no, I'm not here for the service when I glance up at the window again. This time my attention's captured by the list of fallen heroes from the village, rather than being drawn to

Kit Rivers' golden grace. What does it matter how I feel about church or religion? Never mind my own personal issues. Today's about honouring all of those who willingly suffered untold horrors so that people like me could have freedom. I also read Kit's poems last night, and even on a sparkly winter's day like this I'm haunted by the bleakness of his verse and the appalling reality of the Western Front. The least I can do is give an hour of my time to a service in the honour of those who fought for their king and country.

"I hope the logs arrived?" Sue asks as I take the hymn book and slide to the far end of the front pew. "Although the fact you're here and not in hospital with hypothermia suggests they did?"

"They did indeed. Thanks so much for organising it. I don't know what you said but the delivery guy even stacked them for me," I tell her.

"I *might* have hinted something about putting in a good word with my Boss," Sue laughs. "Naughty of me and definitely not in the rules, but needs must! In any case, I'm glad you're sorted and I'm even more glad you're here in church today. We'll catch up about arranging that pizza, OK?"

"OK," I agree, and Sue promises to call in and firm up a date. Then, in a swish of ecclesiastical robes, she's off to welcome her flock. As I return my attention back to Kit's window I think about the poems he left behind, poems that speak of loss and heartache and love of home, and I can't help but think he and his comrades would be pleased to know their sacrifice isn't forgotten. Mulling on this, I settle down to the service.

The packed church is testament to both Sue's popularity and the respect felt for Rosecraddick's fallen sons. I'm moved by the words in the readings as wreaths are laid beneath the stained-glass memorial.

An elderly man reads Laurence Binyon's *For The Fallen*. His voice quavers and I wonder who it is that his cloudy eyes are seeing. A father? A brother? A comrade? I'm seeing Neil because he'll never age either: he'll remain thirty-one in my memory, forever young and strong and fit and full of life, as likely to throw me over his shoulder and carry me up to bed as he was to go running or cycling. That's the Neil I'll always picture, not the tired shell of a man hooked up to drips, who gripped my hand in his thin fingers as though it was all that tethered him to this life.

Maybe it was? He slipped away when I wasn't there to weave my fingers with his. I wasn't by his side at the end to hold him, tell him I loved him and reassure him that it was all right to leave. I'd gone to get a coffee. A bloody coffee. How banal and desperately, dreadfully ill-timed. I don't think I'll ever forgive myself for not being there. It doesn't matter how many nurses tell me that loved ones often wait until they're alone to leave or that he was in no pain or even that he wouldn't have known; it doesn't make the slightest bit of difference to me.

I know.

I let him down. How will I ever get over knowing that? The answer is that I can't and deep in my heart I don't think I deserve to either. Surely it's only a matter of time before the smiling Neil that I've seen lately tells me exactly how badly done this was.

I'm sorry, I say silently as my eyes brim with tears and the whole church wobbles like blancmange. *I'm so sorry.*

"We will remember them," concludes the elderly man.

A tear splashes onto my hymn book. I haven't cried for months and I'm taken aback because I wondered whether I couldn't cry at all, as though I'd used all my tears up in the first few days of choking out angry sobs. These words, coupled with the peace of the church and the beauty of its rainbows of light, have unlocked something in me. Suddenly I'm terrified that after months of drought there could be a flood. I swallow hard and dig my nails into the palms of my hand. Time, Chloe. It just takes time to heal, remember? That's what everyone says.

But the problem is nobody seems to have a clue exactly how *much* time it takes. Are we talking decades? Centuries? Or maybe even aeons?

We observe the two minutes of silence and I study Kit's window again, blinking my tears away and distracting myself by imagining what his real story might be. I wonder what he'd think of this memorial. Would he like it? Or would he laugh and say that he was nothing like the angelic depiction? Did he like girls? Drink? Fast horses? New-fangled motor cars? I guess nobody will ever know now; the true Kit is lost and all that remains is this sanitised version that his mother paid to have immortalised in glass. If I saw him now, could he explain why somebody had added the daisy? Did it mean anything to him?

My head's pounding. So many questions that will never be answered. The dead take their secrets with them, I suppose. Maybe that's just as well? Do I really want to know how Neil feels about his wife missing his last moments because she wanted some caffeine?

The silence hangs as though weighted. The church seems to hold its breath and even the gulls outside are quiet. I know this is fanciful but it's so noiseless amid the old stones and prayers that I half belief even Nature stops to mourn. I watch the dust motes dance around shards of light, and when the brightness hurts my eyes I lower my gaze to the shelf in front of my pew, where the prayer books are kept. The wood is worn smooth from centuries of hands passing over it. Still lost in thought, I caress the cool surface – and then my hand discovers a ridge.

I frown. That's odd. Why is there a scratch in the wood? My fingers journey along and the first ridge leaps into another and another. I look more closely. Carved into the wood is the small but unmistakeable shape of a daisy.

CHAPTER 6

CHLOE

The church quietens as the congregation makes its way out through the arched doorway into the sunshine. Voices recede, feet tap over the flagstones and the organist gathers up his sheet music and heads outside, after which a perfect stillness falls.

I sit in the pew and trace the carving with my forefinger, following the crude lines over and over again. The edges feel rough beneath my fingertips, in contrast to the smooth wood. The design's been scratched in with a penknife. I know this because on one of our first dates Neil scratched our initials into the bark of a tree. When I close my eyes I see that moment frozen in time, the letters bald against the scarred trunk as Neil tilts my chin and brushes his mouth against mine.

"It's written down now, so you'd better not leave me now, Chloe Hughes," he'd whispered. In response I'd laughed, called him an idiot and promised I wasn't going anywhere. I think that was the moment I knew I loved him: I realised I could no more walk away from Neil Pencarrow than I could stop myself from breathing.

"I'll never leave you," I'd said.

I never broke my word either. As it turned out, Neil left me – something neither of us ever imagined. Sometimes I wonder what happened to our initials. Is the tree still there? Did the bark repair itself? Or does the faintest scar remain as evidence of a long-ago promise?

I reopen my eyes and the simple daisy's still there but, even so, I'm not sure I trust my own judgement. I'm only too aware that these days I see things because I want to see them and not because they're real. Neil, for instance, and maybe daisies too? Is Mum right? Am I *not quite myself?*

"Chloe? Is everything all right? Are you feeling unwell?"

Sue's opposite me and her gentle face is full of concern. I must look odd, sitting here all alone long after everyone else has left and staring at the front of my pew.

"Look at this," I say, pointing down at the carved daisy.

She leans over the pew.

"I take it you didn't whittle that because you were bored during my sermon?"

I laugh. "Absolutely not!"

"You're meant to say that my sermon wasn't boring," Sue sighs. She slides into the pew and sits beside me, then runs her hand over the carved flower.

"How odd. Until you pointed out the daisy in the window I'd never noticed it, and now there's this. You do have sharp eyes, Chloe."

"Tell me I'm not seeing things?" I plead. "That's a daisy, isn't it?"

"Certainly looks like one to me, although I must warn you that gardening, a bit like cooking, isn't my strong point!"

It's good to know I'm not hallucinating. "And you've never noticed it before?"

"No, definitely not. But then I wouldn't have, would I? I've never sat here. Far too busy at the front trying to entertain my congregation! Anyway, this looks to me as though it's been here a while, so maybe one of my predecessors wasn't quite as hot on the old PowerPoints and visual aids?"

"Maybe that's it? Somebody scratched it here because it reminded them of something?"

Sue looks doubtful. "It could just be that somebody sat here and copied the daisy from the window? A bored teenager maybe, passing time during a service? Or somebody artistic like yourself?"

She could be right but somehow I don't think so. The scores in the wood aren't fresh: they're age-darkened and grimy. The scratched image has been here a long, long time. Maybe as long as the window? Or longer? Perhaps it even came first? Whatever the answer, I feel certain this image meant something once.

It meant *everything*.

"This meant something to somebody," I say firmly.

"It's a mystery, that's for sure," Sue agrees. "I feel a bit dim actually for not being able to tell you much more about the daisy in the window. I must mug up on my history – once I've got to grips with the cooking and the gardening! And talking of cooking, my husband will be wondering what's happening to Sunday lunch. I'll call you about that pizza."

She stands up, robes swirling and her thoughts miles away from strange symbols and half uncovered mysteries. Now her mind is on roast beef, bubbling pans and a kitchen filled with steam. Her chubby toddler will be perched on the hip of the smiling man who'll greet her with a kiss. She'll pull off her dog collar, change into her jeans and be a mum and wife for a few hours before it's time to return for evensong. A dart of envy makes me catch my breath. Neil loved preparing a Sunday roast. It was the only meal he ever cooked, but he did it with such love and such attention to detail – from the crispy potatoes, to the beef still pink in the middle, to the gravy made with meat juices. He'd roll up his sleeves and stand at the hob, stirring and chatting away while I sat at the kitchen table with the Sunday papers. Looking back, those simple Sundays were some of the happiest times of my life. I wish I'd known then just how special they were.

"You're welcome to join us," Sue adds, probably catching the sadness flickering over my face. "We always make far too much, and Tim will get even fatter if he polishes it off. We've opened a nice red too."

One day I will eat Sunday roast again, but not just yet. I want to join Sue and her family. I want to sit at the kitchen table and hold Caspar on my lap, drink wine and chat away. One day. But not today. Not for many days yet.

"That's really kind but I'll pass today." I stand up too and slip my bag onto my shoulder. I need to get going before she tries to change my mind. I can't hold it together enough yet to face a family Sunday lunch.

"Are you sure? You're very welcome. Tim's dying to meet you."

"Another time. I thought I'd walk over to Rosecraddick Manor and see if there's anyone about to ask about Kit Rivers. The place was deserted yesterday."

"I expect Matt was with his kids," Sue sighs. "Poor guy. I have no idea how he juggles everything. He's doing his best to help with the family business and be a good dad to the twins as well as working for Kernow Heritage Foundation."

"Do you think he'll be there now?"

"I imagine so. He was wreath-laying this morning with the local councillor but he's bound to be there at some point, so you may be in luck. He's a historian, and he's local too – so he might be able to shed some light on things. Let me know if you find anything out about our vandal! Now, I'd better get these robes off and scoot home or I'll be in big trouble!"

We part company, Sue striding briskly through the nave on her way to get changed and me slipping quietly outside into the early afternoon. The wind's got up, whipping the waves into a canter and making me shiver in spite of the sunshine. I gather my coat around me and walk into the village, flattening myself against a hedge when Sue's battered Focus zooms by. She waves and hoots and I wave back, smiling because her energy and enthusiasm are as much a blast of fresh air as the bracing wind. These days I feel as though I'm on autopilot, dragging one foot in front of another to make it through the day, and Sue reminds me of the person I used to be – the Chloe who went running before school, managed the Art Faculty, visited galleries, had a growing career as an artist and adored her husband. That Chloe brimmed with life and I hardly recognise this husk of myself.

And neither would Neil. He'd be horrified.

Well, you're not here! I shriek at him silently. *You went away and left me! It's your fault!*

But this time there's no answer. There's only the calling of the gulls, which never seems to end. I think there'd be a metaphor in this if I could only find it.

I'm halfway to Rosecraddick when the sun vanishes and the world turns grey. Rain starts to fall, lightly at first as it sweeps in from the sea, but growing heavier and heavier with each moment. I haven't got a hood on my trendy city jacket and by the time I reach the Manor I'm drenched. Fortunately the gates are open today and there's a light shining from one of the lower ivy-cloaked windows. Encouraged by this, I trudge along the drive.

You'll only get wet once, I tell myself as I press on and do my best to dodge the puddles in the pock-marked drive. This is some downpour. So much for the sparkling frost and sunshine of the morning. Now it looks as though the village has been smothered by a grey dishrag.

Lacklustre as the weather is, even the rain doesn't detract from the beauty of the house. I sprint up the cracked steps and knock on the door while water drips through the porch and splashes onto the tiles. Ivy's growing through the gaps and I have the peculiar feeling that nature's creeping up on me. If I turn my back for the briefest moment, I'll be caught by stealthy green fingers and smothered by foliage.

The thought makes me shiver and I'm glad the door's wedged open with a pair of muddy boots.

"Hello?" I call, into a dark-panelled hall where two moth-eaten stags' heads regard me mournfully from above an empty fireplace. "Hello?"

My voice sounds hesitant and thin. There's no reply, so I step over the boots and try again.

"Hello? Is anyone there?"

There's still no answer and it feels as though the house is holding its breath. The vaulted hall is deserted and as I step inside the floorboards groan beneath my feet. The air is ripe with the smell of damp and mould, and now the only sounds are the ping of droplets falling into buckets and the drumming of rain on the roof. Unsure what to do next, I look around, taking in the light patches on the walls where once upon a time portraits of the Rivers family must have gazed down on visitors with the haughty confidence of ownership. Dreary light slides in through the ivy-snarled windows but does little to dispel the gloom. It feels as though nobody's been here for decades.

"I'm so sorry, I didn't hear you knock. Hang on a minute."

A figure emerges from the shadows and strides across the room to flick a switch. Instantly the hall fills with harsh electric light. This highlights mould and cobwebs, the crumbling plasterwork and treacherous holes in the floorboards – but it isn't these that make me gasp.

It's the identity of the speaker.

Standing in front of me, and totally at ease in Kit Rivers' childhood home, is none other than the log-delivery man.

CHAPTER 7

CHLOE

"Hello again," he says, not seeming the least surprised to find me here dripping rainwater all over the floor. "I do hope you were warmer last night?"

Thrown, I can only stare.

"The logs for your range?" he prompts when I fail to reply. "You did manage to light it, didn't you? Please say yes. I feel bad enough that I didn't offer to do it for you. I know we talked about girl power but I still ought to have been more of a gentleman."

"Yes. Yes, thank you. I did and I was very warm," I say, dazed. "The logs are great and you've got nothing to feel bad about. It was all fine."

"Phew. That's a relief," he says. "It's always good to pass quality control too! My uncle will be delighted. Now, can I offer you a towel?"

I'm puddling water all over the floor and am soaked to my knickers. Just to add to my joy, my hair's frizzing and my nose is running. I must look a state. Then again, what does it matter if I do? I don't care about any of that stuff anymore.

"I'm fine," I say. "I'm not that wet."

We both know this is blatantly untrue. I look as though I've been swimming. A towel won't even come close to drying me off.

Log Man raises an eyebrow. "You're drenched. I know this makes me sound like my granny, but you'll catch your death of cold like that. I've already got not lighting your wood burner on my conscience, so you're not catching pneumonia on my watch."

Before I can protest he's stretching up and pulling off his hoody.

As he tugs it over his head I catch a glimpse of taut stomach and dark whorls of hair tapering to the waist of his jeans, and I feel hot with something that could be embarrassment. Well I *hope* it's just embarrassment, anyway. Luckily he's wearing a plain white tee shirt underneath the hoody, otherwise I'd have had to flee the room like a coy Victorian maiden. Since Neil, this is the closest I've come to seeing a man's body and it feels… odd. Wrong even.

Guilt stipples my skin and my face is flushed. Yesterday I caught myself thinking he was attractive – and he really is, in a smouldering Ross Poldark kind of way. I look down at my wellies. Oh look! Aren't the pink and yellow spots cute?

Fortunately for me, Log Man is unaware of my thoughts and thrusts his hoody into my arms with great enthusiasm.

"There you go. Mop yourself up with that."

I stare down at the garment that I'm now clutching against my chest. The fabric's warm from the heat of his body. It smells of maleness and fabric conditioner and a lemony aftershave. Just holding it feels intimate and wrong.

Like I'm cheating on Neil.

"Honestly, it's fine," he assures me, understandably misinterpreting my silence as a reluctance to use his clothing as a mop. "It really is. The hoody's ancient and I've got a jacket upstairs too. Besides, I'm really warm. I've been lugging furniture about for hours. It's hard work but I keep telling myself it's good for me to get some exercise at my age. I need to keep up with my kids. They already think I'm practically a geriatric."

In the harsh electric lighting I see he's older than I'd thought. Early forties maybe? The dark hair is sprinkled with grey at the temples, there are lines of sadness etched about his mouth and he looks tired. Then he smiles and the years melt away with the boyish twinkle in his eyes. He's being kind, that's all. I'm overreacting. He's lending me his hoody, not asking to sleep with me.

This thought really makes me blush. I'm not thinking about

sleeping with him. It was just a turn of phrase.

"It's clean," he adds. "Fresh on today."

I feel ungrateful now, and a bit daft. Perky Pippa would love to examine my conflict about accepting help from a handsome man. She'd want to *explore* and *validate* every detail. Well, no thanks. It's just an offer of a hoody. No big deal.

"Thanks," I say and begin to dab at my face and hair.

"So, I'm assuming you haven't come to complain?" the log-delivery man continues while I pat myself dry. "I have to level with you – I really don't fancy having to unstack that lot if you want to return it! If you keep the hoody, maybe we could be quits?"

He smiles and I'm struck again by the perfect teeth and the lines fanning out around his eyes like stars. I like his sense of humour.

"No, the logs have definitely passed quality control, so you've nothing to worry about. Your hoody's safe."

He mimes wiping his brow. "I'm relieved. Uncle Larry will let me out again and my souvenir from the nineties can continue to give my age away!"

Slightly drier now, I hand him back the soggy garment and tuck my hair behind my ears.

"Thanks for that. No, don't worry; I'm not here about logs. I'm actually looking for Matthew Enys? Sue Perry said I might find him here."

Log Man holds out his hand. "The Reverend Sue is rarely wrong. We haven't been formally introduced but I'm Matt Enys."

"You're Matt? You work for the Kernow Heritage Foundation?"

I can't hide my surprise. I'd been expecting a much older man, an academic type in tweed maybe and with long grey hair, but not this muscular guy who lifts logs as though they were matchsticks and wears faded Levi's and Iron Maiden hoodies. His dark wavy hair brushes his shoulders, his jaw's shadowed with stubble and an earring glints in his left ear. His torso, or what little I've just glimpsed of it, is ripped too and he looks more like a rock star than an academic. Why didn't Sue mention he was hot?

This thought makes my face grow warm again. Did I just label Matt Enys as "hot"? I guess I did but in a purely objective way, the same way I can still appreciate Johnny Depp or Brad Pitt. Luckily, Matt can't read my mind. He's draping the hoody over the back of a massive cast-iron radiator and chatting away easily as he does so.

"I certainly am and, yes, I work for the Kernow Heritage Foundation when I'm not moonlighting for my uncle."

"I'm really sorry. That sounded dreadfully rude," I say. I think there's a part of me that's broken; I don't seem to function socially like I used to. I guess I'm out of practice.

But Matt doesn't appear offended.

"I should look like Dumbledore to really be the part, shouldn't I? Still, I promise you that if our budget for this place gets slashed again I'll soon have white hair just like his. This project is certainly responsible for all my grey! I'm a historian and I'm in charge of putting exhibitions together for the Foundation – easier said than done on a shoestring. Anyway, I'll stop prattling on. I take it you're here because you're interested in Kit Rivers?"

I nod. "Sue's been telling me a bit about Kit. I'm afraid I didn't know anything about him before."

"Don't apologise. That's totally understandable. He's not particularly well known, although I'm really hoping that will change soon. He's such a lost talent. The tragedy is that so much of his work and story died with him. He died far too soon."

Sadness flits across his face like moonlight over the sea. It's an open and honest countenance, nothing hides there, and it's a face you instinctively trust. For a moment I teeter on the brink of telling him that I understand because my husband also died far too young, but I stop myself in time. Rosecraddick is supposed to be my new start and the last thing I want is pity.

"Sue says the Kernow Heritage Foundation are restoring the house?"

Matt nods. "That's right. We've got some money together, a mixture of EU funding, lottery money and a legacy – although I've a feeling this will be a drop in the ocean. We're hoping to bring Rosecraddick Manor back to the way it would have been in 1914 when Kit lived here. It's a massive undertaking, as you can probably see just from standing in the entrance hall!"

I glance around. Mildewed curtains hang limply from sagging poles and it's hard to visualise how smart the hall would have looked in the nineteen-hundreds. There would have been a blazing fire in the big hearth at the far end and the wooden panelling must have glowed with beeswax polish. Intimidating family portraits would have eyeballed new arrivals as a butler stepped forward to greet them. I imagine Kit, blond and full of life, striding across the room dressed in riding gear or maybe sitting by the fire reading poetry. Was he an outdoors person? Or did he spend his time in the library? I'd love to know.

"It'll be worth it in the end," Matt's saying, oblivious to my drifting thoughts. "We'll do all the usual stuff with tea rooms and visitor trails, but the real jewel in the crown will be Kit's story. I'm hoping that will attract school parties too, as well as helping his work to reach a wider audience. He was such a talent and deserves to be recognised, so I'm going to do my very best to make sure that happens."

As he says this excitement lifts the tiredness from his face and his eyes light up. This is Matt's passion and suddenly I feel foolish. What am I thinking, bowling up here because I have a hunch about some graffiti on a pew and a growing fascination with a long-dead poet? It's hardly academic stuff. In fact, it sounds ridiculous.

"It sounds like you're really busy. I'm sure you could do without me turning up and wasting your time," I say.

"Not at all. I love sharing what I know about Kit. His life and poetry have been my passion ever since I first read his work when I was a teenager. I think it was partly him who inspired my love of history, so coming here to work on his house is a dream come true, especially for a Cornish lad like me. What can I help you with?"

"I don't know where to start," I say tentatively. "I'm horribly ignorant. I Googled Kit and read his poems. They're pretty harrowing."

"I know," Matt agrees. "Kit certainly didn't pull his punches. *God Hid His Face* gives me nightmares."

I nod. "Me too. I can't put it out of my mind."

It's not an exaggeration. The images drawn in verse haunted me before I fell asleep. My dreams, half recollected when I woke up this morning, were filled with fire and shells and mud, and I've made a mental note that in the future I won't read anything by Kit before bedtime.

"And what did you think?" Matt's dark grey eyes pin me and I really, really want to get my answer right. This matters.

"I thought the poems are terrible but in the true sense of the word," I tell him. "Full of dread and with such heaviness. They made me feel weary and full of despair. It's hard to shake off."

"That's exactly it," Matt agrees. "So how can I help you? Was there something in particular?"

I pause. If I tell him about the daisy carved on the pew, will he think I'm making a mountain out of a molehill? The fear of appearing crazy haunts me these days. The questions. The concern. The worried looks. The spiral.

"Sort of," I say.

"Sort of?"

"OK then, yes. Yes, I want to know more."

His eyes crinkle. "That's more like it. So, more about what? His poetry? His life? His war?"

I take a deep breath. I really want to tell him but I can't find the words. Maybe I don't want to share this strange conviction that there's a message in the window and on the pew.

Matt regards me thoughtfully, as though he knows I want to say something, but when the words aren't forthcoming, he just inclines his head and smiles. "All of it?"

I laugh. "That sounds like a big ask, but yes. I'd like to know more. I'm intrigued."

"How about I start by showing you the house? I'm afraid it's all quite a muddle at the moment. The place has been a school, a hotel, barracks for the army in the Second World War and even a commune in the sixties. The attics are stuffed full of God knows what and I'm going to be sifting through them for quite a while. That's why I'm here on a Sunday afternoon instead of having a life."

"If you don't mind showing me, I'd love to have a look. I'm fascinated by what I've learned about Kit and I'd love to see where he grew up."

And see if there are any daisies, I add silently. It's a long shot, I know, but it's a possibility...

Matt seems delighted to give me a tour and we spend an hour or so exploring the house. It's not a huge stately home built to impress or to entertain monarchs; rather, it's a place that feels as though it's grown organically out of the Cornish earth and settled gently into itself over the centuries. Matt shows me the Elizabethan long gallery, the kitchens, the library and the drawing room, and although the rooms are stripped of furniture and scarred with the additions of blackboards or fire doors, his words paint such a vivid picture that I feel as though I'm seeing the place Kit would have known. We climb up the grand staircase and pause on the return, where a large window faces out over the village. Rainy fingernails scrape the glass and the sea's a low leaden line hemming a smudge of green. From this vantage spot, I can see the cedar tree on the Old Rectory's front lawn, and the roof of my own home.

"You can see the Rectory from here!"

"It's a wonderful view, isn't it?" Matt rests his hands on the banisters. "The family would have owned all the land for miles around, and they'd also have been able to influence the appointment of the parish clergyman. It's hard for us to imagine just how much power they would have had. Most of the villagers would have depended upon them for their employment and their housing."

"It's real *Downton Abbey* stuff," I remark. I can picture it all: the servants, the horses, the elegant dinners…

"Absolutely. The family was very important. They would have owned most of the farms and the parkland around the place too. A lot of that's been sold, of course, and the new housing estate where Sue lives is built on some of it, but in Kit's time it would have been there to ride and walk in. The park was ploughed up and farmed during both wars and I believe the US Military were practising manoeuvres here at one point. There are layers and layers of history in Rosecraddick and I like to think of it as being a bit like an onion; the more I peel away, the closer I get to the heart of it."

This idea chimes with me. Grief is my onion but I daren't peel away the layers because I'm afraid of what I may find at the centre.

"After Kit died the place fell into decline," Matt continues, still gazing out across the rainy Cornish landscape. Dark squalls march across the sea but on the horizon the faintest line of gold is appearing, and I find myself wondering how I'd paint this. I'd need to show the might of the elements and the fury of the storm but temper these with the promise of light to come. Acrylics would work, and bold strokes.

My heart lifts to discover I'm thinking about painting again. Maybe Matt would let me set up my equipment here and try? I think I could start again with this view.

"His father didn't survive him by many years," Matt says softly, almost to himself, as though repeating a familiar and much-loved tale for comfort. "And Kit's mother died in the early 1930s. Without an heir, the estate passed to a distant cousin who rented it out and sold off parcels of land and any valuables. Times had changed anyway and the glory days of big country estates were drawing to a close. Eventually the place fell into disrepair and we managed to buy it last year, albeit with lots of help."

"And if you hadn't bought it?"

Matt shakes his head. "Then I think Kit Rivers' story and his work might have faded away. There's a memorial to him in the walled garden too – I'll show you if this rain ever stops – and I couldn't bear to think of it being lost."

We continue upwards and I think about time and how it erases all kinds of things, from mighty empires to (according to Perky Pippa) grief. This once prosperous house is now dusty and almost derelict, a far cry from its heyday. The stair carpet's worn thin, the chandeliers have long since been sold, bare patches scar the wall where works of art once hung, and the beautiful banisters are blemished from decades of schoolboys scrambling up and down them. Even so, the dignity of the place is intact. It feels as though Rosecraddick Manor is watching Matt Enys to see what will happen next. The lost world of the early twentieth-century upper classes is waiting in the shadows; it hasn't gone away.

"What do you think of this?" Matt asks when we reach the top of the great staircase. He's pointing towards a portrait of a stern gentleman with grey mutton-chop side whiskers and a determined chin, who gazes through his monocle in such a fierce and critical manner that I gulp. He's dressed in full military regalia, with medals emblazoned across his chest, and under his scrutiny I can't help feeling nervous.

"We found this portrait in the cellar," Matt tells me. "It was wrapped up very carefully, one of the few family portraits that we have managed to find. This is Colonel Rivers, Kit's father, who was a decorated hero of the Boer War and by all accounts a very exacting individual."

"I can believe it," I say. Colonel Rivers doesn't look as though he would approve of much at all. I wonder how life with such a father was for his poetic son? Did Kit enlist straight away because he was keen to follow in his father's footsteps, or were there conflicts? Did they argue? Or were they alike?

"I should imagine Colonel Rivers would have been a hard act to follow," Matt remarks. "The Rivers family had a military background and Kit seems to have bucked the trend by being educated at home rather than at public school. From what we know of the family, his mother wanted him kept with her. He was due to go to Oxford when war was declared. He may have flourished there and become famous if he'd had the chance. Who knows?"

"Life can change in a heartbeat," I say before I can help myself. Matt gives me a long and searching look but doesn't ask me to elaborate.

"Very true," is all he says. "Come on. I'll show you the attics. They're full of interesting bits and pieces."

He leads me through some dusty attic rooms where lowly servants would have been quartered, before we retrace our steps to the middle floor. Here the wooden shutters are closed and the rooms swim with gloom, but as Matt talks I picture the nursery and the bedrooms as they would have been, and I almost see Kit sitting in the window reading. Keats, perhaps? Or was he more excited by Byron and Shelley's revolutionary verse?

"Which one was Kit's room? Was this it?" I ask when Matt shows me into a large chamber with three big windows. The shutters are closed tightly but, were they open, we would have a view of the formal gardens and the wooded hills beyond.

Matt sighs. "I have absolutely no idea and I can't imagine how we'd ever find out. It would certainly have been on this floor though and at the back of the house with the views over the gardens. There are bathrooms there too, which again suggests the family used those rooms."

"But you'll never know for sure." For some reason this thought fills me with sadness. Our time here is so fleeting; it's unbearable that we aren't remembered. Who else will remember Neil the way I do? Who else would know or care in a hundred years' time that he slept on his stomach or hated tomatoes or loved a girl called Chloe?

Matt studies me, his dark brows drawing together as though he guesses there's a subtext.

"I suppose not," he says eventually. "There are so many gaps in Kit's story, mostly because he died so young and before he even had a chance to make his mark. If it wasn't for the poems he'd be almost forgotten. Even the stained-glass window in St Nonna's would be little more than a curiosity."

"Doesn't that distress you?"

"What? The not knowing? Or the passing of time?"

I shrug. "Both, I guess. I hate the idea that the years rub us out."

Matt frowns. "But I don't think that's true. I think we all make our mark in some way. OK, not everyone changes the world by landing on the moon or creating great works of literature, but we all make a difference. And what's the world anyway, except our experience of it? How do we know that a kind word or a smile doesn't alter the course of somebody else's history? What seems small to us can be huge to another person. I think the thing I enjoy the most about history is trying to uncover those small acts and the little details that make a bigger picture. I don't know if I'll ever be able to tell you anything more about Kit Rivers, but I'm going to do my very best to tell his story."

I really want to tell him about the daisy scratched on the pew. It could be just the small detail he needs – but Matt is into his stride now and telling me all about his plans for the house.

"So eventually we'll mock up one of the bedrooms as Kit's and create an exhibition. Maybe a trunk being packed for war, a dress uniform and some moving images of the Western Front to accompany recordings of his poems? What do you think?"

I shiver. What I think is that it sounds desolate and unbearably sad, but I don't want to say this out loud. I have an overpowering feeling that something vital's missing from all this, something that's been overlooked, and that from the shadows Kit's trying to tell us so.

It's all fanciful stuff, of course, and my stomach lurches with the fear that I might be having some sort of relapse. I must make sure I don't start to slide backwards. Feelings and instincts are all very well, but doctors don't tend to like my wilder flights of imagination.

"I think it could be interesting," I reply doubtfully.

"But there's a long way to go?" Matt adds on my behalf. Then he sighs. "There's tonnes to do, but that's what I'm here for and I have a great team too. And my kids love playing in the grounds."

He's mentioned his children several times so, to be polite, I ask him about them and am rewarded with a smile of such joy that it feels as though the sun's coming out.

"I've got eight-year-old twins, Merryl and Lowenna, and they're brilliant. They live with their mum in Exeter, but they stay with me some weekends and during their school holidays. They love Rosecraddick."

"I bet they do. My husband spent his holidays here as a child and he was always talking about it, even years on."

The words are spoken before I can stop myself. Instantly I long to reach out and grab them, stuff each syllable back down my treacherous throat. Now that I've mentioned Neil, Matt's bound to ask about him. Where he is. What he does. Alternatively, if it occurs to Matt that Neil's no longer alive he'll be sympathetic – which will be ten times worse. I won't be Chloe anymore but a widow and an object of pity. The easy conversation I've enjoyed will dry up. I hadn't realised until I met Sue and now Matt just how much my life has been governed recently by my status as a widow. It's all people see me as now. I'm not a wife or an artist or even myself, but somebody who inhabits the awkward edges of society. I don't belong anywhere and they have no idea what to do with me.

I hold my breath and wait. Can I talk about Neil without crumpling? What should I say anyway? And when I know, can I even say it without falling apart?

But Matt doesn't ask about my husband.

"Cornwall's made for kids, isn't it?" he agrees. "Beaches and crabbing and ice cream and chips. Heaven for them and not bad for the rest of us, once you're used to reversing in lanes and driving ten miles to the supermarket, of course! And don't get me started on the erratic weather. Although, talking of that, I think we may be through the worst of the rain."

He heads to the window and gingerly prises open a shutter. A stripe of pallid sunshine bisects the floorboards and I realise that the patter of rain and the song of drops falling into buckets ceased a while ago.

"Yep, looks to me as though the rain's eased off. Still, we'd better not take that for granted. Let me show you Kit's memorial before the weather decides we need another drenching."

We leave the bedroom, turning left and ducking through a low door leading to a narrow stairwell. This would have been where the servants hurried up and down, carrying firewood or hot water or even chamber pots. The steps are made of stone and worn from all those feet scurrying to do the bidding of the Rivers family. At the bottom of the stairwell is the kitchen; its huge fireplace is still blackened from centuries of smoke, but the room is empty of all furniture except stacks of school desks.

"They're from when the house was a boarding school in the fifties," Matt says, seeing me looking. "God knows why they've ended up in here."

"I see what you mean about having a lot to do," I say sympathetically.

"In fairness, it's not just down to me. I have a great team of experts and specialists to call upon. Come on, let's go outside. I'll show you the gardens."

There's an arched door at the far end of the kitchen that has two big iron bolts. Matt slides these across and we step outside into a courtyard.

"This would have been the herb garden at one point," Matt says as we walk across it. "The Foundation has plans to restore it, but that's really not my area of expertise. I'm hopeless with plants. How about you? Do you like gardening?"

I consider the question. To be honest, I don't know. Our flat was on the second floor of a converted Victorian house situated on a main road. The only bit of greenery we had was a sparse earthy patch outside the front door where the communal bins were kept. A fine collection of thistles and dandelions thrived there, but without any help from me. Neil and I had hoped to move out to Buckinghamshire when we talked vaguely about having a house with a garden; we took it for granted that we'd have children one day and that they'd need space to play. I supposed he would have mowed the lawn while I'd have attempted to grow flowers. The vision drifts before my eyes and I blink it away. That version of my future is long gone.

"I don't know," I reply. "I've never really had the chance to find out."

"Well, feel free to come here anytime and see," Matt grins. "You could make a start in here if you wanted."

"Here" is a small door set into a crumbling wall, which Matt unlocks before standing back to let me through. Fingers of ivy reach for me as I pass through; I push them away, impatient to see the secrets hidden in this small walled garden with its tangled hedges and its flower beds thick with the remains of long-dead plants. The garden is a perfect square, with paths leading from each corner to converge at the centre. Rosemary bushes, straggling and woody, guard the paths on each side.

"Kit's memorial's in the centre. All paths lead to him because he was the centre of his parents' world," Matt says simply.

"I thought he was lost in action? That's what the window says in the church."

"You're right: he was. This is a private memorial his parents placed here for the family. I guess it gave them something to focus on and a private place to grieve. Some people need that."

He's right. They do. I don't think I'm one of them though. I've not visited the garden of remembrance since the simple ceremony after Neil's funeral. He isn't there: he's in my heart. His mother called me a cold fish when I refused to have him buried with an ornate headstone. She wanted the grave and the ritual and the whole big funeral, but Neil would have hated it. He was all about grabbing life with both hands and wrestling it to the ground, and in honour of this I scattered his ashes on the lake where he loved to sail. That's where he would want to be, with the water and the wind and the freedom of endless possibilities. It was the last thing I could do for him.

"All these bushes are rosemary," Matt says, pointing at the bedraggled hedges. "According to Janet, the Foundation's garden historian, rosemary's associated with remembrance. I think that's a nice touch, don't you?"

I nod but I'm not looking at Matt. Instead, I'm imagining a woman who's walking towards the centre of the garden. Her grey hair is swept into a chignon and she's wearing the clothes of a long-gone era. Her head is bowed and one hand trails through the rosemary, brushing the leaves and filling the air with a pungent scent. For Lady Rivers, Kit would forever be associated with this aroma, just the faintest trace of it enough to bring his memory tearing back no matter where she was. I'm envious because when I think of Neil, no matter how hard I try to conjure up the warm scent of his neck when I nuzzled into it at night, all I get is the choking smell of the hospital. Maybe I'll plant a rosemary bush at the Rectory. If I think of Neil when I brush past it, will this smudge out the horrors lodged in my senses?

Matt and I walk to the centre of the garden. A semicircular stone bench is placed at the midpoint where the paths converge. In front of it is a simple marble slab set into the path.

Captain Christopher 'Kit' Rivers

Beloved son
1896–1916
'Their name liveth for evermore'

It's plain, but its simplicity is more moving than an ornate tomb covered in weeping angels would have been.

"Kit's parents must have sat here and thought of him. I hope the peace of the spot helped them," I say.

"His mother apparently told her friends that she didn't know how she could bear the loss or go on without him. Losing a child must be unbearable. Poor woman. They say she never got over it. How could she?"

"She wouldn't have, but in the end you do your best because there's no choice," I say quietly. "You have to move forwards."

You do, Neil agrees, smiling across the garden at me. *And you are moving forwards, Chloe. You really are.*

"That's true. I think this is a healing place. Maybe it helped her do that?" Matt says. "I never fail to be touched by it. Crazy as it sounds, I feel close to Kit here even though he's buried somewhere in France."

He's right: it is a special place. As we stand quietly and look at the memorial, which is softened by the watery sunlight, I decide I want to tell Matt Enys about the carving in the church. It could be a piece in the puzzle and it was what I came here to talk about. If he thinks I'm making something out of nothing, then I'll just have to deal with it.

"Matt," I begin, "Kit's window in the church has a daisy in it, doesn't it? Have you any idea why? I was looking at it earlier and it seems to me as though it was added later on."

"Yes, I know the bit you mean and the daisy does look like an addition," Matt agrees. "It's very out of place, I think, but I'm afraid if you're asking me why it's there I can't tell you the answer. It's another mystery. It could mean something or it might be as simple and banal as somebody thought it might look nice. It may even be a clumsy repair."

I nod. "That's what I thought too, but when I was in church earlier for the remembrance service I noticed something. It's probably just a coincidence, but I've noticed there's also a daisy carved onto the front pew, on the shelf part."

"What?"

"There's a daisy carved onto the pew," I repeat. "It's nothing special. Just something that looks as though it's been etched with a penknife. If I was at school I'd find similar things scratched onto desks."

Erect penises are usually what the kids I teach like to carve, but I don't share this little gem. I've only known Matt a few hours, hardly long enough to discuss genitalia.

"In St Nonna's?"

"Yes. I was sitting in the front pew on the right-hand side and it caught my attention."

"Interesting," Matt says slowly. "That pew used to be where the Rivers family sat. Back then the most important families had their own pews and, being the foremost landowners, the Rivers were right at the front. On the right-hand side."

"I could have been sitting where Kit Rivers once sat?"

"It's very likely," he replies.

"So the daisy in the window and the one on the pew are linked?"

"They could be, but how we'd ever know that for sure is the big question. I've never heard anyone explain what the daisy emblem is all about."

"But it could mean something."

"Like a message from the past?" Matt's teasing me and I laugh.

"I know that's a bit unlikely. Fair enough. It could have been done by anyone."

"True, but it does sound very intriguing. Come on, then. Shall we go?"

"Go where?"

Matt Enys smiles down at me. "To the church, of course. I'd like to see this for myself."

CHAPTER 8

CHLOE

Matt and I walk through the empty church, our footsteps seeming unbearably loud as we pass through the nave. We slip into the front pew and I point out the etched daisy. Matt's fingers stroke the wood.

"How strange," he says.

"Do you think it means something?"

"To be honest I don't know."

"But Kit would have sat here?"

He nods. "This was the family pew and Kit would have sat here every Sunday until he left to fight, but I couldn't tell you whether this is linked to him. The daisy in the window has irked me for years but I've always assumed it was a clumsy repair. Obviously it wasn't here in Kit's time." His finger skims the design. "Maybe there could be a connection, but I couldn't even begin to guess what that might be."

"So it's a mystery?"

"It seems that way. Kit's memorial window was made at least ten years after his death and the design was nothing to do with him."

"Do you think you can find out what it means? Or if it's linked to Kit Rivers?"

"I'll certainly do my best," Matt promises. "This is where I earn my keep. Maybe there's something in the house that I've overlooked? Or a line in one of the poems? A photo tucked into a drawer? There are hundreds of possibilities, but it's going to take time. You've seen the Manor and how full of stuff it is. I could be a while."

"Needles and haystacks spring to mind," I say, and he laughs.

"If only it was that straightforward!"

We sit in thoughtful silence. The two memorial windows glow in the late sunlight, like laughter after a storm of tears. I think about the poems I read, and I wonder what the significance of the flower might be. Could it have been Kit who carved this one? The etched flower is perfectly placed to be secretly traced with a forefinger, maybe during prayers or a sermon. For a second an idea surfaces, flickering through my mind with bright brilliance before it flips and dives deep, leaving me struggling to cling onto what it was I thought I almost understood.

Matt turns to me. "You could help? If you like?"

"Me? How can I help? I'm no historian."

"I don't need a historian. I need a pair of sharp eyes and somebody who's interested. You see things in a different way to other people, Chloe. You notice details and patterns. If it hadn't been for you then I wouldn't know about this carving."

I shake my head. "It might be nothing."

"Or it might be everything. The point is, I don't know and I wouldn't have known if it wasn't for you. Look, you don't have to make your mind up now, but we're always looking for volunteers at the Kernow Heritage Foundation and I think you'd be a wonderful addition to the team. You're exactly the kind of person we need."

This unexpected praise feels like slipping into a warm bath. I can't remember the last time that somebody told me I might be useful to have around. My mother watches me with a permanently worried pleat between her brows, and when I last stayed with my sister I caught her hiding the steak knives (although Steph always was a drama queen). The doctors have an air of patient resignation, Perky Pippa analyses me as though I'm a lab specimen and, before I finally handed in my notice after my brief return to work, all my colleagues tiptoed around me. To be in St Nonna's with a virtual stranger who thinks I'm worth listening to is really quite refreshing. Matt doesn't know anything about me. He doesn't know about Neil or the past. He just sees me.

"Sorry. I'm being presumptuous. You're probably busy enough

already," Matt apologises when I don't reply. He runs a hand through his hair and smiles ruefully. "Feel free to tell me to shut up. I'm afraid I get totally carried away about Kit. My ex said it borders on obsession and she probably has a point. I'm sure you've got better things to do than spend hours sifting through junk."

He's wrong: I haven't. My grand plan of *leave London and move to Cornwall* never got beyond what would happen when I actually arrived. For months my only focus was escaping the flat and all the memories it held. The minutiae of dealing with estate agents, potential buyers and conveyancers filled my time and, following that, the logistics of storing items and selecting those that would come with me. I never thought about what I'd do with myself once I got here. Paint again was the hope, but I never considered just how vast the Rectory would feel or imagined how my days would yawn ahead, empty and endless.

Do it! Neil's lolling against a pew and looking stern. *Can't have you lazing about all day now I'm not here to kick you up the backside! You'll be watching* Jeremy Kyle *and* Homes Under the Hammer *before you know it!*

He's gone in one beat of my pulse. Still, this is the reminder I need. Neil would hate to think of me alone and lacking focus. Stewing in the Rectory won't bring him back to me, but perhaps finding out more about Kit Rivers and doing some voluntary work for the Kernow Heritage Foundation might help to ease the ache in my heart?

"OK," I say. "Why not?"

"Really?"

"Really. I have some time on my hands and I'd like to help."

"Well, that's great! Welcome to the team!"

He holds out his hand and we shake. It's strange to have my fingers enclosed in a man's grasp, however fleetingly, and I'm startled by the unexpected intimacy of the contact. I slide my fingers away as swiftly as I can. Neil and I held hands all the time and this is a reminder of the loss of something I'd so casually taken for granted.

I'd loved being linked to him as we strolled around the market or sat on the sofa watching a film.

Sometimes it's the simple losses that slice deepest. It's a good thing I have something new to concentrate on.

"When do I start?" I ask.

Matt grins. "At the beginning, of course. You, Chloe Pencarrow, have got a lot of reading to do!"

"And Matt thinks that the image in the window and the carved daisy on the pew are linked?" Sue asks, or at least I think this is what she says. It's hard to tell because her mouth's full of pizza.

As I'd expected, it would have been easier to stop the tide racing up the beach than to find a good excuse not to eat dinner with the vicar and her family. It's Monday evening, the elusive gap in her schedule that Sue was looking for. It turned out that one of her meetings had been cancelled at short notice. When she knocked on the Old Rectory's door to see if I happened to be free, I was bleary-eyed after hours spent mugging up on the Great War and the history of Rosecraddick. For the first time in longer than I can remember, my thoughts have been well and truly occupied by something other than my own grief.

"Happy reading!" Matt had said cheerfully this morning when he'd turned up with a pile of books and papers. "Just something light to keep you going. Owen, Sassoon, Robert Graves, some military history, some social history, and the icing on the cake – my personal notes on Kit Rivers. Don't read it all at once!"

"You do know I teach art, not English?"

"You foolishly said you had time on your hands," Matt had reminded me. "Kernow Heritage Foundation needs all volunteers to be well informed before we let them loose. Let me know when you're ready for your test."

"Test?"

"Absolutely. Nothing too scary. Just a couple of essays and some multiple choice," he'd deadpanned, and for a minute I'd stared at him in horror before he'd started laughing.

"Very funny," I'd huffed, but secretly I was pleased. What better way to take my mind off the present than by immersing myself in the past? The desire to paint was starting to return but I was still afraid to pick up my brushes. What if my gift had died with Neil? What if I couldn't paint anymore? Several times I'd almost tried, had selected a sketchbook and sorted out my watercolours before the dread of failure took hold and I'd put everything away again. Whatever the name was for the artist's equivalent of writer's block, it seemed that I had it.

"Enjoy," had been Matt's parting shot – and then he'd driven away, waving merrily and leaving me clutching an armful of books. I'd supposed I had better get stuck in.

And anyway, *enjoy* wasn't quite the word I would have used for reading about the horrors of trench warfare...

I'd lit the wood burner in the sitting room and curled up in the window seat with the first of the books Matt had lent me. This was a social history of the Great War, and as I'd read I'd been transported back to the early nineteen-hundreds. Then I'd delved into Kit's poetry again before turning to Matt's notes. The mug of coffee I'd made turned cold, lunchtime came and went, and by the time Sue hammered on the door the sun had dipped behind the woods and shadows were tiptoeing across the floorboards.

"I've been trying to call you!" Sue had cried as I'd opened the door. "I was getting worried."

"I think I left my phone in the kitchen. I couldn't hear it."

"Brr! It's blooming freezing in here! I thought you'd got logs?" Sue had stood in the hallway, puffing out clouds of breath. "This is ridiculous! Isn't the range working?"

"It was. I think it must have gone out while I was reading."

Her eyebrows flew up into her curly fringe. "How long were you reading?"

"I'm not sure. Five hours? Maybe six?"

It had been a shock to find myself abruptly returned to the twenty-first century, and for a few seconds I'd blinked and rubbed my eyes. Sue was already marching into the kitchen where, sure enough, the range's firebox had died down to a red glow.

"Thank you, Lord, for the gift of central heating," Sue had said, stuffing logs into the firebox and stoking it up to a roar. Then she'd slammed the door shut and turned to face me, hands on her hips and with her chin set at a determined angle.

"Right. That's sorted now, but it's going to take a while to heat the radiators. In the meantime, you're coming to ours for pizza and some serious defrosting. No arguments!"

Before I'd had a chance to protest, Sue had fetched my coat and bag and herded me out of the house and to her car. Once she'd turned the engine on and the car's asthmatic heater had started puffing out wheezy clouds of warmth, she'd driven me across Rosecraddick to the New Rectory, where the radiators were cranked up and her husband was unpacking a stack of Domino's best. Tim didn't seem at all put out that his wife had turned up with an extra mouth to feed. Instead, he gave me a kiss on the cheek, said he was pleased to meet me and poured us all a glass of red wine. Before long I was curled up on a squashy sofa in a toasty living room, my plate piled high with pizza and my head just the right side of woozy.

"You've got to stop titbitting our dog," Tim scolds his wife now, just as she's about to offer Molly a piece of pepperoni.

"I don't!" protests Sue, hastily tucking the giveaway meat behind her back.

Her husband laughs. "See what kind of a vicar we have in this parish?" he says.

"Well, I may treat her now and then," Sue admits. "She does love pepperoni."

"Her tummy doesn't, and who cleans it up while you're out at PCC meetings or chairing committees?" Tim shakes his head. "Honestly. Who'd be a house husband?"

"You know I couldn't do any of this without you, darling," Sue says. "Honestly, I couldn't." To me she adds, "Seriously, he really is brilliant. Look at how easily he's just got Caspar to bed. It usually takes me an hour and at least three stories."

"OK, don't over-egg the pudding or I'll wonder what else you want." Tim reaches across for another slice of pizza from the box propped open on the coffee table. I like him a lot. He's easy-going and welcoming, and it's obvious that he and Sue adore each other. I wait for the dart of loss that usually comes with this kind of observation, but for once it isn't there. Besides, Neil would have been a hopeless house husband. It took me years to train him to leave the loo seat down...

"Chloe? Are you all right?"

Sue touches my arm and I jump.

"Sorry, I was miles away." I must stop drifting off like this.

"Best thing when my wife's interrogating you," teases Tim, and Sue punches him gently.

"I am not interrogating her!"

"Whatever you say, dear," Tim replies mildly. "I'm going to check on Cas. Feel free to talk about me while I'm gone! Isn't that what girls do?"

"In your dreams!" laughs Sue, shooing him out. Then she picks up the wine to top up our glasses.

"So, rather than talking about my husband, tell me what Matt had to say about that carved daisy. Does he think it's anything to do with Kit Rivers?"

"He says it could be but there's no real link apart from the addition to the window – and nobody seems to know what that's about. He was wondering if you'd be able to unearth any church records about when it was added."

Sue pulls a face. "I'll do my best, but to be honest I don't hold out much hope. They weren't that good at record-keeping here pre Second World War. I know that there are all kinds of documents in

Cornwall Record Office. Maybe it would be worth looking there?"

"Maybe," I say. "I guess Matt will know more about that."

"It certainly sounds promising if he thinks it's worth pursuing, anyway. Matt's the expert on all things Kit."

I nod. "He seems convinced there could be more evidence in the manor house. He says it's just a matter of finding it."

"Good luck with that. The place is in a dreadful state. Kernow Heritage Foundation have their work cut out there, that's for sure. I should imagine they need twice the funding just to get started."

"He's asked me to be a volunteer. That's what all the reading material's for. Matt thinks all the volunteers need to know about the First World War and how it affected the house and the family."

"Matt certainly takes his job seriously." Sue's voice is full of admiration. "It's a shame he isn't paid more but I guess that's the nature of working for a charity. He's actually way overqualified to be buried here in the middle of nowhere. He won't have told you because he's far too modest, but he's actually Doctor Matthew Enys. He was lecturing at Oxford until his divorce. His ex-wife moved to be near her family and he followed to be close to the twins."

Matt mentioned that his children lived in Exeter. There'd been sadness in his voice and I could tell he missed them. I guess at our age everyone has their own private grief to bear. None of us are unscathed.

"He's been divorced for a while, which makes Matt Rosecraddick's most eligible bachelor," Sue says. "Half the women in this village have made a play for him already and the other half are planning to. If I wasn't a happily married woman then I might be tempted myself. He's gorgeous, isn't he?"

I really don't want to be drawn into a conversation about Matt and whether or not he's gorgeous. I can see that he's attractive, but that's purely from an objective standpoint. My heart sinks because I can tell that Sue's quietly matchmaking, which is the last thing I need. Matt's offered me something I can throw myself into and I need this escape from my own thoughts. I don't want anything to complicate matters and I can't imagine Matt does either. He seems more than content to bury himself in his work.

"He's really nice, isn't he?" Sue continues innocently as she places another slice of pizza on her plate. "Any more for you?"

"No, no. I'm fine."

I've eaten two slices but my stomach's so full it hurts. This is the most food I've managed for ages.

"No wonder you're so slim and I'm such a porker," Sue sighs, attacking her fresh slice with gusto. "I'm sure I eat twice as much since I got married. What's your secret? Is it being single?"

Misery? Grief? Not really anything I want to share, but if I'm to live here and enjoy life without any well-meaning matchmaking I know I have to level with her.

"I lost my husband two and a half years ago," I say quietly. "To be honest, Sue, I haven't really felt much like eating since."

Sue's pizza-laden hand freezes between her mouth and plate.

"I'm so sorry, Chloe. What a crass thing for me to say. I'd assumed you're divorced like Matt. I had no idea."

"The village gossip mill's been very remiss. I thought they knew everything," I try to sound light-hearted but my voice cracks.

"They certainly don't know about your husband and it won't go any further than me." Sue looks at her food and it seems that I've cured her appetite after all, because she puts the pizza down and pushes her plate away. "I don't know what to say. I feel terrible."

And now she feels awkward. I hate that.

"You weren't to know," I say. "Honestly. It's OK."

But we both know it's far from OK. There's an uncomfortable silence. Above us the floorboards creak as Tim crosses the bedroom. The light on the baby monitor flickers as Caspar grizzles before his father soothes him. I know Sue's waiting for me to continue, so I dredge up words from the deep place inside where I usually keep them safely pushed down.

"Well, no, it isn't OK – but that isn't what anyone wants to hear, is it? I'm supposed to be moving on now. It's been long enough."

"I don't think there are any rules for these things," Sue says gently. "Grief and loss don't work to timetables. Or not in my experience anyway."

I think about the stained-glass windows in the church and the granite cross on the cliffs, memorials to a loss that can never be tempered by time.

"I suppose not, but I thought a move here might help. Neil spent his childhood holidays in the village and it feels like my last link to him. It's a way of being close but our memories aren't here, if that makes sense?"

"It makes perfect sense," Sue replies. "You want to heal but you still want to be close to him."

"Exactly. I'm not ready to let go. Not yet. Maybe never." My throat's tight and I feel the old beat of panic in my chest. I can't cry. I daren't cry. Poor Sue's off-duty. She wanted pizza and wine and a chat – not a full-on counselling session.

"I don't think we ever let go of loved ones," she says. "They're always in our hearts. I do think time lessens the pain of the loss, but they never, ever leave us. That's what memories are for. Talking helps too, Chloe, and I'm here if you ever want to chat."

I take a big gulp of my wine. Memories are painful. Talking is even worse. Perky Pippa wanted to talk non-stop and it was awful, like digging into an open wound. I have to change the subject. Now.

"Thanks, Sue. I guess in a way this brings us back to Kit Rivers. Somebody remembered him, didn't they? I think that's what the daisy in the window is about."

Kit Rivers is the lifebelt I need to stop me sinking and I grab it gratefully. Sue takes the hint. By the time Tim joins us I've managed to step away from the emotional quicksand and our conversation drifts back to life in Rosecraddick. All is calm, outwardly anyway. But inside? I'm shaken.

The quicksand's much closer than I'd realised and still I'm only a footstep away from plunging in.

CHAPTER 9

CHLOE

November blends into December in a swirl of sea mist and rain. The crisp days of frost and lemon-tinted sunshine are distant memories and I become an expert at drying my damp clothes on the wooden rack hanging over the range. I also learn how to bank up the firebox and load the wood burner so that the Rectory has some semblance of heating and hot water. It's funny how visiting the woodshed and stacking log baskets have become second nature.

I have something of a routine here now, if you can call it that. The Rectory's far too large for me, so I've shut up most of the rooms and restricted myself to the sitting room, kitchen and bedroom. Most of my time's spent in the downstairs window seat, where I never tire of watching the waves gallop across the bay and where I can see the clouds dance across the sky. I've placed my sketchbook on the table and my pencils and water colours are never far away, but I've yet to find the courage to discover whether I can still draw. When the weather allows I walk across the cliffs or wind my way down the narrow path to the rocky cove, where I sit and watch the surf pound the shore. It's comforting to think that the waves have dashed these rocks for centuries and will continue to do so long after I've passed.

The nights have drawn right in. Darkness pools from the wooded hills beyond the Manor and by half four in the afternoon the whole world feels as though it's sleeping. In the evenings I light the lamps in the sitting room, throw another log on the wood burner and curl up to read. I'm gradually working my way through the pile of books that Matt loaned me, and with every page I turn I fall deeper and deeper into the world of Kit Rivers. At times this feels more real to me than my own time, and I'm surprised and grateful at how fast the quiet evenings pass. By the time I haul myself up the steep stairs to bed my eyes are heavy and my head's spinning with images and verse.

Sometimes I picture Neil sitting opposite me, one ankle crossed over his knee and his fingers drumming on the arm of the chair. He was never one for sitting still and reading, so it's no surprise to me that as the shortened days race towards Christmas he's here less and less. He drifts through my dreams, always a fingertip's touch out of reach, and I lose count of the times I wake up with wet cheeks and an aching heart. On these mornings I have to force myself out of bed and, as crazy as it sounds, I'm grateful for the cold shock of lino under my feet and the chilly trek to the woodshed. It's hard to dwell on feeling sad when you have to battle wind and rain to fetch wood. Life in the Rectory isn't easy but it is exhausting and the setting never fails to stir my soul. When I'm ready to paint again I suspect my canvases will be filled with savage skies, driving rain and wild wrecking waves.

Apart from walking and reading and fighting daily battles with the temperamental heating system, I've also joined the team of volunteers at Rosecraddick Manor. We're an eclectic bunch of people. So far I've met a retired head teacher, a pagan, a poet and two elderly sisters who used to race speedboats in the seventies, so as well as learning about Kit's war I'm also learning a great deal about many other things. No matter what our backgrounds or political views, we all come together for one shared purpose: to restore the grand old house to her former glory.

It's not a glamorous job – I seem to spend most of my time in the attic sifting through junk and painstakingly cataloguing it – but it's a wonderful distraction. Matt's busy meeting conservation officers or travelling to London to attend fundraising meetings, so I haven't seen a lot of him. After my conversation with Sue, I'm quite relieved about that; I don't want to be viewed as the latest desperate woman who's set her cap at him.

When Matt and I do meet up, we brainstorm the meaning of the daisy. So far we've come up with precisely nothing. Matt's made a start on the parish records but it's a slow task. Still, as I sort through the strata of junk in the attic I live in hope that something significant will appear. It hasn't so far – but, even so, my solitary work's absorbing. One morning I came across a pile of exercise books from the nineteen-fifties, the pages yellowed with age and the ink as brown as old blood. The round childish hand that had crafted the words in them and spilled blots in many places belonged to a Tommy Waken in class 4b. As I'd flipped through his composition book, I'd learned all about Tommy's school life, his dog Dash and his sad mother. His father had died in the war and Tommy had written about him at great length. One essay entitled *My Hero* brought tears to my eyes. I'd collected up all his books and crawled through the years of detritus in the attic to one of the windows, where I'd read for hours until Tommy's life at Rosecraddick merged with Kit's and both overlay my own with their unique colours and nuances. I wonder what happened to Tommy. Did he have a family of his own? Did he ever become a pilot? Is he even alive? I guess I can Google him and find out, but something stops me from typing his name into the search engine. Maybe I'd rather he stayed forever twelve, a cheeky imp with scraped knees and ink-stained fingers who missed his dog and hated tapioca pudding. In the same way that Kit Rivers is forever twenty and Neil will always be in his early thirties.

Age shall not weary them…

It's a blustery December Thursday and I'm on my way to the Manor, swaddled in my winter coat and wearing my trusty welly boots. The sky's a bruised purple and the clouds are billowing. Rain is fast approaching. I usually walk to the Manor but I've no desire to arrive soaked to the skin again. My little red convertible hasn't done many miles since I arrived, so it will do it good to have a run. I'm busy reacquainting myself with the radio when my phone rings. It's not a number I recognise. I don't usually answer these but for some reason today I take the call.

"Hello?"

"Chloe? Is that you? Thank Christ. What's going on? Why haven't you picked up your emails? Where the hell are you anyway?"

It's Moira Olsen, my agent, and she doesn't sound happy. My heart sinks because I've not checked my emails since I left London and I've been avoiding her for obvious reasons.

And anyway, how did she get my mobile number? She only ever had my old landline one.

"Hi, Moira, how are you?" I try to sound pleased to hear from her but I'm a rubbish actress.

"As pissed off as you sound!"

Moira's never one to pull her punches. This is one of the reasons I was so happy to sign with her. She's feisty, forthright and the best in the business. I could hardly believe my luck when she said she wanted to represent me. Neil and I celebrated by splashing out on the most expensive bottle of champagne we'd ever dared to buy, but we knew it was worth it. My dream of leaving teaching and pursuing a career as an artist was on the cusp of coming true. Moira sold some of my designs for cards and prints, but then Neil got sick and painting was squeezed in between teaching and chemo and visits to consultants, until it finally became something I didn't have the heart to do anymore.

Moira had said she understood I needed time – but I don't think she realised just how much. I'm just wondering how I can explain my unprofessional silence when she steams ahead in her own indomitable fashion.

"Anyway, never mind how I feel. It's you that's the issue. Your mother says you've gone quite mad and run away to Cornwall."

Has she indeed? I make a mental note to have a stern word with my mother and also to tell her not to give out my number. What's the point of escaping to Rosecraddick if the old life just follows?

"I'm having some time out," I say mildly. "Cornwall's very

peaceful."

"Lovely," says Moira. "Pleased for you and all that. Can't bear the place myself. Too far from London for me. Still, it's Mecca for artists and the light and the scenery are to die for. I did pootle down to the Beside The Wave gallery the other day. Would have looked you up if I'd known you were nearby. Have you been there?"

The furthest I've been since I arrived is the vicar's house, but somehow I don't think this will impress my agent.

"Not yet," is all I say.

"Well if you ever get off your arse and paint again I'll see what I can do. Anyway, that's not why I called. I've got you a commission and it comes with some serious money." She lowers her voice and then names a figure that does make me blink.

"Seriously?"

"Seriously. This is it. It's for syndication but you keep creative control and great royalties. This is the bit where you thank me."

In the past I would have jumped for joy. Making money from my passion has always been the dream, but the dream has now become a nightmare.

"Who's it for?" I ask.

"You'd better make sure you're sitting down for this one. It's for Regal Press."

She's right. It is just as well I'm sitting down.

"The big publishing house?"

"Publishing *giants*," Moira corrects. "They need six book covers for a series of novels based on that country house drama – you know, the *Downton* rip-off one that's huge right now – and by chance they've come across that sketch of the castle you sold ages ago. The one that was on the biscuit tins and tea towels."

This was a little more than a sketch: it was a detailed canvas and one I'm still hugely proud of. Neil and I had been on holiday in Scotland and, struck by the beauty of a castle we'd come across, I'd asked the laird for permission to paint it. He'd loved the finished piece and bought it from me. It was eventually used as an image on cards and gifts at the castle shop. It was one of the first paintings I ever sold and Neil and I used the money to have a much longed-for weekend in Paris. I still count this sale as a big success, but if it's not on the scale of Tracey Emin or Damien Hirst then it doesn't register in Moira's eyes. She knows her stuff and wants top dollar.

What she doesn't know is that I can't paint anymore...

"Moira, I—"

"Don't you dare," she warns. "Don't you dare say that you can't or it's too soon or any of that bollocks, Chloe. I've been really patient and I've respected your loss and left you alone like you asked me to, but it's been well over two years. You can't shut yourself away anymore. You've got a talent and wasting it..." She pauses for a minute and I can tell that she's trying her hardest to rein herself in before she says something truly awful. "Wasting it is wrong. And I can't believe it's what Neil would have wanted you to do. If he was here now and knew you'd given up painting, he'd be seriously pissed off."

I gasp. I can't believe she's said this to me.

"I'm sorry if it's upsetting to hear this," Moira continues, while I sit in the car with my mouth as wide open as something the local fishermen might land, "but it's bloody well true. I didn't know Neil for long, but from what I did know of your husband he wasn't the type to sit around and stew. He grabbed life with both hands and he made the most of every opportunity. You and I both know that I only signed you because he was so persistent. His bombardment of emails and portfolios ground me down! Just as well you turned out to be good."

In spite of her blunt words, I laugh. It was Neil who'd decided that I needed a good agent to look after my interests, and once he'd discovered that Moira Olsen was the best in the business he wouldn't rest until I was on her books. Neil never gave up on anything. The only battle he ever lost was his final one with leukaemia.

"I liked him, Chloe," Moira says quietly. "He was wonderful. Determined, pig-headed maybe, and certainly bloody hard to shake off when he had an idea in his head. I'll never forget turning up at my office and finding him waiting for me with your work. He was charming but adamant he wouldn't get off the doorstep until I saw it. I nearly called the police!"

"He never told me that," I say. It's classic Neil though. He never took no for an answer. Like getting married, for example. I was happy with things as they were. We'd been together for so long that my attitude was *if it ain't broke, why fix it?* He wore me down though and we got engaged and then finally we were married. I ought to have known he'd manage to persuade me. I only went on a date with him in the first place because I was tired of being asked. So far as I was concerned, he was just the annoying boy in the year above who did wheelies on his bike and hung out with the cool kids rather than swots like me. One date and then he'd push off because he'd be bored with me, was what I'd thought, but I'd been totally wrong – as he'd known all along. Once I agreed to that first date we were never apart again. We might have looked like opposites but in reality we were mirror images, that was all.

"Well, it's true. He was totally, one hundred percent on your side – and not many people ever have that. You were bloody lucky, woman."

I bite my lip. My luck ran out. It feels as though I had the best of everything and used my quota of happiness up faster than most people. Maybe that's how life works? Perhaps I just had all my joy at once.

"I can't imagine how awful it must have been for you to lose him and I'm so sorry, Chloe," Moira says. "He was a wonderful man and he believed in you with all his heart."

People don't talk much to me about Neil. They avoid the topic. To have him brought to life so unexpectedly makes my eyes fill. I can picture him. Silent tears spill down my cheeks and splash onto my

87

jeans. What would Neil think of me hiding away in Cornwall? I think he'd understand why.

But what would he think of my not painting? And giving up my job?

I think it's running away, Neil says from the passenger seat. He looks sad. *And it pisses me off too. How can you waste what you've been given? How can you throw away a single minute of your life? Would I have done that?*

Of course he wouldn't. Neil grieved and mourned and railed against everything thrown at him, but he never once gave up. Not even when he called for a razor and shaved his head or when he could hardly lift a spoon. He never gave in.

There's silence on the other end of the phone. I lean forward, rest my forehead on the wheel and close my eyes. I'm at a crossroads; which way should I go?

Far away in Pimlico, Moira exhales wearily.

"Look, for what it's worth, Chloe, I really think you should do this. You might even enjoy it. The brief is right up your street. Just check your emails, please? I sent the details days ago. The least you can do is take a look."

She's so insistent and unusually there's a hint of desperation in her voice too. Instantly, I'm on red alert.

"You've already said I'll do it, haven't you?"

Her short pause tells me all I need to know. Oh God, she has. Moira's committed me already. What am I going to do?

"I'm sorry, Chloe, but they were so keen and when I couldn't get hold of you I knew I couldn't stall them much longer. I didn't want you to lose the work, because it could lead to amazing things for you – and yes, before you point it out, me too by default. It's a prestigious job. I thought you'd be thrilled."

Ordinarily, of course, I would be. Neil and I would have been turning cartwheels around our flat. Then he'd have got totally carried away, booting up Rightmove to scope out dream properties in the countryside and planning the rosy future that he was so convinced lay ahead for us. No wonder I just feel empty now. What's the point of success if I can't share it?

"I'll have a look but—" I'm on the point of confessing that I haven't painted a thing since Neil died when I realise my agent isn't listening. As far as she's concerned I've said "yes" and her work is over. Onwards and upwards to the next difficult client.

"Fantastic! You won't regret it, I promise. Email some preliminary sketches over as soon as you're ready and we'll go from there. Anyway, got to go. There's a call on the other line. Talk soon!"

Moira rings off before I can change my mind, leaving me sitting in the car staring at my phone in a state of mingled shock and panic.

This is the biggest commission I've ever had and I have absolutely no idea how I'm going to even start to tackle it.

One thing's for certain though: somehow I'm going to have to start painting again.

CHAPTER 10

CHLOE

I drive to Rosecraddick Manor in a daze. There's a part of me that's hugely proud that such a big client should actively seek me out. However, this feeling's swiftly swamped by sadness that I can't share the news with Neil. I'm also terrified I won't be able to paint anymore and will let everyone down.

This is bad. What has Moira done? What am I going to do?

Panic hurtles around my nervous system. *Breathe,* I tell myself desperately as my head starts to spin. I recognise this feeling and I know I have to take control before it carries me to a very dark place. *Breathe. In. Out. In. Out.*

I need fresh air. I park up and let myself out of the car, leaning against the door and struggling to draw oxygen into my lungs. Hideous images spool before my eyes like a newsreel: I see soldiers frantically pulling on gas masks as clouds of mustard gas start to engulf them. *Breathe, Chloe, breathe. You're not there. This isn't World War One. This is a panic attack, that's all.*

The Cornish sky is thick with mizzle that beads my coat and makes my curls spiral. I gulp the fresh, salty air greedily. I can deal with all this. I know I can.

I need a quiet space to think. Although it's early morning there are already several cars tucked into the layby opposite the Manor where volunteers park, and Matt's Land Rover is among them. This makes my heart lift because Matt's knowledge and vision drive this project. Every conversation we have, however short, I feel I learn something new. I've read Kit's poems, have worked my way through Wilfred Owen's work and just recently discovered Isaac Rosenberg. My mind's continually ringing with lines of verse and images of wire, trenches and mud.

My breathing's calmer and my pulse slows. I haven't had a panic attack for months; I'd almost forgotten how stealthy this old enemy could be. Feeling shaken, I lock the car and walk up the drive. I'm not ready yet to go inside and make small talk with the others in the hall. Since Matt had the chimney swept and a tea urn set up, the entrance hall's become the spot were volunteers gather to have a hot drink and spend a few moments thawing out by the fire. Usually I enjoy making a coffee and catching up with the people here, but today I need to collect my thoughts.

I skirt around the side of the house and cross the lawn to the walled garden. The wet grass carries the scent of rotting leaves, and when I step through the arched door, the weathered wood pimpled with iron studs, the garden beyond feels secretive and adrift from the real world. There's no birdsong today and the only sound is the crunch of my footsteps on the path. Moisture runs along the rosemary boughs like tears, fungus is trodden underfoot and webs of cloud hang low in the sky as though about to shroud the world. Tangles of weeds and brambles might smother the original design, but here the past has clung on to survive into the present. Likewise, Kit's verse might have grown obscure but at least he hasn't left silence behind.

As I brush against the straggling rosemary, the air fills with heavy scent. Unbidden, memories sluice through the floodgates. Roast dinners. Laughter. Gallons of red wine. Replete and watching a movie, curled up and safe. An ease of mind and body that's almost hard to equate with the person I've become. Loss slices me.

Rosemary for remembrance. Will I remember how to paint? And if I can, and my life moves on, does it mean my memories of Neil will start to fade? Can I live with that? It feels like the worst betrayal.

I'm planning to rest on the bench to gather my thoughts, but when I reach the centre of the garden I soon realise that somebody's beaten me to this spot: a man's already there. He's slumped forward with his head in his hands but, hearing me approaching, he looks up.

It's Matt.

"Oh, hi," I say, feeling awkward because I know I've disturbed a private moment. The look on his face is of utter bleakness and I realise he's also slipped away to stitch his ragged thoughts together.

Matt does his best to look pleased to see me, but his smile fails to light his eyes and his voice is weary. "Hey, Chloe. You've caught me lazing about when I should be cataloguing. Don't tell Jill, for God's sake."

Jill's the retired head teacher who seems to have replaced her erstwhile pupils with Rosecraddick's volunteers. The other day I thought she was about to give me a detention for arriving after nine.

I laugh. "I won't dob you in. Fancy a cigarette behind the bike shed at break time?"

"You're on," says Matt but rather listlessly. It's disconcerting to see his usually merry face so sad.

"Sorry to disturb you. I'll leave you in peace," I say.

"No, honestly, you don't need to do that. Have a seat and grab some quiet." He pats the bench. "Don't feel you have to go."

"Thanks."

I sit next to him and for the next five minutes or so we say nothing. The rain's stopped but a sea fret's drifting in; it mingles with the clouds that hang over the garden, creating the disorientating impression that we're cut adrift from the world. There's a strange peace in this and although I'm no closer to knowing what I'm going to do about Moira's bombshell, I'm no longer feeling quite as terrified as I was. I'll paint or I won't. That's all there is to it really.

"You look as though you've decided something? Has the garden worked its magic?" Matt turns to me and I see genuine interest in his expression.

"Do you know, I think it has," I reply.

"Good. I'm glad."

"How about you?" The words are out of my mouth before I can censor them, and I'm horrified. I hope he doesn't think I'm prying. It's just that there's something about being in the misty garden which invites confidences.

"Actually, yes," Matt says slowly. "Looking at Kit's memorial always puts things into perspective for me. Things that seem unbearable soon settle into a different pattern when you remember how many young lives were rubbed out in conditions of unimaginable horror. What those young men went through puts other things into context, like feeling upset that I won't have the kids for Christmas. At least I'll have another Christmas to look forward to."

I'd known that Matt's divorced. He doesn't talk about it much, but the other volunteers do. Over the weeks I've gleaned that his ex-wife can be difficult and that he misses the twins dreadfully. I've done my best not to listen and I never join in. I also now have a good idea how they must all gossip about me when I'm not present.

"That's still hard," I say quietly. "It's a loss of a different kind, I think?"

"That's it exactly. It's the loss of a special day that will never be recaptured. They're only young for such a fleeting moment in time and the magic soon vanishes. I love going to midnight Mass with them and seeing their faces on Christmas morning when Santa's been."

Christmas is a raw time for so many people. The last one I spent in bed with the curtains tightly closed and my eyes closed even tighter.

"I can imagine it's not been fun for you either," he says gently. "I'm sorry, Chloe. It must be hard."

So he knows about Neil. I'm not surprised. I've been here over a month now and it wouldn't have taken the villagers long to figure out my story. I glance down at my rings and sigh.

"It's been well over two years but no, it isn't great."

Matt looks sympathetic. "Christmas makes everything harder."

I nod. To be honest I'm dreading Christmas. My mother's threatening to come and fetch me back to London for the festive season. I've told her I'm more than happy being here and just having a quiet day, but this very idea horrifies her. She says she wants to stuff me with turkey. The truth, though, is that she wants to make sure I don't top myself. I can't think of anything worse than going back to London, sleeping in my old single bed and staring at the same plastic tree my parents have had since the nineties. If anything's going to drive me to the brink of despair, it's *that*. Sue's invited me to her place – apparently she and Tim always gather the local waifs and strays for Christmas dinner – but in all honesty I'd rather channel my inner Greta Garbo and work my way through the Baileys.

"Life has a nasty habit of throwing curveballs," Matt remarks, gazing at Kit's memorial with a small frown creasing his brow. "I guess it's all about how we deal with them? When I'm feeling particularly sore it helps to throw myself into work, but you've probably already figured that out. Why else would I leave Oxford and dedicate myself to an underfunded project?"

"Because you care about Kit and his poetry," I say, and he nods.

"Yes, of course, but not many people understand that. You do though."

I feel the tug of mutual sympathy because I *do* get it. My thoughts are full of Kit and the nagging feeling that there's far more to his story than we know.

"Life threw Kit a curveball, that's for sure," Matt continues. "A dreamer, a poet and by all accounts a thoughtful young man looking forward to Oxford, suddenly pitched into the horrors of the trenches. It must have been like falling into the mouth of hell, yet he stayed the course. Even after his last visit home, when we know from *Far Away* he was terrified of going back, he didn't falter." He shakes his head, droplets of water flying from the thick locks. "Sorry, I'm lecturing, aren't I?"

"A little, but I do enjoy learning about all this. It helps to focus on Kit rather than on other stuff." I decide to tell him what's bothering me. Matt's easy to talk to. "The thing is, I've been thrown a curveball today and I'm at a bit of a loss. That's why I came here. I needed to figure it out."

"Must be the day for it."

"Must be. I've been offered a commission. A really big one, in fact. The sort of thing I'd have killed for a few years ago."

"What they call an opportunity of a lifetime?"

I nod. "Pretty much. I've been commissioned by Regal Press to design book covers based on *Wildeacre*."

Matt whistles. "Even I've seen that show! It's huge. Isn't that good news?"

Rising panic forms a lump in my throat. "Normally, yes, but I'm not so sure this time."

"Anything I can help with?"

"I haven't painted for more than two years, Matt. I don't even know if I can draw anymore. Since I lost Neil I haven't painted a thing. I haven't even sketched."

This is usually the point where the person I'm talking to tells me I'm wrong and insists an ability never goes away. My mother does exactly this, and Perky Pippa and my head teacher too. They have no idea that sadness can freeze more than just your joy and break more than your heart. When Neil became ill, my drawing felt frivolous. How could I waste hours absorbed in sketching when my husband's life was counting down in weeks?

But Matt doesn't argue.

"Poor you. That must be awful."

"Yes." I look down at my feet. The spotty city wellies are speckled with humus and mud. They're working hard and I need to do the same. There's only so long that my savings will last before I start nibbling into the small amount of equity from selling our flat. I need to think about what I do next to earn money. Practicalities are starting to elbow their way to the forefront of my attention.

"So what will you do?"

That's the million-dollar question.

"I want to paint and sometimes I nearly start, but something holds me back each time. I can't bring myself to do it in case I fail, if that makes sense? It's a mess."

"Could you just decline? I think these things maybe work to their own timescale."

This reminds me of Sue's words that night we ate pizza. "A bit like grief?"

He looks thoughtful. "Maybe? Pushing yourself might cause more harm than good."

"The problem is, my agent's already committed me. I don't want to let her down."

Matt nods. "I see. So, what do you have to paint for these book covers?"

Actually I have no idea. It seemed pointless checking, since I didn't think I could do it.

"I'm not sure. My agent's emailed the brief."

"Is there any merit in just seeing what it is? You may have a really strong gut reaction either way. You say that a part of you is longing to start again. Maybe this will inspire you? I'm a big believer in trusting your heart." He looks up at me from under dark eyelashes starred with rain, and my own heart does something strange: it feels as though it rises a little. I feel... hopeful.

"I guess that wouldn't hurt," I agree.

"You can log on to my laptop if you like?" Matt offers. "It practically runs on steam, which drives the twins mad because they can't play Minecraft properly, but it can just about cope with a few emails. We can get a coffee too. I don't know about you, but I'm starting to freeze out here."

The cold from the bench is seeping into my bones and the sea mist is drenching me by stealth. The idea of being inside, warming my hands around a mug of coffee and listening to the chatter of the other volunteers, is suddenly very welcome. Together we walk back to the house. Light spills into the gloomy morning from the diamond-paned windows and inside the hall a fire crackles merrily in the grate, filling the room with the scent of woodsmoke. Several volunteers warming themselves by the flames call out cheery hellos.

"I like to think it would have smelt just the same in Kit's time," remarks Matt, after we've greeted everyone and made our way through a narrow passageway to the back of the house. At one time this would have been part of the warren of sculleries, larders and kitchens. The flagstones are dipped from centuries of wear by leaden feet and in the kitchens the ceilings are still dark from long-ago smoke. At the farthest end, by a small window overlooking the garden, a spiral flight of stone steps vanishes intriguingly into a solid wall. I wonder what colours I would use to create the sense of half-light and shifting centuries? Somebody's placed a poinsettia on the window ledge and the bold splash of crimson against the greyness of stone, together with the sharp green ivy fringing the window, makes me catch my breath. I know *exactly* how I would paint this scene, and I need to see if I'm right.

Is my gift coming back?

Matt's set up a makeshift office in an airy room at the far end of the passageway. At one time this would have been the still room, where the lady of the house would have overseen the distillation or making of medicines and tinctures. Now it's "still" in the sense that it's far away from the main activity and a place where hopefully he isn't disturbed too often. Matt has a desk piled high with folders, papers and heavy books. There are also two wooden school chairs heaped with yet more folders, and in the corner a small electric heater is doing its best to take the chill from the air. In addition, a couple of filing cabinets have been dragged in from where they'd been abandoned in the old coach house, and there's a battered suitcase rescued from the attic as well as some faded sepia photographs of Kit in uniform. The place feels homely and welcoming and I know this atmosphere comes from Matt. He has a gift of setting people at their ease. Look at how readily I spoke to him earlier.

"It's buried here somewhere," Matt says, shuffling some papers together and pushing books aside to locate the laptop. "Excuse the mess. I know it's shocking."

"It obviously works for you," I say.

"Yep, I know where most things are, but I know I'm pretty chaotic. It drove Gina mad. Then again, most things seemed to in the end."

Neil was a neat freak and I know I drove him round the twist with my havoc. He was always restacking the dishwasher if by chance I'd got near it, or sorting out the mess I'd caused in the cutlery drawer. If it would bring him back to me, I swear I'd never muddle up the knives and forks again.

Matt switches the laptop on and while it buzzes awake he scoops more folders and papers from the chair so that I can sit down. I do so carefully because I don't want to cause an avalanche or be concussed by knocking down a pile of books. While I navigate my email folder, which is overflowing with correspondence I've been ignoring, Matt fetches coffees. He peers over my shoulder as he sets my mug on the table. Coffee sloshes onto the desk, adding another brown ring to the Olympic circles already decorating an envelope.

"Another bad habit," he grins.

"There seem to be quite a lot!"

"Far too many. Did I mention I can't screw the lids on jars either?"

"I'm amazed you've made it this far."

"Yeah, it's been tough. The Marmite suffered dreadfully. Anyway, don't let me disturb you. Looks as though you've got a few emails to work through."

He isn't kidding, but I'm not even going to attempt trawling through all these today. Instead I scroll through until I find Moira's email, marked urgent with a scarlet flag. I open it and scan the brief and, as I do, something very odd happens: my stomach flutters with excitement. I peer more closely at the screen and read the details again just in case I'm mistaken and the stomach butterflies are actually terror – but no, this feeling really is the delicious realisation that the project at my fingertips couldn't be more perfect for me.

I have to hand it to Moira: she's good.

"Everything OK?" Matt asks, and I realise I've been staring at the screen in silence for some time.

"Yes, thanks. More than OK, actually. I think this might be something I can do – want to do, even!"

"Really? That's fantastic! What is it?"

"It's six covers set in an old manor house. Mullioned windows, courtyards, spiral steps, walled gardens…" I turn to him and see my own delight reflected in his shining eyes. "Can you believe that? What are the chances?"

"I'd say it's meant to be. Serendipity and all that."

This is exactly how I feel. Already half in love with Kit Rivers and Rosecraddick Manor, I'm now picturing the scenes I want to create and dreaming of the colours and shades that will bring my ideas to life. The first piece of artwork is flowering in my mind's eye: a latticed window overlooking a garden, with the sea in the background beyond the squat tower of St Nonna's. I'll sketch it as it is now and then transport it to the spring when the flower beds pop with colour and sunlight gilds the water.

"This is the first brief," I say, and Matt reads it over my shoulder. "Any ideas of where I could begin?"

"So you'll do it then?"

"I think so. Yes."

"I know the perfect spot to start with this. Shall I show you? It's a bit dusty and cobwebby but I'm sure you're used to that now."

I print the brief out, fire off a quick reply to Moira and then follow Matt up the grand staircase to the first floor. This is the oldest part of the house and where the rooms link to one another. We wander through to the farthest chamber and then he opens a cunningly concealed door in the wooden panelling.

"A secret room!" I exclaim. "I'd never have known it was there."

"You just need to know where to look," says Matt, smiling at me encouragingly. "Maybe it's a metaphor? Anyway, come on."

Behind the low door is a narrow flight of creaky wooden stairs. Matt has to lower his head as he climbs but, being shorter, I manage easily. At the top is a small chamber overlooking the garden. Matt pulls the heavy shutters open and through the ivy and a cage of iron lattice I spot the Old Rectory and the wise grey church.

"Whose room was this?" I wonder.

"We've no idea. This is the tower and part of the original manor house. It must have been a bedchamber once, but not in Kit's time," Matt explains. "I'm assuming in Kit's time the Rivers family used the newer wing, as it's far more convenient. This older part of the house is awkward and tucked away and we've not really done much with it. It was probably used for storage back then. There's no electricity either and it's also quite a long way from the nearest bathroom."

I walk over to the window and lean against the sill. The wood's crumbly beneath my fingers and peppered with the nibbles of long-dead woodworm. Some parts have even fallen away. This room up in the tower is an old and secret spot, the perfect place to hide away to write and dream.

This was Kit's place. I'm certain of it – and when I glance down at the windowsill I know for sure that I'm right. There's no doubt at all.

Scratched into the wood, so close to the stonework that it could easily be missed, is the unmistakable outline of a carved daisy.

CHAPTER 11

CHLOE

"I can't believe I haven't noticed that before."

Matt stares at the carving. There's no mistaking what we're looking at. This crude flower is exactly like the one I found in the church, which can only mean one thing: someone from this household carved them both.

"Could the stained-glass window be linked to the carving in the church, after all?" I ask.

"It would certainly seem that way. The daisy in the church window's a much later addition, though." He pushes his dark hair back from his face as he peers at the flower more closely. "This looks identical to the one we saw in the church."

"Do you think Kit carved it?"

Matt spreads his hands in a gesture of helplessness. "I have no idea."

"And there are no clues in his poetry?"

"None whatsoever. Believe me, I've been back over every single poem and studied every line. I've gone cross-eyed looking for mnemonics or acrostics but there's nothing. My fear is that whatever this means was lost with Kit."

Kit carved this daisy. I know he did. The room has the most beautiful views, even on a gloomy winter's day, and there's a sense of stillness and peace. I can even see the attic windows of the Old Rectory and the melon slice of Rosecraddick Bay. I'm certain Kit wrote up here. And how do I know? Because I feel that I can paint here. It feels creative.

It feels *right* and I know I'm not the first person to think like this.

"He left no diary or letters either, or at least not as far as we know," Matt tells me. "Any belongings of his must have been tidied away by the family or thrown out when the house changed hands. We only have the poems because his mother had them published. The Kit Rivers Society own those now and all the publishing rights to them as well."

"How come?"

"Kit's last remaining and very distant relative, Eunice Rivers-Elliott, died in the early 1960s. She left the Kit Rivers Society the body of his work, all the rights to it, and also the rights to any more poems that may come to light. Sadly, that hasn't happened, and it probably never will, but we live in hope. I can show you the original poems sometime, if you like?"

"I'd love to see them. But surely Kit wrote home from the Front? There would have been letters?"

I've seen countless exhibitions featuring time-faded ink on notepaper; these letters are usually displayed in glass cabinets next to photographs of the young men in uniform, shiny faced with youth and hope, and amid the scarlet splashes of paper poppies.

"If he did then Lady Rivers didn't keep any of his correspondence. She didn't even keep the telegram that said he was missing."

I'm a little confused by this because I have belongings of Neil's that I could never part with. Surely a mother would feel this way too?

"Isn't that a bit odd? You'd have thought she'd treasure all Kit's possessions."

Matt shrugs. "The Colonel died in the early 1920s and Lady Rivers passed away in the next decade. That was when the house was taken over by a distant branch of the family, who decided to rent it out and who later sold it. People weren't so sentimental about the past as us and lots of things were thrown out. Kit's belongings would have been included in that, I suppose, and probably his mother's personal effects too. The worry I always have is that his early work must have been lost and other poems as well. I find it hard to believe he only wrote eight."

"But the Manor's attics are full of stuff," I point out, feeling well-qualified on this score having spent days lugging furniture around the dusty and dim rooms. As well as the schoolbooks, I'd found biscuit tins crammed with cigarette cards, a recipe book bristling with yellow cuttings, and a beautiful hat with drooping scarlet feathers. The people who'd lived at Rosecraddick Manor hadn't worried about throwing things out; they'd just shoved them in the attic and forgotten about them.

"Maybe we'll find something that helps in all the junk?" Matt's saying. He gives my shoulder an encouraging squeeze. "That's the whole point of going through it all so carefully and taking expert advice. Who knows what treasures we'll find next?"

I study the simple carved flower and feel a tug of sadness that the significance of something once so important, something that meant enough to be scratched in at least two places and commemorated in another, has been lost.

"I hope we can find the answer to what this meant."

"We'll keep sifting away and see what we can find out," Matt says staunchly. "Welcome to the exciting world of historical research. Something will hopefully come to light at some point, just like this has today. This is really exciting, Chloe. It's another piece in the jigsaw. Albeit a very slow one!"

We make our way back through the house. Matt returns to his office and I'm pressganged by Jill into cleaning the kitchen. As I work, my head is full of questions I simply can't answer, and I distract myself by running through Moira's brief again and planning my preliminary sketches. I'll start with the window in what I'm calling Kit's Room. Then maybe a view of the Manor through the wrought-iron gate? That would look intriguing and romantic, I think. And the walled garden glimpsed through the just-open door could work.

"Right. I'm breaking for lunch." Jill straightens up and unties her headscarf. "Coming for a bite to eat and a cuppa?"

"In a bit," I say. To be honest I'm not in the mood to listen to gossip about who said what to whom in the village shop or hear discussions about grandchildren. Instead, I want to return to that quiet tower room. I'm longing to fetch my sketch pad, pick up a pencil and lose myself in soft 2B lines, and this fills me with growing impatience. I need to get sketching. I wonder if Matt has any paper?

I tip my bucket of grimy water down the sink, the same sink where scullery maids in Kit's time would have scrubbed pans until their fingers bled, and then peel off my Marigolds, feeling glad I live in the twenty-first century. While my fellow volunteers brew tea and munch their sandwiches in front of the fire, I return to Matt's office on the hunt for some paper and a pencil. My heart's hammering against my ribs as though I'm about to run a race, and I laugh at my own ridiculousness. I'm going to do a simple sketch. There's nothing to worry about.

Matt's not at his desk. Maybe he's with the Project Manager and talking to the builders who are in to quote? Or perhaps the book-restoration guy's arrived?

I dither in the doorway. Maybe I should just go back to my work in the attic?

You're procrastinating, Neil scolds. He's standing by the old sink, arms crossed and with a stern expression on his face. *Grab a pencil and get on with it!*

My husband was always bossy. Why should death stop him? Shaking my head, I overcome my reticence and help myself to several sheets of printer paper, a book to rest on and a pencil. That's all I need to make a start — that and a huge dose of courage. When I look up again Neil's gone, so before I can change my mind, I retrace my steps to the first floor, through the linked rooms and up the hidden stairway to the tower room.

The rain's eased off now and the sea fret's lifted, revealing the world beyond the Manor. A finger of sun gilds the pewter sea and lights the ivy around the window to a vivid emerald. My breath catches; it's magical. I'm sure this spot inspired Kit and I have the strongest feeling it's going to inspire me too.

Go on, says Neil. He's standing by the window and smiling encouragingly. *You can do this, Chloe. I believe in you.*

"You always did," I whisper, but he's already gone. Imagined though they are, his words warm me from head to toe as I sit down opposite the window and lean my back against the wall. The pencil feels as thick as a tree trunk between my fingers and my head's spinning.

I take a deep breath and wait for the strange alchemy between eyes and lead to begin. Slowly, tentatively at first, the pencil tip begins to make marks on the paper, feathering lines and cross-hatches as textures build and shading steals over the whiteness.

It's happening! I'm drawing again!

Of course you are, says Neil, from just over my shoulder. *Did you ever doubt it for a second?*

My pencil's skating across the page as though it has a mind of its own. I draw and draw and draw until my fingers ache and each sheet of paper is full. It's as though a floodgate has been opened. I can't stop. I don't want to stop! I can still do this!

"There you are. We were getting worried."

I jump, having been so engrossed in sketching that I hadn't noticed Matt's arrival. I hadn't noticed much at all except the need to draw, which is as instinctive and vital as my need to breathe. How long have I been sitting here? The sky beyond the window has grown gloomy and the corners of the room are thick with shadows. It feels like minutes but it must have been hours. I blink at him, dazed and disorientated.

"Hey, you're freezing." Matt crouches down beside me and places his hands over mine. His breath clouds as he speaks and suddenly I realise just how cold I am. My fingers are numb and I'm trembling. Up here I'm far away from any heating and my hoody isn't enough to keep off the chill.

"I'm fine," I tell him.

"You're not," Matt says firmly. "Come on, we need to get you warmed up."

He gently unpeels my fingers from the pencil and, with my hands in his, raises me up. Pins and needles gush into my legs and I stagger against him. I feel lightheaded, as though I've been drinking, and for a few seconds the room spins while Matt steadies me.

"It's OK, Chloe. Take a deep breath."

I breathe in and out several times and the world rights itself. I haven't been so absorbed in something for months – unless you count grief of course – and it's strange to return to reality.

"I've been sketching," I explain, rather pointlessly since Matt's busy collecting up my work, which is scattered on the floor like autumn leaves.

"So I see. I think we can safely say you can still draw. Come on, let's get you a hot drink."

Matt places his hand in the small of my back and gently propels me out of the room and down the steps. Once in the hall he makes me a mug of tea and fetches a couple of biscuits.

"You need the sugar," he insists when I protest. "Don't argue. Just eat them while I find a folder for those sketches. I don't want you passing out on me."

I do feel lightheaded, but once I've had the tea and biscuits the room stops swimming quite as much and I feel more like myself – whoever that is these days. Matt returns with a plastic folder tucked under his arms, which he hands to me with a flourish.

"There! Can't have works of art getting creased or wet."

The rain's started again. Before long the skies are flinging fistfuls of water against the windows and sending spiteful gusts that rattle the glass. As the December evening wraps itself around the house like a scarf, the volunteers are putting on their coats, fishing out umbrellas and making dashes to their cars. I guess I should do the same and drive home, but the idea of returning to the echoey Rectory with its blinded shutters and ravenous wood burner is rather bleak. The place will be in darkness, a shadowy reminder that I'm all alone. Usually the solitude soothes me – it's why I'm here, after all – but today the thought makes me feel lonely. The wild weather, crackling fire and comfort of having people around have disconcerted me.

Matt's busy switching off the heaters and turning off lights. He's settling the house for the night and he'll need to set the alarms. I'm holding him up by loitering here.

"I'd better get going," I say, reaching for my coat, which he's draped over the arm of my chair.

"It's only just five. Do you need to rush back? I thought we could go to the pub."

Caught off guard, I stare at him. "What? Why?"

"To have a drink? Isn't that what's usually done in pubs? I thought we could celebrate your return to the art world. That's got to be worth a glass of wine. We could even be really crazy and have some food too. I don't know what it's like at your place but I've nothing in."

I think of the huge larder at the Rectory and the big fridge, both of which are totally wasted on me. There's a loaf of bread, which may or may not be going mouldy, and a tin of beans, but apart from that I'm out of supplies. Maybe I should have heeded my mother's warnings about the lack of a Tesco Express and the vast distance between here and Waitrose?

"I can't face another Pot Noodle," grimaces Matt. "Honestly, you'll be doing me a favour. I'll probably get scurvy if I don't have some vegetables soon."

I'm disarmed by his humour. "How can I live with myself if that happens? Especially since you've saved me several times from hypothermia!"

"That's true. Give me ten minutes to lock up here and set the alarms and I'll meet you there. Buy yourself a drink and pop it on my tab. And mine's a Guinness!"

Leaving Matt to do the final checks, I scurry down the drive, my head bowed against the rain and trying not to feel spooked by the way the tangled rhododendron branches reach for me like skeletal hands. By the time I reach my car I'm dripping all over the seat but my sketches, tightly zipped inside my coat, are dry – which is all that matters. I already know that these have that certain something that will lead to a special painting.

The drive to the Fisherman's Arms only takes a few minutes, the headlamps cutting a pale swathe of light through the night and the wipers swishing away the rain. I park up and run for the door. Immediately, I'm hit by the fug of warm bodies and woodsmoke.

The pub is a pretty, low-beamed building with a large inglenook fireplace where a merry blaze leaps and dances. Locals playing dice have commandeered the prime spot next to its warmth, while other drinkers lean against the bar and chat. Conversation bubbles away and the dark night is shut out behind thick crimson curtains. Couples sit at tables working their way through plates heaped with golden chips and steak pie, the puff-pastry crusts rising like clouds. After living on toast and soup for weeks, my mouth waters.

I order a Guinness for Matt and a white wine for myself before settling down at a small table set into the far window. It's a great spot for people-watching, and as I sip my drink I glance about with interest. I recognise some familiar faces from the village shop, whereas others in their Joules and Barbour clothing stand out a mile as second-homers. I wonder how I appear to them? I'm neither a local nor a holidaymaker. As always, I don't fit anywhere.

"There you are! Sorry if I kept you waiting. I was hoping it might ease off. It's foul out there."

Matt unwinds his scarf and shrugs off his coat. Raindrops shimmer in his hair and as he leans across to grab a menu, droplets speckle the tabletop.

"I don't know why I'm even looking. I always have the pie and chips," he grins.

"I thought you were supposed to be having vegetables?"

"Chips are vegetables, aren't they?"

"I suppose so," I say doubtfully, although I'm not convinced a plate of fries counts as one of your five a day.

"Well, there you go then. Problem solved. What would you like?"

The simple question floors me. I have no idea. Food hasn't featured much recently. There's no pleasure in cooking for one and, as I told Sue, my appetite departed around the same time Neil did.

"I'd go with the pie," Matt suggests, and I nod. Why not? It doesn't really matter.

He goes to order at the bar and I notice how many people wave at him or want to engage in conversation. It takes a good ten minutes before he returns and, when he does, I notice several pairs of female eyes following his movement. Oh Lord. By meeting him here I've instantly made myself a subject of huge interest, if Sue's to be believed.

"Sorry about that. Jim Pendennys was grilling me about priest holes for his son's history project. We poor parents do all the homework for our kids!" Matt sits down and picks up his pint. "I need this!"

"Priest holes? As in where Catholics would hide?"

"Yep. I reckon Rosecraddick Manor would have had at least one. The de Mainault family, who owned the place during Elizabeth the First's reign, were Catholics. Times were volatile and they'd have had to have been on their toes and ready to hide the priest away at a moment's notice."

"How fascinating. Where is it?"

"As I just told Jim at the bar, filled in or sealed up is my guess. It's another of the Manor's lost secrets, like the daisy. The concealed room in the tower could have been one, perhaps? Not a very good one, though, if you're counting windows from outside! Anyway, enough of work. To mystery daisies, poetry and paintings!"

I clink my wine glass against his pint and we drink quietly. The noise of the pub washes over me like the tide on the beach and I start to relax. This is normal. This is what most people do after work. They don't hide in big, empty houses and hold conversations with their dead husbands.

"So are you pleased with the sketches?" Matt asks eventually.

I consider this question for a moment. "Yes, I think so."

Matt says nothing. He's waiting for me to elaborate and I find this is OK; I'm happy to tell him more.

"I'm relieved I can still do it. I know that probably sounds crazy, but it's been so long and I was starting to think I'd never draw and paint again. Now though…" I shake my head in disbelief. "Now I find I don't want to stop. I've got so many ideas for this project that it feels like a tsunami. You'll have trouble getting me to do anything useful at the Manor now, I'm afraid."

His dark grey eyes hold mine. "I'm so pleased for you, Chloe. Draw as much as you like at the Manor. There are plenty of us to do the other bits."

"So I can skive off? You won't put me in detention?"

He laughs. "No, but Jill might. She still thinks she's running a school. Some days I half expect her to give me lines."

I laugh too.

"You look different," Matt says softly.

"Do I?"

"Yes. Less haunted? In the sense of not fearing what might happen, I mean. Not ghosts."

I think about Neil. I know he's just a hallucination born of longing, but Matt's right. Something dark has lifted. Perhaps it's the fear of failure that's been trailing me, clanking chains and wailing?

I swirl my wine thoughtfully. "I feel ready to paint again. I think I'll even make a start on clearing the attic at the Rectory and make a bit of a studio up there. The letting agent said I could do what I liked with the place."

"Haven't you had enough of sorting out junk? Or is this some weird dust fetish? You don't really want to be my friend; you're just using me for my attics?" he teases.

Matt wants to be my friend. *Is* my friend. I prod this idea a little to see how it feels and the answer is: nice. Matt's funny and clever and he makes me smile. He's the kind of person I would have wanted to be friends with before. Neil would have liked him too, I think. They're opposites in many ways but they're both honest, funny and easy to talk to.

"You've got me. I can't stay away from cobwebs and grime," I laugh. "Seriously though, the light up there is fantastic. It's the perfect spot."

"Well, feel free to use the Manor as much as you like for inspiration. It could be good publicity for us when the books are launched. It all helps."

"Brilliant. I'll sketch like mad and take lots of pictures for later." I'm already planning my next cover. I know exactly the spot I want to use. Maybe tomorrow I'll drive into Truro and buy new supplies.

"The builders aren't arriving until the New Year, so there's plenty of time to get your sketches done," Matt's saying. "Hopefully they won't find extensive rot or deathwatch beetle or anything awful. I'm sure the conservation experts would be able to deal with it, but I'd hate to be held up by that kind of thing. I'm itching to get on with the exhibition."

At this point our food arrives and conversation turns from the house to our dinner. The pie's delicious, just as Matt promised. The gravy's thick and rich, the pastry cloud melts in the mouth and the steak falls apart on my tongue. The chips are crispy and fluffy inside and perfect for mopping up my plate, which I'm amazed to clear.

Matt's right. I am different. I'm painting. I'm eating. And I'm having a lovely evening with an attractive man who isn't my husband.

I'm having a lovely time with a man who isn't my husband?

Suddenly I'm cold from head to toe and the food in my stomach feels millstone heavy.

Neil's dead. Dead. What am I thinking? I shouldn't be out in a pub enjoying myself and enjoying the company of another man. I feel sick with shame.

I have to get away.

"I've got to go."

I jump to my feet and root in my purse for some cash to settle the bill.

Matt looks taken aback. "Now? It's still early."

"No. No. I've got to go home."

I throw the money across the table and yank my coat on so fast that I knock my empty wine glass over. I scarcely notice. Nothing matters apart from escaping.

"OK. Well, thanks for dinner. It was fun," Matt says.

Yes, it was. That's the problem. I had fun. What sort of woman has *fun* when her husband, the man she promised to love, is dead? I'm disgusted.

"Please, let me pay," he says, as I snatch up my bag and scarf. "It's the least I can do for all your hard work."

There's no way I can let him pay. That would feel wrong, as if this were a date or something, and I shake my head frantically.

"No. No. It's fine. Keep it, please."

I just want to be out of here and out of my own skin preferably. Guilt crawls all over me.

"Is everything all right? You're not ill, are you?"

"I'm fine. I just need to go home. Thank you."

I turn to walk away but Matt catches my arm.

"I'll see you tomorrow? At the house?"

There's concern in his voice but I don't reply. I can't because I have no answer. The guilt bites into my heart and makes my stomach churn, and all I can do is nod and make a bolt for the door.

Outside the rain's still falling. As soon as I reach the car park my stomach heaves in revulsion at my unforgiveable ability to forget so easily. With this, the food and wine are purged. Shaking and weak, I walk to my car and lean against it. The food's gone, but the betrayal of Neil stays with me. I can run away to the Rectory and hide but this knowledge is something I can't escape.

I was happy. I had fun. I liked spending time with Matt.

I forgot I was grieving for my husband.

What sort of person am I?

CHAPTER 12

CHLOE

It's the light streaming through the bedroom window that wakes me from restless dreams. The beat of raindrops against glass and the rattle of the sash windows have been the backing track to life at the Rectory for days now, and it's disorientating to hear instead the cry of gulls and the rasp of waves racing up the beach.

I sit up, bewildered by this brightness after the relentless gloom, and rub eyes that are swollen and sore from hours of crying. When I came home last night I didn't even pause to lock up, load the range or switch on the lights. I didn't bother to draw the curtains or get undressed. Instead I burrowed under the duvet, still clad in my jeans and sweater, and cried until I could hardly breathe. I cried for everything that had gone and would never return, for the unfairness of Neil's death and for the guilt I felt after enjoying my meal with Matt. I wasn't the first to cry like this and I wouldn't be the last, but right then I'd felt like the loneliest person in the world.

This morning ice sparkles on the inside of the bedroom window and my breath rises like smoke. I pad to the bathroom to wash but of course the water's cold, so I make do with a facial wipe and drag a brush through my hair. I daren't change my clothes until the house warms up.

The next job is lighting the range and the wood burner. I'm getting good at this now; if I can just get to grips with not letting the fires go out, then I might make it through the winter without freezing to death. I fetch two baskets of wood from the shed, then lay and light the fires. Once these are blazing, I brew some coffee. Being busy helps because it stops me from thinking.

114

And thinking is something I daren't do. I have to keep moving or else I'll fall apart.

Keeping moving is the key. While the house warms up and the sun rises higher, I grab my coat and faithful spotty wellies and walk out through the graveyard. My feet leave dark green prints in the wet grass. At the far end of the graveyard is the cliff path – which I usually follow up to the memorial, where I sit and gaze out to sea. It feels like a healing place and when I'm there I think about the unknown Gem Pencarrow, the poetic Kit Rivers with his biting verse and daisy emblem, and all their lost friends who knew this view so well. How they must have longed for these silver ripples of water and this shimmer of the light on the waves when they were far away. Did they dream of this spot when they shivered in the trenches? Was it this place that they thought of at the end? Do they know that they're still remembered here? So many questions and so much loss. Loss is everywhere, then and now.

I can't bear to think any further about young lives cut short, so I take the turning just past the church and follow the steep path that plummets to St Nonna's Cove. It's not an easy walk, which is why not many people attempt it. Even in the middle of winter the track is overgrown. Rocks and ruts do their very best to trip me up and gorse snatches at my clothes, but I slither and leap my way down until I'm on the shore, where the waves grasp at pebbles and seaweed fingers cling to the rocks. The suck and sigh of the sea slows my heart and I walk along the tide's edge, skimming stones and watching them bounce across the water before they sink into infinity.

The far end of the beach is guarded by a ridge of snaggle-toothed rocks, revealed now at the ebb but almost invisible when the tide is in. Beyond this point are smaller, secretive coves only accessible at low tide or by boat – the perfect places for picnics and romantic assignations. I've tried to spot these from the cliff path but all I could see was foaming water. Being so well hidden, these coves must have been perfect for smugglers. I can't imagine anyone really makes the effort to visit them. I'm tempted to clamber over and see for myself what's there, except that I have no idea how fast the water sweeps in. I might not have lived in Cornwall for very long, but I'm wise enough to know that you don't play games with the sea.

Not unless you really have had enough...

My return climb up to the church is hard work, and by the time I reach the Rectory I'm puffing and red-faced. I'm certainly not cold either. The exercise and fresh air have cleared my head, the sunshine has lifted my spirits and the guilt's receded to the dark shadowy places where it's now lurking with all the other things I hide from.

You can't hide from the fact that I'm dead, Neil says bluntly. He's at the gate, ahead of me because he always was a fast walker. *I'm not coming back, Chloe. You have to accept it.*

"I can't," I say, but my words are snatched by the wind and they fly away into the scudding clouds, taking Neil with them. I can no more reach him and bring him back than I can wing my way over the cliffs and into the sky.

Neil's right: he isn't coming back. All the same, I'm a long way from accepting this. As I return to the house, much warmer now, I know that I overreacted last night and that I owe Matt an apology. He didn't deserve to bear the brunt of my grief when all he's done is be a friend. I'll find him and I'll explain. I hope he'll understand.

The range has done its job and there's plenty of hot water. I run a bath. A combination of low pressure, blocked pipes and an enormous cast-iron tub means this takes ages, so while the water spurts and splutters through the taps I fetch the folder of sketches and flick through them, my eyes narrowed critically. I'm fully prepared for these to be dreadful but to my delight they're not bad at all.

OK. I'm being modest. They're good, very good, and I know they'll be a great foundation for the first design. Rosecraddick Manor is exactly the right place to use as a setting. I can't wait to go back and do some more sketching.

First though I'll need to apologise to Matt.

I glance at my watch. It's just gone nine. I'll have my bath and then head over to the Manor and find him. I can take some photos in the sunshine too, which will help, and I'll check out some other possible locations. If Matt's free I'll do my best to explain what happened last night. He'll probably think I'm crazy – which is fair enough, since I'm starting to think the same – but I do owe him an explanation. He was being a friend and didn't deserve to be walked out on.

Quite what I'll say I do not know. I guess I'll have to take some time in the bath to figure that out. Most likely I'll end up very wrinkly.

"Matt's not here today. I thought he might have told you."

Jill announces this as though she's delighted to be telling me something I don't know about Matt. I suspect this is *exactly* the case because she's very possessive of him, always wanting to discuss history or mentioning her first-class degree whenever she gets the chance.

"No. No, he didn't."

A brief flash of triumph in her eyes confirms my suspicion.

"Oh. I am surprised, since you two are so pally lately, eating dinner together and everything."

I should have expected this. Sue did tell me that Matt was Rosecraddick's number one bachelor. By having supper with him in the pub I've probably made a few enemies.

"Where is he?" I ask.

Jill's clearly desperate to keep me in suspense but her desire to share a tasty snippet of gossip is too strong to resist. "His daughter's broken her leg. She fell down some steps last night, apparently, and it needs pinning. He's gone to be with her in hospital. He's beside himself."

Poor Matt. He hasn't spoken much about his children but I remember his stricken face when he sat on the bench contemplating a Christmas spent apart from them. This will have broken his heart. I've been so self-absorbed. Maybe Matt needed cheering up last night? Did I think of that?

Of course I didn't. Grief can make you selfish.

Jill's busy running through today's to-do list but I tune her out. I'm not going to scrub the cellar or clean the windows with vinegar or whatever other grotty task she's lined up for me. I'm going to call Matt and apologise for running out on him, and then I'm going to get some material together for these pictures. The house will have to wait for a few days.

"I was going to ask Matt about doing some sketches. I wanted to use the drawing room and the long gallery," I say when Jill stops to draw breath.

"Those are closed."

"I know but—"

"So you'll have to wait until he's back, dear." Jill turns her attention back to the pile of books she's dusting, her white-gloved hands deft and determined. No speck of dirt stands a chance. "Now, there's lots to do in the kitchen. Why don't you start there?"

Our conversation is over and there's no way Jill will let me loose to sketch, so I make my excuse that I need to work. Not that this is an excuse. I *have* to work now that Moira's committed me. Matt would understand if he was here. Leaving Jill stony-faced with disapproval, I walk back to the Rectory feeling rather deflated. I attempt to call Matt a couple of times but there's no answer, so I leave a brief message apologising and sending him my best wishes. I don't expect to hear back. He's got enough to deal with.

The Rectory feels very empty in the daytime, and as I drift around I realise just how much time I've been spending at the Manor. I throw a few more logs into the range, check the wood burner too and even call my mother to make more excuses about not coming home for Christmas. Once I've run out of things to do I face the fact that I can procrastinate no longer: it's time to tackle the attic and put together a makeshift studio. With this new project of Moira's to occupy me, I'll need a decent space in which to work.

I make a mug of coffee and, scooping up the fan heater, scale the stairs. The attic door creaks open and instantly I'm bathed in glorious light from either side, both land and sea. I was right. Even on a dull day this room will still be bright enough to work in. The days are getting shorter and although it's only lunchtime the cedar tree throws a long shadow across the front lawn. Nevertheless, the attic's still perfectly usable. I feel the same tingle of excitement I felt yesterday when I drew the view from the tower room.

I know I can work here. Maybe things will be all right?

From here I can just make out the rooftop of the manor house through the lacework of naked trees. One of those windows glittering through the knotted branches must belong to the room where I was drawing yesterday: the room where Kit Rivers – for I'm certain it was him – once scratched a daisy onto the windowsill. It's strange to think that he must have gazed across and seen the very window I'm staring through now.

The hairs on my forearms stand up.

I must be chilly. Rubbing at my arms I turn my attention to plugging in the heater and getting to work. This was once a bedroom, maybe even several, and it's full of a jumble of old boxes, chairs spewing stuffing, and various other odds and ends of broken furniture. I drag as much of this as I can to the far side of the attic, sending disgruntled spiders scuttling into corners and making myself sneeze as I disturb several decades' worth of dust. I'm getting good at this now. If the painting doesn't work out, maybe I'll get a job as a removal woman?

I unearth an old table with a wonky leg, then shift it to the middle of the room, where the light floods it from all angles. I'll place my easel here and loop string across the beams so that I can peg my paintings and photos up. There's no running water here, so I'll have to carry that up in a jug – but there is an ancient washstand that will come in handy for rinsing brushes when I use watercolours. Finally, I salvage a saggy floral armchair, which I can imagine curling up in. As I stand back to admire my handiwork, I decide that I already like this space. It may have hideous eighties flock wallpaper and an even older brown and orange carpet that gives me a headache, but it feels as though it belongs to me.

I take a break for some toast and more coffee, followed by some reloading of the range, before returning to the attic. The sun's lower now but the room has a lovely golden glow. The walls turn peachy and dust motes twirl in the light like ballerinas. All feels warm and still, as though I'm suspended in honey. Nearly done. Just one last task.

I flex my fingers. Time to peel back the ghastly carpet. The corner has already lifted and peeking out, like a shy girl glimpsing the world from beneath her fringe, is a beautiful wooden floor. I'm going to pull the migraine-inducing carpet up and let the floorboards breathe.

This is my plan, anyway, but ripping up a carpet that's been undisturbed since the seventies isn't as easy as it sounds. The underlay's stuck in several places and it takes a lot of tugging and swearing for me to even peel back a third of it. I'll be here for hours at this rate and my fingers are already sore.

I sit back on my heels and push my hair behind my ears. My hands are black with grime and the air's thick with dust. I'm hot, dirty and contemplating leaving this until tomorrow when something catches my eye. One of the half-uncovered floorboards seems to be higher than the others. It's close to the skirting but it doesn't lie flush to the parallel board. Intrigued, I crawl forwards and push the carpet back further until the whole area's uncovered. This reveals a loose board where the nails have been removed. It's a crude hiding place, the sort I made behind my bedroom sink when I was a teenager, and out of curiosity I curl my fingers around the edge and try to lift the wood. My nails scrabble for a hold and splinters dart into my fingertips, but all for nothing – the board doesn't budge. It's only when I fetch a palette knife from my painting kit and use it as a lever that the board starts to come up.

Heartened, I wedge the handle of a paintbrush into the gap, followed by a succession of thicker brushes until my fingers can claw underneath. Now I have greater leverage and I prise the board up, preparing myself for spiders and silverfish to come scuttling out. There are several of these, but my attention is drawn to the rusting lid of what looks like a tin, rather than to creepy-crawlies. I go to switch on the light, then return to the void in the floor, where I lean forwards and peer in. Sure enough, inside this home-made hiding place, nestled between joists that are garlanded with spiders' webs, is a dented and very old biscuit tin.

I'm about to pick it up when it occurs to me that, by doing this, I'm intruding into somebody's private belongings – belongings someone once went to great lengths to hide. It scarcely matters that whoever owned this tin is probably long dead. Whatever is in here isn't mine. Should I be prying? Are they watching me from the shadowy corners? And, if so, are they willing me on or are they angry?

The room feels charged. My breath catches in my throat. I can't leave this hidden. It meant something once and it's part of the history of this place: it's evidence from a long-gone age. Whatever's in this tin might teach us about that time and about ourselves too. That's what Matt would say, surely? Where's the difference between opening this tin and reading Tommy's exercise books or trying on moth-eaten feather hats? Neither the exercise books nor the hats were mine, but in finding and logging them I was able to add a little more detail to the Manor's history.

Buoyed by this thought, I lift the tin out and wipe the dirt away with my sleeve.

It is a biscuit tin, just as I thought. It's mostly copper-coloured, but with a pretty design of soaring bluebirds and pink blossom. Whose fingers last touched this? Who closed the lid, lowered the tin into its hiding place and then pushed the section of board back? Did they know they would never see it again? It looks old, certainly last century, and as I lift the lid I have a strange sensation that I'm travelling back in time to the moment when it was last opened.

Somebody's treasures are in here. Worthless in money, but priceless in the way that only sentimental belongings can be. There's a thick notebook with a leather cover, a faded red ribbon tying a curl of blond hair, a marble bottle stopper, some seashells, an envelope addressed in an elegant sloping hand, and a daisy chain. Dried almost to dust and ready to crumble, yes, but instantly recognisable. A daisy chain.

A *Daisy* chain.

The realisation of what this means is like a shaft of sunlight. I don't need to look any further or open the notebook. I know exactly what this is. With trembling fingers, I gently replace the long-dried flowers into the tin. I know I've stumbled upon something very private. Something that once meant the world.

Captivated, I carry the biscuit tin to the armchair and sit down. Then I open the notebook.

Daisy Alice Hills

1914

Diary

My teacher's eye recognises the round and confident style of a young hand, the writing neat and well formed with elaborate loops and flourishes. The ink is pale brown and faint, but the nib was once pressed firmly into the paper, scratching the words into life – as though with the force of her pen Daisy Hills was claiming every blank page.

Daisy Hills.

Daisy.

Of course. Why didn't it occur to me before? This was never about a flower. This was all about a girl.

Kit Rivers' girl?

Maybe.

Without even reading a word I'm certain she must have been. This unknown girl, this Daisy whose diary rests in my lap, was never far from Kit's thoughts in life; even in death she was close, judging by the window in St Nonna's. It's all been about her. Daisy Hills might have vanished from history, been erased from the official story of Kit Rivers, but someone made sure they left clues behind. They've been waiting for us to work out what these meant, that's all.

With the knowledge that I'm holding something very precious, I turn the first page and begin to read...

PART 2

CHAPTER 1

DAISY, MAY 1914

Daisy Hills stood on the platform, watching her train become a grey smudge feathered with smoke, hoping somebody had remembered she was arriving today. The fellow passengers who'd alighted alongside her at Rosecraddick Halt had already been collected by gigs and traps, and there'd even been a very smart carriage pulled by beautiful bay horses and driven by a groom in green and gold livery. As much as Daisy had longed to ride in it, she'd known straight away that it hadn't been sent for her. Vicars couldn't afford such luxury, and in any case such a carriage wouldn't have been sent to fetch a humble doctor's daughter. Her godfather, the Reverend Cutwell, was far more likely to send a farm cart. A carriage would encourage vanity – and vanity was a sin.

On the rare occasions when her godfather had visited them in Fulham, he'd struck Daisy as strict. With his mutton-chop sideboards, swirling black robes and bushy grey brows, he resembled a distinguished gentleman from the old Queen's time. When her godfather had last visited, four years ago now, Papa had warned Mama that under *no circumstances* was she to mention women's suffrage. The Reverend apparently had very strong opinions on such matters and would not be impressed, Papa had said, and although she wasn't pleased Mama had tried to keep the peace.

And I must do the same, Daisy told herself as she stood on the platform. It was kind of her godfather to invite her to stay and she must do her very best to make sure she didn't upset him.

Daisy's godfather was an old family friend and Papa had lodged with him when he was an undergraduate at Oxford. Reverend

Cutwell had long since moved to a parish in Cornwall and Charles Hills had settled in London. Their paths seldom crossed nowadays, but Papa recalled him with fondness and the Reverend was certainly a devoted godfather, regularly writing to Daisy to enquire after her spiritual welfare. Daisy was more than a little jealous of her brother's godfather, who was always good for ice creams or a penny. These may not secure entry to heaven but they were a lot more fun than having to memorise Bible verses and be on her very best behaviour.

Daisy had never visited Cornwall before, but Papa had gently explained that it was a quiet place, rather old-fashioned, where the radical ideas of the city would seem somewhat alarming. Daisy really hadn't understood this four years ago but now, at the practically ancient age of sixteen, she thought she did. Daisy had once overheard Cook say that Mama was a "bluestocking", which had confused her for a long time given that Mama's stockings were woollen and black.

"That's an old-fashioned name for a woman who's intelligent and enjoys intellectual pursuits," Mama had said when Daisy asked her to explain. "It's much easier to be scornful than to admit that women like us are men's intellectual equals. Not everyone thinks like your dear Papa, my love."

Daisy had beamed at the "like us" comment. She was immensely proud of her pretty and clever mama, who'd studied at Oxford and often argued the case for women's suffrage. An avid reader herself, Daisy was determined to be just like Mama when she grew up. Maybe she would write too? Daisy loved to write and for as long as she could recall had kept a diary, which she updated every evening. The early entries were all very dull and mostly about what pudding Cook had produced at dinner, but Daisy had always been sure that once she grew up they'd become far more exciting. She could scarcely wait to see what happened.

Standing on a deserted railway platform on a beautiful May afternoon, listening to the trembling calls of wood pigeons and wondering if the stationmaster would ever return, Daisy was very glad that her twelve-year-old self hadn't known what was ahead. There'd been an awful lot to write about since then, but excitement wasn't always such a good thing after all.

Daisy bit her lip. She wasn't going to dwell on *that*. Mama was dead, Eddie had been sent away to public school, Papa was sad and tired, and she was lucky to still be alive – even if she was stranded on an empty railway platform. It was time to count her blessings. That was what their nursemaid, Meggie, used to say when she made Daisy and Eddie kneel down to say their prayers: they had to think about all the good things to be thankful for. As she squinted into the distance, feeling disconcerted by all this emptiness and space after a lifetime spent gazing at rooftops and chimneypots, Daisy did her best to dredge up a few blessings. Surviving polio was one, and surviving with *just* a limp and a weakened leg was another. Maybe this counted for two or even three blessings? Lots of the other patients in the sanatorium hadn't been as lucky. Neither did many of them have a godfather who lived by the sea and who was willing to have them come and stay for fresh air and saltwater bathing. Papa said these things were what she needed – and although Daisy had wept bitterly to leave him and her home, with all its memories of Mama, she knew that in all matters medicinal Papa was always right. Some of the other doctors might scoff at his ideas but she was still alive, if thin and weaker, wasn't she? And if Papa said that fresh air, good country food and saltwater swimming were what Daisy needed, then she didn't doubt him for a minute. Yes, she was lucky that her godfather was willing to have her come to stay.

So her godfather was another blessing, Daisy decided as she dragged her trunk along the platform. She was very fortunate to have this chance to become strong again. If she had to do some light duties around the house, help to clean the church and keep her opinions on women's suffrage to herself, those would be small prices to pay. Perhaps if she had some spare time she could also ask to borrow a bicycle. Such exercise would probably strengthen her leg and she'd have some fun cycling along the lanes. With this idea in mind, she felt slightly less downcast at being marooned in Cornwall.

Meggie was right. Counting your blessings worked and was certainly preferable to thinking about all the things you'd lost...

The battered brown trunk bumping into her calves made her limp worse and her leg ached, but Daisy gritted her teeth and ignored this. Instead she thought about what was inside. There were two new dresses, one a deep green serge for dinner and the other a sprigged cotton, threaded with green ribbons. She'd also packed a knee-length bathing costume, a pretty straw bonnet for Sundays and a pair of brand-new boots. There were new hair ribbons too, which a weeping Meggie had given Daisy just before the hansom cab had drawn up. Meggie, who'd been valiantly wielding the comb for as long as Daisy could remember, knew that if Daisy was left to her own devices she would let her wild mane of red curls tumble to her waist.

The final blessing Daisy could think of was tucked safely at the bottom of the trunk, deliciously wrapped up in brown paper and possibilities. Just thinking about it made her shiver with anticipation. It was a new journal, a present from Papa and the most treasured gift ever, with its smart embossed cover and pages of unmarked creamy cartridge paper. Throughout the long journey westwards, Daisy had itched to open it and write her first entry but had somehow managed to contain herself. The train had rattled and jolted over the tracks, and smuts had blown in while the windows were open; such a beautiful book didn't deserve blots or wobbly characters. Instead she'd sat up straight with her back against the scratchy fabric and watched as the fields and sky slipped past in a blur of startling green and bright blue. There would be time enough to start writing properly once she arrived at Rosecraddick Rectory, she'd decided.

So now, as she waited on the quiet platform, Daisy wondered what she would do if nobody came to fetch her. Although this would certainly be an adventure to record in her journal, she had no idea how she would find her godfather's place. It was only thanks to the stationmaster calling, "Rosecraddick Halt!" that she'd known where she was at all. Anxious not to hold anyone up, she had reached out of the window and opened the door almost before the train had lurched to a stop. Then Daisy had retrieved her trunk from the luggage car and waited for the steam to clear and for someone to step forward and claim her.

It was yet to happen. So far she was alone, and all that hissing of steam and slamming of carriage doors felt as though it had occurred an entire lifetime ago.

Daisy frowned. This wasn't what she'd expected. From what she did know of her godfather, he was a stickler for good timekeeping. She recalled him constantly checking the big pocket watch Eddie had so envied, and tutting if anyone had been so much as a minute late to meals. Apart from a few vivid details like this though, Daisy didn't remember a great deal of her godfather's last visit to Fulham. She and her little brother had been confined to the nursery for much of it. Mama had been very irritable for the entire stay and at one point had made Eddie rinse his mouth out with soap and water for cheeking her. This was most unlike Mama, and Eddie had spat out saliva for hours. Daisy had had to wear her best pinafore, so starched by Meggie that the frills scratched like brambles, and had been expected to be seen but not heard at the dining table. Usually Daisy loved to chat and Papa and Mama were happy to listen to her, but her godfather, it transpired, had very strict opinions on children – and pretty much everything else too. When the Reverend had departed, the whole household had heaved a sigh of relief, life had returned to normal and Daisy hadn't given her godfather another thought.

At least, not until recently. Daisy hoped that now she was a very grown-up sixteen she might find his company a little easier. Maybe she could be of use to him about the parish and help with sermons, like Dorothea in *Middlemarch*? Or perhaps she would visit the sick and read them words of comfort, like Beth in *Little Women*? These ideas cheered her hugely because, as Meggie could testify, Daisy's strengths lay firmly in intellectual pursuits rather than housework. In any case, Daisy felt certain that lots of adventures lay ahead and that in no time at all her journal would be crammed full of them.

As the spring sunshine played peekaboo with strands of cloud, Daisy ignored Meggie's dire warnings of freckles and dark skin and raised her face to it. The warmth promised happiness and hope, and her heart lifted. Somebody would be along soon. Putting her trunk down and pulling a battered edition of Keats from her bag, she settled down to read.

"Excuse me, are you Miss Hills?"

Daisy's head whipped up. A young lad with a nut-brown face and eyes as blue as the bright sky was staring at her with interest. A lock of chestnut hair slipped from beneath his cloth cap to fall across his face, and he pushed it away with an impatient gesture.

"I am," she said. "I'm Daisy Hills."

"Phew! Glad you're still here, Miss!" said the lad. "I'm Gem Pencarrow and the Reverend Cutwell sent me to meet your train."

Daisy stood up. She was very aware that her hat had slipped from her head, her hair was a mess and she probably had soot on her nose. None of this had mattered a jot when she'd thought an elderly groom would be collecting her, but now that she was aware of Gem's blue-eyed scrutiny taking in her faded poplin, old shawl and scuffed boots, she felt her face flush. Unlike her, he was at ease. She noticed not only his breeches and polished country boots, but also the way his lawn shirt was rolled up to reveal his strong, tanned forearms.

"You're very late," she said, standing up and putting her book away. "I thought I'd been forgotten."

Gem laughed easily, not seeming offended that nervousness had made her short with him. "No chance of that, Miss Daisy. The Reverend never forgets anything. His eyes mightn't be what they were, but he's as sharp as ever and he'd skin me alive if he knew I was late meeting you. I'm sorry about that, Miss, but Merlin threw a shoe so I had to go by the smithy."

129

Daisy assumed Merlin was the horse. "That's perfectly fine," she said, straightening her spine and making sure she had the upright carriage Meggie insisted a young lady should exhibit, regardless of polio and weak legs. "I was reading Keats. Reading always passes the time, don't you think?"

Daisy certainly thought so. While she'd been in hospital she'd read and read and read until she'd thought her brain couldn't possibly absorb any more words. The Brontës, Austen, Wollstonecraft, Byron, Shelley... all these old friends had transported her away from the pain and the long bedbound hours, just as they'd been her escape when Mama had passed away. Reading and writing meant everything to Daisy. Perhaps one day the words she wove would make that magic happen for somebody else. She very much hoped so. That would be the most rewarding thing in the world.

Gem, picking up her trunk and swinging it easily onto his shoulder, laughed. "It'd take me all day just to read a few lines, Miss! Not much of a scholar, I'm afraid."

"Oh, but books are wonderful!" Daisy began earnestly, but Gem only smiled and reached for her bag.

"I'm sure you're right, Miss."

That ended that conversation, Daisy realised as she followed Gem out of the station. The long journey had been lonely and, apart from an elderly lady who'd sat opposite in the compartment and talked about her daughter without pausing from Paddington to Reading, there had been little chance of conversation. Daisy, who usually spent hours discussing literature and politics and art with her father, was longing for someone to talk to. She already knew that her godfather wouldn't think these topics suitable for a young woman, and now Gem had gently reminded her that they weren't social equals. Maybe, thought Daisy, watching Merlin's swaying rump as the dog cart carried them along the leafy lanes, she'd have to chat to the horse instead. Away from the safety of home everything was so complicated.

The ride to Rosecraddick took the neat little dog cart (*exactly* the kind of vehicle Daisy would have expected her godfather to keep – functional and tidy but definitely sans livery and footmen) up and down some very steep hills. Having been a Londoner for most of her sixteen years, Daisy hadn't spent much time in the countryside. Now, as Gem clicked his tongue to Merlin and the dog cart sped up a little, she glanced about with interest.

Rather than bustling with horse buses and hansom cabs and the odd motorcar, the Cornish roads were rough and empty. All around was a patchwork of fields, each scrap of colour stitched together with dark hedges and embroidered with woods of deep green. When they passed the occasional hamlet or isolated dwelling where chickens scratched in the dust and cats snoozed on windowsills, Gem waved and called to people. Apart from this, the only sound was the clop of Merlin's hooves and the squeak of the harness. The world seemed too slow, sun streamed through the leafy canopy above and golden fields either side of the lane glowed with the burnished promise of a good harvest. Although Daisy felt more nervous with every mile that brought them closer to the Rectory, she was heartened by the prettiness of the hedgerows foaming with cow parsley and dotted with swathes of pink campion. Wordsworth and Coleridge could have waxed lyrical about the spot, of this Daisy felt certain.

Gem clicked his tongue again and, in response, Merlin picked up pace as the road swung to the left. Soon they were passing a pair of imposing wrought-iron gates hung from stone pillars topped with huge stone orbs. An immaculate drive stretched ahead to an impressive manor house; at the foot of the front steps stood the smart carriage Daisy had admired earlier.

"Whose house is that?" she asked Gem, so intrigued that she forgot to worry about protocol and whether she ought to be talking to the groom. Besides, Gem with his dimpled smile and easy manner was the first person she'd spoken to for hours.

"That's Rosecraddick Manor, Miss," Gem said, following her

gaze. "The family who live there own most of the land around here."

"It's beautiful." Daisy's gaze was drawn to the tower over the arched front door, the windows as dark and secretive as closed eyes. What a wonderful view that room must have. She could imagine reading for hours up there or simply sitting and looking out over the rest of the world. In such a spot you'd feel like a princess in your own private kingdom. How magical.

The Manor was left behind now as Merlin trotted on with a sudden enthusiasm that suggested home wasn't far away. Gem drove the dog cart through a lane edged with small cottages with lobster pots stacked outside and nets strung out for mending. The street here was as busy as the rest of the route had seemed deserted. Women wrapped in shawls and with baskets over their arms were going about their business, while a group of grubby children bowled a hoop along – earning themselves a reprimand from Gem when it wobbled too near the cart. Men in darned jumpers and smocks sat outside the inn, smoking and talking as they drank from metal tankards. The air was sharp with salt, and when the cart rounded the corner and the road continued to drop away, Daisy gasped to see the endless blue of the sea.

Her eyes were wide. She'd read about the English Channel, of course, and had seen the vast marshes and leaden line of the Thames, but never before had Daisy understood the vastness of the sea. The cliffs swept away into the deepest azure and the rolling water glittered as though the entire contents of Aladdin's cave had been poured into it. Seabirds soared high above and her ears were full of their calls and the crashing of waves on rocks.

It was possibly the most breathtaking sight she'd ever seen.

"Rosecraddick Rectory, Miss."

The dog cart turned towards a short drive where a Georgian house draped in ivy presided over a clipped lawn and immaculate flowerbeds. A stately cedar tree held centre stage on the lawn and, as she looked at it, Daisy's pulse skipped a beat. There was a memory, yet not a memory; she was aware of something she had to remember but that slipped out of reach as soon as she tried to think of it. The warm air shimmered and for a moment she felt the heat of fire and saw the limbs of the tree become a charred skeleton.

"Are you all right, Miss? You're awfully pale," Gem said.

Daisy couldn't answer. The whole world was starting to tilt. She hadn't had the dream for years – so long, in fact, that she had all but forgotten it – but now her heart was racing as though she was waking up in the grey dawn, her nightgown cold with sweat and her entire body trembling. Meggie used to come running and Mama, before she was sick, would always fetch a hot posset and hold her close until the night terrors faded.

Oh! She was being ridiculous. It was just a dream, a foolish dream she thought she had grown out of.

Gem halted Merlin in front of the Rectory's shiny front door and looked across at her. His blue eyes were filled with concern.

"Is it the heat, Miss? Are you coming over faint?"

Daisy took a deep breath and forced herself to smile. It was the heat, but not in the sense that Gem meant. It wasn't the golden warmth of a spring evening that had affected her: it was something far more intense, from a place of unknown horrors.

"I think it must be," she said as he helped her down from the dog cart. "Yes, I'm sure that's it."

But her words sounded doubtful even to her own ears because, as absurd as it might seem, she had the overwhelming feeling that she'd been here before.

Her old dream meant something, Daisy thought. It felt like a warning.

CHAPTER 2

DAISY, MAY 1914

"You must be Miss Daisy! Welcome to Rosecraddick Rectory!"

The front door swung open and a plump woman stepped forward. She was dressed in black and her white hair was scraped back from her round face in a bun; the overall impression would have been rather severe had it not been for her smiling face and warm greeting. Still a little dazed, Daisy found herself being ushered into a gloomy panelled hall where the air was cool and a longcase clock ticked sonorously at the foot of the staircase.

"Don't just stand there gawking, Gem Pencarrow," the woman called over her shoulder. "Bring Miss Hills' trunk in and carry it up to her room. This week, mind. No dawdling or detours to the pantry!"

"Yes, Mrs Polmartin," said Gem, catching Daisy's eye and giving her a ghost of a smile as he lifted the trunk. Daisy's lips twitched. Smiling at her was probably not at all appropriate, but she liked the sense of camaraderie and there was something about Gem that reminded her of her brother. Daisy had missed Eddie terribly when he'd gone away to school. Maybe her godfather would allow her brother to come and visit in the holidays? That could be fun and the idea cheered her.

Once Gem was on his way with the luggage, the older woman turned to Daisy.

"I'm Mrs Polmartin, the Reverend's housekeeper. You must be tired and thirsty after your long day? Can I offer you some refreshment?"

Daisy realised she hadn't eaten anything since breakfast, hours and hours ago — and that had only been a boiled egg. She was lightheaded from hunger rather than sinister premonitions. That was all. She must have been reading too many gothic novels.

Relieved, Daisy followed the housekeeper's swishing skirts along the corridor and into a big kitchen. There was a large range at the far end with a kettle set on the hotplate whistling away while a young woman sat at the big table chopping carrots, oblivious to the cloud of steam filling the room. She was curvy, with a beautiful complexion like something straight out of an advert for Pears soap, and locks of her golden hair were making a break for freedom from her mob cap. She was obviously the kitchen maid, but from the dreamy expression on her face and the very slow carrot-chopping, Daisy guessed her mind was on other things than the kitchen chores.

"Nancy Trehunnist!" bellowed Mrs Polmartin, making both Daisy and the daydreaming Nancy jump. "I asked you to prepare the vegetables this morning. After you'd aired a room for Miss Daisy. Have you done either?"

Nancy Trehunnist couldn't have looked more confused if the housekeeper had been speaking French. Daisy wondered whether she'd find carrots in her bedroom and pillowcases served up for dinner. She smothered a giggle.

But the housekeeper wasn't amused in the slightest.

"Gem has taken Miss Daisy's trunk up, Nancy. You'll need to unpack it and make sure you've lit the fire, as it still gets chilly in the evenings. Oh, and fill the jug for the washstand too. Well? What are you waiting for?"

Having spent a great deal of time in hospital, Daisy had become adept at reading people. The long months spent recovering from her illness had passed slowly and when she'd felt too ill to read her books, Daisy had studied her fellow patients and the staff. The arch of an eyebrow or the flicker of an eye held a wealth of secrets and it didn't escape her notice that at the mention of Gem, Nancy's gaze had shot up from the half-chopped carrots.

"Yes, Mrs Polmartin. I'll see to it right now," the girl said, bobbing a hasty curtsey and then dashing from the room with an energy that moments before would have seemed impossible. Daisy smiled to herself. So, Gem Pencarrow had an admirer. She could see why.

"Take a seat, Miss. You must be tired from your journey," Mrs Polmartin said, pulling out a chair.

"I am. Thank you," said Daisy.

She took her place at the large kitchen table and looked around her while Mrs Polmartin brewed tea. She could see that there was a large sink at the far end and, beyond that, a scullery and larder. The smell of roast beef drifted from the range and Daisy's stomach rumbled. Hearing this, the housekeeper cut her an enormous slice of fruit cake.

"Reverend Cutwell generally likes to dine at half past six," she said, placing the cake in front of Daisy. "I expect you'll usually join him but he's dining at Rosecraddick Manor this evening, so I thought you could eat supper in here with us. Unless you'd prefer me to set the dining table? Whatever you think proper, Miss."

Daisy had been wondering when she would see her godfather and was rather relieved to learn he was out. The thought of trying to make polite conversation over dinner when she was tired and on edge was unnerving. As was the idea of eating all alone in the dining room.

"I'm very happy to eat supper in here," she said. "I wouldn't want you to go to any extra trouble."

Mrs Polmartin looked pleased with this answer. "Well, I won't pretend it doesn't save me a little work. We tend to eat in here at seven. Why don't I show you to your room when you've finished your tea and you can settle in?"

Once she'd eaten her cake, Daisy followed the housekeeper up the staircase. Being south-facing, the Rectory should have streamed with light on an afternoon like this, but all the windows were shrouded in heavy net curtains and the doors leading from the landing were tightly closed as though jealously guarding secrets. There was a musty smell and deep shadows lurked in corners. Papa had mentioned that after the Reverend's wife and son had died he'd shut himself away, but Daisy had thought this was just a turn of phrase.

Now she wasn't quite so certain.

"The master doesn't like these rooms opened," Mrs Polmartin explained as they passed by. "They were used by the mistress. After the Lord took her, we left the rooms. It didn't feel right to use them."

Papa had told Daisy that Reverend Cutwell's wife had died in childbed a very long time ago and the baby hadn't survived. The shadows seemed to stir and Daisy shivered. This part of the house smelt old and sad.

"The bathroom is at the end of the corridor." Mrs Polmartin pointed to the farthest door. "We have an indoor water closet here."

Daisy was glad to hear it. She didn't fancy venturing out into the graveyard to find the privy or, even worse, having to use a chamber pot. She was about to ask where her room was when the housekeeper gestured to a narrow flight of stairs leading from the landing.

"We've made the attic bedroom ready for you, Miss. Nancy arranged it all, as I have trouble with those stairs on account of my knees."

Daisy thought it more likely that the rather large housekeeper wouldn't fit up the staircase, but she nodded politely. "Thank you."

"I hope you find it to your taste, Miss."

Daisy hoped so too, although she was rather surprised to have been given an attic room. Usually servants occupied such quarters. Was this a clue that her godfather was expecting her to earn her keep? What was her status here exactly? Family? Servant? Or something in between? Perhaps she wouldn't belong anywhere. She glanced at the steep stairs. Her bad leg, already tired, started to throb at the mere thought of climbing them. *You'll just have to get sea bathing and make it stronger*, she told herself firmly. *That's why you're here, after all!*

"I'm sure it will be lovely," she said. The climb was exhausting, yet when she reached the top Daisy instantly forgot about any discomfort.

Her hands flew to her mouth in surprised pleasure. This was like arriving in a brave new world! Unlike the gloom of the floor below, the attic room was bright with sunshine flooding in from windows on both sides. The floorboards glowed in the warm light and to her delight she could see out to sea, where the waves sparkled and the sky stretched to infinity. The opposite window boasted a view towards Rosecraddick Manor; when Daisy craned her neck she could just make out the magical tower she'd admired earlier. Now she could be a princess in her own tower!

The room wasn't elegant but it was very pretty. It had faded floral wallpaper, a bright rag rug on the smooth floorboards and a colourful patchwork eiderdown covering a big brass bed. There was a washstand, a comfy armchair piled with cushions, a dressing table, a big chest and a rail for hanging clothes. A merry fire danced in the grate and an age-speckled mirror hung above the mantelpiece, making the room feel even bigger. Everything had been cobbled together from bits and pieces but the overall effect was feminine and welcoming.

Gem had left her trunk at the foot of the bed, so Daisy opened it and began to put her belongings away. Little by little the room began to feel as though it was her own, and by the time she drew out her new journal Daisy felt far more cheerful. There would be a great deal to write about, she was certain – starting with a description of the waves, perhaps? Or maybe a few lines about her journey? She carried the diary to the window that overlooked the sea and wondered where to begin. The pages and pages of blank paper were ripe with possibilities and she could hardly wait to fill them. Her new life in Cornwall started here.

Daisy lay the book on the windowsill and, opening it slowly, pressed the first page flat with the palm of her hand. Then she fetched her fountain pen, pulled off the lid and wrote with a firm and determined hand:

Daisy Alice Hills
1914
Diary

The nib hovered over the page for a moment before she drew breath and began to write.

CHAPTER 3

DAISY, MAY 1914

"I trust you have something edifying with which to occupy yourself today?"

Reverend Cutwell peered over his newspaper like an old bespectacled tortoise peeking out of its shell and Daisy, who'd been reading his newspaper across the table rather than eating her boiled egg, was thrown for a moment. She struggled to think of a suitable reply while her godfather regarded her with thinly veiled irritation. The Reverend Cutwell, Daisy had quickly discovered, was not a morning person.

"Yes, thank you," she said.

"And would you care to elaborate on what this might be?"

Daisy had only been at the Rectory for a few days, but she'd been quick to work out how best to handle her godfather. Set in his ways, old-fashioned and exceedingly grumpy, he hadn't seemed particularly pleased to see his goddaughter. So far, she'd sat through two painful suppers with him, making timid attempts at conversation; there had been several equally awkward breakfasts too. She had decided that she much preferred to take her meals in the kitchen, in the company of the servants. It might not have the elegance of the dining room with its deep crimson walls, gold-brocade curtains and vast mahogany table, but at least there she was able to enjoy her food without worrying about saying the wrong thing. Already the sea air had given her an appetite –something she'd lacked for months. There had been some very lively conversations in the kitchen too, albeit kept firmly in check by Mrs Polmartin, and these had helped Daisy feel more settled. She'd been pleased to learn that she would be eating in the kitchen whenever the Reverend was away from home.

Eating with her godfather was a nerve-racking affair. He was a stickler for table manners and proper behaviour, and his scrutiny put Daisy on edge. Anxiety turned her food into cotton wool and she could scarcely choke down a mouthful – a fact that caused the Reverend to scowl. Last night he'd made several sharp comments about appreciating what the Lord provided.

"Well?" said her godfather impatiently. He folded his newspaper, placing it face down on the white tablecloth, and regarded Daisy as if she were an idiot. "The Devil makes work for idle hands."

Daisy only just stopped herself from rolling her eyes at this.

"I'm going to go saltwater swimming, Godfather," she said sweetly.

Reverend Cutwell made a noise that was something between a snort and a bark. He didn't approve of sea bathing and he especially didn't approve of young ladies doing so. Nonetheless, Daisy's swimming was for medicinal purposes and it was the primary reason for her coming to Cornwall, so he had no grounds for objection. This didn't stop him making his feelings clear though: as she forced herself to eat her egg, Daisy was treated to a lecture about decorum. Young women had to behave a certain way and, above all, they had to preserve their modesty. Their very lives, as well as their immortal souls, depended upon it.

Daisy had spluttered into her teacup at this and swiftly had to pretend to have a coughing fit when her godfather shot her a suspicious look. Having already attempted to swim in the sea in her woollen bathing costume, she was quite decided that the opposite was true: modesty was rather dangerous.

And with this thought, the seed of an idea was planted...

As her godfather's words continued to drone through the dining room like one of his sermons, Daisy didn't hear a word. She'd learned to swim with Mama and was a confident, if not particularly stylish, swimmer. The idea of swimming in the sea had excited her and yesterday she'd had a wonderful morning meandering along the cliff path, her hands trailing through swathes of wild garlic and purple thrift, before picking her way down a steep path to a rocky cove. Her hat had slipped from her head and bounced merrily against her back as she'd skipped and hopped her way down the track, her boots sending scree and earth skittering to the ground and her straw basket swinging from her hand. Her heart had pounded as the glittering water below drew her like a magnet. The fact that her leg was aching from the physical exertion barely mattered to her.

When she was finally on the beach, she'd craned her neck upwards in the direction of the cliff path, just to make sure she wasn't visible from above. She would need to change into her bathing costume, and the last thing she wanted to do was scandalise the locals – or, indeed, the good parson. Being on her best behaviour was exhausting and it had been a relief to exchange his scrutiny for that of the beady-eyed gulls and cormorants.

Honestly, Daisy had laughed to herself as she'd located the perfect changing spot behind some large rocks, who would be wandering by or make the effort to walk all the way down here? Her godfather spent most of his day closeted in the study with the door most firmly and determinedly closed (it hadn't taken Daisy very long to realise she wouldn't be playing the part of Dorothea Brooke), and Mrs Polmartin and Nancy were busy with household chores while Gem and the menfolk worked the land or tended the horses. She'd noticed a sailing boat skipping across the horizon and supposed that the fishing fleet was probably far beyond, but nobody else was around. The place had been deserted.

Daisy was alone. Totally and utterly alone.

She couldn't recall a time in her life when this had ever been the case. Reading in her room didn't count because Papa or Meggie were always in the house – and besides, how could you ever be alone in London? The city teemed with life. This was the first time she had ever been properly alone.

And it was glorious!

Somehow Daisy had managed to undo all the lace on her corset and change into her bathing costume. Once she'd wrestled the woollen garment on, it had felt scratchy against her skin. She'd pulled the matching cap onto her head, folded her clothes neatly into her basket and draped her towel over the rocks to warm in the sunshine. Then Daisy had stepped into the sea, shrieking as the icy water nipped her skin and the waves raced in and foamed about her ankles. Then she'd forced herself to start swimming. At first the cold sea had made her gasp, but it hadn't been long before her body had grown accustomed to the chill. She'd spent a very contented hour splashing about and floating on her back to watch the clouds. When at last her teeth had started to chatter, she'd struck for the shore – only to discover that the weight of the sodden wool made it very difficult to swim. The wet fabric wanted nothing more than to drag her limbs beneath the waves.

By the time she'd reached the beach, Daisy had been exhausted and her leg aching so much with the effort of dragging the costume through the water that she'd wanted to weep.

Modesty was no fun! Daisy had reflected as she'd towelled herself dry. Who was there to see her anyway on a deserted Cornish beach? A few seagulls? A crab or two? Nosey shannies in the rock pool?

So today, which promised to be another glorious sun-drenched affair, Daisy had a plan and it was one she could hardly wait to put into action. As she let herself through the Rectory gate and skirted past St Nonna's to the cliff path, Daisy laughed out loud with joy. She felt so much better for being here. The sea and the clear Cornish air were already working their magic, and if meals with her godfather weren't so stressful she'd probably have put on lots of weight too. These days she was always ravenous. The mere thought of thick doorsteps of bread smothered with yellow farm butter and accompanied by hunks of cold mutton was enough to make her mouth water. Maybe tomorrow she would pack a picnic. With Keats in her basket too, she would be able to read in peace.

Still smiling, Daisy followed the steep path to the cove. Once she was safely out of sight, she pulled off her hat and tugged the hairpins from her bun so that her wild curls tumbled to her waist. She felt alive and happy. Even the heaviness and aching in her leg had subsided, and once she was on the beach she could hardly wait for the cool kiss of the green water and to feel the waves carry her.

And this time there wouldn't be any heavy wool to drag her down!

She'd selected the sheltered spot behind the bigger rocks at the far end of the bay as a perfect place to change. As before, Daisy checked she was alone before tugging off her boots, unrolling her woollen stockings, stepping out of her dress and unhooking her corset. Oh, the relief of taking that garment off! Yet another unfairness that women had to bear. How wonderful it would be to move and breathe easily all the time.

Clad only in her drawers and camisole, Daisy glanced about the cove. As she teetered on the brink of doing something so shocking, her heart was racing and her hands were shaking. How ridiculous! There was nobody here to see. But even so, maybe she should clamber over the rocks to the next cove along. That was even more secluded and perfect for what she had in mind.

This was the moment when she ought to be pulling on the itchy bathing costume and tucking her hair up into the knitted cap, before inching her way into the water in a modest and ladylike manner. Yes, that was what she *should* do, but Daisy Hills wasn't the kind of girl who always did what she was supposed to do, especially when the joyous freedom of slicing through the water beckoned.

Before she had time to change her mind, Daisy abandoned her belongings and scrambled over the rocks to the next beach. Her feet slithered on the seaweed and she slipped a couple of times, grazing her knees on rough barnacles, before she found herself in a small cove that was little more than a bite out of the cliffs. This was the perfect place, she thought delightedly. It was totally hidden.

With a whoop of pure exhilaration, Daisy ran to the sea and hurled herself into it, gasping as the icy waves hit her chest. Without the weight of the woollen costume she was soon splashing through the water with her legs kicking up a wake of salty diamonds. Swimming unencumbered was a joy and so easy! Daisy bobbed with the waves and then floated on her back. As her camisole fanned out in the water and her hair floated like a halo of seaweed, she imagined herself as a tragic heroine. The Lady of Shalott maybe? Or Ophelia?

Daisy closed her eyes, relishing the sunlight that turned her lids to flame and the whooshing of her blood through her veins as the water blocked her ears. All was tranquil and she floated in a pleasant haze of daydreams – until strong hands closed around her waist and shocked her back to the present.

What?

Daisy's eyes snapped open but salt water sloshed over her face, filling her nose and mouth. For a moment she began to sink. Surfacing again, she fought for breath. Somebody was pulling her through the water and she twisted and turned, kicking out at whoever it was and thrashing with her arms.

The hands tightened their grasp on her waist and Daisy was towed through the waves, unable to protest. Whoever her captor was, he was a strong swimmer; despite her best efforts to escape, he powered through the water until the sea grew shallow and Daisy felt pebbles roll beneath her toes. As a big wave broke, she pitched forward and landed on her hands and knees, panting and spluttering.

What just happened?

"Are you all right, Miss? Can you breathe?" asked a man. His voice was gentle and beautifully spoken. He took her arm and raised her to her feet. "You're safe now. You haven't drowned, I promise."

"I wasn't drowning! I was swimming!" Daisy protested. She was shaking, although whether from cold, shock or anger she wasn't sure. It was infuriating. Couldn't a girl swim in peace even in a secret cove?

"Swimming?" he echoed. "On your own? Are you insane? The

currents are utterly deadly here when the tide turns. Nobody swims then. Or they don't unless they want to drown."

"I didn't know that, did I?" Daisy snapped. She felt cross and more than a little stupid.

"Well, now you do. Anyway, isn't it customary to wear a bathing costume when one swims, rather than undergarments?"

Daisy pushed her wet hair out of her face and blinked away seawater. As the world came back into view she saw eyes as green and deep as secret rock pools regarding her with concern, tinged with amusement. The eyes belonged to someone not much older than her, with thick golden hair slick with sea spray pushed back from a sun-kissed face. His linen shirt and pale trousers clung to his body and the water turned the fabric translucent, tracing every line of his muscled arms and strong shoulders. He reminded her of one of the Grecian statues she'd looked at once when Papa had taken her to the British Museum. Until now, this was the closest she'd ever come to seeing a real-life young man disrobed.

"The water's wonderful for swimming in, but not so great for modesty," he grinned, catching her looking.

This was when Daisy realised that her long camisole was just as saturated as the stranger's clothes. Sure enough, when she looked down she saw that the thin white cotton was clinging to her legs and breasts. Her godfather would combust if he ever saw her in such an indecent state. Her garments were transparent and she may as well be naked!

With a howl of horror, Daisy crossed her arms over her chest while the young man chivalrously turned his back – but not before she'd seen his face flush and the green eyes flicker with an emotion she couldn't quite name.

Whatever it was though, it made her pulse start to race.

"My jacket's over there. Drape that over yourself to cover up – I mean warm up," he suggested.

Daisy didn't protest. Her original plan of drying off in the sunshine abandoned, she tore up the beach, oblivious to the stones bruising her soles, and seized the tweed jacket that was draped over the rocks at the back of the cove. It was heavy and, as she burrowed into it, Daisy caught the tang of musky cologne and cigarettes and strong young male. She shivered again but this time it wasn't from the icy seawater.

"May I turn around?" he asked.

"Yes."

Huddled into the jacket and sitting with her knees drawn up to her chest and her arms clasped tightly around them, Daisy thought she was probably as decent as a shameless girl who went swimming in her undergarments would ever be. Whoever this young man was, she hoped he wouldn't tell the Reverend about this incident. She'd be back on the train home before you could say *hussy*.

The stranger strolled up the beach to join her. His lips looked a little blue and, warmly wrapped in his jacket, Daisy felt guilty.

"If you look behind those rocks you'll find my basket. There's a towel in it. Please, use it," she said.

He shot her a grateful smile. Two dimples danced in his cheeks and it felt a little as though the sun had come out. "I'm a tad on the damp side, I must say. Thanks."

Daisy didn't answer. Instead she fixed her gaze on the horizon while he rummaged in her basket. She felt all wobbly and strange. It must be the exercise and the water.

"Hey!" he called over his shoulder. "You're reading Keats?"

"I am," Daisy replied. "I love his poetry."

"Me too!" said the young man with feeling. "The way he uses language is just beautiful. *Ode to a Nightingale* is simply exquisite. If I can ever write verse even half as well as that, then I'll die happy."

"You're a poet?"

"I wouldn't go that far. I dabble a bit, that's all, but nothing in his league."

"I wish I could write poetry," sighed Daisy. She had tried many times but had soon realised it wasn't her gift.

"Me too," he laughed. "I keep trying!"

Moments later he returned with the towel. The sun had climbed higher in the sky since she'd left the water and there was a real strength to it. She'd dry soon, Daisy thought with relief, and then she could change into the spare undergarments she'd packed. Once he'd left, obviously.

The young man passed Daisy her towel.

"Here, Miss, you need this more than I do. You're still looking cold."

The towel was a little damp and as she held it in her hands Daisy shivered to think that the fabric had passed over his body. The idea was intimate and strangely thrilling.

"Thank you," she said, starting to blot her curls, which were turning into springs.

"I'm Kit, by the way," the young man said, holding out his hand as though they'd just been introduced at a garden fete. "Kit Rivers. How do you do?"

"Daisy Hills."

She took his hand and their fingers slid together in a perfect fit, as though they'd done so a thousand times before.

I know you! she thought, and she knew by the flicker of surprise in Kit's mesmerising eyes that he felt exactly the same.

"For saints have hands that pilgrims' hands do touch," he said softly, his fingers closing around hers.

Romeo and Juliet. Of course, Daisy knew the next line of the play, but her heart was racing too hard to speak. Unnerved, she slid her hand away and the moment was lost – if it had ever really happened at all.

"I really was swimming, by the way," Daisy said quickly, partly to counteract the rather strange cartwheeling sensation in her stomach. It was something she'd never experienced before. "It's the reason I'm staying in Rosecraddick. I have to bathe in salt water every day for my health. My father is a doctor and he says it's the best thing to bring back strength to a limb."

She waited for him to ask her what was wrong – most people did – but Kit Rivers just nodded.

"There's nothing better for the soul than swimming in the sea. I swim as much as I can. I love the water. Sailing's fun too. Do you sail, Miss?"

Daisy laughed. "Not much sailing goes on in Fulham. I've never even been on a boat. Truth be told, until a few days ago I hadn't even seen the sea."

Kit Rivers looked outraged. "That's terrible. I have a little sailing boat and you'll have to come out on the water. I insist." Then he grinned. "But maybe fully dressed this time?"

She blushed but found she liked his teasing. Kit was putting her at ease by making a joke of the situation.

"I do have a bathing costume, but it's made of wool and so hard to swim in. It becomes full of water and pulls me under, so today I decided to chance swimming without it. That's why I was swimming off this smaller cove. I thought nobody would see."

"You were right there. They wouldn't usually. I only climbed down the steep way on my walk back to the village because I was..."

Kit paused and an expression of sadness crossed his face. Daisy waited and he exhaled slowly.

"I had a bit of a row with my father, and I needed to get away. This is somewhere I often go to when I need to think and have some solitude. Nobody comes here. Usually."

Daisy wondered what this argument had been about, but she didn't ask. They'd both sought the cove for personal reasons and some things, like her health and her swimming in her camisole, were private. And talking of that...

She took a deep breath. "You won't tell anyone I was doing this, will you? Please?"

He shook his head. "I swear I won't breathe a word. Besides, I

149

always think swimming in all that lot is utterly rotten. I hate wearing a bathing costume and I avoid the things as much as I can."

"So what do you wear instead?" Daisy asked and then wished she could sink beneath the sand as Kit's mouth curled into a grin. She was such an idiot!

"Let's just say I'm creative," he said. "Swimming's supposed to make you feel free, isn't it? I can't say I ever feel like that when I'm weighed down in a knitted costume that stretches to my knees."

"It isn't much fun," Daisy agreed. It was time to change the subject and she twirled a ringlet around her forefinger before letting it spring free, a habit she always reverted to when she was anxious. "My godfather isn't worried about fun, though. He'd send me straight home if he knew about this."

"Is that who you're staying with, your godfather?"

"Yes. He's the Vicar of Rosecraddick."

"Killjoy Cutwell is your godfather?" Kit exclaimed. "Sorry, that's dreadfully disrespectful of me, Miss Hills. I apologise if I've caused offence."

But Daisy was too busy giggling to be offended. Killjoy Cutwell! It was the perfect name!

"No offence taken, Mr Rivers. He is a misery but he's an old family friend. Do you know him?"

Kit pulled a face.

"I certainly do. He's christened and confirmed just about everyone here, and preached enough fire-and-brimstone sermons to put the fear of God in me and the rest of the parish."

"Yes, I can imagine he has," Daisy replied with feeling. "I'm sure he thinks I'm destined for hell."

"It's not a destination exclusive to you, you know! We're all going there as far as he's concerned. Heaven will be very empty!"

"Goddaughters who swim in their underclothes get there sooner," Daisy sighed. She'd lasted only a matter of days at the Rectory and Papa would be so disappointed in her for letting him down. She had a feeling her mama would have understood though. Her mama would maybe even have done the same herself.

"Reverend Cutwell won't hear a thing about this from me, Miss Hills, I promise. Cross my heart and hope to die," Kit Rivers said.

Daisy burst out laughing at the old schoolyard vow. "Cross your heart and hope to die? How old are you?"

"I'm eighteen," he said proudly, "but I'm not too old to cross my heart! How about you?"

"Too old to cross my heart? Certainly, I am."

He nudged her with his elbow.

"I bet you you're not."

"I am."

He gave her another nudge. And another. And another. His elbow was bony and Daisy soon relented because it was digging into her ribs and making her giggle.

"All right! All right! I'm nearly seventeen."

"So you're sixteen."

"Yes! I'm sixteen."

Already counting down until her birthday in September, Daisy suddenly found she was even more eager for the day to arrive. Seventeen sounded far more grown-up than sixteen and it was certainly closer to eighteen. Why this suddenly seemed to matter so much she wasn't sure, but she suspected it had something to do with the way her insides swooped when Kit's laughing green eyes held hers – just as the dusting of goosebumps on her arms had nothing to do with temperature and everything to do with being near to him. She was fizzing like shaken ginger beer.

It was odd. And inexplicable. And utterly, utterly wonderful.

They basked in the sunshine for a little longer and talked easily. Kit explained to Daisy where the safest spots for swimming were to be found and told her a bit about the village. In turn she told him about her polio and the long months spent in the sanatorium reading and losing herself in literature. Kit was widely read, and it was a joy to

151

be able to discuss Byron and Shelley with him as well as listen to him confess that he aspired to be a poet. By the time they'd dried off in the sun, they knew a great deal about one another and it was a surprise to discover that the tide had receded, leaving glistening wet sand where gulls pecked and rock pools shimmered. Kit said this meant he would safely be able to scramble over the rocks to the next bay and head along the coast.

"Only do that on a spring tide like this," he warned. "Otherwise it's very dangerous. You must take care."

Daisy had thought that, after London, Rosecraddick would feel like a safe place, but she was swiftly realising she had been wrong in making such an assumption: Cornwall was full of dangers she'd never even dreamed of. As Kit Rivers bade her farewell and continued on his way, Daisy watched him and knew deep down in her heart that meeting him was without doubt the biggest danger of them all.

"And palm to palm is holy palmers' kiss," she whispered, gazing down at her hand. How could it feel so different yet be totally unaltered? The skin was the same fair colour and her nails were the same pale pink ovals they'd been before, yet it felt as though her hand now belonged to a new version of herself. Suddenly all the plays and all the poetry she'd ever read made perfect sense. She'd barely understood them until this moment. She hadn't known what they really meant.

But she did now – and she knew why.

In just the blink of Kit's green eyes and the touch of his hand, Daisy Hills had fallen headlong and hopelessly in love.

CHAPTER 4

DAISY, MAY 1914

The following morning dawned wild and stormy. It certainly wasn't the weather for venturing down to the cove for a swim. Even if the skies had been ink blue and the sea silky smooth, Daisy suspected she wouldn't have been able to swim a stroke anyway because she'd barely had a wink of sleep. The dream had come again.

As always, the nightmare faded moments after she opened her eyes, but this morning the nagging unease had taken longer than usual to leave. Unable to fall back asleep, she'd tossed and turned until the light had stolen through the thin curtains. It was just a silly dream, she'd told herself sternly. Even so, the sense of foreboding was enough to cast a shadow over her morning and the bleak weather only exacerbated her mood.

As the light had crept in and the nightmare had ebbed away, she'd lain in her big brass bed, listening to the old house settle and creak around her. Her thoughts had raced back to Kit with the swiftness and inevitability of an incoming tide. Since their meeting she'd been able to think of little else.

On her walk home after yesterday's swim, Daisy had replayed every second of the time they'd shared on the beach. Her mind had been so full of Kit's ocean-deep eyes, perfect bone structure and curling blond hair (which she could imagine needed constant cutting) that she'd scarcely noticed the steep path or felt the burning ache of her leg. Instead she'd floated back to the Rectory, where she'd hardly been able to eat a mouthful of the mutton stew Mrs Polmartin had served for supper. Several times she'd drifted into a daydream over her plate. This had led to some worried remarks from the housekeeper about illness, but Daisy had known her lack of appetite owed nothing to polio and everything to the chance beach meeting. Nancy, also picking at her supper, had raised her eyebrows at Daisy in a knowing way.

After supper Daisy had been dispatched to cut flowers for the house; Mrs Polmartin had explained that they lasted longer if they were picked in the evening rather than the heat of the day. Daisy had snipped the blooms at random while her mind had wandered back to Kit. The housekeeper had tutted in disapproval at Daisy's dreadful flower-arranging skills, but this had barely registered with Daisy; she was far too busy wondering if Kit had quoted from *Romeo and Juliet* because he'd felt the same charge of energy and the flicker of recognition that she'd experienced.

He must have done, surely?

Once she was safely up in her attic room, Daisy had lain on her bed and written all about their meeting in her new journal. It seemed wholly fitting that this new diary with its beautiful blank pages should record the event; nothing less was worthy of it. Something important had taken place and her life had spun away on a different tangent. She would never be the same again. When she closed her eyes she saw again Kit's slow smile, heard his soft considered voice, felt his fingers as they took hers.

She was in love. There was no logic to any of it, but it was a fact.

Daisy had put the lid on her pen and gazed thoughtfully out of the window at the sky, where a small smile of moon glimmered among the clouds. So this was love. This skittering of the pulse and swooping sensation in the stomach was what falling in love felt like. She'd read all about this emotion, of course, but until a few hours ago it had seemed as relevant to her own life as Homer's tales or Beowulf. Now Daisy wished she'd studied more carefully.

It made no sense. Apart from his name, she knew almost nothing about Kit Rivers. As she'd put her diary away, Daisy had tried to tell herself that she was being ridiculous. Maybe she was coming down with a fever from bathing in the cold water. That would explain her wobbly legs and vanishing appetite. It might even be the reason for her racing heart.

But it didn't account for why, whenever she closed her eyes, all she could see was Kit – or why her heart squeezed with longing.

Eventually Daisy had drifted off, but then the dream had come again. After that she knew she wouldn't sleep. With eyes that were gritty and heavy, Daisy had watched the world grow lighter as the day crept in, in a thousand hues of grey. The sea was topped by white horses and the cloud was a thick scarf obscuring the sunshine. There would be no swimming today and no chance of coming across Kit Rivers again. The disappointment made her heart feel as bleak as the world outside.

Daisy had spent the morning cleaning silver with Mrs Polmartin until her fingers were sore and her head was pounding from the smell of the polish. The Reverend had made noises about her cataloguing his sermons, and the thought of spending the rest of the day trapped inside with her godfather was unbearable. By the time lunch arrived Daisy knew she *had* to go outside and breathe, before the Rectory with its shut-up spaces and constant smell of boiling cabbage suffocated her.

Giving up on luncheon – a gristly affair today of mince and potatoes – Daisy lay her knife and fork down.

"Nancy, may I ask you a favour?"

The other girl shrugged, which Daisy took to be an affirmative. Nancy didn't say a great deal apart from "Yes, Miss" and "No, Miss", which didn't make for much of a conversation – unlike Gem, who was more than happy to chat away. Daisy wasn't sure whether her status as the Reverend's goddaughter was the reason for this awkwardness or whether Nancy viewed her as a rival for Gem's affections. Neither issue should have given Nancy cause for concern. As much as Daisy liked Gem, it wasn't the stable lad who made her heart shiver, and a doctor's daughter wasn't so very far removed in status from a farmer's niece.

"May I borrow your bicycle?"

Nancy bicycled to and from the Rectory each day. She looked surprised by the question though. "Where do you need to go, Miss?"

Now it was Daisy's turn to shrug. "Nowhere, really. It's just that I'm supposed to strengthen my leg every day. Saltwater bathing is the best thing but the sea's too rough today. I thought riding a bicycle might help a little."

"Never mind too rough! You'd catch your death in the water," shuddered Mrs Polmartin. "I honestly wonder what doctors are thinking nowadays."

Daisy opened her mouth to explain the benefits of hydrotherapy but thought better of it. Modern ideas, she had soon discovered, were viewed as little more than a step away from witchcraft in these parts.

"I'll need it back by six," Nancy said. "And don't get it muddy, mind. Pa will kill me."

"I won't! Thank you!" Daisy jumped to her feet, beaming. She could have hugged Nancy.

"You won't be so happy in a minute. The hills here are hellish," Nancy warned, pulling a face. "Everywhere is uphill from here."

But Daisy didn't care. She'd willingly cycle up a mountain just to feel the wind rush against her cheeks and to see the delicious blur of passing scenery. Before long she was peddling up the lane, her skirt billowing behind her and her straw hat slipping from her head. Nancy wasn't wrong about the hills and by the time Daisy had travelled through the village, past the manor house and towards the woods, the muscles in both her legs were screaming and her breath was coming in harsh pants. Once she reached the summit of the next hill she'd have a rest, Daisy promised herself. Then she could have fun freewheeling back down. The exhilaration of the descent would more than make up for the effort of the climb. Besides, peddling hard meant that she could hardly hear her chattering thoughts about Kit Rivers above the thudding of her heartbeat.

Once she reached the top of the hill, having conceded defeat for the final half mile and pushed the bicycle instead of riding it, Daisy paused to admire the landscape. Unlike London, with its endless rooftops peeling away to infinity, the view from here stretched to wooded hills and valleys in one direction and back to the sea and Rosecraddick in the other. The swirling pewter sky seemed to hold the world in its arms and as she recovered her breath Daisy felt her spirits rise. There were possibilities in this openness and broad sweep of sea and sky that she'd never felt in the city. The air was sharp with salt and rich with the smell of earth and rotting leaves and freedom. Her godfather – the awkward conversation at mealtimes, the closed doors and general air of reproach – felt very far away, and so did the long months of her illness and the even longer months of recovery.

"I'm on the top of the world!" Daisy shouted to the wind and the scudding clouds. Something wonderful was waiting; she could feel it in the promise of the green leaves on the trees and the new crops in the fields. Life was all around her, rich and teeming with energy, and being sixteen and filled with hope she felt a part of it. Bad dreams were forgotten, along with her stern godfather. Even her troublesome leg seemed to be causing her less discomfort than usual as she hopped back onto the bicycle and pointed it downhill. Soon Daisy was freewheeling faster and faster, her hat and hairpins long lost and her red curls streaming behind her. The air whipped tears from her cheeks, her feet slipped from the peddles and she felt as though she was flying. This was far more exciting than the flat streets of Fulham!

Faster and faster Daisy flew until the countryside was a sage blur. Eventually, when the gradient levelled, the world came back into focus – but still the bicycle carried her along with ease and she laughed out loud. As she steered towards the village, Daisy decided she would write to Papa and tell him about this. She was sure he'd agree that cycling was beneficial for her health, that there was no better way to see the countryside and—

The nearer the lane drew to the village, the more rutted it became from the passing wheels of carts. Intoxicated with the heady blend of speed and exhilaration, she hadn't been paying attention – so when the front wheel hit a deep rut and the bicycle swerved, Daisy flew over the handlebars. For a sickening moment the world spun around as she lay winded, gazing up through an ocean of weeds to a sky webbed with cloud.

Her head was throbbing and something sticky dripped into her eye. There was an awful lot of it...

It was blood, Daisy thought abstractedly as she lay in the ditch. It was probably nothing to worry about though; Papa said head wounds always bled horribly. All the same, it would stain her new blouse and that was a shame. And what about Nancy's bicycle? Had she damaged it? Stricken, Daisy tried to sit up – but the world cartwheeled and, with a moan, she sank back onto the lane. Oh dear. This was quite a tumble.

"My God! Are you all right?"

Daisy knew then that she must have hit her head very hard, because it seemed that Kit Rivers was peering down at her and looking most concerned. She must have thought about him so much that she was dreaming him into being. Papa had talked at length about Freud and the subconscious mind, so Daisy knew just how powerful dreams could be.

"You're not really here," she said crossly. "Are you?"

"I promise I am," said Kit, his arm behind her head supporting her weight. "Do you think you could sit?"

Daisy wasn't certain but she nodded, which made her brain feel as though it had come loose in her skull. She did her best not to groan. She wasn't concussed, she decided, and she didn't think any bones were broken.

But talking of broken—

"What's happened to the bicycle? Is it all right?"

"Never mind the bicycle! You're bleeding!" Kit pressed something

158

soft against her forehead (his handkerchief, she realised) and dabbed the wound. "That's a nasty cut. It'll need cleaning, and some arnica. Are you dizzy? Do you think you might have concussion?"

But Daisy was far more concerned about Nancy's bicycle than her own injuries, especially when she caught sight of it upside down and with the wheel still spinning.

"Is it broken?"

Kit sighed. "If you insist on worrying about the bicycle, it looks fine to me. The chain's still on and the wheel doesn't appear buckled." His hand brushed her hair away from her face so that he could get a closer look at the cut. Daisy's breath caught in her throat as his forefinger traced her cheek. This touch and his closeness were making her feel far shakier than the tumble. She hadn't imagined a thing! These feelings were real – and from the way his hands trembled, she knew Kit felt them too.

"Your bicycle's safe," he assured her.

"It's not mine. I borrowed it. I promised to be careful."

Kit laughed. He had a nice laugh; it made Daisy feel as though she was wrapped in sunshine.

"We're not well acquainted, Miss Hills, but I don't think being careful is one of your most striking personal qualities. Swimming off dangerous coves and hurtling down hills at breakneck speed are hardly careful activities. What will be next? Maybe you'll learn to fly an aeroplane?"

"Explaining this to my godfather is next," Daisy said gloomily, touching her hand to her forehead and wincing. Reverend Cutwell would never allow her to bicycle anywhere now. Her hat was lost, her hair was a mess and she'd probably shown her ankles to a young man, although thanks to the swimming episode Kit Rivers had already seen far more exciting parts of her than her ankles. She was so cross with herself. "Of all the stupid things to do!"

"You hit a rut," Kit said kindly. "Anyone would have come off." He paused, the green eyes twinkling at her with amusement.

"Although I do admit, not everyone might have hurtled towards it at such speed!"

"You saw?"

"I most certainly did. You flew past me as I climbed the stile out of the woods. Nearly took me out, actually."

"I'm so sorry. I didn't see you," Daisy apologised.

Kit laughed again. "I'm not surprised. You looked as though you were having a marvellous time. Before you fell off, of course."

"Oh, I was," she agreed. "It felt like flying. It felt free. And anyway, I didn't fall off. I hit a rut, like you said. That's different."

"Totally different," he agreed, lips twitching. "Hurtling downhill on a bicycle sounds wonderful. I must try it some time. I'm quite certain it beats hunting for thrills."

Daisy wasn't sure what to say to this. Not a great deal of hunting took place in Fulham, so she didn't feel qualified to comment.

"Can you stand?" Kit was asking.

She nodded cautiously. "I think so."

Slowly and gently, he raised her to her feet. The earth felt a little uncertain beneath her boots and the sky rolled once more, but to Daisy's relief she didn't feel faint. Even the cut on her head seemed to have stopped bleeding.

"How's that? Can you walk, do you think?" Kit asked.

She nodded again. "If I go slowly. Thank you for helping. I'll be fine now."

Kit looked affronted and his fingers tightened their grasp. Daisy liked the way it felt to have him hold onto her, tethering her to the earth. It felt safe.

"You don't think I'm going to abandon you and go on my way? That wouldn't be very gentlemanly. I'm going to walk you back to the Rectory, if you think you can make it that far? Otherwise I'll send for the trap."

"Of course I can walk!" Daisy said indignantly, although she wasn't certain she could. Her legs felt as soggy as the overcooked vegetables Mrs Polmartin liked to serve up.

"I'll wheel the bicycle and you can hold my arm," suggested Kit. "We'll go exceedingly slowly and if you feel unwell you're to let me know and we'll stop. I can always fetch help if you think you require it."

Daisy thought she would rather crawl back on her hands and knees than have the Reverend send Merlin and the trap. She was rather hoping that she'd be able to find Gem and ask him to clean and return the bicycle, while she stole inside to wash and change before anyone else noticed her torn skirt and cut head. Some careful rearranging of her hair before dinner should hide the injury. It was fortunate that her godfather was short-sighted.

When Kit had managed to right the bicycle, spinning the wheels to make certain the chain was intact, they walked slowly back to the Rectory while Daisy leaned heavily on his arm and stole sideways looks at him. Even simply dressed in corduroy trousers and a battered tweed jacket with leather patches on the elbows and plain cuffs, he made her breath catch. A cap was rammed onto the thick blond hair, and golden stubble dusted his jaw. He was wearing scuffed country boots and was dressed for a walk, but she noticed that the top of a notebook was sticking out of his pocket. Had he been walking to seek inspiration for his writing? Like Wordsworth? She would have loved to ask but it felt like a rather personal question. If Kit Rivers wanted to talk about his own poetry, Daisy knew he'd do so without any prompting from her.

They walked through the village, the men touching their caps respectfully as they passed, and finally they reached the Rectory, choosing to take the back path past the woodshed rather than walking to the front door. Daisy breathed a sigh of relief when she saw that the stable yard was empty and the trap missing; Reverend Cutwell must be out on parish business, which meant he would be none the wiser about her misadventure. Here was another secret she would need to ask Kit to keep. There seemed to be a pattern

161

emerging.

"Back safe and sound," Kit said, leaning the bicycle against the outhouse wall and smiling at her.

"Thank you."

"It's my pleasure – although I must say, Miss Hills, rescuing you is starting to become a habit!"

Daisy pretended to be outraged. "May I remind you that I didn't need rescuing from the cove? I was swimming perfectly well."

"In your undergarments!" Kit grinned.

"Shh!" mortified, Daisy glanced around, but fortunately nobody was about to overhear. "You promised that was a secret."

"And so it is, but not between us," he pointed out. He stepped forward and quietly added, "Since we were both there, and I believe we've both thought about it a great deal since, it's hardly a secret is it?"

He'd thought about it since? There were goosebumps on Daisy's arms now.

"No," she said finally. "I suppose not."

They stood for a moment, not knowing quite what to say to one another, smiling shyly. Daisy wondered if he was recalling how it had felt to hold hands, however briefly. If only she could ask him, could talk to him properly, but somewhere they weren't in danger of being overheard.

As though reading her mind, Kit said in a low voice, "The weather forecast is set fair for the next few days. Will you be swimming at the cove? Maybe at low tide? Tomorrow?"

Daisy's mouth dried as though the beach had been poured into it. Was Kit arranging to meet her? Did he want to see her again? She swallowed.

"Yes. Yes, I will."

"Wonderful. Well, until we meet again. Maybe by *chance* at a cove? Tomorrow? For a swim?"

Daisy nodded and Kit looked as though he was about to say

something more, but the clop of iron-shod hooves on cobbles and the appearance of Gem stopped him.

"Good afternoon, Mr Kit," Gem said, doffing his cap and looking startled.

"Good afternoon, Gem," said Kit evenly. "If you have a moment, would you be so good as to take Miss Daisy's bicycle and give it a clean and maybe some oil? That would be marvellous."

Gem glanced at Daisy in surprise and then back at Kit. "Yes, sir, of course."

"Thank you, Gem."

Kit turned to Daisy and smiled, a slow smile so full of unspoken promise that it squeezed her heart until she thought it would burst. He took off his cap and bowed his head. "Until next time, Miss Hills. Good afternoon."

"Good afternoon, Mr Rivers," Daisy echoed.

Together she and Gem watched him walk away. Then, once Kit was out of earshot, Gem whistled.

"What was *he* doing here, Miss?"

Daisy decided to tell the truth. Gem was no fool and she could tell he'd already noticed the cut on her head and the rip in her dress.

"I fell off Nancy's bicycle and Kit was kind enough to help me walk back."

Gem's dark eyebrows shot into his thick fringe. "Well, you know how to fall on your feet and no mistake, Miss Daisy! Walked home by Kit Rivers himself. Get you!"

"What's that supposed to mean?"

"You! Being escorted home by Kit Rivers!"

Daisy stared at him. She had no idea what Gem was talking about.

"You don't know who he is, do you?" Gem said, and she shook her head.

"What more is there to know?"

"Mr Kit is Colonel Rivers' son and heir," Gem told her. When she still looked nonplussed, he added, "From Rosecraddick Manor. The big house you admired when we drove here from the railway station? Kit's the Honourable Christopher Rivers and one day he'll own just about everything around here. He'll only be the lord of the manor, Miss! The likes of him don't usually speak to the likes of me and you, do they? It's all titles and fancy folk for them, although Mr Kit's not so bad as most of the toffs. He's a pretty decent sort."

Daisy stared at Gem.

"Really?"

"Really," he said.

It was just like a fairly tale! Maybe Kit wasn't quite the handsome prince, but she'd been rescued by the lord of the manor's son. Gentle Kit, with the sea-green eyes and angel's smile – the unassuming young man who loved poetry and made her heart race – was the heir to the enormous house and surrounding land. He was the only son of the most important family in the area. The funny, teasing, laughing Kit was landed gentry.

She couldn't take it in.

She didn't need to. What did it matter who Kit was? Daisy already knew how she felt about him. Her heart had told her everything that mattered.

CHAPTER 5

DAISY, JULY 1914

"Heavenly day for a dip!"

Daisy, who'd been dozing in the sunshine, looked up to see Kit striding across the beach with a wicker basket swinging from one hand. He was simply dressed in linen trousers and a white shirt, and as he approached her the sun turned his hair to gold. For a brief moment he looked like an angel. When he sat down beside her and produced a bottle of ginger beer, Daisy decided this must be *exactly* what he was. After a morning spent swimming in the salty sea (wearing the hated woollen suit this time) and basking in the sunshine, she was thirsty.

"Fancy seeing you here!" she teased, sitting up and tucking her hair behind her ears as he handed her a bottle.

"I know. We must stop bumping into one another like this." He flipped the stopper on his bottle and clinked his drink against hers. "Here's to saltwater swimming and its myriad health benefits."

"Myriad? Is that one you're trying to work into a poem? I can't imagine it's easy to rhyme," Daisy said, and he rolled his eyes.

"You'd be surprised at the extent of my poetical skills, Miss Hills. I'm a very well-read man. I don't suppose Shakespeare had to put up with such disrespect!"

"You're comparing yourself to Shakespeare now? I feel very honoured such a future bard would spend time with me!"

He tickled her ribs until she gasped and shrieked for mercy.

"There's nobody I'd rather spend my time with," he said gravely and once she'd recovered her breath.

"Same here," Daisy replied, and they sipped their ginger beer in companionable silence while the waves broke on the shore and the gulls danced and called to each other high above.

Daisy meant every word. She had never had a friend like Kit or felt about anyone the way she did about him. In the weeks since their first meeting they'd seen each other every day, either at the cove for a swim or on the cliffs for a walk, and Daisy could no longer imagine a world without him playing a part in it. She was becoming accustomed to life at the Rectory, where she had taken over organising the daily meals and helping to keep house. Already she'd adopted a routine: after breakfast she would help Nancy clear the plates and then clean some silver or organise the flowers in St Nonna's, before slipping away to meet Kit. Reverend Cutwell was delighted to observe that all the swimming and fresh air were working wonders for her health, even going so far as to concede that saltwater bathing might not necessarily be the work of Satan – but Daisy knew that the sparkle in her eyes and the flush of colour in her cheeks were attributable to something other than the fresh Cornish air and swimming. Her appetite was good, she brimmed with energy and she was always singing as she went about her chores. Falling in love was a far better cure for her health problems than anything her papa could have devised. She'd put on weight, her skin was dusted with a cinnamon sprinkle of freckles, and her brown eyes were bright. Even the red curls tumbling to her waist bounced with health. When she regarded her reflection in the speckled bedroom mirror, Daisy was pleased. She even thought she was developing a bust at last; she'd spent ages turning sideways to admire it until Nancy, coming in to clean, had interrupted her mid-preen.

"Who is he, Miss?" Nancy had demanded, hands on hips and blue eyes full of curiosity.

"I don't know what you mean," Daisy had retorted. There was no way she was telling Nancy anything about Kit, even though the two girls had become friends of a sort. No, Kit was Daisy's wonderful, magical secret.

Nancy had snorted. "You must take me for a fool, Miss Daisy. It's as plain as day you're mooning over a fellow."

"I am not!"

"You are too! It had better not be my Gem," Nancy had warned, wagging a finger. She and Gem were officially courting now.

"Don't be absurd. I was just looking at my new dress," Daisy had said, but she'd caught Nancy's eye-roll in the mirror and knew the other girl wasn't fooled. No doubt Nancy would be speculating over the identity of the man who'd won Daisy's affections. There would be gossip amongst the servants, and if Gem mentioned how Kit had once walked Daisy home then her secret might be discovered. Kit hadn't said a great deal about his family, but Daisy knew there were tensions between him and his father. She was also realistic enough to understand that the daughter of a doctor would never be seen as a good match for him. She made a vow to be less cheerful (outwardly, at least), but it was proving difficult to suppress her happiness.

"You need to be careful, Miss," Gem had remarked the other morning when Daisy, humming to herself on the way back from picking peas, had passed him in the scullery.

"Careful about what?" Daisy had said.

Gem wouldn't be drawn into any further discussion but his blue eyes were dark with concern.

"You know what about, Miss," was all he would say. "You know."

Troubled, Daisy had stared after him for a moment before the promise of another golden day spent with Kit had made any misgivings vanish like sea mist in sunlight. What on earth was there to be careful about? Gem was just being grumpy – probably because Nancy was always breathing down his neck about getting married. Their relationship seemed like very hard work indeed, especially for Gem, who was constantly having to please his beloved.

Daisy and Kit, though, were two halves of the same soul and they never argued. They picnicked and walked and read poetry together, each equally amazed by the fact that the other thought and felt exactly the same way. Sometimes Kit shared the poems he was writing, asking her opinion and jotting pencilled notes in the margin of his notebook when she voiced her thoughts; other times he just sat and wrote while she swam. Poetry was his passion and his verses were poignant, catching moments and preserving them as if they were insects in amber. She did the same in her diary but never breathed a word of this to Kit. Daisy knew that her writing was by far inferior to his. Kit had a gift and when she read his work Daisy was certain he was destined to be as famous as his literary heroes.

She only wished the days they spent together wouldn't fly by so fast. She had a secret horror that their time together would soon run out. It wasn't so much the recurring nightmare that had instilled this dread in her, as the realisation that they came from entirely different worlds. At some point Kit would return to his life of garden parties and hunt balls (where willowy debutantes would vie for his slow, sweet smiles), and she would journey back to London and become a teacher. She would never see Kit again except in her memory.

Daisy's heart sank at the thought. If only this summer could last forever.

Although they never spoke of the differences between them – and in any case these didn't seem to matter a jot when they were together – Daisy was all too aware that Kit was as out of her reach as the stars and the moon. A doctor's daughter was not Kit's social equal. Daisy's papa wasn't even a smart society physician: he was a doctor who worked with some of the poorest folk in London. Kit's parents would no more approve of their friendship than her godfather would if he knew about it.

Yet, even so, Kit understood her and she understood him. They thought the same way and he teased her and she teased him. She never called him "Mr Kit" as Gem did, and Kit never spoke to her the way he did to Gem. Daisy recognised that there was a class barrier between them, and to begin with she'd been very conscious of it – but when she'd raised the subject with him, Kit had brushed it aside impatiently.

"We're just people, Daisy," he'd said, taking her hand and tracing the inside of her wrist with his forefinger, so that her soul ached with longing. "It's nothing but chance what circumstances we're born into."

"You don't believe in God assigning each of us a place and wanting us to stay there?" Daisy had asked. Her godfather certainly did. Every Sunday they prayed for the King and Queen and the Rivers family, and Reverend Cutwell was always telling her how women should behave.

At this suggestion, Kit had spread his hands in a gesture of exasperation. "I don't think God works like that. No, it's only a matter of luck that I was born into Rosecraddick Manor and not a slum somewhere. There's nothing clever about an accident of birth. Being born to a title doesn't make me any better than anyone else."

Daisy had nodded. Papa often spoke like this, but he and Mama held opinions that lots of others found shocking – disapproved of, even. Reverend Cutwell had called Papa a radical and, on her arrival, had made it clear that he hoped Daisy didn't hold the same ideas. She wondered what he would say if he knew the lord of the manor's son shared them. He'd probably be apoplectic.

"So the fact that I'm the lord of the manor's son and your papa is a doctor doesn't stop us being friends, if that's what you're worrying about," Kit had said firmly. "It might matter to my parents and their generation, but times are changing, Daisy, and I believe a day is coming when intellect and ability and character will matter much more than the luck of who one's parents are." He paused and looked out to sea, his green eyes troubled. "Especially if war comes. Death is a great leveller."

"Do you think there'll be a war?" Daisy had been frantically reading the back of the Reverend's paper over breakfast. It was all exceedingly complicated and trying to unpick it all over the marmalade wasn't doing a great deal for her understanding.

"I hope not," Kit had said quietly. His top teeth worried at his bottom lip and his brow furrowed. "My father thinks it's a possibility and he even sounds quite excited about it. Stupid old fool!"

"You oughtn't talk about your father like that," Daisy had said reprovingly, but Kit had answered her with a bitter laugh.

"You haven't met him, Daisy. He's a difficult man and very hard to reason with."

Daisy and Kit's conversations always flowed as naturally as the tides, and Kit knew all about Daisy's illness, her grief at the loss of her mother and her passion for the women's suffrage movement. He understood how frustrated she felt about the restrictions that accompanied her gender, and he sympathised with her desire to write. They'd also discussed at length the increased strain upon his relationship with his father. Kit longed to be a poet and was hoping to take up his place at Oxford, but Colonel Rivers felt his son should abandon these plans and follow the family tradition of joining the army. Although Kit never said as much, Daisy gleaned that these weren't new conflicts but rather old ones that were being thrown into harsh relief by the increasing tensions in Europe.

"I suppose it's hard for him, no longer being able to fight," she'd offered.

"Maybe he does feel frustrated," Kit conceded. "Still, this is no conversation for such a beautiful afternoon! Come on, never mind all that now. Race you to the water!"

And they'd left talk of war and class and religion behind, unable to think about much more than the sting of cold water on their limbs and the pure joy of slicing through the waves. But today, sitting in what she'd come to think of as their cove, Daisy shivered. In the daylight hours her old night terror was just a stalking horror, but sometimes snatches of it peered out of the shadows. Burning. Dead trees. Terrible, terrible heat. Was war coming after all?

"You're shaking. Have you caught a chill?" Kit asked now. "Here, Daisy, have my towel."

He reached into his basket and draped a stripy towel over her shoulders, gently patting her down as though she were a horse he was drying off. Daisy shivered again but this time it wasn't from the cold. She was sure Kit felt the same way, even though he had never been anything but the perfect gentleman. Quite unable to stop herself, she reached out and touched his face, tracing the delicate planes with a wondering finger. His stubble rasped beneath her fingertip and in a heartbeat the ease between them evaporated like the salt water on Daisy's skin. Then Kit's hands were cupping her face and his mouth was on hers.

The touch of his lips made Daisy's brain reel. Kit's mouth was warm and strong against her lips, caressing her, teasing her and exploring. Instinctively, her lips parted as she kissed him back. Kit's fingers wove into her hair as he kissed her deeply, like a drowning man seeking air. Daisy felt as though she could dissolve into him, and her senses swam with a longing for something she barely understood.

His breathing ragged, Kit broke the kiss and pulled her close, cradling her head against his chest. Beneath his shirt Daisy heard the drumming of his heart. She held onto him tightly, unable to believe the intensity of what they'd shared.

"You're so beautiful," he said.

Daisy couldn't speak. She had never known anything could feel this way; she'd had no idea that something could feel so powerful, so overwhelming and so utterly, utterly right. She never wanted to let Kit go. She wanted to stay close to him, hear his heart beating and feel his skin pressed against hers. The dream flickered through her mind's eye and then vanished, but her heart quailed and she held him even closer.

"I love you, Kit," she whispered. The words fell from her lips before she even knew she was going to say them, but somehow this didn't matter; she couldn't have stopped them even if she'd tried. Loving Kit was as natural to Daisy as breathing, and to tell him so was the sweetest relief she'd ever known.

"And I love you, Daisy Alice Hills," he said quietly, punctuating each word with a kiss. "I've loved you since the first moment I saw you. When I'm not in your company I'm counting the moments until I see you again and looking forward to telling you all the things I've been storing up. You're my first thought when I wake up and my last before I sleep. You're everything to me and you always will be."

Daisy nodded. "There will never be anyone else for me. Never."

Just as she whispered these words, the sun slipped behind a cloud and a sharp wind whipped across the bay. Shivers rippled her skin and no matter how closely Kit held her or how tenderly he spoke, Daisy simply couldn't get warm. She had the strangest feeling that she'd just sworn a sacred oath and that the rest of her life would be bound to honouring it.

Daisy would love Kit Rivers until her eyes closed for the very last time. There would never be anyone else.

CHAPTER 6

DAISY, JULY 1914

"You look very pretty today, Miss Hills. Green suits you. You ought to wear it more often."

Daisy, who was on her way out of church, looked up, startled by this confident address. Having spent the past hour staring longingly at the back of Kit's golden head in the front pew and willing the hours to fly by until their next meeting, she hadn't noticed that a stocky young man had fallen into step with her on the path.

She recognised him straight away as Nancy's cousin, Dickon Trehunnist, whose father owned the farm on the westerly side of Rosecraddick and supplied the Rectory with milk and cheese. Dickon was often to be found in the kitchen being fed by Mrs Polmartin and bossing Nancy about. Daisy supposed he was a handsome enough lad, well-muscled from physical work and with a head of thick straw-coloured hair and a determined sun-browned face, but there was something in the mocking curl of his lips and coldness of his blue eyes that made Daisy's skin crawl. She generally avoided him. He seemed very inclined to chat to her, however, and Gem had teased Daisy on several occasions that Dickon was sweet on her.

"You'd better watch out for him, Miss," he'd said yesterday evening, waiting in the scullery for Nancy to finish washing up before he walked her home. "He's a right one for the ladies, is Dickon. All the girls in Rosecraddick think he's a catch and he knows it. I reckon you're next on his list of hearts to conquer!"

But Daisy's heart was already conquered; her thoughts were brimful of Kit and the magical kisses they'd shared on the beach and during all their snatched meetings since. Kit was the sun and his brilliance eclipsed everyone else to the extent that she could barely see them. Yesterday they had picnicked on the cliffs, feasting on cold pease pudding, hunks of cheese and crusts of bread washed down with lemonade. As she'd lain on the grass with her head in his lap, Kit had tenderly stroked her face while reading out his poems. This image drifted through her memory, as beautiful and pulse-quickening as the language of his verse. Handsome Kit Rivers – with his extraordinary ability to weave words, those delicious kisses that made her smile inside, and his delicate, heart-shivering touch – was her world, her love and her everything. The very idea of Dickon Trehunnist taking his place was ridiculous. There was simply no comparison!

"He's definitely sweet on you," Nancy had agreed, clattering the china in the sink. "I heard he's planning to ask you to the next village dance."

Daisy had laughed out loud at this idea, but Nancy wasn't laughing and neither was Gem. Rather, his brow was creased in a thoughtful expression and when he pushed his dark hair out of his eyes he did so with impatience, as though he was pushing worries aside too.

"Be careful, Miss Daisy. I've known Dickon all my life and lads like him can turn when they don't get their own way or if they notice certain things," he'd warned. "I'd hate you, or *anyone else*, to be on the wrong side of him. I reckon he could be right nasty."

Daisy, unloading the Reverend's tea tray, had almost dropped a cup and saucer. Did Gem know about her and Kit? Surely not? That would be impossible, given that they'd always been so careful. Nobody could have seen them together. The only thing Gem knew was that Kit had once walked her home after she'd fallen off a bicycle. Admittedly she'd written every detail of her relationship with Kit in her journal, but she'd taken the precaution of hiding it beneath a loose floorboard in her room, further concealed by a rug. Daisy now kept all her treasures there in a pretty biscuit tin Mrs Polmartin hadn't wanted. In addition to her journal, the cache included a marble stopper from a bottle of picnic lemonade, several seashells they'd collected from the tide's edge, and two poems Kit had written for her – the paper already worn on the folds and the ink smudged from constant rereading. Although Daisy adored them, Kit was embarrassed by these writings. ("Honestly, Daisy! They're truly dreadful. The rhyme doesn't scan and the language is so clichéd!") These artefacts were worthless to most people but priceless to Daisy; when she was unable to sleep at night and instead sat up in bed with the draughts blowing through the window and her wavering candle causing shadows to leap, she pored over the contents of her tin like a miser would count his gold.

This was her secret! Her wonderful, incredible, heart-stopping secret. There was no way Gem could know any of it, and Kit wouldn't have breathed a word. His father was so terribly stern that if he thought his son was spending time with a humble doctor's daughter he would probably birch Kit, eighteen or not. Kit had spoken a little about his parents' expectations for him, and Daisy knew that Kit's romance with her would never feature in his parents' plans, regardless of her feelings for him. A glittering military career to match the Colonel's, marriage to a suitable girl with a good fortune, and continuing the Rivers line at Rosecraddick Manor: these were all part of the future that his parents had laid out for their son since birth. It was little surprise that Kit found the weight of their expectations so hard to bear. He baulked at the idea of the army, longing instead to be a poet, and he loved her. A shadow always fell over his face when he talked about how he had to write in secret in a seldom-used part of the manor house. From this place he could see the roof of the Rectory; blushing, Kit had confessed that he'd even carved a little daisy into the windowsill there, to remind him of her. Whenever she could escape her godfather or Mrs Polmartin (who was always finding her sheets to mend or errands to run), Daisy would creep upstairs to her room and wave a handkerchief out of her window just in case Kit could see and know she was thinking of him.

If she was able to get away to swim, she would tie one of her red hair ribbons to the latch and let it flutter in the breeze, a little streak of rebellion flying in the sky and a silent banner declaring her feelings.

Although he never said as much, Daisy knew it pained Kit greatly that he had to keep their love secret, and so she never told him how much this hurt. She knew Kit wasn't ashamed of her, but it made her heart ache to have to hide her feelings when every cell of her body wanted nothing more than to declare them to the world. No wonder Romeo and Juliet had only lasted a day before they'd asked Friar Laurence to marry them, Daisy had once reflected when scribbling in her diary by the light of a cold moon. Somehow, she couldn't imagine her godfather would be nearly so obliging. He'd be much more likely to send her home on the next train. She'd sighed at this thought. The Reverend certainly wouldn't understand. Rather, he would give her a big lecture on *knowing one's place*. Having already had the misfortune of suffering such a sermon after the Reverend had seen her giggling with Nancy while pegging out washing, Daisy had no desire to be subjected to another. As if his dull Sunday sermons weren't already torture enough!

So, apart from this deep and secret sadness, Kit and Daisy talked about everything under the sun. The more they spoke, the clearer it became to Daisy and to Kit that the life mapped out for him was not the life he wanted. Daisy had come to realise just how unusual and how fortunate her own upbringing had been. There might not have been the privileges Kit enjoyed, but Papa (and Mama too when she was alive) had only wanted Daisy and Eddie to be happy.

Daisy had considered probing further to discover whether Gem did know anything about her clandestine romance, but at this point a loud snort from Nancy had ripped into her thoughts.

"There's no reckon about it, Gem! Dickon's mean and he's spiteful too. I once caught him drowning kittens just for the fun of it. I begged and begged him not to, but he said they were pests and laughed when I cried. I think he enjoyed watching them suffer and it gave me nightmares for years."

At this Daisy had shivered. So she hadn't been mistaken when she'd thought Dickon's eyes were like chips of ice. What sort of person enjoyed watching another's suffering? A dangerous one, was the answer. She would listen to Gem's warning and be very careful. But it was so hard when she was drawn to Kit like a moth to a candle and when he made her feel so alive and joyful. Daisy was sure the returning strength in her leg and her new curves were down to him rather than the saltwater bathing and the fresh air.

She mustn't let her gaze drift over to Kit when she sat in church, his golden head three rows in front of her pew. Kit couldn't look at her either but confessed he'd scratched a daisy onto the front of his pew, concealed behind his prayer book. He said that he often traced it with his fingers during the service as he thought about her. When Daisy had worried that this was blasphemous, Kit had just laughed and said that God was love, wasn't He? And Kit was certain that his heavenly Father had sent Daisy to him. She was an angel fallen to earth, and holding her in his arms was the closest thing to paradise he could imagine.

Kit was skilled with words but this had to be one of the most romantic things he'd ever said to her. Daisy had written it all down in her diary before kissing the words on the page and pressing the book against her heart. She was so happy she thought she might burst. She'd never imagined it was possible to feel like this!

Still, just to make certain nobody suspected anything, she wouldn't cycle past the Manor quite so often when she borrowed Nancy's bicycle. That was quite a giveaway. She must also make sure that any new poems Kit wrote for her were hidden beneath the floorboards, along with the others. Kit, shy and self-depreciating, thought all his poems were mere scribbles and tried to throw them away, which Daisy couldn't bear. Instead she kept them all. Early drafts in his beautiful cursive hand, peppered with crossings out, were tied up with a red hair ribbon and stored in the biscuit tin. However, the latest one, a sonnet about the sea, was still tucked inside her copy of Keats. Kit had been redrafting it for days, frustrated with the conceit. She must make sure she placed it in her tin just in case…

"He's just a bully," Gem had said gravely, giving Nancy's shoulder a reassuring squeeze. "Don't look so glum. Not all men are like him, Nance. I promise."

"They think they're a cut above the rest of us, that side of the family," Nancy had replied bitterly. "Just because they own a farm and land, they think they're gentry now. Dickon even thinks he's good enough for a doctor's daughter."

Although Nancy was washing up with her back to Daisy, it had been obvious by the stiff set of her shoulders that she was fuming.

"He's set his sights on you all right, Miss," Gem had agreed. "He's been telling everyone so. I heard him boasting in the pub that you're going to be his girl. He thinks it's a done deal, so be careful."

Daisy had been about to tell them both that this was nonsense and that she didn't think she was any better, or worse, than anyone else. However, at that moment Mrs Polmartin had interrupted, telling Nancy to hurry up, tutting at Gem for being inside with dirty boots on and shooing Daisy back to the drawing room to read to her godfather. Nancy had finished the washing up, Gem had walked her home and Daisy had forgotten the conversation amid all the excitement of falling in love with Kit.

But now, standing outside St Nonna's with the brawny Dickon towering over her, Daisy recalled every word and was immediately on her guard. Dickon might be handsome to look at, but something very ugly lurked beneath the surface. Thinking of soft scrabbling paws and pitiful meows, she swallowed nervously.

"Thank you," she said politely. What else was she meant to say to such a comment? Her eyes flickered to the gate. Just beyond, Kit was helping his mother into a smart carriage, but his attention was wholly focused on the task; he was unaware of Dickon. Daisy's godfather was behind her in the church porch, deep in conversation, and Gem and Nancy were already strolling back to the village. Although Daisy was surrounded by parishioners, in effect she was alone with Dickon.

"You don't need to thank me when it's true," he said. "You're a very pretty girl and I think we have a great deal in common."

Daisy couldn't imagine what this could be. From what little she knew of him, Dickon Trehunnist was more interested in wrestling and drinking than he was in reading poetry or discussing literature. She craned her neck in Kit's direction once again, but the carriage was heading away at a spanking trot and her heart sank. She was stuck.

Dickon took her elbow and guided Daisy along the path, nodding to neighbours as they passed and holding court with the villagers. Daisy allowed herself to be swept along, even though the touch of his hand on her arm was repellent. At least it was only a short distance to the gate before she could turn to the Rectory and make her escape. A little like holding her breath beneath the water, she could do this. She just hoped he wasn't expecting a conversation.

Fortunately for Daisy, Dickon wasn't interested in anything she might have to say. Instead she was treated to a monologue about how many bales of straw he could lift, how he'd won the steeplechase last season, his love of fox hunting and how many acres he would stand to inherit. All she was required to do was listen. She attempted this for a while but eventually drifted away on thoughts of Kit.

They were due to meet at the cove that afternoon and she could hardly wait. Seeing him across the church and not being able to speak to him, barely being acknowledged save a polite nod as he passed her pew, was agony. All she longed to do was touch him, trail her fingertips along the ridge of his collarbone and slip her hand underneath his shirt to feel his warm skin. Daisy wasn't sure how she could wait for two more hours to see him. She loved Kit so much it hurt.

"So, as you can see, I have prospects and good ones too," Dickon finished proudly. "I know there are a lot of girls in this village who would love to come to the dance with me but I've decided I want to take you. We're perfectly matched in every way. I'll come to collect you up next Saturday at six."

Daisy wasn't quite able to believe what she'd heard.

"I beg your pardon? You'll collect me for what?"

"The summer dance at the village hall," Dickon repeated. There was a flicker of something in his expression that looked a lot like impatience, but he squashed it quickly. Again, the image of drowning kittens darted through her mind's eye. "There's one held every month. I'm going to take you, Miss Daisy."

No, he wasn't!

"Thank you for the kind invitation, but I'm afraid I won't be going to the dance," she said politely.

"What? Don't be ridiculous. Of course you will. It's a big event. Everyone from the village will be there."

"Not me," said Daisy firmly.

"Of course you'll be there. It'll be great fun. You'll see." His grasp on her elbow tightened and Daisy pulled away sharply.

"I'm not going to the dance with you," she said.

Dickon's brows drew into a scowl. "Has somebody asked you already? Don't worry about that. I'll have a word with them. It isn't a problem."

"Nobody's asked me. Thank you for the kind invite but I don't want to go to the dance. Not with you or anyone."

Except Kit, Daisy added silently. How wonderful would it be to feel his arms around her as they danced cheek to cheek beneath a sleepy harvest moon? Imagine if they could court openly like Nancy and Gem. How marvellous would such openness be?

Dickon looked stunned. "I'm asking you to go with *me*. As my partner. Lots of girls would be pleased."

"Then you must ask one of them," Daisy told him. "As I've said, I'm very flattered to be asked but I don't wish to go to the dance with you."

Dickon's mouth was swinging open on its hinges.

"But I've told everyone you're going to be my partner," he spluttered when he eventually recovered himself.

"That was rather presumptuous," Daisy replied, irritated by this.

Dickon's face was red with a mixture of embarrassment and anger. It must have been the first time in his life that a girl had refused him.

"There's someone else, isn't there?" he said, his eyes narrowing. "Don't bother to deny it. I can tell just by looking at you. Who is he?"

"There's nobody," Daisy insisted, but Dickon shook his head and for a moment she thought he was going to shake her until Kit's name rolled from her tongue. There was certainly power in those bunched biceps and Daisy didn't doubt that Dickon would use it if he thought he would get away with it.

"You're lying," he declared. "There's someone else. You'd have said 'yes' otherwise. Who is he? I'll deal with him. No one makes a fool out of me."

"I think you've done a very good job of that by yourself," Daisy snapped.

The words flew from her mouth before she could stop them. Mama had always said her redhead's temper was going to get her into trouble, and now it seemed that she'd been right. Dickon stepped back. His eyes were dark with fury.

"You've made yourself very plain, Miss Hills," he hissed. "Don't trouble yourself any longer. I won't be asking you again. There are no second chances with me. Ever."

And with this parting shot he spun on his heel and marched away, every line of his body rigid with indignation. Even his hands were balled into fists as he fought to keep his temper, although she guessed he itched to hit her. There was rage and menace there and a low cunning too, Daisy thought, and her heart sank when she remembered Gem's warning.

I'd hate you, or anyone else, to be on the wrong side of him. I reckon he could be right nasty.

As she watched Dickon slamming the churchyard gate behind him, Daisy feared she'd made a very dangerous enemy indeed. She and Kit would need to be doubly careful from now on.

CHAPTER 7

DAISY, JULY 1914

July was a hot and hazy backdrop to falling in love. The days were dappled with sunshine and the nights were warm enough for Daisy to leave her window open so that salty breezes lifted the curtains and cooled the attic. She had never known a happiness like it and Daisy knew she would remember this time for the rest of her life; she would always look back upon it as the most perfect summer. She and Kit snatched every moment they could together, and whenever they were apart they longed for one another. Sometimes they met at the cove, other times on the clifftop and occasionally even in the woods at the far side of the village. The more time they spent together, the more intense their feelings grew. Daisy knew beyond all doubt that she had found her soulmate.

Yet as perfect as all this was, Daisy had an uneasy feeling that something was hovering just over their horizon. Sitting beside Kit on the clifftop, watching the seabirds plunge and the waves roll to the shore, it was easy to forget that their time together wasn't infinite. It was even easier to allow herself to weave dreams for the future – dreams that she knew in her heart could never come true.

"What's wrong?" Kit asked, catching the wistful expression on her face.

Daisy shrugged. It wasn't anything she could put her finger on or explain, more of a feeling that time was running away from them. Whether it was the tense headlines she read across the breakfast table or the nagging unease since Dickon Trehunnist had asked her to the dance, Daisy couldn't tell; she only knew that knots were starting to tighten in the pit of her stomach. Like intense heat before a thunderstorm, these sunny days felt as though they were a prequel to something momentous. This bubble of happiness couldn't possibly last forever. At some point, Kit would have to embrace the life he was born for, and where would that leave her?

Broken-hearted. That was where.

"It's nothing," she said, but Kit wasn't fooled.

Putting aside the daisy chain he'd been fiddling with, he drew her against him and pressed his lips into her sun-warmed hair. "I don't believe that for a minute," he said quietly. "Something's worrying you, Daisy. Tell me what it is."

Daisy wasn't sure where to begin. "This?" she said, spreading her hands.

"But this is good, isn't it?" Kit asked. A lock of hair fell over his face and she smoothed it away tenderly. As she did so, he caught her hand, pressing a kiss into the palm and then closing her fingers as though sealing it in. "Isn't it?" he repeated.

"Yes, this is wonderful, Kit, so wonderful that it frightens me. How can something so good last?"

He laughed. "Because it's meant to be. It's written in the stars. It's fate!"

Daisy, recalling Romeo and Juliet, didn't feel encouraged. There was something about the idea of fate that terrified her; it made her feel like a puppet and as though any sense of control was merely an illusion. Rather than allaying her fears, Kit's words had exacerbated them. What if this growing sense of unease and the creeping dread of her dream weren't mere fancies at all but premonitions of something darker?

"I know things aren't straightforward for us," Kit said, leaning his forehead against hers so that even their eyelashes kissed, "but I'll find a way around that, I promise. I'll make my father understand."

"How?" Daisy asked. She doubted that Colonel Rivers, a stern man who even on a Sunday and seated in the family pew bristled with disapproval, would ever countenance a humble doctor's daughter marrying his son.

"I'll talk to Father and tell him how I feel about you. I'll make my parents understand. Trust me."

"And if they don't?"

A determined expression stole across Kit's face and his jaw clenched. "Then it's their choice. They can disown me, disinherit me. They can do whatever they like but I won't give you up, Daisy. I can find work to support us. It will all be fine, I promise."

His hands tightened on hers. Daisy knew he meant every word he said, but Kit had never had to support himself. He was clever and brave, but he had scant experience of the world beyond the Manor.

"I know you're thinking that I'm spoiled and privileged and have no idea," he continued. "Don't deny it, Daisy! I can see everything in those beautiful brown eyes of yours! But I can do this. I can write, so maybe I could become a schoolmaster? Or a curate? Or even, and here's an irony, join the army? Whatever it takes, I'll take care of you. I swear it."

"I know you will," Daisy said.

There was a "but" hanging over her words, like the heat haze that hung over the water. Before she could say any more, Kit pulled Daisy close and kissed her.

"Never mind how. All that matters is that I love you," he said firmly. "And you love me. We're meant to be together and nothing can keep us apart. I love you so terribly, Daisy Hills, and I cannot be without you."

She nodded and was going to reply when Kit looked straight at her. It was a look that made Daisy feel as dizzy as she sometimes did when she stood a little too close to the cliff edge. Her words evaporated.

"I love you and I want to marry you," he told her softly. "I want you to be my wife, Daisy Hills. I'm sorry if this isn't the most romantic proposal, and I know I should have spoken to your father first and I should be on one knee and with a ring and all that, but I don't think there's much time to waste, truth be told." He looked out to sea for a moment before turning back to her. "Times like these make a man think about what counts."

"There's going to be a war, isn't there?" Daisy whispered.

Kit nodded. "I think so, yes."

An image of blackened skeleton trees and scorched earth flashed through Daisy's mind. Her stomach lurched. Was this what her dream had shown her?

"Would you fight if there was?" she asked, even though she already knew the answer. The Rivers were a military family and nothing else would be expected.

Kit exhaled wearily. "Of course, I would. And if that happens then I want to know I'm fighting for something that really matters. All this," he jerked his head towards the green cliffs and glittering sea, "and you, Daisy. Most of all you. I love you, you know that."

She nodded, even though her mind was still stumbling through the remembered remnants of her nightmare dreamscape. "I love you too."

"So, do I take that as a yes? Will you marry me?"

Daisy flung her arms around him and covered his face in kisses. Her heart was racing.

"Yes! Yes! Yes! Of course it's yes!"

"In that case we need a ring." Reaching for his abandoned daisy chain, Kit wound the delicate strand around the third finger of her left hand and regarded it critically.

"It's hardly a diamond but it will have to do for now."

"I love it!" Daisy cried. "I don't need a diamond. I'll keep it forever!"

Kit grinned. "I should hold you to that and save a fortune. Besides, I'd be surprised if that daisy chain lasts until suppertime."

"You wait! I shall press it and keep it with all my treasures. I'll still have it even when I'm a very old lady. You'll see!"

Kit held up his hands. "I believe you! I'm not going to argue with my beautiful fiancée!"

Daisy's heart skipped a beat when she heard this said out loud. She was Kit Rivers' fiancée! She really, truly was! How was it possible to be so happy? At this moment his parents, her godfather and even Dickon Trehunnist couldn't have mattered less, because Kit was kissing her and nothing else registered at all. He was her world and Daisy wanted nothing more.

The afternoon slipped into the early evening and, after many kisses, she and Kit parted company. As she walked back to the Rectory, Daisy turned the afternoon's events over and over in her mind. The daisy chain was safely pressed inside her volume of Keats and, except for a smile on her face, lips swollen from Kit's kisses and a head full of dreams, there was little to show that she was an engaged woman. When the time was right, Kit was resolved to break the news to his parents and then Kit and Daisy could make their plans. Until then, this was their wonderful, delicious secret. The practicalities didn't matter a jot. All that mattered was that they were engaged and in love.

The walk back was uphill but, buoyed by happiness, Daisy scarcely noticed the incline. Her limp was almost gone now and the muscles in her legs had been strengthened by weeks of climbing up the cliffs and swimming in the cove. When she peered into the speckled looking-glass, she hardly recognised the reflection that stared out at her. Who was this girl with roses in her cheeks, a sprinkling of freckles on her nose and sparkling eyes? She didn't resemble the thin and hollow-cheeked shadow who'd left the sanatorium only three months before. She was different in every way.

Her head full of Kit and their secret engagement, Daisy floated up the path to the Rectory and came tumbling down to earth when she saw that Mrs Polmartin was waiting for her on the doorstep with a stony expression.

"About time too, Miss! The Reverend wants to see you in his study," she said, taking Daisy's basket and holding out her hands for her hat. "He's been waiting over an hour for you to return and you know how he hates to be kept waiting."

Daisy did indeed and her bubble of happiness popped. What was this about? Her godfather rarely saw her in the daytime if he could help it.

"Did he say what he wanted?" she asked, undoing the ribbon on her straw hat and hoping that her hair wasn't too messy; Kit wasn't much use when it came to pinning it back up. She prayed there were no telltale grass stains on her skirt either.

But the housekeeper was too busy shepherding Daisy down the corridor to worry about Daisy's dress. The stiff set of Mrs Polmartin's shoulders and the pursed mouth that resembled a cat's bottom didn't bode well. By the time she arrived at the Reverend's study, Daisy felt quite sick. What was this about? Dredging up her courage, she knocked on the door.

"Come in," barked her godfather, and Daisy stepped into a dark panelled room, the walls of which were lined with books. Even on this summer's day a fire blazed in the grate.

"You wanted to see me, Godfather?" she asked, amazed that her voice sounded even.

The Reverend Cutwell was seated at his desk and didn't speak for a moment. Instead, he pinched the bridge of his nose between his thumb and forefinger until the flesh glowed ghostly white and his shallow breathing steadied. He was fighting for control, Daisy realised, and she knew why.

He'd found out about her and Kit. Somehow they'd been discovered.

Daisy waited for her godfather to ask her to sit down, but the invitation was not forthcoming. He glowered at her from behind his desk, reminding Daisy uncomfortably of the headmistress at her old day school. She hoped he wasn't about to reach for the ruler and tell her to hold out her hand.

"Something most unfortunate has come to my attention," he said finally. "Something I would hope is untrue."

He paused. A log shifted in the grate, sending a fantail of hellish embers up the flue. The combination of heat and tension made sweat break out between her shoulder blades.

"Tell me, have you been consorting with Christopher Rivers?"

His question threw Daisy momentarily, until she remembered that Christopher was Kit's real name. Her brain scrabbled for an answer.

"Consorting?" she said. "What on earth is that supposed to mean?"

"You know very well what it means!" Reverend Cutwell barked. His eyes bulged and a vein throbbed in his temple, a fat blue worm of fury. "Have you been partaking in illicit meetings with Mr Rivers? Have you betrayed my trust?"

Daisy stared at him, aghast. Put this way, her cherished times with Kit sounded sordid and shameful.

"I assume your silence is an admission of guilt," her godfather said tightly. His entire face was white apart from two spots of high colour on his cheekbones. "Don't deny it. You were seen together and your unseemly conduct was brought, quite rightly, to my attention. The young man who came to speak to me was most concerned for your reputation."

Dickon, thought Daisy bitterly. He must have been spying on her and biding his time. Gem had been right: he was a dangerous person to cross. How much did he know? What had he seen? What exactly had he said? Did Kit's family know? For an awful moment she feared she would be sick. The clock on the mantelpiece seemed to tick more slowly and twice as loudly.

"Have you nothing to say?"

Daisy gathered her nerves together. There was nothing to be ashamed of. She had done nothing wrong. Why, Kit had just proposed! They were to be married. This thought was all Daisy needed to be brave and she raised her chin.

"Yes, Kit Rivers and I are friends. We discuss poetry and his writing, Godfather, and we walk together. His intentions are entirely honourable."

The worm-like vein wiggled. "Have you no shame?"

"There's nothing to be ashamed of. We've done nothing improper or wrong." Daisy's hands, tucked in the folds of her dress, bunched into fists as she fought to keep calm. "Kit has been nothing but a gentleman. In fact, he's asked me to marry him and I've agreed. We are engaged to be married."

There was a sharp intake of breath at her revelation and the Reverend's mouth fell open.

"I beg your pardon?"

Daisy hadn't meant to say anything about the engagement; it was a delicious secret that she'd wanted to hold close, to dream about and to explore in her diary before facing the reality of announcing it. Being Kit's fiancée was new and precious and untainted and Daisy had hoped to keep it that way, but her godfather's harsh words had been too much to bear.

"Kit Rivers and I are engaged to be married," Daisy repeated. The words sounded strange and wonderful and she saw again Kit's beautiful smile as he wrapped the daisy chain around her finger. "We're going to be married as soon as he's spoken to Papa."

"You most certainly are not engaged, you silly, foolish girl! What have you done? What have you given that young man in return for his empty promises? Have you compromised your honour?"

"No!" Daisy cried. "Of course not! We're getting married and Kit would never—"

"That young man has absolutely no intention of marrying you, no matter what he might say!" roared Reverend Cutwell. "He's led you into a fool's paradise because his parents would never allow such a thing. Marriage to you is out of the question."

There was no colour whatsoever in her godfather's face now. He was as white as the sermon pages spread out on his desk.

Daisy's own face was flaming at his assumption of loose morals.

"I have done nothing wrong!" she flared. "Kit and I love each other and we want to be married."

"Love!" spluttered the Reverend Cutwell. "Love! Love does not come into marriage for the likes of Christopher Rivers. Duty and family and position come first – and none of those, young lady, are related to any dealings he may have had with you. He doesn't come into his majority for three more years and, even then, his parents would never countenance such a thing."

Daisy knew this. Kit had already mentioned it as they'd climbed the cliff path, slowly because their hands were entwined and they'd been unable to stop kissing every few steps...

"I'm not expecting you to elope with me or anything improper," Kit had said softly, brushing her curls away and dropping another kiss onto her upturned face. "I'll do whatever I can to offer you some kind of a future. I'll get a job, save some money and then we'll get married properly, with or without my parents' blessing. It may take a few years, though. Do you think you can wait that long?"

Daisy had risen onto her tiptoes and kissed him back. "I would wait forever for you."

She meant it too. There would never be another for her.

"You had better forget all about this ridiculous infatuation and return to London at once, where maybe your father can talk some sense into you," her godfather was saying now, his angry tones battering into her reminiscences. "It's high time you sought gainful employment. Your father has indulged you far too much in my opinion. It does no good to allow a woman ideas above her place. He was the same with Marie. Small wonder she had such peculiar notions."

Hearing her mother's name jolted Daisy and also gave her courage. Her clever and fiery mama would not have stood here in silence and allowed herself to be browbeaten.

"Kit and I are aware of the difficulties and we're prepared to wait," she said quietly. "Whether I am here or in London, it will make little difference to my feelings."

Her godfather regarded her for a moment. "No, I imagine not," he said at last. "However, I think you'll feel very differently when you realise you've been taken for a fool and that the young man in question has never had any intention of behaving honourably towards you. Yes, I do believe you'll see circumstances rather differently then."

Daisy frowned. There was something about the quiet certainty of the Reverend's words that made her falter.

"What do you mean?"

Reverend Cutwell reached for his spectacles and, sliding them off, gazed at her with weary eyes.

"I mean that Christopher Rivers has been taking advantage of your naivety, you silly, silly girl! He has no serious intentions towards you. How can he have *when he's already engaged to be married?*"

CHAPTER 8

DAISY, JULY 1914

Daisy hadn't believed Reverend Cutwell. He was trying to upset her, she decided as she fled his study. Kit would never lie about something so important. He was honourable and true. He wouldn't dream of proposing to her if he was already engaged. It was preposterous! She would find him and tell him what her godfather had said and then Kit would hold her close and tell her that he loved her, because these were all lies. Already she felt better. She would cycle to the Manor at once and talk to Kit. She'd find a way to see him and all would be well.

But as soon as Daisy reached the kitchen, Nancy dashed this hope.

"Oh, Miss Daisy, I'm so sorry!" she said before Daisy could even draw breath to ask about borrowing the bicycle. "I wasn't listening at doors, I promise, but our Sal works at the Manor and she told Ma about Mr Kit and you. I would never have thought it! And him matched to Emily Pendennys practically from the cradle. What a to-do!"

Daisy had the sensation of her blood draining from her limbs. The kitchen, already hot with boiling pans, began to swim around her and she had to clutch the table.

"You would never have thought it of him. Young Dickon, maybe, but not Mr Kit," Mrs Polmartin agreed, shaking her head sadly.

"Thought what of him?" Daisy demanded. There was a whooshing in her ears, above the background sound of the pans bubbling on the hob. She couldn't believe that everyone was talking this way. Dickon had certainly done a good job of spreading his poison.

"Thought that Mr Kit would take advantage of a lass," tutted the housekeeper.

Daisy rounded on her. "He *never* took advantage of me. Kit's a gentleman."

"Yes, he is, and that's exactly why he should never have led you up the garden path. Gentry don't marry beneath them, no matter how pretty a girl or how much book learning she has. They stick with their own kind. That's how it is," Mrs Polmartin retorted.

Daisy wanted to scream.

"He is handsome though," sighed Nancy. "He'd turn any girl's head, with his poems and his sweet-talking ways. All the secret meetings must have been so romantic."

"Don't be so ridiculous! Get back to your work," snapped Mrs Polmartin, but Nancy ignored her.

"You never breathed a word, Miss!" Nancy exclaimed. "If you'd have said something I would have told you to stay away from Mr Kit and I would have warned you to be on your guard with Dickon. I wouldn't have let him cause you both so much trouble."

"Kit's in trouble?"

Nancy nodded. "There'll be hell up at the Manor. Our Sally says she wouldn't be surprised if the Colonel takes a strap to him. He's livid."

"That's enough of your gossiping about your betters, my girl!" Mrs Polmartin said sharply. "Get on with draining those potatoes! Unless you want to look for another position?"

Daisy made an excuse to leave and raced into the privy to throw up. She wasn't sure quite what shocked her more: the idea of Kit's father hitting him or discovering that Kit was engaged to another girl. Everyone knew this except her, it seemed, and she felt stupid and betrayed. Had it all been a game to him? Had she got him wrong?

No. It wasn't possible. Daisy's love for Kit was the most real and precious experience of her life. To have it snatched away so suddenly left her floundering and lost. She believed him when he said he loved her. There had to be an explanation. Kit wouldn't do this to her. He loved her. She knew he did. She just had to talk to him.

But unfortunately Daisy's godfather wasn't inclined to let her out of his sight now, which made seeking Kit an impossibility. Instead, Daisy spent the rest of the evening mending bed linen under the beady eye of Mrs Polmartin, and then she was treated to another stern lecture from Reverend Cutwell. He had been to visit Kit's parents and on his return he made Daisy's position very clear. If she wished to remain at the Rectory, and not to have her father involved, then she must stay well away from Kit Rivers. Unless Kit was willing to be disinherited, he would have to marry a girl of whom his parents approved and keep away from Daisy. Emily Pendennys was a suitable match and apparently one that had been unofficially agreed between the families for many years. The Colonel also swore that Kit's hopes of Oxford would be over if he persisted with the foolish idea of marrying beneath him. This tore Daisy into pieces because she knew how much Kit longed to study and how much his poetry meant to him. He was fiercely talented and had a glittering future ahead; how could she be responsible for denying him this?

She couldn't ruin Kit's life. Daisy loved him far too much.

"Have I made myself clear?" the Reverend asked her. "If you insist on pursuing this ridiculous and utterly unsuitable infatuation, then Christopher's parents will cut him off without a penny. If you care for the boy at all, you must promise not to continue seeing him – and then we can leave the matter there and your father need not be troubled with it."

Her godfather would probably prefer not to confess to her father that she'd been able to meet a young man in secret while she was in his care, Daisy realised; he certainly looked relieved when she agreed not to see Kit again. It was fortunate that the Reverend Cutwell couldn't see her fingers crossed behind her back. Daisy was confused, and she felt hurt, but she wasn't prepared to give up on Kit or be bullied into walking away. Until she'd spoken to Kit and heard his version of events, Daisy was determined not to give in.

Quite how she would manage to find Kit was another matter. Her godfather had declared that saltwater swimming and walking out alone were now banned. Henceforth, Daisy was to be accompanied by Nancy (when they could spare her) or confined to reading edifying sermons in the study and helping about the house. The very thought was unbearable. How would she be able to find Kit and speak to him now? She would be like a prisoner.

That night, once the moon had risen and stars freckled the sky, Daisy lay in bed with tears sliding silently from the sides of her eyes and soaking into her pillow. If it was true that Kit was already engaged then her heart was broken – worse than broken, because broken suggested it could be mended. Could Kit truly have lied to her with the same mouth that had trailed kisses over the soft skin of her neck? He may as well have plunged a knife in. Nothing Daisy tried could make the pain of this betrayal go away. No amount of tears or diary writing could quell the churning despair. She felt as though she was an empty shell and Kit had taken the part that was stars and glitter and joy; without him there was nothing left apart from a terrible yawning emptiness.

Oh, surely he hadn't been toying with her? Kit loved her as she loved him. Daisy knew he did.

She was staring miserably at the ceiling, afraid to fall asleep in case the dream came again, when a scrabble of pebbles on glass made her start. Uncertain at first that she hadn't imagined it, Daisy didn't move until she heard the sound again. Somebody was throwing gravel at her window and taking a considerable risk in doing so, since her godfather's bedroom was directly underneath. She kicked off her covers and padded across the floorboards to pull aside the curtains. Sure enough, a shadowy figure was beneath the cedar tree, poised to hurl the next salvo. It was dark but Daisy would have known that dear frame anywhere. Kit!

Kit placed his finger over his lips and jerked his head in the direction of the tree. Daisy laughed out loud and then her hand flew to her mouth because she must be quiet! Snatching her shawl and shoving her bare feet into her boots, she crept down the stairs, freezing for a second as she heard her godfather's rumbling snores, before tiptoeing past his door and slipping along the passageway to the scullery. Holding her breath and praying that the bolts on the back door wouldn't squeak, she slid them open and then ran across the lawn to the kindly shield of the cedar tree and the shadows beneath it. In the next instant she was in Kit's arms and pressed against the heat of his body.

"I was so afraid you wouldn't come," he said, cupping her face in his hands and staring down at her as though he wanted to memorise her features for all time.

"And I was so afraid you were engaged to somebody else," she wept. "They said you were."

"Never!" said Kit fiercely. "I love *you*, Daisy Hills. There's no other engagement, no matter what my father might like to believe. The Pendennys estate adjoins ours and a marriage would have been convenient for our families, but it's all wishful thinking on their part. There's never been any formal arrangement between me and Emily, even though our parents might have liked one. I swear it, Daisy. Emily is not my fiancée! There's no one else for me but you. There never has been since the first moment I saw you."

"Nor I you," she sobbed, and Kit pressed his lips against the crown of her head.

"I'm going to find the means to support us, just you see," he promised. "I don't care if Father cuts me off. It doesn't matter."

"But it does matter. You want to go to university."

"I want to be with you more," said Kit. "I will find a way we can be together. I promise. I know we can't marry straight away; I'm not that naïve, and I know I need your father's blessing. But I'll make my fortune somehow and then I'll come for you. I love you, Daisy, but it may take time. Will you wait for me?"

"Of course I'll wait for you. I'd wait forever," Daisy promised. She closed her eyes, anticipating his kiss. When it came, the bliss of it made her senses swim.

It was a kiss like no other they'd shared before, full of determination. There were no pauses for poetic turns of phrase or flowery language. These weren't necessary: Kit's lips and touch told Daisy all she needed to know. He loved her and that was all that mattered. They would be together. They just had to find a way.

"Was your father very angry?" she asked eventually once they'd broken apart.

Kit sighed. "You could say that. I've had the full lecture about the family name and doing my duty. I thought he was going to hit me at one point. It was only because my mother begged him to calm down that we didn't come to blows."

Daisy's eyes filled with tears. The difficulties seemed almost insurmountable. "Oh, Kit. What are we to do?"

"Make our plans and hold on to them," Kit said firmly.

"My godfather was furious too. He thinks I've behaved shamefully."

"He certainly made his feelings very clear when he visited. I thought my father would combust. I assured them both that you were totally blameless and I swore to them that nothing improper had passed between us."

"I was so afraid the Reverend might send me back to London," Daisy said. The very idea sent dread rippling through her. How would she see Kit then? Without him, she would shrivel to nothing like a flower denied water.

"I think it's best we play our cards close to our chests for a few weeks while we work out what to do and how we can be together. This has to be our secret. Everyone else needs to believe we've parted. When we meet we'll have to be exceedingly cautious. I believe my parents had word in the first place from a lad in the village who was more than happy to spy on us."

"Dickon Trehunnist," Daisy said bitterly.

"That sounds familiar," Kit agreed. "I think we can outwit him though. From what I've seen of him he doesn't appear to be the smartest chap."

"No, but he's cunning and he's still angry that I wouldn't go to the dance with him," Daisy sighed. "We'll have to be careful. If I slip out from time to time, Nancy might cover for me and maybe Gem will too?"

Kit nodded. "Only leave if you think it's safe – and if you can get away, hang something from your bedroom window. I'll do the same from the tower room. That way we can know when to meet in the cove."

"There's a removable stone in the wall by the church gate too," Daisy added excitedly. She had come across this quite by accident while standing there making polite conversation with her godfather's parishioners. Her fingers had stolen across the crumbling stones and discovered that one of them was loose; later investigation had revealed a perfect hiding place. "We can leave messages there as well. If I have to turn back for any reason, I'll slip a note inside."

"I'll leave you a sonnet every day," said Kit. He squeezed her hands. "It won't be forever, Daisy, I promise. A few weeks at the most. I'll find a way. My uncle's a barrister in the city and may help us. He's a decent chap and might even take me on as a clerk. That would be a start."

The moon, which had been sulking behind the clouds, stole out and filled the garden with silvery light.

Kit caught her to him and kissed her again. "I should go. We mustn't take too many risks. Not until we have some plans in place."

Daisy nodded. Despite the almost physical pain of having to wrench herself away from him, the heaviness in her heart had lifted. It wasn't forever. They would find a way. As she watched Kit retreat into the shadows, she raised her face to the night sky and took comfort from its vastness. They were meant to be together, and so they would be. Kit loved her as she loved him. There was no one else.

Smiling, Daisy gathered her shawl about her shoulders and crept back into the Rectory. When she slipped into her bed, sleep was just moments away – and this time her dreams were calm and peaceful.

CHAPTER 9

DAISY, AUGUST 1914

Reading the paper across the table was a bad habit, Daisy knew, and one she generally did her best to hide from her godfather, but on the morning of the fifth of August she simply couldn't ignore the headline. How was she supposed to concentrate on lumpy porridge when Britain was apparently at war with Germany? And how on earth could her godfather manage to eat kippers when their world was turning upside down? Daisy couldn't face a mouthful. The half-recalled images from her old dream suddenly felt like premonitions and she pushed her bowl away with such violence that the Reverend Cutwell looked up in surprise.

"Are we really at war?" Daisy asked.

Her godfather laid the paper down.

"I am afraid so, my dear. As from last night."

Daisy's stomach lurched. She and Kit, meeting sporadically and secretly whenever they could, had talked of this a little but Daisy had been so focused on finding ways to see him that she'd barely registered just how badly affairs were escalating on the continent.

"War's inevitable," Kit had said, only days before when they'd snatched a few precious minutes together. "If Germany won't give the Cabinet the same assurance on Belgian neutrality that France has given, then I don't think Mr Asquith will have any choice."

He would have explained in greater detail, but then Daisy had kissed him and all thoughts of politics had been forgotten for a few magical minutes.

Now though, sitting at the breakfast table with her eyes straining to decipher the small print, Daisy wished she'd let Kit say more.

"Is this because Germany won't respect the neutrality of Belgium? They've forced Mr Asquith's hand?"

The Reverend's bushy brows flew upwards. "And what, pray, do you know of these matters?"

"I heard it somewhere," Daisy improvised quickly. "I think maybe after church? Dr Parsons was speaking to you."

"Indeed?" Her godfather didn't look convinced. "Well, in answer to your question, yes, I believe that's the reason. We must protect our nation's integrity and that is what this declaration of war will do."

So Britain really was at war. Daisy felt cold all over. Young men would have to go away and fight.

Young men like Kit.

"Don't look so glum, my dear. It will all be over by Christmas, just you mark my words," her godfather declared, tucking into his kippers.

This wasn't what Kit thought, but Daisy prayed her godfather was right.

In the days that followed the announcement of war, Daisy was to hear these sentiments expressed over and over again. There was almost a carnival atmosphere in Rosecraddick. Gem was full of excitement about it all, desperately keen to do his bit, and on the following Sunday her godfather preached a patriotic sermon, calling upon all able-bodied men to enlist and fight for their King and country. Daisy, sitting in the church, could only stare at the back of Kit's golden head and pray that he wouldn't be one of them, although she knew deep in her heart that of course he would be.

They hadn't been able to meet up all week but after the service she managed to slip a note into their hiding place, her heart rising when she saw that one had been left for her. It was another sonnet, and by the time she'd reached the Rectory Daisy already knew it by heart. There was no mention of a meeting, however, and although she checked Kit's tower constantly he didn't signal to her. Daisy supposed she would just have to wait for him to snatch a moment.

All their dreams of Kit joining his uncle in London and sending for her suddenly seemed childish and naïve in comparison to what was happening around them. Daisy began to fear that these hopes might never come to fruition. She missed Kit dreadfully and her dream came again with a vengeance.

She was terribly afraid it was a warning...

Somehow Daisy managed to hide her fears – and if there was one good thing to be said about the declaration of war, then it was that her godfather no longer seemed interested in what she was up to. Instead, he was preoccupied with preparing rousing sermons and doing his bit to spread Kitchener's message throughout the parish. Soon Daisy found herself free to roam again. She left more secret notes for Kit and eventually they managed to meet at the cove, falling into each other's arms and holding tightly.

"Darling Daisy, I've missed you so, so much," Kit gasped, pressing kisses onto her mouth and her cheeks and then, as he raised them to his lips, her hands. "I think about you all the time."

"You too," she choked. After days apart, it felt so wonderful to be close to him that she was on the verge of tears. She never wanted to let him go.

Kit raised her chin with his finger and brushed her lips with his. His kiss, as soft as a butterfly's wing, made Daisy shiver all over. "My beautiful, beautiful Daisy."

She laughed. She knew she was far from beautiful at this moment: she was wild-haired and red-cheeked from running nearly all the way with her boots slipping on the rocks as she'd pitched forward and grazed her knees. Nevertheless, Kit made her feel as though she was the most exquisite creature on the earth. When he held her, she was in paradise.

Hand in hand they walked along the tide's edge. It was an overcast grey day, the clouds heavy and fat with rain, and Daisy wondered whether this was an omen. She hadn't been able to cast off her leaden sense of dread, and the more she learned about the growing fervour for war the more worried she became. She was so afraid that Kit would enlist. With his sense of honour and his family's military background, it was impossible he would do anything but join the army. So far though, he'd said nothing about this.

Gem could hardly wait to sign up when the recruitment drive reached the village. Nancy and Daisy had walked into Rosecraddick that day on the pretext of doing some shopping for Mrs Polmartin, but mainly because the distracted Nancy was a liability in the kitchen and as likely to chop her fingers off as slice runner beans. The village had been alive with celebrations as soldiers, marching in swinging rhythm, paraded through the street to cheers and claps. Drums were beaten, bugles sounded, women threw flowers, and bunting had been strung across the shopfronts. Photographs were taken (Nancy and Daisy had posed for theirs) and a brass band had played while a line of local men waited to sign up at the table set up outside the pub. Gem, standing among them, had beamed at Nancy and waved.

"He's so excited," she'd said to Daisy, a catch in her voice. "He says he'll earn good money and when the war's over we can get married and buy a little farm all of our own. He says he has to stop the Huns coming and taking it all first though."

Daisy hadn't known quite what to say to this. Her shadowy night terrors had seemed at odds with the music and the sunshine and she'd felt terribly unpatriotic. For all her surreptitious reading of the newspaper, she didn't understand this war and she really couldn't imagine any Germans wanting to steal a lowly Cornish smallholding. She wished she could talk to Papa about it all. The thought of him caused a wave of homesickness to wash over her. Fulham and her upbringing there felt like another lifetime. She would write to him tonight, Daisy had decided; she missed Papa and she owed him a letter.

"We'll get engaged before Gem goes," Nancy was saying in a determined tone. She'd wiped her eyes on her sleeve and had visibly brightened at this thought. "We'll choose a ring in Truro next week and get married when he comes home on leave. That won't be long. Everyone says it'll be over by Christmas anyway."

Daisy certainly hoped so. She'd been about to congratulate Nancy when Dickon Trehunnist had swaggered over looking very pleased with himself. A pretty brunette was on his arm, gazing up at him adoringly.

"I was the first man to join up," he'd announced, his gaze flickering over Daisy as he'd treated her to a *see what you could have had?* smirk. "I'm the first from Rosecraddick to take the King's shilling and fight for King and country. I'm a cracking shot already, as everyone knows, and the Sergeant said they need men like me to kill the Huns."

Daisy imagined the Sergeant was spot on. Dickon Trehunnist, with his cruel streak and native cunning, was perfect killing material. He wouldn't question or think too much but instead would follow orders and even enjoy fighting. Not for him tortured thoughts of bullets burrowing through flesh and crunching into the bones of his fellow man. He probably wouldn't see the Germans as his fellow man anyway. Men like Dickon had no imagination. Maybe they were the fortunate ones? Kit's latest poems were filled with imagery of death, and her dream was returning with increasing regularity.

"It'll be a hard slog but if we don't stop the Huns from taking France then we'll be next," Dickon had continued, his chest swelling with importance. "One glimpse of us and they'll run away like girls."

"Let's hope so," Daisy had replied. The creeping dread was there and in spite of the warm August sunshine she'd felt chilled to the marrow. Every instinct she had was telling her Dickon was wrong, yet what did she know? All the older people seemed certain victory was only months away.

"I've done it! I've enlisted!" Gem had joined them. He was grinning from ear to ear and his eyes were sparkling. "Now then, Nancy, is it true that all the girls love a soldier? Can I have a joining-up kiss?"

Reaching for Nancy, he'd picked her up and spun her around until she'd shrieked with laughter and begged to be released.

"You're an idiot, Gem Pencarrow! You didn't have to join up for me to kiss you," she'd gasped, clutching her side.

"Ah, but think how smart I'll look in my uniform for our wedding photos!" Gem had grinned. "We'll look back on those when we're old and grey and think how handsome I was!"

"I want a Christmas wedding," Nancy had demanded, her tears all dry now and looking thrilled to be on the arm of a soldier. The talk of wedding pictures had perked her up no end. "And I want a decent ring, Gem Pencarrow. I want a diamond!"

Kit's daisy-chain ring was tucked inside Daisy's journal and hidden under the floorboard. It was dry and crumbly, but it couldn't have been more precious if it had been made of the most expensive diamonds. Leaving the happy couple making plans while Dickon continued to brag, Daisy had wandered away, taking the lane past the manor house just in case Kit might see her and follow. There'd been no sign of him though. The doctor's dog cart had bowled by as she'd turned into the woods to take the circular route back to the church, but apart from this and a bright-eyed blackbird that had flown ahead shouting, there'd been nobody around. She'd walked down to the cove and watched the waves breaking on the shore, and wept for something she couldn't name and didn't understand but which felt like utter despair. Then she'd turned for home, drained and exhausted.

Today at the cove with Kit, the same sense of hopelessness had returned and it was overwhelming. Daisy felt as though she was standing on the edge of a precipice and that at any moment she would tumble over.

"Are you going to fight?" she blurted, unable to keep her fears to herself any longer. Her skirts trailed in the water but she barely noticed. All her attention was trained on Kit. "Have you enlisted? Is that why I haven't seen you? Are you hiding it from me?"

Kit's fingers tightened on hers. "Daisy, I would never stay away from you or hide anything. Never. My father's been taken ill and I haven't been able to get away. Dr Parsons says he mustn't be placed under any strain."

"I'm so sorry, Kit."

He smiled wryly. "It's no fun to see the old man in such a bad way. Mind you, he's still well enough to lecture me about my duty and the family traditions."

Dread lapped over her like the waves at her ankles.

"You've enlisted, haven't you?"

She saw the anguish in his eyes.

"What else can I do? Every able-bodied man will be asked to do his patriotic duty. How can I be any different?"

"Because I love you!" Daisy cried. "You're not a soldier, Kit. You're a poet!"

"And I love you too, Daisy, but how can I not go and fight? How can I let everyone else go and not do my bit? I love my country, my home, this village and most of all I love you. I have to go and fight. Pa's right there: it is my duty. I'm joining his regiment, so at least I'll go to war knowing I've finally done something he approves of."

Oh God. This was it. Daisy knew she had to hold on to him, had to keep him safe – but at that moment she understood that, no matter what, she wouldn't be able to do so. The creeping terror of the dream was here and it was real.

"Please, Kit," she whispered. "Please don't go. Don't leave me."

He stared down at her, distraught. "Daisy, what sort of man would I be if I didn't fight to keep my girl safe? If I didn't do my bit for my country? How could I live with myself?"

At least you'd live! she wanted to cry, but she bit the words back because there was no point arguing: Kit had already made up his mind. Besides, he was right. What choice did he really have? Enlisting might be voluntary in theory but the reality was very different. As Kit spoke to her about how he wanted to protect the land of Shakespeare and Keats and do the right thing by his King and country, Daisy knew there was nothing she could say to change his decision. In that moment, her heart broke.

"But they say you have to be nineteen to fight," she said in a final attempt.

Kit nodded. "Yes, that's true, and I'll be at a training camp on Salisbury Plain for a few months first. I can't imagine I'll see action until the autumn and I'll be nineteen by then anyway."

So there were a few months of safety at least. Daisy held him tightly and buried her face in his chest.

"I love you, Kit. So much."

His arms closed around her. "And I love you, Daisy. I'll love you forever. The war won't change that. We'll be together one day. I promise."

And as he kissed her, Daisy knew that Kit meant every word. Nonetheless, the churning in the pit of her stomach reminded her that there were some promises even he wouldn't be able to keep.

CHAPTER 10

DAISY, AUGUST 1914

War fever gripped Rosecraddick. One by one more men enlisted and before long the exhilaration of the sign-up was replaced by the sadness of farewells. Gem and some of his friends from the village were among the first to leave for a training camp in Sussex. There was a tremendous send-off at the station, with bunting, a brass band, a blessing from the Reverend and lots of cheering and flag-waving. Gem, who had never left Cornwall before, had been almost unable to contain himself, and as the train had pulled away he'd been waving and smiling as though off on an adventure rather than to war. Dickon had strutted along the platform and even this had brought a lump to Daisy's throat. They were so optimistic, so filled with excitement at what lay ahead. Was it only she and Kit who feared something terrible? Perhaps his poet's imagination was running away with him, and maybe she was too obsessed with a childhood nightmare that ought to have been outgrown a long time ago.

It felt like something more significant than that though. Daisy was convinced something awful was lurking just over the horizon. A subdued atmosphere had fallen over Rosecraddick since the young men had departed, and the Rectory was a sombre place without Gem's cheerful face and the banter of the gardeners now that only one of them (an old man) remained. Meanwhile Nancy, after a flurry of heady days showing off her engagement ring, had become silent.

Kit, having passed before the medical board, was to take up an officer's post in his father's old regiment, and was due to leave imminently for training on Salisbury Plain. With every second that brought his departure nearer, Daisy felt closer to panic. She wanted to hold onto him and prevent him from leaving, yet she knew this wasn't what Kit wanted. He was determined to play his part – and Daisy loved him even more for his quiet bravery, which was so at odds with Dickon's swaggering and the jingoistic words her godfather hurled from his pulpit every Sunday.

The coming of the war had changed so much already. The close scrutiny Daisy had been under previously soon vanished as Mrs Polmartin became preoccupied with the departure of her only son and the Reverend busied himself with sermons. Daisy found herself free once more to walk the cliffs and swim in the cove, but with Colonel Rivers' health still in question and Kit's time being taken up with helping with estate business, her fiancé was seldom able to join her. When they did manage to snatch some time together, Kit told her he was keen to speak to her father so that they could make their engagement official. However, Daisy had begged Kit not to breathe a word about their plans to marry. She couldn't bear the thought of Kit leaving Rosecraddick on bad terms with his family because of her. Kit argued that he'd been at odds with Colonel Rivers for a long time anyway and that he had a duty to do the right thing by Daisy. He wanted everyone to know she was his girl. Eventually, though, she persuaded him to wait until he was back on leave. That way, Daisy told herself when she lay in bed with tears silently slipping onto her pillow, Kit would *have* to come home to her. There was something to fight for and to keep him alive no matter what. The thought that he might not return was simply too dreadful to countenance.

He would come back, and when he did they would speak to his parents and to her father, Kit promised. Then, if Dr Hills gave his consent, they would be married. Daisy, who had no doubt that her papa would approve of Kit, was cheered by this thought and knew it would be what sustained her through the time they were apart.

The secrecy of their relationship meant that Daisy couldn't say goodbye to Kit at the station. Not for her the kisses, promises and waving of handkerchiefs that Nancy and the other sweethearts and wives had taken for granted. Instead, Kit and Daisy had agreed to meet the day before he left. As a result, Daisy was now torn between longing to see Kit again and the bitter knowledge that every moment this time came nearer was also a moment closer to saying goodbye. How she would bear it she didn't know; she only knew that bear it she must, and that if Kit could be brave enough to fight then somehow she would have to find the strength to be left behind. She would have to be strong, Daisy told herself sharply. She didn't want their last moments together to be tainted by tears and sadness. Daisy wanted Kit's memories of her to be filled with sunshine and smiles and tenderness.

Their final day together dawned fine, with baby-blue skies above a sea as smooth as silk. As always, Daisy ate breakfast with her godfather, but this morning she averted her eyes from the newspaper. Instead she looked to the window and concentrated on fat pink roses twined together and nodding in the soft breeze, and on the white sails of a boat dancing across the bay. It was the perfect summer's morning to be young and alive and in love, and she was determined to hold every moment close.

"I'm going for a swim," Daisy told Mrs Polmartin, after breakfast. "May I pack a picnic?"

"There's cold cuts in the pantry, Miss," said the housekeeper. Luckily she didn't ask why a girl who'd scarcely touched her food for days suddenly needed so much cold mutton, cheese and bread.

"Take some apples too, Miss," she added, fetching some from the pantry and tucking them into Daisy's basket, along with a bottle of home-made lemonade. "It's a beautiful day and should be enjoyed. Nancy here will help me in the kitchen. You make the most of the sunshine and your day."

There was sympathy in her voice and a lump rose to Daisy's throat. The housekeeper's son Bertie had enlisted too, and Daisy had heard her weeping piteously in the scullery on several occasions. Daisy suspected that Mrs Polmartin had guessed she was meeting Kit to bid him farewell; after all, everyone in Rosecraddick knew that Kit Rivers was leaving for Salisbury. It was hard to keep secrets in a small Cornish village, but the war was changing everything and what had mattered so very much a few weeks ago no longer held the same significance.

With the basket on her arm, Daisy left the Rectory and crossed the churchyard. Her hair, loose today and curling to her waist, lifted in the light breeze, and her white cotton dress drifted like the sails on the boat she'd watched earlier. She scarcely noticed the cliff path beneath her feet or the sharp fingers of yellow-starred gorse snatching at her skirts. Pink valerian swayed as she passed, and her namesake daisies crowded the grass. Above her, swifts darted. All of nature was teeming with vitality and Daisy had never felt so alive. She raised her face to the sunshine and, in spite of her sadness, her heart was gladdened by the warmth and the surrounding scenery.

Kit was waiting on the beach, holding onto a small sailing boat that tugged and danced in the shallows. His back was to her and his white shirt was rolled up to his elbows, revealing forearms that were corded with muscle as he fought to hold the vessel. The sunlight turned his hair to gold and Daisy gasped, dazzled by his beauty and the strength of her love for him. She loved him so much it was a physical pain in her chest; the wonder of it took her breath away.

"Daisy!" Kit waved at her with a smile of pure delight. "Come on! We need to catch the tide!"

"We're going sailing?"

"There's no sailing in Fulham – wasn't that what you told me? Believe me, there's no better way to see Cornwall than from the sea and today's perfect for it. Come on, slowcoach!"

The sea looked very big and the boat very small, but Daisy would have set sail in a teacup if Kit had been there too, so she hurried down to the water's edge. He took her basket and placed it into the boat, then lifted her after it, holding her against him for a moment and kissing her.

"You're so beautiful, Daisy," he said softly. "The first time I saw you I thought you must be a mermaid. Your hair was fiery seaweed and your skin pure alabaster in the water. You were like a creature from another world."

"Is that the start of another sonnet? I'm starting to think you only want me for your poetry!" she teased, but Kit was solemn.

"The truth. I loved you the first moment I saw you and I've loved you every moment since." Having lowered her into the boat, he regarded her with a serious expression. "I'll love you and write about you for the rest of my life. There will never be anyone else. It's always you, Daisy. You have my heart, now and forever."

She smiled and glanced away. She didn't want him to see that his words had made her eyes fill with tears, not when this was their happy day.

Kit pushed the boat into the surf, the water up to his knees as he caught the next big wave and pulled himself up into the vessel and next to her. He raised the sail effortlessly and let it bloom with air then surge forward. Daisy felt the wind in her face as the boat picked up speed and danced across the bay.

Oh! It was wonderful! Glorious! She felt as though she was flying! Daisy looked across at Kit, whose focus was trained on the tiller and the sails. His shirt was open and she watched the muscles of his chest swell as he held the power of the vessel and made it obey him. The ease with which Kit handled the boat, commanded it to sing beneath his touch and thrill to his desires, made her shiver deep inside. She longed to feel his hands on her with that same gentleness and skill. She knew the experience would be every bit as joyful and heart-stopping as this flight across the sparkling waves.

Sensing her gaze, Kit gave her a smile.

"Do you like it?"

"Like it? I love it! It feels free!"

The smile blossomed into a huge grin. "You're right. Out here nothing matters. Just the water and the freedom. I feel alive."

"Me too!" Daisy knew she'd never felt as alive as she had since she'd known Kit. Everything was brighter, more beautiful, more vivid and in many ways more painful too. It seemed to Daisy that loving someone so much was a blessing and a curse all mixed into one.

They sailed across the bay, tacking and racing the white horses, with the wind whipping Daisy's hair across her cheeks. For a blissful time nothing mattered save the hull slicing through the water; when Kit lowered the sails and guided the boat into a small inlet, Daisy was sorry to stop.

"It's time to eat!" Kit said when she complained. "All that fresh air makes me hungry and exhausted."

Kit appeared far from exhausted though: as he tossed the anchor overboard, his eyes were shining. She doubted his mind was really on food either. When he glanced at her, Daisy knew he was thinking about the solitude of the deep blue inlet and being alone with her. Something awoke deep inside her, yawned and stretched into life, and as their eyes met she felt warmth rush into her face. Something delicious and unknown was beckoning and Daisy understood that her life was about to change.

Waves lapped the hull. Seabirds called. The blue sky arched above. This was the most perfect moment and the most perfect place imaginable. There was nobody here but them, and for this brief moment nothing else existed. This was their time and they had to take it.

Daisy turned to him, holding out her hands.

"I want to be with you, Kit."

He nodded, taking them and kissing each one in turn. "I want to be with you too and we will get married, I promise."

She blushed. "I didn't mean that. I meant I want to *be* with you. Now."

His green eyes widened. The pupils were so dark she saw herself swimming in them. "Daisy, I didn't bring you here expecting... thinking..." Now it was Kit's turn to flush. "I don't want you to feel that was my intention. I would never—"

She stopped his words by leaning forward and kissing him, and in that embrace her lips told him everything she wanted him to know: that she loved him, adored him and wanted him more than she had ever known it was possible to want anyone.

"This has been the most wonderful summer of my life," she said when they finally broke apart. "Whatever is ahead, Kit, meeting you is something I can never be thankful enough for. I'll never, ever regret it."

He nodded. "It's perfect, Daisy. Before I met you I thought I understood love, thought I could write about it. But the instant I saw you I realised I knew more in that one heartbeat than I ever did from all those years of reading. Those were just words on a page. I never got it *here*." He slipped her hand inside his shirt and lay it over his racing heart. "I never let love in until I saw you. You are here forever, Daisy. There's only you."

Daisy was intensely aware of how close they were. His skin beneath her fingers seemed to burn like fire and she wanted to be closer still. When Kit leaned in again and kissed her softly, Daisy closed her eyes and lost herself to everything except the sensation of his lips on hers. Then his mouth moved to her eyelids, her cheeks and her neck. Daisy found herself unfastening his shirt completely and pulling him towards her until his naked skin was against her palms.

Kit groaned and his eyes were dark with desire – desire for *her*, Daisy thought – and the thrill of this made her giddy and reckless.

"Daisy, I—"

"Shh," she whispered, slipping the shirt from his shoulders and burying her face in his chest. She was drowning in the thousand sensations that came from being so intimate. "Just love me, Kit. Please."

The sun shone and the waves slapped the hull as Daisy lay in Kit's arms and gave herself up to the joy of his touch. He kissed her as though he worshipped every inch of her body, slowly loving and teasing her until she thought she would die from bliss. Then he pulled her closer and she knew that they really were one heart in two bodies, his soul and hers forever twinned and destined to be as one. Kit was gentle and strong and tender all at once, and if there was anything she was certain of, it was that this moment was meant to be theirs. It was right and it was beautiful, and Daisy had never dreamed there could be anything like this.

She'd had no idea.

"I love you so much," Kit said wonderingly as she trembled in his arms. He was dropping kisses on her eyelids and her tear-wet cheeks. "I love you, Daisy Hills."

She wrapped her arms around him, unable to speak. There simply weren't the words. How could there be? Daisy was certain nobody had ever felt like this before.

They spent the next few hours wrapped in a rough boat blanket before feasting on the picnic, ravenous from the salt air and each other. Then they held each other close and, lulled by the motion of the boat, dozed in the sunshine. By the time the tide turned they were tired and heavy-eyed and their mouths ached with kisses and smiles.

How could everything in her world feel so right when soon it would all feel so wrong? Daisy wondered. How could she have found such exquisite happiness while teetering on the precipice of such despair? And how had she ever thought she'd loved Kit before this moment? Those earlier feelings were nothing, nothing, compared with the overwhelming ones she had now as she cradled his head against her breasts and drifted in and out of sleep. Kit was her everything – and to find him only to let him go so soon was agony. She never wanted to leave his side again. He was her and she was him; where one ended the other began. They were meant to be together.

This was what Heathcliff and Cathy had known, she thought drowsily, and what Shakespeare had understood when he'd written

Romeo and Juliet. Even her love of literature had come into a sharp and wonderful new focus.

When they could no longer risk missing the tide, they set sail for home without speaking of the future that loomed ahead. The boat flew across the bay far too fast. With every second that brought them nearer to the end of the journey, a greater sense of loss tightened Daisy's throat. The moment of their first parting was racing towards them and, just like the turning of the tide, she was powerless to stop it. This morning Daisy had believed she was about to face the worst, but she'd been ill-prepared for the apprehension she felt now.

She stole a glance at Kit and saw at once that he felt the same way. His eyes were bright jade with emotion and his jaw was clenched in an attempt to keep himself in check. Daisy knew then that she must be brave for his sake, because Kit was facing so much more than she could ever comprehend; she couldn't bear for him to leave her feeling anything other than love. Fear and grief had no right stealing their time today. She must believe that all would be well and that Kit would come home to marry her. She must have faith that they would live happily ever after in a little cottage with roses around the door, where Kit would write poetry and she would raise smiling babies with his rock-pool eyes and her wild curls. That beautiful life was waiting for them. It *was*. She just had to hold the thought close and believe it.

For both of them.

The boat sailed towards their cove and Kit leapt out, pulling it up the beach so that he could lift Daisy onto the shore. They stood on the sand for a moment, holding hands and drinking each other in, knowing that this day would have to sustain them during the separation that lay ahead.

Kit squeezed her hands.

"Daisy, I love you more than my life. You're everything to me. But if I don't come back or you don't think you can wait, then I wouldn't blame you. I would still love you and I would understand."

"You think I could ever want anyone else? Especially now?" Daisy could hardly speak; the lump in her throat was swelling almost enough to asphyxiate her. "Could you love anyone else after today?"

"No! Never!"

"Then don't say it! There will never be anyone else for me, Kit, do you understand? Never! I'll wait for you however long I have to – forever, if needs be. We'll see each other again though. Of course we will!"

He held her tightly as the sea retreated and then came back up the beach. The boat bashed against her ankles and her skirts grew heavy but Daisy didn't care. She clung to Kit as though she was drowning and only he could keep the waves from closing over her. She was already drowning in her imminent loss.

"But if we don't, Daisy," he said quietly, raising her chin and tenderly wiping her tears away with his thumb, "and if the worst does happen, I want you to know that I do love you and one day, maybe in another place, we will be together. I love you. Never forget that. I love you and I promise I will come back to you. I promise. I'll write to you too. Every poem I write will be for you."

"I'll write to you too," she choked. "I'll write every day, Kit."

He kissed her once more, the gentlest and most bittersweet kiss they'd ever shared, before his hands began to slip from hers, the fingers sliding away from her own until just the very tips of them brushed hers. Then her hand fell away from his in a rush of empty air as he leapt into the boat.

Would she ever touch Kit Rivers again? Hold him? Kiss him? Feel her body melt into his? Daisy didn't know. Her world was spinning around her, and then she was wading into the water and desperately trying to grasp the hull. She couldn't let him go. She couldn't. She had to catch hold of Kit and keep him safe. Nothing was more important: not the war, nor her godfather nor even her family. None of this mattered.

"Kit!" she cried, blinded by tears and panic. "Kit! I love you! Please don't leave me! Come back! Please!"

But the wind snatched her words and Kit couldn't hear her cries above the slapping of the sail. All Daisy could do was watch as the little boat drew further away from the shore. Kit was waving and his hair glinted in the sunlight, but she could no longer see his face. Moments later the boat rounded the headland and he was lost from sight.

Daisy sank to her knees, not caring or even noticing that the sea was swirling around her and soaking her skirts, but knowing that somehow she would have to find the courage and the strength to face whatever lay ahead. Kit had gone, had slipped out of her reach, and she would live now only for letters and the hope that the man she loved would hold her in his arms once more. Until that day came, Daisy knew her nightmare was no longer confined to the darkness; it would stalk her through the daylight and be her constant companion until she saw her beloved Kit again.

CHAPTER 11

DAISY, 1916

The nightmare returned with heart-pounding regularity over the many months that followed. Sometimes Daisy dreamed she caught up with Kit and briefly grasped the rough fabric of his uniform in her fingertips, only for it to slip from her touch as he moved away, forever out of reach. She now knew it to be more than a child's night terror: it was a vision of what had come and what was still to pass.

The difference was that the dream had become less nebulous. The waking remnants were mixed now with details gleaned from Kit's letters and ugly imagery from his more recent poems. Gone were the gentle stanzas in homage to Keats or the elegant Shakespearean sonnets; in their place was a heavy, harsher rhyme that weighed her heart down. Kit's verse had grown powerful and devastating and Daisy wept to read it. His letters might be scant in terms of military detail but somehow his poetry, which conveyed the horror of the mud and the shells and the artillery's mocking laughter, managed to escape the censor's heavy pen.

She would kiss the precious pages Kit's hands had touched (it was the closest she could get to kissing him), before tucking them safely into her tin with all his letters and her sorely neglected journal. The hours she'd once spent poring over that and her dreams of being a writer felt as though they belonged to a stranger. Daisy no longer knew who that girl was; she bore no resemblance to the person Daisy had become. Her leg had long since healed, with only a trace of a limp remaining, and her skin glowed from being outside; all thoughts of keeping the freckles at bay were long forgotten. When at last she fell into bed after each long day working in the garden, she was too tired and unhappy to pick up her pen.

Sometimes it seemed impossible to Daisy that there had ever been a time before the war. The summer of 1914 felt as though it belonged to a different life altogether: a golden age when cricket matches had been played on the village green late into the light evenings, and the fields had rippled with wheat before the clatter of reapers had come and piled the wagons high with the harvest. The horses that had pulled these carts were long gone, having been taken away by the army. They were now far from home, just like the men who'd once harnessed them and harvested the crops. Women worked in the fields now and the grass was long on the village green because there were no young men left to mow it, let alone to bowl or field. Most of them would never return and their names were spoken of in quiet tones and with many tears.

Gem was one of those for whom the village grieved. The young man who'd left with such high hopes and a head full of dreams of coming home to marry his girl had been killed in action, and with him three other lads from Rosecraddick. When the news came, poor Nancy had fainted clean away in the kitchen and had been unable to speak for days. She was quiet now, twisting her engagement ring around and around with a haunted expression, unable to comprehend what had happened to the merry boy she'd loved.

"He could have died while I was making meat pies," she'd choked once, when Daisy had walked into the kitchen and found her sobbing over the saucepans. "My Gem died far from home, Miss Daisy, and I was probably thinking about making pastry or chopping vegetables. Why didn't I sense it? I should have known, not carried on making dinner when all the time he was dead. What kind of fiancée was I? How did it all still feel so ordinary?"

There was nothing Daisy could say to this; Nancy was right. The banal nature of everyday chores juxtaposed with the horrors abroad appalled her. She'd written about this to Kit, whose response had been a bleak poem, *Home Fires,* and weary agreement that none of it made any sense.

So far Kit hadn't come home. His first leave had been spent at a field hospital, following a shrapnel wound that became infected. A "scratch" was how he'd described his injury, although Daisy knew this was an understatement purely for her benefit. She'd been terrified when she'd heard on the village grapevine that Mr Rivers had been injured, and beyond relieved to receive a letter from Kit that put her mind at rest. His second leave was due very soon and he'd promised Daisy faithfully that this time he would make it home to Cornwall. Colonel Rivers was also very unwell – his health had never fully recovered – and when Daisy had seen him in church she'd been struck by how frail he'd seemed. There was talk in the village now of a serious illness, and Reverend Cutwell was often in attendance at the Manor. Daisy knew that Kit was afraid of leaving it too late to see his father and she worried that time was running out.

So much has passed since I last spoke to Father that I am certain the issues of the past will no longer seem of such importance, Kit had written, in his last letter. *Mama tells me he is very weak. I would like to seek his blessing on our marriage before it's too late. We have been at odds in the past and I would like us to be reconciled. Being in this place has made me view so much in a different way. How could my father have understood what the nature of this war would be? We who are here can scarcely comprehend it. I am ready to speak to your father and I am prepared to speak to mine. When I am home we shall be married.*

This letter had filled Daisy with elation and terror in equal doses. She longed to be open about her love for Kit and wanted nothing more than to be his wife, yet she also knew that Kit was very much mistaken: his father hadn't changed his views. Social status was everything to the Rivers family. Even in these troubled times, they insisted upon rank and protocol being adhered to, and Daisy suspected they would still see a union with her as deeply degrading. She was also afraid that if Kit and his father argued, a rift could form that might never have an opportunity to heal; in the future, this could poison everything between them. Daisy hated the thought that she could be the cause of a family estrangement. She hadn't said as much to Kit, but she was resolved not to announce their engagement or marry until the war was over and Kit was safely home for good. Then he would have time to make his parents understand that he and Daisy loved each other. Surely that day couldn't be too far away? The fighting had been going on for so very long now, and at the outset everyone had said it would be over by that first Christmas. The end had to be close, didn't it?

Yet no end to the conflict was forthcoming. Poor Mrs Polmartin was now mourning her son, and she wasn't the only one to have lost someone dear. Daisy was tortured by the thought of the danger Kit was in. He was Captain Rivers now, promoted after his injury (which had been sustained when he'd returned to a shell hole for an injured comrade), and as much as Daisy's heart had swelled with pride at his courage she was also terrified by it.

Daisy lived for Kit's letters and seeing him again, and she hoped he wouldn't be disappointed in the changes he would find in her. Working in the garden now that the lads had left had roughened her hands, her hair was longer and wilder than before, and her face was freckled and rosy. She was stronger too from the physical work and no longer as slight as she had been in those first few months in Cornwall.

Daisy's brother Eddie, who was fifteen now and still at school, was bitterly afraid he would miss the chance to see action. He wrote endless letters bemoaning his age, and when he came to stay in Rosecraddick for the holidays he drove Daisy demented with all his talk of wanting to "join in the game" before it was over.

How could Daisy explain that the reality was as far from *Boy's Own* stories of gallant drummer boys and noble deeds as anything ever could be? Kit's poems portrayed unimaginable horrors taking place in what was surely hell on earth.

Daisy hadn't acquired her knowledge of the Front just from Kit's poems or even gleaned it from the newspapers – most of which were buoyed up with patriotic talk anyway. Rather, she'd heard it first-hand from her father, who'd enlisted and joined the Royal Army Medical Corps as a surgeon. With Eddie safely at boarding school and Daisy remaining with her godfather at the Rectory, Charles Hills was serving in a field hospital on the Western Front and had ordered the Fulham house to be closed up. He'd been home on leave just once, making the long journey to Cornwall for some much-needed rest and fresh air. Daisy had been shocked by how haunted her papa's face was and how thin he'd become, and she'd heard him shouting out in the night on more than one occasion. When they'd gone for a stroll together on the cliffs one afternoon, he'd told her a little of what he'd seen – and her heart had quailed for Kit.

They'd walked up to the headland and looked out over the sea, as grey as shrapnel that day and topped with white spume. It seemed impossible that across this bleak expanse were France and Belgium, where men drowned in mud or, blinded, stumbled into tangled wire. Daisy had read somewhere that the gunfire could even be heard in Kent. Kent? Impossible! How loud must it be for the men who were fighting? She had heard too that the terrible noise caused men to collapse and lose their reason. "Shell shock", they were all calling it now. Apparently even Dickon Trehunnist had succumbed and was in hospital, unable to speak or feed or even, some said, toilet himself. Daisy had been no friend of Dickon's, but to think of all that swaggering confidence reduced to such a piteous state had brought tears to her eyes. Nobody deserved that.

"Tell me the truth about the Western Front, Papa. I need to know the truth. I have friends there," Daisy had said.

And the man I love.

Here Papa had bowed his head. His curls, once the same deep red as her own, were now frosted with grey.

"Sweetheart, just keep on doing your bit. What you're doing is important too. You don't need to know the details."

"Just keep on knitting socks and scarves and pretend everything's fine, you mean? I'm not an idiot, Papa!"

"I know that—"

But Daisy hadn't been in the mood to listen to a lecture. "I should be there too! I could join the VAD. Nobody needs to know how old I really am."

The thought of joining the Voluntary Aid Detachment had crossed her mind many times. Growing up as a doctor's daughter and having spent time in a sanatorium had taught Daisy a great deal about the realities of sickness. She wasn't squeamish. She was practical, and Daisy knew she could be of use at the Front. Just how many socks could she knit? How many meals could she help Mrs Polmartin, a hollow-eyed shadow of her former plump self, prepare? The Reverend would manage without her to help around the house, and he could eat his meals in the kitchen. Daisy needed to be doing something more useful than this. She had to do something that counted – and although she wasn't old enough to join the VAD, plenty of boys lied about their age to enlist. Daisy fully intended to do the same if Papa wouldn't help her.

"I'm eighteen, Papa. I can deal with the truth," she'd said.

"Can you? I don't think I can."

"The truth is better than not knowing," Daisy had insisted.

Her father had looked out over the sea.

"I'm not sure I agree, my dear, but I won't lie to you," he'd replied, so quietly that Daisy had had to lean forward to catch his words over the breaking waves. "It's carnage. There are injuries I couldn't have imagined, not even in my worst dreams."

"But aren't we winning, Papa?"

The papers were full of how one big push was needed, but her father just gave a harsh and mirthless laugh.

"No side can ever win a war like this. There are shells and bayonets and every possible invention designed solely to maim and kill. There are men who've lost limbs, had their faces blown off, been blinded and shredded by shrapnel. Some cry for their mothers and their wives. Others lie in mud for days dying in craters with the dead bodies of their comrades decaying around them and praying death comes soon."

Daisy couldn't speak. She could hardly breathe.

"The lads are lame because their boots are useless and their feet rot away in the wet trenches. They have lung infections and pneumonia too. Some men become insensible as though their wits have fled with the horror of it all – and those poor souls are trapped in their own private hell, pushed right over the edge of sanity by the brutality. They scream and howl and claw at their own faces. The scenes are burnt into their brains. Do I need to go on?"

She shook her head. "No, Papa."

He'd turned to her then and, to Daisy's distress, there were tears running down her father's cheeks. "I despair of it and, above all, I despair of mankind. We've found a way to kill and maim on a scale that's unimaginable, and we're using it with impunity. The lucky ones are those who die quickly or those who died early. For the rest there? It's a living death. Believe me, Daisy, this war will be remembered as the bloodiest in human history. Generations will be wiped out. Whole villages will see their menfolk cut down in their prime – and for what, I no longer know. All I can do is my best to ease their suffering."

Her father's bleak words had echoed Kit's verse and Daisy had cried too then. She'd wept for Gem and Nancy, for Dickon and Bertie, and for her foolish little brother who longed to fight. She'd cried for the fear of what might happen to Kit and for the sheer waste of it all. When her tears had all been spent, Daisy and her father had walked back to the Rectory in reflective silence. The next day, Papa had kissed her goodbye and returned to his posting. Daisy thought of him often and was so proud of what he did that it hurt. Papa was brave and good and clever and was doing his bit to help. Reflecting on his words, Daisy had vowed that after Kit's leave she would make plans to join the VAD, and her age was not going to prevent her. She needed – wanted – to do her bit. Remaining here in suspended animation was not enough.

In the meantime, she helped Mrs Polmartin run the house, worked in the Rectory garden and shouldered Nancy's chores. She soon gave up knitting socks for the soldiers though.

"The soldiers have enough to bear without having to wear these!" Nancy teased, holding up Daisy's attempts at knitting for victory. "Are you working for the enemy by trying to cripple our boys? I'd stick to helping in the garden if I were you, Miss!"

Daisy had to agree. Her newly acquired gardening skills were superior to her knitting. Sometimes when she caught sight of the back of the Colonel's head (when he was well enough to attend church), Daisy wondered what Kit's father would make of his son's future wife working with the soil. She imagined he would be utterly horrified, and this made her even more resolved to get Kit to understand that they needed to wait to announce their engagement.

Whenever she had a spare moment, Daisy still wrote in her diary, catching up on the day-to-day business of life in Rosecraddick, but most of her writing time was dedicated to penning letters to Kit. She wrote to him every day, pouring out her feelings but always doing her best to avoid telling him her fears. She wanted to be brave for him. She sent news from home, including funny anecdotes that she hoped would make him smile, and wrote of her dreams for their future. As long as she could write to Kit, it felt as though he was never far away. Daisy liked to imagine him reading her letters in his bunk, comforted by the knowledge that she was thinking of him always and that both she and Rosecraddick were waiting for him.

In reality though, the glorious summer days of swimming with Kit in the cove or walking hand in hand with him through the cool woods had taken on a dreamlike quality. Sometimes Daisy was afraid that his face was starting to fade from her memory. When she closed her eyes she could see him again, but whenever she tried to focus on him he slipped out of reach, just as in the old night terrors. Some nights she could lie in her bed and see his features vividly – the dear face she'd last seen before he'd sailed away from her, his eyes warm with love – but on other nights she could scarcely picture him at all. This was when she would have to leave her bed, prise up the floorboard and open the tin. Shivering on the bedroom floor, Daisy would spend the darkest hours piecing Kit back together by candlelight through the tender words of his letters, the old entries in her journal and, most treasured of all, the lock of blond hair tied with a strip of red velvet. Kit had left this hidden in the church wall with a letter telling her how much he loved her, and when Daisy had found it several days after their parting, the loss of him had floored her anew. She would close her eyes, trace her lips with that lock of hair and imagine that the soft touch was Kit's mouth brushing hers as he pulled her close. Their magical afternoon in the boat was one memory that was still as bright and as vivid as the sharp Cornish light.

When she was free of her chores and when the Reverend, whose eyesight was failing, didn't need her to read to him, one of the best ways Daisy had found to feel close to Kit was to walk down to the cove and wander along the shore. Here she would skim pebbles across the cold water or collect pieces of sea-smoothed glass from the sand, her favourites being the ones that were as vividly green as Kit's clear gaze. It was here in the solitude, with just the sigh of waves and the call of gulls for company, that Daisy could think about the time they'd spent together. They'd been snatched moments, but nonetheless they'd been the happiest ones of her life. Often she would sit on the rock at the far side of the cove, smiling at the memory of the day they'd first met, when Kit had fetched his jacket to cover up her wet undergarments. She could almost believe that at any moment he would appear at the foot of the cliff path waving and smiling.

One Tuesday, when she had a rare afternoon to herself, Daisy was seated in this exact spot with her arms wrapped around her legs and her chin resting on her knees. The May afternoon was chilly and stormy. The sea and sky seemed to meet in one heavy leaden line and the sulky sun slipped in and out of the clouds whenever the mood took it. She'd brought with her a brown paper parcel containing a ham sandwich, and a book was open on her lap, but Daisy wasn't really in the mood to eat or read. Wrapped in her shawl, she felt as unsettled as the weather. When the capricious sun slid out from behind the clouds again, she thought it was just a trick of the light making it seem as though a figure was emerging from the cliff path.

The figure descended the final few feet and then crossed the rocks with ease, his long legs striding over the sand and his arms swinging casually. Daisy frowned. He was dressed in khaki and wearing a peaked cap. He looked like a soldier, and she'd seen lots of soldiers since the war had started, but on a beach? And one as hard to reach as this?

The soldier was walking towards her. She blinked. Surely not? It couldn't be...

He would have written.

Or told her.

But it was!

Daisy leapt to her feet. The sandwich and book tumbled to the sand, but she didn't care because she was running towards him with the blood rushing in her ears and her heart pounding. Then she was in his arms and he was holding her close, one hand stroking her hair as she pressed her face into the scratchy fabric of his uniform. He was here! He was! The buttons on his uniform were hard against her cheek; she wouldn't feel these if this moment wasn't real, surely? Neither would she shiver at the rasp of his stubble against her scalp as he buried his face in her hair.

"You're here," she sobbed, undone by being held by him again after so long apart and so many nights spent in fear. "You're really here!"

His answer was to tighten his arms and pull her even closer, until she could feel the drumming of his heart against her skin and his lips kissing away her tears.

"Didn't I promise I'd come back to you, Daisy Hills?" said Kit Rivers.

CHAPTER 12

DAISY, MAY 1916

Kit had only been granted six days' leave and two of these were dedicated to travelling, which made every moment doubly precious. His parents were overjoyed to have him home and Daisy was adamant that his time with them mustn't be tainted by family conflicts, especially now that Colonel Rivers was so unwell. Besides, Kit and Daisy would only be able to have a few snatched hours together; she didn't want to squander so much as a second by getting into any disagreements.

"I don't want you to mention us," she'd told Kit as, hand in hand, they'd followed the line of the tide. "There isn't time to resolve it all now and I don't want your leave ruined by arguments."

His fingers had tightened their grip on hers. "I want to marry you, Daisy. I want you to be my wife."

"And I will be when the war's over and you're home for good. Please, Kit, don't let's spend what little time we've got now fighting with your family. I love you and you love me. Isn't that enough?"

He'd shaken his head. "No. I want it to be official. You're my girl and I want everyone to know how we feel about each other."

"*We* know. Isn't that all that matters? The rest we can deal with when the time's right. And, Kit, with only a few days' leave and your father so ill, this isn't the right time."

Kit hadn't looked happy at this, but he'd nodded reluctantly. "You're right, Daisy, but I wish to God you weren't. I wish that things were different and that we had more time. Sometimes I'm so scared there isn't going to be enough for you and I."

"If we had a thousand lifetimes it wouldn't be enough," she'd told him, her heart bursting with love and fear. "There's never enough time when it comes to being with you. Let's just make the most of what we do have."

And never had she spoken a truer word, Daisy thought four days later. How was it possible that four days could fly by like four minutes? Time had been doing some odd things since the war had been declared. Since August 1914 it had seemed to limp by, with one day seeming much the same as another; it had been an endless round of duties and tasks, although there'd also been the dreadful scanning of the casualty lists, her breath held in case Kit's name was there. However, the past few days had rushed past at the speed of bullets. When the final morning of Kit's leave had dawned, Daisy had wanted to burrow back beneath the counterpane. It was the nightingale singing and not the lark, she'd told herself over and over again. The sun wasn't rising: it was still night-time, and Kit's final day of leave hadn't arrived.

They'd squeezed a lifetime of love and memories into the past few days. In between seeing his family, Kit had met with Daisy and together they'd walked miles over the cliffs and wandered through the woods. Everything was sodden, as though the whole world was weeping, and eventually they'd surrendered to the weather and hidden from the rain in one of the barns on Home Farm. Here, in the hay, they'd held each other close and talked away the rainy hours in their own sweet-smelling kingdom. If the Reverend Cutwell had wondered where his goddaughter was going in a downpour or Mrs Polmartin had been curious as to why Daisy was packing a picnic basket on a wet day, neither had said anything – and for this Daisy was grateful. Time was compressed, the usual niceties swept aside by circumstances, and there was a sense of freedom that she hadn't experienced before the coming of the war.

"I'm tired of hiding in the shadows," Kit had said, kissing her softly as he'd stroked the hair away from her flushed cheeks. "I want the world to know I love you, my beautiful, wonderful Daisy."

Daisy wanted nothing more too. Would there ever be a day when that was possible? She could only pray so.

Eventually Daisy had to admit that it was Kit's last day and that she had to rise, help Mrs Polmartin prepare the Reverend's breakfast and then clear everything away. By the time Nancy was washing the plates, the weather had cheered up and the rain-washed world outside was new and sparkling. The sea was blue rather than the dishwater grey Daisy had become accustomed to, and the sky was clear. Maybe it was a good omen, she thought as she sat in the drawing room writing a letter to Eddie. Maybe everything would be all right after all? Her godfather had just departed in the dog cart, bound for Bodmin, which meant that she was free for the day. Hopefully she would spend some of it with Kit. Daisy had checked Kit's tower window and, having seen the white handkerchief fluttering from it, was hoping to meet him at the cove. Beyond that she didn't dare think; the imminent parting filled her with terror and she didn't want it to cast its shadow over their last day.

She was hunting for some blotting paper when she heard the scrunch of wheels outside on the gravel and, through the window, saw a smart blue Rolls Royce pull up in the lane. Her eyes widened as Kit climbed out, dressed in his uniform and looking so handsome that her pulse skipped. Kit was calling here? That was bold!

Moments later, Nancy came to the drawing room looking more animated than Daisy had seen her for months.

"Captain Christopher Rivers, Miss," she said, her lips twitching with suppressed amusement. "Whatever can he want?"

Daisy arranged her features into what she hoped was a nonchalant expression.

"I have no idea," she replied. "You'd better show him in, Nancy. We don't want to leave Captain Rivers waiting."

Kit strode into the room with his cane and cap tucked under his arm. He bowed formally and Daisy, who only the day before had been picking hay out of his golden hair, smiled at this.

233

"Can I offer you some refreshment, Captain?" Nancy asked, while Daisy said nothing.

Kit shook his head. "Regrettably I don't have time. I have an appointment in Truro. I was wondering if the Reverend Cutwell would like to accompany me there for luncheon? And maybe you too, Miss Daisy?" As he said this, he gave Daisy the ghost of a wink and she knew at once that Kit had waited until the Reverend's dog cart had bowled safely past before turning the Rolls Royce towards the Rectory. Excitement fluttered in her belly.

"What a pity; you've just missed my godfather," she said evenly.

"What a pity," Kit echoed. "Well, while I'm here I don't suppose you'd like a ride in the motorcar, Miss Daisy?"

Daisy glanced outside at the open-topped car and felt a surge of excitement. She'd seen motorcars, of course, but had never travelled in one. How would it feel to whizz down the lanes in this, with the wind rushing against her cheeks and the possibilities of the open road unravelling before her?

Behind Kit, Nancy was nodding dementedly.

Daisy smiled. "I think I would like that very much," she said.

Kit beamed at her. "Marvellous. Let me warn you though, it may feel cold in the motorcar – so wrap up."

Daisy flew upstairs to change. She put on her warmest clothes, including a winter coat and woollen gloves. Wherever they were headed, she didn't want to arrive there frozen to death. When she joined Kit at the car, she saw that he was pulling on a long leather coat, a muffler and leather driving gloves, as well as a driving hat and goggles. She wasn't overdressed then!

"Ever been in a motorcar before?" he asked.

Daisy shook her head. "No."

"You'll love it," Kit promised. "It's like being on a bicycle but even better; you'll see. Mark my words – one day everyone will be driving motorcars."

She laughed out loud at this. It seemed unlikely. Motorcars were so terribly expensive.

"Mock me if you want," Kit said, "but I'm right, just you see. Now, put these on," he added, handing her a pair of goggles and a driving hat and scarf. "And hop in."

Daisy did as she was told and soon she was sitting inside while Kit solicitously tucked a rug around her and made sure her goggles were secure.

"Ready?" Kit asked shortly afterwards, jumping into the driver's seat.

She nodded. "Ready!"

Kit was right: Daisy loved driving. From the sense of barely contained power to the thrum of the engine to the rush of air as they flew along the narrow lanes, to the way the gears worked, every second of their journey was a joy. She was almost sorry when they reached the city and Kit parked the car in the high street.

"So you really did need to go to town?" she asked.

He pulled an outraged face. "Of course! You didn't think I'd bring you here under false pretences just to have my wicked way with you?"

An image of Kit's face buried in her breasts darted in front of Daisy's vision.

"I think we both know you don't need to bring me all the way to Truro for that, Kit Rivers," she murmured.

He chuckled and a flush spread over his cheeks. "Much as I would rather spend every moment hidden in coves or barns with you, I really do have some business to attend to. Can you guess what it is?"

Daisy, slipping off her goggles and untying her scarf, was mystified.

"See your tailor?"

"Not even close. Guess again."

"Have lunch?"

Kit laughed. "Yes, of course lunch, but we could have had lunch at any number of roadside inns. I can't keep it a secret any longer,

Daisy. I've brought you to Truro because I want to buy you an engagement ring."

"I thought we'd agreed that we'd leave all that until after the war?"

"We said we'd get married after the war's over and deal with my parents then – at your insistence not mine, remember? I don't recall saying anything about not buying my fiancée an engagement ring. I've seen the perfect one too. It's meant for you. Now, are you going to sit in the car all day or are you going to come to the jewellers with me and try it?"

Daisy gave up arguing. Truth be told, she was thrilled to be in Truro with Kit. As they strolled arm in arm through the narrow streets, looking up at the cathedral soaring high above, she could almost believe that it was a normal day and that they were a normal couple. The war had never happened, her bad dream was just that, and Kit's parents had given their blessing. It was a pleasure to be able to walk with Kit and not have to keep their relationship a secret. For all her protestations, for all the excitement of hiding places and stolen moments in secluded coves, Daisy was finding being a secret fiancée something of a strain. She couldn't wait until the war was over and they could be married.

Kit took her by the hand and led her into a jeweller's shop tucked away in a small alley deep in the cathedral's shadow. There, on a bed of royal blue velvet, sat a delicate ring. Just as Kit had promised, it was perfect. It was a dainty daisy fashioned from diamonds and set into a gold band and, when she tried it on, the jewelled flower sat on her engagement finger as though it was made to be there. Daisy heard yet another click of Fate's wheel, the same turning wheel that had brought her to Rosecraddick and to Kit. This ring, like their love, was always meant to be.

Once the ring had been purchased, they visited a photographic studio where they posed for an engagement picture as well as individual shots. As Kit stood still and serious and faced the camera, Daisy thought just how handsome he looked in his uniform. She wasn't so sure that in her simple sprigged cotton dress she was his equal, but Kit made her promise that as soon as the pictures arrived at the Rectory she would send them on to him.

"I can see you whenever I close my eyes," he said as they strolled back along the street arm in arm and with the sun making Daisy's new ring sparkle, "but to have your likeness to look at would be wonderful. It will make the other chaps terribly jealous to see how beautiful my fiancée is."

Daisy rolled her eyes. She knew she wasn't beautiful. Red curls, freckles and bony limbs weren't at all fashionable.

"Don't you dare pull that face," Kit scolded. "You *are* beautiful, Daisy. In every way. And today you've made me the happiest man alive. Come on, soon-to-be Mrs Rivers! It's time to celebrate our engagement."

They were outside a hotel with a white façade as elaborate and pretty as an iced wedding cake. The gleaming glass door was held open by a footman in a green uniform laced with gold braid, who doffed his hat at them when they passed through. This gave Daisy the giggles and made Kit grin.

"You'd better get used to all that when you're Lady Rivers," he said.

Daisy's eyes widened. She'd not thought at all about what marriage to Kit meant, apart from being with him. He was just Kit and it came as a shock to remember that he was also heir to a big country estate, as well as being the future Lord Rivers. Small wonder his parents had wanted him to marry Emily Pendennys. Daisy could staunch a wound and discuss politics – but when it came to hosting society parties or going hunting, she was lost. For the first time since they'd decided to get engaged she felt a lurch of doubt.

"You'll be the most wonderful Lady Rivers," Kit whispered, raising her hand to his lips. "I'll be the proudest man in the world to call you my wife."

Daisy smiled at him and felt reassured. She could only pray that the day would come when her biggest concern was how to host a house party and which fork to use.

Kit was greeted effusively by the hotel manager and Daisy's patched overcoat was taken to be hung with as much reverence as though it were mink. As she and Kit were escorted to the best table in the restaurant, Daisy tried hard not to gawk too much at the enormous chandeliers and the sweeping staircase with its crimson carpet. She supposed the Rivers family was accustomed to this kind of thing – a fact that reminded her of Colonel and Lady Rivers' wealth and importance. Undoubtedly, Kit would have remained as out of reach as the moon had matters been left to his parents. She sent up a quiet prayer of thanks that they were still unaware of the relationship.

"We'd like some champagne, please, the best you have," Kit ordered, and moments later a bottle was uncorked and two flutes were filled with foaming bubbles.

"Celebrating something, sir?" the waiter asked as he replaced the bottle in a metal cooler filled with ice.

"Oh yes, I think you could say that – ouch!"

Kit yelped as Daisy's boot kicked him hard on the shin. She couldn't risk him giving too much away. The Rivers family was clearly well known at this hotel.

"We're celebrating my leave," Kit said hastily, and the waiter nodded, shooting Daisy a knowing look which made her flush. He thought she was Kit's fancy woman!

"You nearly gave us away," she scolded when they were alone again.

In answer, Kit reached across the table and took her hand, his thumb tracing the newly placed ring. As he did so, a look of wonder bloomed on his face. "I don't want to hide what I feel for you. I'm so proud you're my fiancée, Daisy. I want to shout it from the rooftops because I'm the luckiest man alive."

"And I'm the luckiest girl," she said.

Kit raised his champagne flute. "To my fiancée, and to being lucky."

They clinked glasses – but try as she might, Daisy couldn't shake off a growing sense of unease. It was because time was running out before Kit left, she told herself, and nothing more sinister.

Later on, whenever she tried to recall that afternoon, Daisy could never remember what they had eaten. Luncheon must have been exquisite, but the food passed her lips without her noticing and she drank the champagne without tasting it. Instead, she feasted her eyes on Kit. When she wasn't gazing at him, she was admiring her ring. She'd not be able to wear it openly but would keep it in the little Christmas 1914 tin Kit had given to her as a keepsake. When he came home he would speak to his parents properly and then she vowed she would never take the ring off again.

Once their engagement lunch was over, Kit drove home slowly with one gloved hand resting on Daisy's knee and the other loosely holding the wheel. The heaviness of their imminent parting was weighing on them both. When he turned off the road and guided the Rolls along the bumpy track to the old hay barn, Daisy wasn't sure she could bear the pain of being close to him, as close as two people could ever be, only to be parted.

Her heart was already breaking even before he'd left.

The early promise of sunshine had been swept away by late afternoon. Grey clouds rolled in across the sea and, as Kit stopped the car, fat raindrops began to fall, lethargically at first before gaining enthusiasm.

"Run!" he cried, flinging the door open and dashing around to help Daisy out. "I'll put the hood up – just run!"

She did as he said but, even so, Daisy was soaked by the time she reached the barn. Kit, who was only moments behind her, was equally sodden. Laughing and shaking raindrops from their hair, they climbed the rickety ladder up to the loft and collapsed into the sweet hay.

"Drenched!" he groaned. "Can you believe it? Some May this is."

"It's just an excuse to get me in here again, isn't it?" Daisy teased.

"Do you think I organise the weather for my own nefarious purposes?"

"Of course! I think you can do anything. Besides, aren't I worth a little effort?"

Kit pulled Daisy against him and pressed kisses onto the crown of her head. "You're worth everything," he said fiercely into her hair, his breath like fire against her scalp. "Nothing matters more to me than you, Daisy Hills. You're all I think about and the thought of coming home to you is what keeps me going."

"Thinking of you coming home is all that keeps me going too," she whispered. Their laughter had evaporated now, the mirth rolling away like the raindrops from the barn roof. "I live for your letters, Kit. Hearing from you and knowing you're coming home is all that keeps me from going insane."

He tightened his arms around her. "I read your letters over and over again until I know them by heart, and when I write my poems I'm telling you how it really is and how I really feel. I can't say that in a letter or out loud – but, Daisy, I need to say it. I know my verse might not be romantic or easy to read, but it's true and I'm writing it for you – and I swear my feelings for you are in every line."

Daisy hid her face in his chest. Kit's poems certainly couldn't be described as romantic sonnets. The imagery was raw and shocking, but she saw through Kit's eyes the ugliness of this war. The pity and the pathos and the barbarity, and his honesty in depicting these things, had brought them closer than any flowery lines could ever have done. This way she was sharing Kit's new world. Some men, he'd once explained, came home on leave only to be angry with their womenfolk for not understanding what they'd gone through. They found themselves relieved to return to their comrades at the Front, where they could get on with the job and not have to pretend all was well.

"You make me see," she said. "You make me understand at least a little of it."

"How else could we build a life together when it's forming who I am?" Kit asked, his face still buried in her hair. "It's impossible to explain what it's really like there: men alive one moment and dead the next, and forced to commit acts of unimaginable savagery. I'm not a hero. Christ, Daisy, I wouldn't want you to ever fully know some of the things I've seen and done. My poems are the only way I know to beg you to still love me and to bear with me and to understand if I seem changed."

There was a lump in her throat. "I'll always love you."

Kit moved so that he was looking directly at her. "I know you mean that, but war changes a man, Daisy. We're engaged but if you change your mind or something happens that alters me irrevocably then I want you to know that I would never hold you to this engagement. I'd want you to be happy even if that meant letting go of me. I love you so much I would rather a million times over that you were free to be happy."

His green eyes looked down into hers. They were no longer like sunlight filtered through seawater, Daisy realised. They now seemed darker and haunted, like deep-sea caverns where unknown monsters lurked. Those eyes had seen things Daisy couldn't imagine, and at this thought a sliver of fear pierced her heart.

"I'll love you no matter what happens," she promised. "I'll never stop and I'd never leave you. Never."

"If I lose a limb? All my limbs? My sight? Suffer from shell shock?"

Daisy raised her chin. "'Love is not love / Which alters when it alteration finds, / Or bends with the remover to remove.'"

"'O no, it is an ever-fixed mark'," Kit quoted back. Then he leaned his forehead against hers, exhaling wearily. "I might not come home, Daisy. I might not be able to make you my wife. Or I might never be the same again. You need to understand that, and you need to be prepared for it."

Daisy felt icy cold all over, reliving again the fruitless search of the dream, the nightmare feeling that he was always just out of reach.

"Don't say that. Don't talk like it, do you hear me? You will come back. Of course you will."

Kit looked away. "There's nothing I want more than to come home, marry you and build our family. A whole tribe of Kits and Daisies to run around on the beach and learn to sail and swim. I want a future with you, but I wouldn't blame you if something happened to me and you found another man to make you happy."

"There will never be anyone else, Kit. Never. I will only ever marry you," Daisy vowed. "I'm your fiancée now and I'll wait for you forever. It's you or nobody! Look at me! Look at this!" She held up her left hand, and the daisy ring caught the light. "*This* is what matters. This," she cried, thumping the heel of her hand into her chest, "and *this!*" She waved her hand at him again, thrusting the ring almost into his face. "I'm your fiancée!"

"Daisy, I might not come home. I might be k—"

Before Kit could bring ill fortune on them by speaking the words out loud, she covered his mouth with hers. The discussion was forgotten now, as need flared in them like tongues of fire licking through dry gorse. They had spent so little time together, but Daisy's body knew his instinctively and kissing him was as natural as breathing.

Trembling with longing, Kit kissed her back. It was a kiss that went on and on and on. Kit Rivers kissed Daisy as though he could never get enough, as though he was starving and she was the substance he'd been craving. Daisy was ravenous in turn, wanting nothing more than to touch and taste and explore him in a homecoming she'd been dreaming of since the moment he'd sailed away. In this moment nothing else mattered to Daisy except giving herself up to the bliss of Kit's love, and every fibre of her body was alive and rejoicing at their intimacy.

She had been born for this, Daisy thought as Kit tenderly lay her back into the hay before lowering his mouth to hers again as she arched to reach him. Daisy Hills had been created for Kit Rivers and he for her. She meant every word she said: there would never, ever be anyone else for her. How could there be when there was no way of telling where he ended and she began? Engagement rings and marriage and certificates didn't mean a thing. This dusty barn was their church, the hammering of rain on the roof their music and the scuttling field mice the witnesses.

Kit's touch and love were all the vows Daisy needed. He was her all, her one and her only love. She would wait forever to be with him.

CHAPTER 13

DAISY, AUGUST 1916

The news came on a day much like any other. There was none of the pathetic fallacy so loved by writers: instead of howling gales, swirling steel-grey skies and dismal rain, the bright sun was out, salty air blew in through the open kitchen window and birds sang in the garden.

Daisy was seated at the kitchen table shelling peas for supper and listening to Mrs Polmartin complaining about the poor quality of the mutton she was stewing. Meanwhile, Reverend Cutwell had closeted himself in his study after visiting Rosecraddick Manor. He was calling there an awful lot lately and always looked so upset when he returned to the Rectory that Daisy feared the Colonel's health had taken a turn for the worse. In the garden, Clarence, their remaining and ancient gardener, was hoeing so slowly that Daisy was certain the weeds were growing faster than he could work. All in all, it was a quiet and ordinary afternoon.

The garden was far too much for Clarence, Daisy reflected as the pods popped and the peas pinged into the dish, but with all the young men at the Front, finding help was increasingly difficult. Daisy knew they needed to plan ahead though, especially when it came to producing food. The Rectory flower garden might have to become a casualty of war, so that it could yield crops rather than blooms. The front lawn could be dug up too, and planted with cabbages if need be.

As Kit had said, the war had changed everything.

It had changed everything except her feelings for Kit, Daisy reminded herself. Kit filled her thoughts constantly. Saying farewell to him again couldn't have been more painful if she'd been cutting away a part of herself. Sometimes his features smudged in her memory and she ached to remember him, but then she would shut herself away in her bedroom, prise up the floorboard and pull out her tin. Tucked inside with his letters and her diary were the photographs they had posed for on what she had come to think of as Engagement Day. The photographs had arrived exactly two weeks to the day since he'd departed. Daisy wept to see Kit captured in time like this, his dear face so serious and his uniform so smart, but it was a comfort to be able to look at him. She hoped he'd received the likeness of her that she'd posted on. She wondered whether he traced her features with a forefinger, as she did his, and whether he kissed her image and held it to his heart. She hoped that, if he did, these things comforted him. The daisy engagement ring was kept safely in her secret tin, but Daisy often slipped it onto her finger and admired the sparkling reminder of Kit's love and the promise he'd made to marry her. She couldn't wait for the day to come when he would make that promise come true.

Kit's last letter had been heavily censored, thick black lines obscuring information that the British Army felt would be dangerous in the wrong hands, but two poems had made it through. Maybe the army censors weren't into poetry, Daisy thought wryly. If they had been, then they might have objected to *Handful of Men* and *Regret to Inform*. These two poems told of how a young officer and his men were shelled by Germans and had hidden in their shell hole for three days while the battle raged around them. One by one they died, until only two were left clawing through the mud and eventually made a break for safety. Then the officer, Kit of course, had to write home to the families and inform them of their losses. As always, Daisy had been moved to tears by Kit's verse.

There were twenty poems now and Daisy kept these with Kit's letters. She'd tied them all up with her hair ribbon and tucked them into the tin with all her treasures. The poems were special – she had read widely enough to know this objectively – and instinct told Daisy that they had to be protected at all costs. What Kit saw and how he conveyed it was important and it was her job, her calling, to guard his work until he was able to return. What to do with it after that would be Kit's decision. The poems were profoundly troubling and Daisy was certain they wouldn't be popular, but they were truthful.

The world needed to hear what Kit Rivers had to say.

"Penny for them," said Mrs Polmartin.

Daisy looked up, startled to find herself in the Rectory kitchen shelling peas rather than cowering in a shell hole or wading through a mud-clagged trench.

"I don't think my thoughts are worth even a farthing," she laughed.

The housekeeper gave her an arch look. "I'm not convinced of that, Miss Daisy. You looked as though you were miles away. A couple of hundred miles away, maybe? With a young man?"

Daisy chose not to bite.

"I was actually thinking about turning the lawn over to cabbages or potatoes. We don't need the flower beds either," she said. It was partly true. "And I was thinking about asking the Trehunnists if we could buy some chickens and a cow from them too."

"A cow? Whatever would we do with a cow, Miss?"

"Milk it? Make cheese?" To be honest, Daisy wasn't certain. She would pay a visit to the farm, ask kindly after Dickon (who was still in hospital) and give his mother her condolences for the loss of her other sons. With Mr Trehunnist away fighting too, maybe she would be glad to sell some livestock and make some money.

"Cheese and milk. Whatever next?" said Mrs Polmartin wonderingly.

As the pods popped and more peas rolled into the dish, Daisy let Mrs Polmartin chatter away. The words became bubbles of sound cushioning her and allowing her thoughts to drift again, this time to plans for the future. Daisy was hoping to join the VAD but she didn't want to leave the Reverend in the lurch with just Mrs

Polmartin, Nancy and Clarence left. Her godfather was a funny old stick, firmly stuck in the old Queen's era, but she'd grown fond of him. In many ways he was generous, opening his home to her and also to Eddie during the school holidays, and Daisy suspected he had even turned a blind eye to her romance with Kit. The war had shaken everything about and in spite of his original disapproval he had never again mentioned Kit's mooted engagement or reminded Daisy to know her place. Instead he had quietly turned the running of the house over to her and retired to his study, leaving her with great tracts of free time to write and walk and swim. He was looking old and tired lately though, and she wondered if—

"Miss Daisy! Miss Daisy! I came as soon as I could. I'm so sorry, I've only just heard the news."

Nancy whirled into the kitchen, her face scarlet with exertion. She was at Daisy's side in an instant and she was weeping.

"I'm so sorry, Miss. I know it's all supposed to be a big secret, Miss, but Gem and me guessed a long time ago. I'm so sorry. This bloody war!"

"You watch your mouth with such cursing in the Reverend's house," scolded Mrs Polmartin, but Nancy ignored her.

"It *is* a bloody war, Mrs P! First my Gem and then Aunty Anne's boys and your Bertie, and now even Mr Kit. When's it going to end?"

Daisy stared at her. "What are you talking about?"

The high colour drained from Nancy's cheeks. "You don't know? Oh, Miss Daisy. I thought *you'd* have heard. It's Mr Kit. He's missing in action."

For two years Daisy had dreaded this moment. She had spent hours fretting and worrying, scanning the casualty lists in the newspapers and living for Kit's next letter. She'd always known there would be no telegram for her and any news would have to be gleaned second-hand, but if the day did come Daisy had always thought she would faint away or have hysterics. Oddly, now that the worst was upon her all she felt was a sense of icy calm. Was this because this was what she had been waiting for?

No. It couldn't be that. She felt this way because it wasn't true. If Kit were dead, Daisy would know. A part of her would have died with him and she would have felt it. She and Kit were twin souls. There was no possible way he could die without her knowing. No way at all.

"Kit isn't dead. You're talking nonsense," she said.

"I wish I was, Miss, but it's all over the village. Colonel and Lady Rivers have had a telegram. The blinds are down too in the manor house. It's awful news, Miss, and I'm so sorry."

There was a rushing sound in Daisy's ears and the table seemed to melt beneath her.

"It isn't true," she insisted, her voice sounding very far away. "Kit isn't dead. I'd know if he was. He isn't dead. He isn't. He isn't. He isn't."

"She's in shock," Nancy said to Mrs Polmartin. "You know she's sweet on him. What do we give her for shock?"

"I'll fetch some brandy," Mrs Polmartin was saying. "Or should it be sweet tea?"

"Both," Nancy decided.

The room was whirling and although she could hear this conversation Daisy felt a thousand miles removed from it. This twisting terror that Kit would always be a fingertip's distance out of reach was the fulfilment of her old nightmare. The dream had been a message; she wasn't to believe this news or to give up hope. Kit was still alive and if she looked hard enough Daisy knew she would find him.

"Kit isn't missing. I didn't see his name in the casualty list," she insisted.

"Oh my love, you must have missed it," said Mrs Polmartin.

Daisy didn't think so. She scoured the lists every day.

"You've got it wrong," she told Nancy sharply.

Nancy, setting the kettle on the hotplate, shook her head.

"Sorry, Miss, but there's no mistake."

"Are you totally sure?" demanded Mrs Polmartin. Her hands on her hips, she gave Nancy a hard look.

"I heard it from our Sally when I was just in the village. The Colonel and Lady Rivers had a telegram and they told the staff just this morning." Nancy's eyes brimmed. "Sal said they called everyone into the hall and broke the news. Mr Kit's been missing for weeks, since the early days of the Somme apparently, or so the Colonel said. It's come as a terrible shock to them."

"To all of us," said Mrs Polmartin, dabbing her eyes on the corner of her apron. "The Rivers are part of Rosecraddick and to lose Mr Kit feels like losing family."

"You haven't lost him. Missing isn't dead," Daisy said angrily. A cold hand laid itself on her heart. She chose to ignore it. "What's the matter with you all? He's not dead."

Kit couldn't be dead. He was coming home to marry her. He'd promised.

Nancy and Mrs Polmartin exchanged a look that made Daisy want to scream. This wasn't the same as Gem or the housekeeper's son, both of whom had been killed outright and buried in foreign soil with no chance of a mistake being made. Kit was missing. And missing didn't mean dead. He was somewhere waiting for her to find him.

Daisy supposed she must have gone into shock at this point because it all became something of a blur. There was hot sweet tea followed by brandy, maybe several brandies, which she must have drunk because her stomach started to churn and her head felt odd. Nancy and Mrs Polmartin talked in hushed voices but Daisy scarcely heard a word they said. Nor did she much care that her big secret wasn't quite as secret as she thought. What did any of that matter now?

She needed to talk to Kit's parents and find out what they knew. If she discovered where Kit was last seen and where he'd been fighting, then she could pick up a breadcrumb trail. He could be injured. He could even be a prisoner of war. There would be a way to find him because Kit couldn't be dead. If he was, Daisy would know. She would feel it.

How could you not feel your heart being wrenched out of your body?

While she sipped the brandy, Daisy's mind was shuttling back and forth as questions and ideas jostled to be at the forefront. Perhaps the army had got the details wrong. That happened. Maybe he even had amnesia? There could be all manner of explanations. But death? Daisy would never, ever accept that. She knew he couldn't be dead, that their love couldn't be drifting away like dandelion seeds in the wind.

Kit was alive. All Daisy had to do was find a way to prove it and then find Kit.

She pushed her glass aside and stood up so abruptly that her chair fell over. The loud clatter stopped Nancy and Mrs Polmartin mid conversation.

"Where are you going, Miss?" Nancy asked as Daisy headed to the door.

"To find out what happened to Kit," Daisy said.

She would discover where Kit was last seen and then she would search for him and bring him home – but to do this she needed all the facts, which would mean having an extremely difficult conversation.

Daisy was going to pay Kit's parents a long-overdue visit.

CHAPTER 14

DAISY, AUGUST 1916

Although she'd passed Rosecraddick Manor a thousand times, Daisy had never had occasion to visit. As she paused by the impressive stone-pillared entrance and looked down the drive, her stomach flipped with nerves. The old manor house was beautiful against the summer sky, yet forbidding in its grandeur. Much of it was Elizabethan, but some of it was even older; there were battlements and arrow slits in the oldest parts, and myriad mullioned windows glinted in the sunshine like eyes heavily browed with boughs of twisting wisteria. Elsewhere, ivy laced the stonework. With walled gardens, green lawns and deep woods beyond, and silvery grey lichen velveting the roof, Rosecraddick Manor was like something out of a fairy tale. As in any good fairy tale, there was a handsome prince – but in this story he was the one in need of rescue.

Daisy leaned Nancy's bicycle against one of the pillars and stood for a moment to recover her breath after the uphill journey from the Rectory. She'd been in such haste to reach the Manor that she'd bicycled hard and fast, and now there was a stitch in her side and her breath burned in her lungs. Maybe she wasn't thinking straight. Perhaps, as Nancy had warned, she was making a huge mistake by coming here. Nevertheless, she had to speak to Kit's parents. If they could tell her where he'd been fighting when he was reported missing in action, then she would have a starting place for her search.

Once her breath was less ragged, Daisy smoothed down her skirts and patted her hair back into place. The engagement ring was on her finger, and tucked safely in her pocket were Kit's letters. These items should prove to his parents that she was indeed their son's fiancée.

She'd toyed with the idea of bringing his poems too, but then she'd decided against it. In some ways, Kit's poetry was far more personal than his letters: the poems had drawn Daisy deep into Kit's soul and taught her how to view the world and the war through his eyes. No person had ever read them apart from her, and until Kit was home and willing to share them, Daisy was determined they would remain a secret. Besides, the imagery they evoked was stark and Daisy couldn't bear to distress the Rivers further. It was best that the poems remained hidden beneath the floorboard for now.

"I'm Kit's fiancée," she said aloud, squaring her shoulders and gulping down her nerves. "I have every right to visit his parents and every right to know the truth, don't I?"

But her only reply was the call of a woodpigeon from across the valley. Even the seagulls and the rooks were silent on the matter.

Daisy raised her chin and began to walk up the drive. With every footstep that took her closer to the house, she wondered how it was possible that her gentle and compassionate Kit came from a world such as this. When they'd been together, the realities of wealth and social standing had rarely featured, but now, as she dredged up the courage to approach his parents, Daisy was desperately aware of the differences between them – differences that had upset his parents so much and still kept Daisy and Kit apart. How could she ever have forgotten these?

The reality was that Kit wasn't just Kit. Her fiancé was more than the poet who'd read to her on the beach with her head cradled against his shoulder and his fingers threaded into her curls. He was more than the man who'd held her close and loved her with every fibre of his being. Kit was the heir to everything as far as the eye could see. One day this beautiful manor house, with its thousands of acres of land and collections of priceless artwork, would all be his – to say nothing of the tenant farms and the properties in London.

He was the landowner's son and she was a doctor's daughter from London. This was respectable, Daisy reminded herself. She might not be from the upper classes but marriage to her was hardly dragging the Rivers' noble lineage into the gutter. It might have caused a little gossip and raised a few eyebrows, but it wouldn't be the awful scandal they seemed to think it might be. Cornwall was the kind of place that was slow to change, but even here the war had altered things. People were adapting, thinking was becoming more modern and marriage between the heir to the estate and the Reverend's goddaughter wouldn't ruffle too many feathers. Her mother had told her all those years ago that the new century would bring changes she couldn't imagine. Recalling Mama's words now made Daisy even more determined to see Kit's parents. She was Kit's fiancée. He loved her and had wanted to marry her before he left – and he would have done so too, had she not dissuaded him.

Oh! If only she had listened! Then nobody would be able to keep anything from her. As Kit's wife Daisy would have been informed first and told where her husband had been fighting. She wouldn't have had to hear the news second-hand or scrabble for information. Tears burned behind her eyes and she blinked them away furiously, knowing that if she started to cry now she was in danger of never stopping. She had nothing, *nothing,* to be ashamed of.

As Daisy grew closer to the house it soon became clear that the war hadn't left the Manor as untouched as it had initially appeared from the entrance. Weeds were shooting upwards through the drive, the overgrown lawn was rippling and sighing like the sea, and the roses around the porch were rampant and desperately in need of deadheading. Old blooms hung heavy and rotted from the wire clipped to the stonework, reminding her of Kit's description of bloated corpses strung along the barbed wire or blooming hellishly in shell holes. She shuddered and looked away. There were too many images of death and decay, as though nature was grieving for the waste of life across the water.

She must share that concept with Kit in her next letter because he'd appreciate it, Daisy thought. Then she brought herself up short.

There would be no more letters. She'd have to wait until she saw him. And she *would* see him again, because he wasn't dead. He wasn't.

Daisy inhaled and exhaled to calm herself – an exercise Papa swore by – and then climbed the steps and tugged at the bell pull. There was a deep clanging from within, but it seemed an age before the door was answered by Nancy's sister, Sally.

"Miss Daisy!" Sally's blue eyes were wide as she showed Daisy into the vaulted entrance hall. *I'm not expected then*, Daisy thought grimly. "So sorry to keep you waiting, Miss. Blame the conscription because we've no footmen left now and I'm fair rushed off my feet, let me tell you. Mr Emmet's busy with the master most of the time but thank goodness he's too old to fight!"

Mr Emmet was the Rivers family's butler, a dour man well known in the village for his unwavering loyalty to the family and lack of humour. With his pale face, beaky nose and grim expression, he reminded Daisy of a character from a gothic novel.

"He scared the hell out of me as a boy," Kit had told her once. "He looked just like an undertaker and I had nightmares about him nailing me into a coffin. He was Father's batman in the army and he's loyal to Pa, I'll give him that, but he gives me the shivers."

He gave Daisy the shivers too, and she was relieved the butler was occupied. She'd been the recipient of several disapproving looks from him during Sunday services, and on one occasion she'd been certain that he'd spotted Kit turning and smiling at her. *He knows*, she'd thought, and a feeling of unease had crept over her which had never quite left.

"I've come to see the Colonel," she told Sally now, taking off her hat and passing it over. The hall was gloomy now that the window blinds had been lowered as a mark of respect.

"Begging your pardon, Miss, but you won't be able to. He's in bed and he's being ever so odd. Only Mr Emmet's been allowed upstairs. The master's health has taken a dreadful turn for the worse these past weeks, and with Mr Kit dead he's in a terrible state."

"Mr Kit is not dead. He's missing," Daisy snapped. "It's not the same thing at all. If the Colonel is indisposed then I'll see Lady Rivers and," she added when Sally opened her mouth to protest, "I'm not going away until I do. This is about Mr Kit and it's important."

Her mama had possessed an *I won't be argued with* tone that nobody in the Hills family had ever dared disobey, and Daisy was now thrilled to hear it ringing through her own voice. Before long Sally was showing her through to the drawing room. Daisy was so nervous that she scarcely noticed the beauty of the house or the impressive portraits lining the panelled walls. Even the sad-eyed deer and the polecats trapped in glass cases didn't fully register.

"I thought I made it clear I was not to be disturbed?" said a voice when Sally opened a heavy door.

"I beg your pardon, ma'am, but Miss Hills has called and says she needs to speak with you."

"I said nobody was to disturb me! Is there no respect? No shame? I am in mourning for my son!"

Before she could be sent away, Daisy ducked beneath Sally's arm and stepped into a large room richly panelled in oak. Family portraits hung all around, fixing Daisy with challenging stares as though outraged that she'd dared to enter without permission. A longcase clock ticked the time away from the farthest corner and, even though it was high summer, a merry fire danced and crackled in the grate. Yet despite this heat the atmosphere was chilly. Daisy shivered, wishing she hadn't been in such haste to leave the Rectory that she'd forgotten her shawl.

Lady Rivers was seated at a writing desk. Slowly replacing the cap onto her fountain pen, she folded her hands and regarded Daisy with distaste, as though Daisy were an unpleasant insect that required squashing. Kit's mother was dressed in black but her eyes, Daisy noticed, weren't red from weeping. For someone who had recently learned that her son was dead, Lady Rivers appeared remarkably composed.

"I wondered how long it would be before we were graced with your company," she said, reaching into a drawer and pulling out a slim leather wallet. "Very well. Name your price."

For a moment all Daisy could do was stare, taken aback to be this close to Kit's mother. She'd often seen Lady Rivers at church, but never closely enough to study any similarities to Kit. Her ash-blonde hair, swept up in an elegant chignon, must once have been the same corn-bright hue as Kit's, and her face had the same high cheekbones – although it lacked Kit's openness and ready smile. Whereas Kit tended to laugh and draw people in, his mother's features were set in a defensive expression and her downturned mouth implied that she found life perpetually disappointing. She would have been beautiful once, as her portrait above the fireplace testified, but today her lips were a tight slash of coral in a lined and powdery face, while her green eyes were as cold as sea-washed glass.

"Well?" One slim brow arched quizzically. "How much will it cost for you to leave us and our son's memory in peace?"

Daisy felt as though she had received a physical blow.

"I haven't come here for money! I came as soon as I heard the news about Kit because I had to speak to you. He isn't dead! I know he isn't. Kit is alive."

Kit's mother blanched. One hand fluttered to her throat.

"How could you possibly know that?" she whispered. The blood even seemed to vanish from her lips. "It's impossible you'd know that. Nobody knows that. They can't."

"I do!" Daisy cried. She stepped forward, her hands pressed against her heart. "Lady Rivers, I would know if Kit were dead. I would feel it in here!" She struck her chest with her hands. "My heart would tell me. You see, we love each other and—"

Lady Rivers gave a shrill laugh. She seemed oddly relieved by Daisy's answer.

"What nonsense is this? Feelings? Love? *Your* heart?" Her lips curled scornfully. "Have you deliberately come here to mock me? Do you not think I would *know* if my son were alive?"

"I'm only telling you what I feel!" Daisy cried. "I would know if Kit was dead!"

"*You* would know? *You?* Who are you to presume to barge in here and speak to me about my son like this?"

Daisy took a deep breath. This was it.

"Lady Rivers, you need to know that Kit and I are engaged to be married. I'm his fiancée."

Lady Rivers was on her feet now and glaring at Daisy.

"I beg your pardon? Engaged? You most certainly are not. On the day I have to announce that my son is dead, you choose to come here and tell such lies? In any case, we would have flatly forbidden it. Christopher had his reputation to consider. He would never marry a slut like you. Never!"

Daisy was finding it hard to breathe. It was as though the air was poisoned.

"I know a great deal about you, Miss Hills. More than you think," said Lady Rivers. "I know all about your secret meetings and your sordid little trysts with my boy. I know about all of it. You thought you'd fooled us, didn't you? But I know your type, so we had you watched. We wouldn't let a girl like you get her claws into our son."

Daisy stared at her.

"You look surprised." Lady Rivers crossed the room, her skirts swishing as though with an ire of their own, until she was standing in front of Daisy. She was taller than Daisy by far. When she reached forward suddenly and took hold of Daisy's chin, her thumb and forefinger bit into the flesh and Daisy cried out in pain.

"You're pretty enough, I suppose, and I can see why my son would find you becoming, but do you honestly think you're the first village girl Kit's enjoyed? Are you really so naïve? He was just having fun, as young men do before they settle down. Christopher would have told you anything to lift your petticoats – and I can see by your face that you've let him. You silly, foolish girl! He was never serious about you. He was just sowing his oats."

Daisy was shocked. She wanted to clap her hands over her ears to block out the ugly language. None of what Lady Rivers was saying was true, she told herself sharply. To know the truth, all Daisy had to do was recall the magical summer moments she'd spent with Kit: the days passed wandering the woods around Rosecraddick Manor, the hours spent swimming in the cove and then dozing beneath the midsummer sun, and finally the engagement trip to Truro. Then there were his letters and the engagement ring, not to mention the poems that he'd only shared with her.

Kit loved her. He did. He really did.

"Kit is – was – our heir. He knew full well that any prospective bride would have needed to meet with our approval, and you most definitely do not. There is no way my son would have proposed marriage without our permission. Kit understood that the future of the estate rested on making a good match. It was the only way to keep everything safe – and if it hadn't been for you, he would have done his duty and married an heiress."

Now Daisy understood everything. The Rosecraddick estate, like so many across the country, was probably burdened with debts and taxes. A good name and a noble lineage were all that shored up their bad credit. Kit had often mentioned how many American heiresses had swapped their papas' millions for marriage to an aristocrat; he'd teased Daisy by wondering whether he ought to follow suit. Then he'd kissed her and promised that all the treasure in the world didn't compare to his love for her. His parents must have pinned all their hopes on an advantageous marriage, Daisy realised. No wonder they'd been so bitterly opposed to Kit and Daisy's relationship. Kit's future marriage had been part of a bigger plan for the family's prosperity. When he'd decided that he wanted something more, there had soon been conflict. Love, like poetry, had never been part of Colonel and Lady Rivers' plan for their only son.

Daisy curled her hands into fists and dug her nails into her palms as she fought to hold her nerve. Mama would never have allowed herself to be bullied in this way, and neither would she. Daisy would keep her dignity and she would remain polite, but she would not be cowed.

"I'm sorry you feel that way," she said evenly. "However, you're wrong about your son's intentions towards me. They were truly honourable. Kit and I are engaged to be married."

Disbelief flared in the older woman's eyes. "Never!"

Slowly Daisy pulled Kit's letters from her pocket and passed them over. They made a thick bundle and her heart swelled to think of the words of love and the promises they contained. A mere glance at these would be all it took to make his mother accept the truth. Then Daisy could ask where Kit had been lost in action and leave the Manor as fast as she could. If she never saw the house or Lady Rivers again, it would be too soon. If she didn't know better, Daisy would have said that Kit's mama was insane.

Lady Rivers scanned the letters.

"And the ring?" she said eventually. "It exists?"

Daisy held out her hand. Without uttering a word, Lady Rivers reached for Daisy's fingers and held them up so that she could scrutinise the ring in the light. The diamonds sparkled with the same brilliance as Kit's love, Daisy thought, and she could tell by the frown creasing his mother's brow that she understood the significance of it. This was no shallow fling. Kit Rivers had been serious about marrying Daisy Hills.

"My son has exquisite taste in jewellery, at least," was all she said.

"We are engaged," Daisy answered quietly. "I love Kit and he loves me. We'll be married as soon as we can."

"Nonsense! Even if you were engaged, he's dead!"

"Lady Rivers, Kit's not dead!" Daisy cried. "I know it makes no sense but I trust my feelings. If you'll only tell me where he was posted when he went missing, I can travel there and start to search for news. My father's a surgeon with the Royal Army Medical Corps.

He'll know how to look for Kit and we'll find him. I know we will."

A spasm of peculiar emotion crossed Lady Rivers' face. It looked rather like fear.

"You won't find him. Christopher's dead and he's never coming back. Accept it."

What was the matter with this woman? She was Kit's mother. She should be fighting too.

"I can't and I won't accept that. Not ever. I love him and he's my fiancé. You have the proof in your hands."

Lady Rivers glanced down at the letters and her face darkened. "Well, I'd better do something about that."

Then, before Daisy could stop her, she hurled Kit's letters onto the fire.

"No! No!" Horrified, Daisy leapt forward to try to snatch them back, but it was too late: the precious pages had burst into bright flames. With a cry of dismay she dropped to her knees, the heat searing her fingers as she tried to salvage the charred remains, only for them to turn to dust.

Daisy was so distraught she couldn't speak. Silence filled the drawing room, punctuated only by the hiss of the fire and the weary tick of the clock. Daisy marvelled at the pain that stabbed through her; it was as though she had lost Kit twice in one day. All his words, his thoughts, his outpourings of love were ash. Thank goodness she hadn't brought his poems with her. Those were even more precious. She must find a safe hiding place for them, she realised now – one that Kit would be able to find should he return before her.

Lady Rivers turned to Daisy. "Was there anything else you wanted to discuss or is our business here concluded?"

"Kit's letters," Daisy whispered. "You burned them."

"Yes. How very unfortunate that they slipped from my hand. Now it's as though they – and you, for that matter – never existed."

In a swish of skirts Lady Rivers returned to her writing desk and picked up her pen. "See yourself out, Miss Hills. I have letters to write and arrangements to make. I would appreciate it if you could show some respect at this time of *family* mourning and leave Kit's memory to his *family*."

As she walked away from the Manor, Daisy couldn't stop shivering. The meeting with Lady Rivers had shocked her to the core. It broke her heart to have watched Kit's letters burn, but she knew that her love for Kit didn't abide in these items but in her heart – and no matter how bleak things felt and looked today, Daisy's heart was telling her that Kit was alive. She would find him and they would be together.

She would never stop looking. Tomorrow, her search would begin.

CHAPTER 15

DAISY, AUGUST 1916

Daisy had no time to waste. Kit's parents might be willing to accept that he was dead, but she never would. As she cycled home from the Manor, her soul stinging from Lady Rivers' spitefulness and the loss of her precious letters, she blotted her eyes with her sleeve and gave herself a stern talking-to. She couldn't crumple now; she had to be brave. After all, Kit and all those who were away fighting had suffered far worse. What were unkind words compared to shells and bullets? Lady Rivers' insults had hurt her dreadfully but Daisy would survive them, just as she would survive the loss of her treasured letters.

What Daisy couldn't survive was losing Kit. How could she face a lifetime without him? She would have to begin the search as soon as possible, Daisy decided. Even without Lady Rivers' help she would surely be able to trace him somehow. Getting in touch with his regiment might be a start. Perhaps Papa would be able to help. Her father was bound to have contacts at field and auxiliary hospitals. If she joined the VAD and was sent to France, she would at least be nearer to finding out where Kit had last been seen.

This was not the end, Daisy vowed as she freewheeled down the lane with her hair flying, having left her hat in her haste to leave the Manor. She would search for Kit and she would never give up on him. Never.

The Rectory was quiet when she returned. Daisy wheeled the bicycle around to the back of the house, then let herself in through the scullery door. There was no sign of Mrs Polmartin or Nancy, and the absence of the dog cart suggested that Reverend Cutwell was about on parish business. Daisy knocked softly on his study door and when there was no reply she opened it, exhaling with relief to find the room empty. Having selected some writing paper and envelopes from the drawer, Daisy headed to her room, where she spent the next hour writing a long letter to Kit, telling him her plans and promising that she would come to find him. This letter would never be posted but it helped Daisy to pour her heart out to him. Nobody disturbed her, and by the time she finished the letter and tucked it into her hiding place beneath the floorboards, twilight was seeping in from the woods. Then, and only then, did Daisy soak up the horror and the shock of her day and, in full grief, begin to cry.

Tears fell down her cheeks as the fire of determination was quenched by cold reality. She cried for Kit and herself and for everyone whose lives had been blighted by this war. She sobbed and sobbed, stuffing the quilt into her mouth to muffle the sound, but images of Kit continued to tumble through her memory, followed by Gem's laugh, Nancy's once happy face and even Dickon's swagger, all belonging to a lost and golden time when none of them had truly understood just how blessed they were. If only they had realised! If only she could go back to those sunny carefree days, even if just for a minute! This thought only made her cry harder, and by the time the sun vanished Daisy could scarcely breathe from weeping. Eventually she slipped into an exhausted sleep with the letter to Kit clutched in her hand.

That night the dream came again and, as always, Daisy awoke in the small hours. Fragments of the nightmare fluttered past her eyes, but this time they didn't panic her as they had in the past. Instead Daisy drew a strange comfort from them because Kit – she was certain now that it was Kit she sought in the dream – was still there, even if he was out of reach. He was waiting for her to catch up with him.

So that was what she would do. First she would hide his poems in a safe place where only she or Kit, should he return before her, could find them. Her diary and treasured things Daisy would leave here in the Rectory, safe and undiscovered until she came back to fetch them. Although it would pain her to part with these, she had already lost Kit's letters and she couldn't risk losing anything else on her travels. If she was to journey abroad to eventually help with nursing the injured there, it would be best to pack only the essentials to take with her. She would send Papa a telegram and prepare to join him.

There was nothing left for her in Cornwall now.

"My aunt's having a séance," Nancy told Daisy two weeks later. "Do you want to come before you go gadding off to France?"

"Hardly gadding," Daisy said mildly.

Her skin rippled with anticipation. The telegram had worked its magic and her father had agreed she could join him in France. Daisy was too young to volunteer, but Papa thought he might be able to circumnavigate this issue. Even if he couldn't, Daisy was determined to find a way.

It seemed impossible that in just a few days' time she would be sailing across the English Channel, with every mile bringing her closer to locating Kit. Daisy had refused to mourn or give up. All her energy was focused on finding Kit and their being reunited. Any tears had been shed in secret and she was resolved to move forward.

"All the more reason to come to the séance," Nancy was saying. "You'll be able to know for sure then if he's alive, won't you? Save you wasting your time wondering."

Daisy stared at her. "What are you talking about?"

"The séance," Nancy repeated. "You do know what one is don't you, Miss? It's when dead people talk to you through a medium."

"I know what a séance is," snapped Daisy. Spiritualism was growing increasingly popular since the war had started and she understood how some might find comfort in the idea that the dead could pass on messages. Papa said it was all a confidence trick with shysters preying on the grief-stricken, and Daisy was inclined to agree. The thought that the dead were floating about in some kind of foggy afterlife, where they may or may not be able to reach mediums, made her shudder.

"It's utter nonsense," she said firmly. "Dead people can't contact us."

"Do you know that for sure?" asked Nancy.

Daisy shook her head. She didn't know for sure, of course, but such a notion didn't sound very likely.

"Well, then. What's to lose? Our Sal went to see a medium to speak to her Sid, who was killed at Wipers. Sal said she really did speak to him because he knew all kinds of things that only *he* would know."

"What a conversation to have in the house of a vicar!" exclaimed Mrs Polmartin. She glanced nervously around the kitchen just in case the Reverend Cutwell happened to be passing the scullery, and then added, "When's this séance then, our Nancy?"

"This afternoon," Nancy said. "I'm going in case Gem comes through."

The thought of vibrant Gem with his dancing blue eyes, floppy dark fringe and infectious laugh being summoned from the afterlife made Daisy shiver. Surely it was nonsense?

"Do you think this medium could talk to my Bertie?" Mrs Polmartin pressed. Her eyes were bright with hope.

"Sal says she's ever so good and she has all kinds of messages come through."

"You can't believe all that claptrap?" Daisy asked.

Nancy shrugged. "It has to be worth a try. Lots of people do believe it. You'd be surprised, Miss."

"I certainly would," Daisy agreed.

"It would be so wonderful to speak to Bertie again," sighed Mrs Polmartin. She was stirring her tea round and around as she spoke, until the cup became a miniature whirlpool. She looked out of the window and her chins wobbled. "Do you know, Nancy, I may just go along. It can't hurt, can it? And if she's genuine then she'll know I called him Bobo. That could be our test, couldn't it?"

"You don't need to test her. Our Sally says she's the real thing," Nancy said, finishing her tea. "Up to you though."

"I think I will go," decided Mrs Polmartin. "Will you come, Miss Daisy? Just to see?"

Daisy wasn't keen but in spite of her scepticism she found herself agreeing to accompany Mrs Polmartin, who was so excited she'd started to shake. Besides, it was a nice walk across the fields to the Trehunnists' farm, with the last butterflies of summer dancing in the long grass and the skylarks soaring high above. She would miss Rosecraddick when she left, Daisy thought. It was here that she'd regained her strength and become a woman, so Cornwall would always hold a special place in her heart. This was her and Kit's place and it was beautiful and bittersweet to her.

The Trehunnists' farm was on the westerly side of the village. When Daisy had arrived in Rosecraddick it had been neat and well managed, with smart fences, closely grazed paddocks and hedges that were regularly maintained. The fields had been filled with crops and the lane to the house had been gravelled and tidy. The women of the village and the assortment of men left behind had done their best to work the land, but it was a growing struggle. The fields they hadn't managed were a tangle of long grass splashed with vivid ragwort and spiked with tall thistles, and the lane leading to the house was rutted and rough.

Even the farmhouse looked desolate. The curtains were drawn in the windows, weeds grew through the path and tiles had slipped from the roof. The stables at the side, which Daisy recalled had housed the strong plough horses, were now dilapidated and smothered in ivy. Bees hummed in the wildflowers, heavy with pollen, and somewhere a pheasant called from the encroaching covert. The boys had been so keen to go away and fight that they hadn't spared a thought of what might become of the home they were fighting for. Would any of it still be there when they returned? And how many of the lads who'd left so eagerly would return to restore order to the fields and the fences?

None of it made any sense to Daisy. This war was a bad dream that showed no sign of ending.

"Poor Anne Trehunnist," remarked Mrs Polmartin, as though reading Daisy's thoughts. "Two boys gone and her husband. What a cross to bear."

"There's still Dickon," Daisy pointed out, although in truth nobody had seen anything of him since he was invalided out of the army. The bully she remembered who'd taken such joy in causing trouble for her and Kit was suffering from what they were now calling "shell shock". Kit had written of it in his poem *Madness*; the macabre images of men clawing at their eyes and rocking forwards and backwards muttering were straight from Hades. Nobody deserved that fate, no matter how vile that person might have been, and Daisy pitied Dickon with all her heart.

Mrs Polmartin sighed. "Young Dickon's not himself, Miss. Maybe he never will be again. Some say it would have been better if he'd died."

"That's a wicked thing to say!" Daisy was shocked but the housekeeper shook her head.

"There are some things worse than death," was all she said.

Daisy wanted to ask what this meant but Mrs Polmartin's face had taken on a shuttered look. Although the sun was shining, Daisy felt chilled and drew her shawl across her shoulders. She felt as though she was being watched. Maybe it was the shrouded look of the house?

When Anne Trehunnist welcomed them at the front door, Daisy was taken aback to see the change in Dickon's mother. She had been a plump woman when Daisy had arrived in Rosecraddick, always beautifully dressed on Sundays, and with the same thick blonde tresses as her sons and Nancy. It was impossible to believe that this thin and stooped figure with sparse grey hair scraped back into a bun was even the same person. Grief, Daisy thought, was like poison. Deep lines scored the sides of Mrs Trehunnist's mouth now, and her eyes were the faded blue of a rained-out sky, as though all the tears shed had washed away the colour.

Daisy and Mrs Polmartin were shown into the dining room, where the brocade curtains were drawn and the lamps were lit. The fire was burning in the grate and shadows leapt across the walls. Nancy was already seated at the table with several other women Daisy knew from the village. The only one she didn't recognise was a tall lady dressed in deep purple and with dark hair pulled back into a bun from a high forehead. She looked just like a headmistress, Daisy thought as she took her seat. There was nothing particularly mystical about her. Was she really a medium?

Then she wanted to laugh at herself. Honestly. What was she expecting? A crimson cloak? A broomstick? Black cats? How Kit would tease her when she told him about this nonsense!

The medium glanced at the gathered women and one by one they stopped chatting, until a hush fell.

When the medium spoke, it was almost in a growl. "Lay your hands out," she told them, indicating that they should starfish their hands on the table in a circle, with their fingertips touching. Daisy, in between Nancy and Mrs Polmartin, began to feel nervous. It wasn't that she believed any of it; rather, this stuffy room was so filled with desperation and despair that she wished she hadn't come here. Daisy longed to be outside and in the fresh air. Kit would never be in a place like this – alive or dead. She wished she could leave but the medium had already started, breathing heavily in and out through her nose and with her eyes closed.

"With whom do we wish to speak today?" she asked.

"My son!" Mrs Polmartin cried, pushing a picture across the table.

The medium opened her eyes. They looked odd, Daisy thought: blank and far away. For a while the medium was silent. Then she began to speak in a low and halting voice. "B… There's a B. That's the start of his name. I'm getting B… B wants to speak to Em."

"That's Bertie!" exclaimed Mrs Polmartin. "And I'm M! I'm Maude. Oh, it's him! It is!"

"I have a message from Bertie to Maude," said the medium slowly. "Bertie wants to tell Maude that he needed the socks. The socks are warm, Ma. I'm so cold."

"Bertie?" Mrs Polmartin whispered. "Is that you, love? Are you there?"

"So cold, so cold, so cold. It's wet. So cold, so cold, cold. Cold, Ma. Bobo's so cold!"

Mrs Polmartin gasped. Daisy felt ice sweep across her body and her scalp prickled. How was this possible?

She met Nancy's eyes. *Told you*, the other girl mouthed.

The medium's voice was growing lower and with every word it sounded different. It was much deeper now – masculine, Daisy would have said. The fire was blazing but the room was so chilly she could see her own breath rising in clouds.

"It's cold, Ma, and it's wet. So cold, so cold," moaned the medium, swaying and rocking now. Her eyes had rolled up under the lids to show only the whites. Even her face seemed altered – twisted and tortured and grotesque in the firelight.

"Oh love, I'm sorry. I knitted lots of socks and I sent them to you," Mrs Polmartin sobbed. "We all did our bit to keep you warm."

Daisy couldn't believe what she was hearing. How many hours had they spent knitting socks to send to the troops? She'd wanted to scream sometimes with the tedium of it all and the incessant click-clack of needles ticking in her ears day after day. How did this woman know? Was it all just a lucky guess?

"Ma! Ma! It hurts, Ma!" The medium's voice rose to a shrill cry. "So cold, so cold, so cold. The mud, Ma! Where are you? Ma? I can't move, Ma! Bobo's cold! Where are you, Ma? Ma!"

"I'm here, love!" the housekeeper wept. "I'm here, Bobo!"

Daisy's skin was covered in goosebumps. The sucking, cloying mud and the cold that bit into the bones, as well as the endless booming of artillery, was the stuff of Kit's verse. Quite what she was witnessing now she couldn't say, but she didn't like it. As the medium shuddered and slumped forwards onto the table, Daisy rose to her feet. She didn't want to hear any more.

"Kit Rivers!" Nancy called out. "Is there a message from Kit Rivers?"

The medium sat upright.

"I'll ask my guides," she said.

Daisy glowered at Nancy. This wasn't what she wanted. It felt wrong.

"Please don't," she began, but the medium wasn't listening.

"Is Kit Rivers here?" Her eyes closed, the lids flickering and the eyes beneath rolling. Her voice became husky and urgent. "Can Kit Rivers step forward from the afterlife?"

Daisy was holding her breath so tightly her chest hurt. *Don't be there,* she prayed. *Don't be there, Kit! You're alive! I don't want to speak to you!*

A log shifted in the grate and there was a pop of resin which made one of the ladies shriek, but the medium didn't flinch.

"There's no one of that name here," she said, with the same authority as a head teacher. "I have no message or contact from this man and he isn't known to my guides. He hasn't crossed over. He hasn't passed."

"What does that mean?" Nancy demanded, but the medium ignored her, addressing Daisy instead. Amber eyes, dark with a knowledge that couldn't be explained, held hers. The message could not have been clearer.

"It means Kit Rivers is still alive," she said.

PART 3

CHAPTER 1

CHLOE

Where's the rest?

I turn the page, frantic to know what happens next, but there's only blank paper. The hand I've grown so accustomed to never wrote another sentence and Daisy's story stops as abruptly as her calamitous downhill bike ride. I flick through each empty page just in case she missed a couple out by mistake, but I already know this won't be the case. If the entries stop at this point it's because she intended them to. Daisy's time in Rosecraddick was over; a chapter of her life had drawn to a close and a new one was about to start. No matter how many times I flip through the pages or how far I stretch my arm out to reach beneath the floorboards in the hope there might be another tin full of information, I won't find anything else.

I feel utterly bereaved. Daisy Hills has vanished – and after all these hours spent reading her thoughts and sharing her adventures, this comes as a shock.

The voice I've been listening to for all this time has fallen silent and has left me with more questions than answers. I'm not ready to say goodbye. I want to know what happened. Did she go to France? Was she able to find out what really happened to Kit? What did she do after the war? Why didn't she come back for her treasures? There are so many things I need to know, not least what became of her.

271

Why did Daisy, and most of Kit's precious poems, vanish from history? Where did she go?

I screw my eyes up and try my hardest not to cry, but it feels as though I've lost a friend. I know this makes no sense. Of course there's no logic in crying for somebody who surely died decades ago – but from the moment I opened her diary, Daisy's been sharing her innermost thoughts and taking me on a journey back in time to the last century. She feels as real to me as any of my own friends. More real now, in many ways: she's become part of my new life in Cornwall.

I know about Daisy's nightmares, her favourite foods, her views on politics, her naughty brother and her dreams of being a writer, but most of all I know about her love for Kit Rivers. Those golden days before the war are perfect moments preserved in faded ink; with every glimpse of Kit there was a burst of joy as she walked across the cliffs to meet him, happiness swelling when she felt his arms close around her. For a while, life had bloomed into something wonderful for Daisy. Her stay in Rosecraddick was no longer a prison sentence with a crotchety old godfather as a gaoler. Instead, Rosecraddick had become the setting for her love story. Her words transform Kit from a stained-glass saint into somebody real: a golden boy from a gilded world, for certain, but one who laughed and teased and loved and who wanted nothing more than to share his feelings for Daisy with the world.

I wipe my eyes on my sleeve. If only she had let him. If Kit had married Daisy as he'd longed to do, then her story wouldn't have vanished – and his other poems, the ones she hid away from his horrible mother, would be as well-known as those of Owen and Sassoon. She would have been Kit's wife and their love story wouldn't have been consigned to dust and hidden under floorboards. That decision, however selfless, was the one small flutter of a butterfly's wings that changed everything. The timeline was shifted because of it, and a multitude of chances were lost without ever being discovered.

I have these thoughts a lot, about the "if onlys" and the sense that the world is loaded with possibilities that slip through our fingers like sand. If only Neil had been diagnosed earlier. If only the chemo had worked. If only we'd had longer. If only Daisy and Kit had been married. How different might our stories have been? Now there are only fragments left, memories disintegrating like autumn leaves and answers always tantalisingly out of reach. The "if onlys" are the saddest things in the world.

Our story ended the day Neil died. I know all the details. There are no questions left to answer and no gaps history needs to fill. The facts are there for anyone who might want to find them. For Daisy and Kit, however, their story is still waiting to be told. The clues are there if I can solve them. The window in the church. The carvings. The poems Daisy hid away after Kit's mother burned his letters. There's so much more waiting to be revealed. My arms are dusted with goosebumps at this thought. I'm so sure Daisy needs to finish telling her story. It can't end here. It can't.

I must have been reading for hours. I remember taking a break at some point, but having been immersed in Daisy's world I'd not noticed that the evening had since turned to dawn, nor how cold the attic had grown. I'm huddled in the chair and my hands are chilled. When I look up, I'm surprised not to see a fire dancing in the grate or a comfy bed covered in a pretty patchwork eiderdown. That old bedstead must have been hers, and maybe the age-spotted mirror too. How strange to think that a young girl with brown eyes and long red curls once peered into it, pinching her cheeks and trying to pin up her hair before running down these same treacherous stairs to meet the young man who made her insides fold so deliciously. I've peeked behind time's curtain and now nothing looks quite the same as it once did.

I glance out of the window into the December gloom. I wonder if I'll glimpse Daisy running across the garden with a basket swinging in

273

her hand as she races to the gate. Here and now the cedar tree looms against the blandness of a winter's dawn, but I'm seeing it in the spring moonlight with a young couple beneath, folded into one another and whispering promises. Swimming out of the greyness is the tower over at the Manor, where a handkerchief signal flutters in the breeze. These are views I've enjoyed every day since I first came here, but now I'm seeing them through Daisy's eyes too. Despite the murk, it feels all bright to me, newly minted and sharper with my new understanding.

I place the diary on the arm of the chair. On the floor are seashells, a marble bottle stopper from a long-forgotten picnic and, most precious of all, the soft lock of Kit's hair. And of course, inside the tin is the crumbling daisy-chain ring Kit gave her. All these are Daisy's treasures, so precious that she hid them away for a lifetime. To see them laid before me after reading about them feels almost voyeuristic. I kneel on the floor, splinters from the worn boards catching my jeans, and gently return everything else to the tin. Strange how these objects no longer seem like tatty odds and ends now that they've travelled across time. I close the lid, struck by the realisation that the last person to do so was Daisy.

Did she have any idea that she would never return to collect her belongings? And how would she feel if she'd known that in a hundred years' time a stranger would be party to her most secret thoughts and would handle her precious things? Would she be angry? Or is she there in the shadows urging me on and willing me to piece her story together? I'm certain it's the latter. Daisy and I are a century apart, but love and loss haven't changed. As I loved Neil, so she loved Kit; and as I fought for my husband's life, so she had vowed to fight for her fiancé's. The Daisy Hills who swam in her undergarments, who defied convention to see the man she loved and refused to give up on him, wouldn't want her story to be forgotten. I feel certain of this.

The morning's arrived. The view of the bay where Daisy and Kit's sailing boat once skimmed the waves is pearly and new. I glance at my watch, wondering if it's too early to call Matt. He's probably awake but it's Saturday now and this is family time for him, so I decide to leave it. Besides, before I do speak to him there's something I need to do, something that's just occurred to me. It's a crazy impulse and I could be wrong, but I have to act on it. Maybe Daisy's urging me onwards? The thought makes me smile as I place her diary on the chair with the biscuit tin beside it. I think she's just given me a clue.

I abandon the attic and make my way through the Rectory. I have the sensation that two worlds are overlapping. The landing with the bedrooms and the big bathroom shimmers and I find myself tiptoeing, not wanting to alert Reverend Cutwell to my presence.

The old stairs creak beneath my tread as though wanting to give my movements away. I grab my coat from where I'd draped it over the banisters, half expecting to bump into Mrs Polmartin and be tutted at for such slovenly behaviour. The people who lived here in Daisy's time don't feel very far away at all, and as I pass the dining room I think about the awkward meals eaten there. Reverend Cutwell could still be shut away in the study, penning his latest sermon. If I turn right along the panelled corridor and go to the kitchen, I'll find Nancy chopping vegetables while Gem, who I know looks just like Neil, will be teasing her and flirting. Merlin the horse will be looking out from the long-abandoned loose box and Clarence will be busy tending to the cutting garden. Each character is so vivid that finding the house empty makes me feel abandoned.

I'm being ridiculous. How can I miss people I've never met and who are long dead? I'm sure Matt would understand; he once told me that history is all about people and their stories, and I wish I could talk to him. As soon as it's a reasonable time I'll call him. He's the only person who appreciates the importance of Daisy's story. And it *is* important. She was Kit's inspiration just as much as the dreadful war that inspired his greatest work.

The big range will still be smouldering and there's a couple of hours to go before I'll need to feed it with logs – the same job that must have fallen to Gem – so I don't venture to the kitchen just yet. It will seem even quieter now and I'll be wondering whether shadows of the past are gathering to watch me as I empty the basket and place my kettle on the hotplate. I need to go outside and find out whether my intuition is right or if it's just my imagination running away with me. My stomach flips over with nerves. What if it's only the latter? It's not so long since my wild thoughts were a cause for being signed off sick.

The longcase clock at the foot of the stairs is ticking away the seconds, now as then, and beyond the window the same weathered gravestones gaze out across the wide sweep of Rosecraddick Bay. Nothing and everything has changed since Daisy Hills put down her pen, placed her diary and the last letter to Kit in the biscuit tin and hid them beneath the floorboard for the very last time. Yet I don't think this was all she left behind. In fact, I'm certain it wasn't.

I pull on my coat, unlock the front door and let myself into the damp Cornish morning. There's mizzle in the air, and the two seagulls huddled on the Rectory roof look rather fed up, but I scarcely notice the weather. I'm too excited. Like Daisy a century earlier, I scurry across the garden, pass through the gate and walk through the churchyard. It's too early even for Sue Perry to be up and about. St Nonna's is dark and silent, the windows dull without the light behind them; they seem to follow my passage like knowing eyes. The path turns left past the church and around to the lane. This was where the Rivers' carriage collected the family after the Sunday service and where a certain young couple once zoomed away in a shiny Rolls Royce. However, I haven't come here for those reasons. I'm thinking of something else Daisy mentioned.

I push the gate open. Droplets tremble on the metalwork before letting go, and my hands are wet and chilled as I step into the lane. They're even wetter when I start to run them over the churchyard wall, my nails scrabbling at crevices and clawing at weeds. There's ivy and bindweed lacing the stones, and I rip this greenery away as my hands read each surface as though seeking a message. *By feel* was how Daisy first noticed something special, I think as my fingers scrabble some more. She'd discovered something that was to become vital for her and Kit as they conducted their secret love affair. Didn't she write that she was standing by the churchyard wall one Sunday, bidding parishioners goodbye, when she felt—

A loose stone.

I feel it too. It's here!

In my haste to pull out the wobbling slice of granite, my nails split and I scrape my knuckles – but these things don't matter. Excitement unfurls deep inside me and even before the stone thuds onto the earth and my fingers have reached into the gap, I know what I'll find. Something, a beetle perhaps, scuttles over my hand but I don't care and my fingers don't recoil. They're too busy pulling out a small tin embossed with a feminine profile and the date *Christmas 1914.*

The Princess Mary Christmas tin! I can hardly believe it's still here. Daisy and Kit's hiding place is as good now as it ever was. If I hadn't found the diary then this tin would have remained hidden for another hundred years, maybe even five hundred more, perhaps even until there are no more years to come.

I open the lid and, even though I'm half expecting it, what I find within kicks my heartbeat into a gallop and sends my blood whooshing to my ears.

Curled up tightly and fastened with pieces of frayed velvet ribbon are yellowed pages torn from a notebook and crammed with narrow lines of handwriting. Even my untrained eye knows what this is. I can scarcely breathe, given that what I'm looking at is so precious.

Resting in my hands, and seeing daylight for the first time in over a century, are Kit Rivers' lost poems.

CHAPTER 2

CHLOE

"This is incredible. I can't quite believe it's true." Matt shakes his head for what has to be the thousandth time. "And all the time these were here hidden. All we had to do was know where to look."

It's late afternoon and we're sitting in the Rectory kitchen with Daisy's diary, the treasures and Kit's poems laid out in front of us. I'd read them over and over again as I'd waited for the hands of the clock to creep around to a time that was acceptable to call, and with each line I'd been transported to the Western Front. Kit's poetry is raw and brutal, and even I recognise a marked change in style and tone compared with his early work. These verses are angry at times, resigned at others. There's one, entitled *Mermaid*, that's so beautiful. It immortalises a girl with long red hair, who captures a young man's heart before he leaves for war. By the time I'd reached the final line I was so choked I could hardly speak.

The moment nine o'clock had arrived, I'd called Matt. Having asked about his daughter, who was desperate to have her friends visit and sign the cast now that her broken leg had been pinned, I'd told him about my discovery. He went so quiet that I thought we'd been cut off. Then I realised he was speechless. Once he'd recovered, Matt had asked so many questions I'd not known which to answer first. In the end I'd given up trying.

"Everything's here at the Rectory. Why don't you come and see for yourself when you're back?" I'd suggested. "It's all been here for over a century, so a few more hours won't make any difference."

"It will to me. I think I'm going to burst," Matt had groaned. "I can't believe it, Chloe, I really can't. I'm planning on leaving mid-morning, so I'll be with you sometime after lunch. See what else you can find by then, if you like? I'm half expecting you to track down the Holy Grail now, or maybe Lord Lucan!"

I'd laughed as I'd ended the call, and then I'd spent the rest of the morning rereading the poems and bits of the diary. By the time Matt arrived, I knew the story off by heart and had explored the Rectory from top to bottom, replaying scenes and trying to picture the house as it had been back in the early twentieth century. It was hard to be in the kitchen without imagining Mrs Polmartin ruling the roost or Nancy daydreaming about Gem. When I returned to the attic, fully intending to carry on with creating my studio, I found myself rooting through the piles of junk stacked in the corners, just in case there was anything there that might have belonged to Daisy once. There wasn't, but it was enough just to look out of the window towards the Manor and picture a handkerchief blowing in the wind and imagine how her heart must have lifted to see it.

Matt hasn't stopped reading since he sat down at the table. He can hardly bear to take his eyes off these precious items – and when he first saw the poems I thought he was going to pass out. A mug of stone-cold tea sits beside him, the second one I've made that's been neglected, and the plate of biscuits is also untouched. I nibble one but I'm far too keyed up to eat, and I know that Matt feels much the same as I do. When he picks up the poems, the paper trembles in his hands. He has yet to read the diary in full, of course, but as he turns its pages I see him blinking hard. I realise that I like him even more for being as excited about these discoveries as I am.

Hold on. What do I mean *I like him even more*? Do I have feelings for Matthew Enys?

He's an OK bloke. You could do a hell of a lot worse, remarks Neil, who's leaning against the range, his arms folded across his chest and with an amused curl to his mouth. *You have my blessing, Chloe, and it's nearly Christmas. Better stock up on the old mistletoe!*

At least, I think this is what Neil says. It's hard to tell because he's flickering like the picture on an old analogue TV set with poor reception, and the wintery light pouring through the kitchen window makes it hard to see him. He's less distinct than usual but he doesn't seem to notice or mind. Oddly, neither do I – although a few weeks ago the thought of Neil disappearing completely would have panicked me. So too would the teasing about mistletoe and other men. He may have gone but his words linger, and I find that I feel at peace.

I glance down at the rings still sitting on my left hand. Unlike Daisy and Kit, Neil and I did have some time together as husband and wife. It wasn't nearly enough but at least we had it, and for that I'll always be thankful. Poor Daisy's pretty ring was never joined by a simple band of gold. I've been blessed. I see that now.

"Chloe?"

Matt's voice pulls me back to the present. The diary is shut and the poems are stacked neatly beneath it, the weight of the book resisting their urge to curl up again.

"Sorry, Matt. I was miles away."

I wait for him to ask what I'm thinking about, but I should know by now that this isn't Matt's way. Instead he reaches across the table and gently wraps his hands around my wrists, his fingers skimming the pulse points. My heart shivers.

"You're amazing, Chloe."

"Hardly. I was just tidying out the attic. I didn't do anything clever."

"Is that what you truly think?" He shakes his head. "You really have no idea quite what you've found, do you? Chloe, this is huge! There are twenty new poems here from one of the most talented poets of the last century. It's like finding a new play by Shakespeare! Some of us dream about this kind of thing! I know Kit's work hasn't really had the recognition it deserves, but after this... Well, it's bound to make people look at him in a whole new light."

I remember how Daisy teased Kit for his literary pretensions and likened him to the Bard. How she'd smile now to hear this!

"*Home Fires. Regret to Inform. Madness. On Salisbury Plain.* These are really something else. There's a rawness in them and they're so bleak, but beautiful nonetheless."

"He was writing for Daisy. Kit wanted to tell her everything."

"Sometimes you feel that way about a person, don't you? There's no logic to it but you know that they share your way of thinking and match you thought for thought. It's a mutual sympathy that can't be explained or denied. Maybe it's even predestined?"

As he says this, Matt's fingers continue to skim my flesh. My breath catches and, unnerved, I slide my hands away and retrieve the poems from underneath the diary, hoping he hasn't noticed just how startled I am. While I do my best to regain control, I uncurl each piece of paper gently, smoothing it with my fingertips and marvelling at how, after all this time hidden in the wall, they appear as though they were written only yesterday. I locate *Swimmers* and *Mermaid* and lay them out as flat as possible, aided by cutlery and salt and pepper shakers as makeshift paperweights.

"Daisy's story's here too," I point out. "Without her, I don't think Kit would have been able to write so openly. Or, if he had, he wouldn't have been able to show anyone else what he'd written. You said the other poems only survived because they were sent back with his personal effects. I'd bet anything that those ones were also intended for Daisy's eyes only, rather than for his parents."

"You're right. Who would want their parents to read about the ugliness of war and the suffering? Then again, why would you want the woman you loved to know of such horrors? It seems cruel."

"It was *because* she was the woman he loved. Kit wanted to share everything with Daisy. She says that in her diary. They'd agreed that they had to have total honesty if they were to build a life together. Marriages have to be based on honesty, don't they? Otherwise why bother?"

A shadow crosses his face.

"You're right. There's no point otherwise. No point at all without honesty."

Matt's wife cheated on him, didn't she? Oh, well done for reminding him, Chloe. Nice one.

"I didn't mean—"

He holds up his hands. "Hey, it's fine. I'm OK with it. Well, maybe not OK exactly, but it's ancient history and it's true what you say: honesty is the most important thing. These poems are honest. I just wish we had Kit's letters too. Can you imagine?"

"I can, but maybe some things should remain private?"

He nods. "True. I can't believe that Lady Rivers threw them in the fire. What a terrible and spiteful thing to do."

I see Daisy falling to her knees and reaching into the flames, not caring that the heat burned her fingers as she tried to save the precious letters.

"Daisy writes that Kit's mother looked afraid," I say. "Maybe she thought she had to destroy the letters to make sure Daisy never returned to the Manor?"

"What could she possibly be afraid of? The worst had happened. Her son was dead. Whatever marriage the Rivers might have had in mind for him, it would have been irrelevant with him gone. I mean, it's not as if Daisy was a threat to their plans anymore."

"I know. It doesn't make any sense to me either. I'm just telling you what Daisy thought. You'll see it for yourself when you read the diary properly. It's all in there."

"I'll be up all night doing that," he promises. "I'll sit at Lowenna's bedside and read until morning. This is going to change everything, Chloe! It's already altered the way I see Lady Rivers. I've always had this picture in my mind of a grieving mother who worshipped her son and spent her last years fading away from heartbreak, with her only consolation being creating memorials to him – hence the walled garden and the window in St Nonna's – but now I'm having a rethink."

I think of the beautiful window in the church with the angelic Kit being raised to heaven. The stained-glass version of Kit doesn't look like the kind of young man who would defy his parents to marry a lower-class girl, tear about in his father's car or make love to his girl in hay barns and sailing boats. If it wasn't for the clumsy stained-glass daisy, this key part of Kit's life would have been totally erased.

"Those memorials are made in the image Lady Rivers wanted to leave of her son," I say. "But there's the daisy in the window which we know was added later on. Somebody put it there, Matt. Somebody else knew the truth and wanted to make sure she wasn't forgotten – but who? Kit was dead, Gem was dead, and Daisy seems to have vanished from history."

"Her father? Her brother? Maybe Daisy told them? She spoke to her father about becoming a nurse, so maybe she told him about Kit too?"

"Maybe."

"Or how about Reverend Cutwell? He was her godfather. Perhaps it was him?" Matt runs his hands through his hair in a gesture I've come to know means he's thinking hard.

"Seems unlikely," I say doubtfully. "Daisy's godfather disapproved of the relationship and I can't imagine he would have changed his opinion. Anyway, would he still have been alive? I had the impression he was frail."

"One of the things I've learned over the years is that, when you rule in the most unlikely scenarios, you sometimes discover that they're not quite as unlikely as they first appeared." Matt delves into his big leather satchel and pulls out a notebook and pen. "There are no records of the addition to the window, not according to Sue anyway, and so far I've not unearthed anything. We'll have to start at the very beginning and make a list of possible contenders."

"We?"

Matt smiles at me, a slow smile that makes my stomach fold over like cake mix turned with a wooden spoon.

"Absolutely *we*. You're a part of Kit's story too."

"Am I?"

"Of course! You're the person who found Kit Rivers' lost poems. More than that, you're the one who found his fiancée's diary and discovered this amazing love story which puts everything into context. This is a huge find! People are going to discover Kit's work for the first time and they'll fall in love with the story behind it."

I feel very protective suddenly of Daisy and her diary. I know she wanted to be a writer and thought carefully about her words, but what she wrote was personal. She never expected anyone else to read it. How would she feel if her private thoughts and the moments she shared with Kit were to become common knowledge? Would she be pleased? Horrified? Angry?

"It's their story, Matt. Shouldn't it stay private?"

"Lots of it will definitely remain that way," Matt assures me, "but the thing is that the Daisy element makes Kit Rivers human, if that makes sense? He's a person who loved and laughed and drove too fast and did all the things young guys do. He wasn't a paragon or a saint any more than the rest of us – and sometimes there's a danger of that happening with these First World War poets. So many of them paid the ultimate price and it's hard not to see them as saintly. Your discovery's made Kit come alive, Chloe. He's no longer a distant figure in a stained-glass window or a sombre young man in uniform frozen in sepia. He's real. So yes, you're woven into this tale as much as any of the others."

I hadn't thought about it this way. The concept of being stitched into Kit and Daisy's story along with Nancy and Gem and all the others makes my head spin. It's as though there's always been an invisible thread pulling us all together. Neil Pencarrow's there too, because without his love and his name and even his loss I would never have come to Rosecraddick and would never have started to wonder about the daisy in the window. Something led me here.

Of course it did, Neil says softly. He's in the doorway, although he's fading even as the words drift through my mind. *Did you ever doubt that for one moment? Nothing happens by mistake, sweetheart, but by design. It's just a matter of how we look at things.*

Sitting in the Rectory kitchen, at a table where I'm certain Daisy shelled peas and dreamed about Kit, I'm struck by the sudden realisation that life isn't a sequence of haphazard events at all. Everything that's happened, every kink in the road and every crossroads I've reached, has brought me to this point. Some of it was painful, some of it was wonderful and some of it I barely noticed beneath the minutiae of day-to-day living, but it's all placed me here with Daisy's diary and Kit's poems spread out before a man who occupies my thoughts far more than I ever expected.

Matt and Neil are both right. I was meant to come to Rosecraddick. It's the place where my story will also unfold.

CHAPTER 3

CHLOE

Matt took Daisy's treasured items back to Exeter with him a short while ago. He needs to untangle the legalities of who owns the newly discovered poems, and before he departed he spent an hour on the phone. The poems were found on Church property, but given that Eunice Rivers-Elliott bequeathed her distant relative's work to the Kit Rivers Society, it seems likely the poems belong to them – although Matt says this needs legal clarification and not just asking Sue Perry. The ownership of the diary, the tin and Daisy's final letter is also a grey area. Are they Mr Sargent's? Mine? Or do Daisy's relatives have a claim – if indeed she has any relatives? I call the letting agents, who are adamant that the landlord had given them written permission to clear the house. They promise to check with their client and get back to me just in case, so I have to be happy with this answer, although I already know I don't want to part with my find.

As the evening creeps in I pull the curtains, light the lamps and wonder what on earth I'm going to do now. There's a part of me that's itching to start searching for Daisy, yet there's also another part of me that's afraid of what I may find. For the time being, she's still eighteen, with wild red curls, a merry freckled face and a steely determination that fills me with admiration – and I'd like her to remain that way. I guess I feel that she belongs to me at the moment. Only Matt and I know about the diary and the poems, and I hug this secret knowledge close to my heart. There'll be time enough for the academics to pick it over.

"What will you do now?" I'd asked Matt as he'd carefully placed the diary, letter and poems in his bag and tucked the biscuit tin under his arm.

"Drive back to Exeter," he'd replied. "I'll read the diary properly once Gina goes and while Lowenna sleeps."

Matt had been trying to wind his scarf around his neck one-handed. It wasn't working well, so I'd stood on my tiptoes and done it for him. The scent of lime and basil and masculinity had made my senses reel and I'd wanted to reach up and find out how his dark stubble would feel against my fingertips. Unnerved, I'd stepped back – but not before I'd seen something flare in the depths of his eyes. It had looked a lot like desire and my heart had quailed. Whatever it was that was between Matt and myself, I wasn't ready for it. Maybe I never would be.

"And then what will you do?" I'd asked, keeping my distance and tucking my shaking hands into the sleeves of my sweater.

Matt had looked down at me. His mouth had curled upwards and his kind grey eyes had crinkled at me.

"About what, exactly?"

"The poems of course!" I'd said. My heart was thudding and I had no idea how to calm it down.

"Ah, yes, the poems. What else?" Matt had said wryly. "Well, first off I'm going to speak to a solicitor about who owns the poems. Then I'll call a colleague of mine from my time at Oxford, who's something of an expert on the Great War poets. He's written several books on them and he's as good a place to start as any. He'll know exactly what to do to check whether these are authentic."

"But the poems are genuine!"

"Of course they are. We both know that, but he'll be able to confirm it, which has to be done. Then I suppose the future of the poems is in the hands of solicitors and the Kit Rivers Society. I should imagine they'll want to publish them in due course and there'll be a lot of interest in Kit's life and poetry. I'll be honest, any publicity at all will be very good news for Kernow Heritage Foundation as well as for the Kit Rivers Society."

"And Daisy? Will you pass her diary to your colleague as well?"

I was holding my breath because so much was pinned on Matt's answer. I'd have been hugely disappointed if he'd been happy to give her diary away so soon and let strangers pore over the pages of her thoughts and dreams. It may be irrational of me, but I feel that Daisy belongs to us for now and that we're the only ones who can find out her story. Surely Matt's fizzing with excitement at the thought of tracing her?

"Daisy's your call," Matt had said softly. "You found the diary and her belongings, not me. I think you'll have to see what Mr Sargent wants you to do. But if he's happy for you to have Daisy's belongings, then I'd love to help you find out more and piece the story together, just as I'd love the story of her romance with Kit to form the foundation of what we do at the house – but that's a long way off yet. We'll need to try and trace her, which will take time. Then Daisy's family, if she has one, may want a say on what happens next. How about we focus on tracing Daisy Hills while the literary world does its thing and the legal people decide who the poems belong to?"

I'd liked this idea. It had integrity, although I wouldn't have expected anything else from Matt. Then he'd kissed me on the cheek, so fleetingly I thought I might have imagined it, and was gone into the gathering dusk. Once his headlamps had sliced through the gloom, I'd returned to the attic, where I'd sat in the chair staring out across to the Manor until the very last of the light was gone and the world was blotted out by nightfall. I would have stayed there for hours, lost in thought, but just now a frantic hammering on the front door made me spring to my feet and race down the stairs.

By the time I throw back the bolts, my heart's crashing against my ribs. It does so even faster when a potted spruce tree is thrust into the hallway.

"Surprise! And don't say you don't want it, because I won't take no for an answer. Nobody should be without a tree at Christmas!"

It's either a talking tree on the Rectory doorstep or Sue Perry holding a non-talking one in her arms and shoving it at me. Needles pierce my sweater and narrowly miss my nose, so I step back hastily. Call me old-fashioned, but I quite enjoy having two eyes.

"Sue! What are you doing? I don't need a tree!"

"Of course you don't. Nobody *needs* a tree, do they? But it's Christmas and what kind of vicar would I be if I sat by and let you be without one? I wouldn't be doing my job."

"I don't think Christmas trees are biblical," I protest, but Sue isn't listening.

"Now, before you say you haven't got baubles and lights, don't panic. I've got it covered. Tim and Cas are on their way to help decorate. We've got stacks of decs and we'll soon have this place looking festive. It's the least I can do, since you refuse to come and join us for Christmas dinner!"

I'm quite happy not to be festive at all. So far I've managed to put my mother off and I've been looking forward to a quiet Christmas all alone. I'd planned to paint all day, eat toast and have an early night without a bauble, tree or Santa hat in sight. Still, I know Sue well enough now to give in. Like she said, she's not one for taking no for an answer.

"Where were you anyway? I was knocking for ages," the vicar grumbles as I step aside to let her in.

"Up in the attic. I'm making a studio there."

"Oh! What a fantastic spot. I bet the light's amazing and the views must be incredible. Good for you. Let's put this down and you can show me what you've done."

Without asking where I want the tree, Sue charges down the corridor, pushes open the door to the sitting room and all but drops the spruce onto the floor. Needles scatter around it and I know I'll still be sweeping them up in June.

"Phew. That weighed a tonne! I've just done St Nonna's one too.

I'll be as skinny as Kate Moss at this rate," she laughs, brushing needles from her jumper and flexing her fingers. "Just as well I've brought some biscuits with me, else I might pass out. How about we stick the kettle on while we wait for Tim?"

I make tea and we take our drinks up to the attic. As I show Sue around my unfinished studio, I explain how I've been distracted by the discovery of the poems. Of course, I have to tell her about finding Daisy's diary too, and by the time I've finished retelling the story we've worked our way through a packet of chocolate digestives.

"There goes my diet," Sue sighs, glancing down at the empty wrapper. "Ah well, never mind. At least we shared."

I hide a smile because I've eaten one.

"But never mind biscuits," she continues. "What an amazing story! How wonderful that there are more poems. The Kit Rivers Society will pop with excitement!"

"I think quite a few literature professors will pop too. The poems are amazing, Sue. They gave me shivers."

"It's great news for Rosecraddick and the Manor if we have more background on Kit. To think that all the clues were right under our noses all along! Daisy lived here and she was the love of Kit's life. How romantic and, now I think about it, how obvious. Of course it was all about love! Isn't that what makes the world go round?"

"You old romantic!"

Sue blushes. "I guess I am. I want everyone to have their happy-ever-after. Don't you?"

I do. It's just a shame mine was so short. Still, it was longer than anything Nancy or Daisy or millions of other young women were able to hope for during or immediately after the war. I may have lost Neil, but at least we were together for all those years, even married for a couple of them, and I have a whole treasure chest of memories to sift through.

"Do you think the Church will claim the poems?" I ask Sue.

She looks thoughtful. "I'd say that's unlikely. They never belonged to the Church in the first place and, from what little I know, it was made very clear that all Kit's work was left to the Kit Rivers Society. Matt shouldn't have an issue there – unless Daisy Hills had hidden a few of St Nonna's candlesticks too? Or some chalices?"

"No, nothing like that," I smile.

"Did you find a photo of Daisy? We've all seen Kit but she's a mystery. I'd love to know what she looked like."

I shake my head. "I know there was an engagement photo because she wrote about it, but I never found it. Daisy must have taken that with her."

"Do you know where she went after here?"

"Not a clue, although she mentions joining her father at a military hospital. Matt and I are going to try and trace her. He has some ideas where to start looking, and with her father being a doctor we should be able to find something fairly quickly. I take it you've never heard of Daisy Hills? Or come across her name in the parish records?"

"Not that I recall," Sue replies, "but then she was here for a very short time really, and she wouldn't appear in the registers unless she married or was buried here. I have heard stories about Reverend Cutwell though. Village legend has it he was a right tartar! A real fire-and-brimstone man, by all accounts. I can't imagine living with him was a barrel of laughs for your Daisy."

"Killjoy Cutwell," I say, recalling Kit's nickname and Daisy's attempts to read the newspaper over the breakfast table. "So you don't think he was the one who put the daisy in the window then?"

"Unlikely, from what we know of him. And anyway, I'm pretty certain he died before the original was installed. He's buried here, I think."

So it wasn't Daisy's godfather who made certain that her story wouldn't be lost. The mystery deepens.

"There's nothing here left of his? No records?"

"I doubt it. The C of E sold this place off in the eighties and anything left would have been destroyed or shoved up here in the attic. Your best bet is to start trawling through the parish records for information about the people who lived here – and the same for the Fulham area, if that's where Daisy was from originally. Lots of records are online now. Hills is quite a common name, though, so it may take a while."

"Her father was a doctor and her mother went to university, which was unusual then," I remark.

"That should make it a bit easier then, surely? If Daisy became a nurse too, then that might help. The Red Cross might be a point of contact? There's lots of places to look."

Sue isn't wrong. The amount of possibilities is overwhelming and I hardly know where to start. "This is all Matt's area of expertise. I'm sure he'll know exactly what to do and where to begin."

Sue gives me a sideways look. "It sounds as though you and Matt are spending quite a lot of time together. Anything you want to confess to your vicar?"

I know she's teasing but I feel my face growing warm – which is amazing really, since the attic's icy cold. Luckily I'm spared any further interrogation by the doorbell announcing the arrival of Tim and Caspar, armed with carrier bags that are lumpy with baubles and stuffed full of lurid coloured tinsel. Tim has brought a takeaway too, so Daisy and Kit recede to the past as I'm swept up in the Perry family's tidal wave of tree decorating, fairy-light hanging and filling up on Chinese food. By the time they leave, the Rectory's looking festive and cheerful, if a little garish. Before I fall into an exhausted sleep, I can't help reflecting that Daisy would have thought all of this was great fun, even though her godfather would have been most disapproving.

The next morning finds me at Rosecraddick Manor by half past eight. As I walk up the drive I see the house through Daisy's eyes, a symbol of everything that stood between her and Kit, and I'm in awe of her courage. Even in the twenty-first century the Manor is imposing; with the added concerns about her relative position in society, it must have taken a great deal of bravery for Daisy to come here and speak to Lady Rivers.

Somebody's placed a small Christmas tree in the entrance hall. It's bravely twinkling away, but the cavernous space needs an enormous spruce reaching to the ceiling and smothered in white lights and red bows. I make a coffee, say hello to Jill and a couple of the other volunteers and then slip away on the pretext of sketching. I fully intend to do some work, and my fingers tingle with the longing to pick up a pencil, but before I start on my sketches I need to revisit a few rooms and overlay the present with my knowledge of the past.

It isn't hard to locate the drawing room where Daisy met with Kit's mother. The long corridor leads to a heavy door set within a granite arch, beyond which there's dark panelling inside. The room feels oppressive. The windows are now choked by wisteria, which blocks out most of the light, and there's no fire today to take the chill from the air. In my imagination I see the flames leaping in the hearth and hear Daisy's cry of distress as Kit's letters turn to ash while his mother watches. My skin prickles and I back away hastily. Is it fanciful to believe such unpleasantness leaves a ripple in the atmosphere?

I wander around the Manor, peeking into other empty rooms and picturing the servants and family going about their daily business. Finally, I drift through the oldest wing of the house and climb up to Kit's tower, where I trace the carved daisy in the crumbling window ledge and wipe the grime from the pane so that I can see the Rectory. The attic window glints in the sunshine and I smile to think of Kit tying his handkerchief to the catch while Daisy looks across, her heart leaping when she spots his signal.

"Where did you go, Daisy? What happened to you?" I say aloud. But of course there's no answer, only the haunting cries of the seagulls and the creaking of the old floorboards beneath my feet as I cross the room. When my phone starts to ring I jump, snatched back to the present.

"Morning!" says Matt when I answer. "I'm not interrupting another literary discovery, am I?"

"Hardly. I'm at the Manor looking at all the places Daisy mentions in her diary. It's fascinating, like seeing them for the first time."

"I bet," he says. "Look, I can't talk for long because I've just nipped away from Lowenna, but I wanted to let you know that I've spoken to the guy I was telling you about who's an expert on war poetry, and obviously he's really excited about all this and frantic to see the poems. I just wanted to make sure you were happy for me to pass them on?"

"What about who owns the poems?"

"I've taken legal advice on that, and there's no doubt that they belong to the Kit Rivers Society. I'm the Chair and passing them on is fine with us, but I want you to be sure before this all goes public."

I'm impressed he's asked and not just ploughed ahead. Matt's a thoughtful guy.

"It's fine by me. Those poems definitely need to be shared."

"I knew you'd feel like that." Matt's voice is warm. "I'll meet him and personally put them in his hands. Be prepared though; this will be a big story. The romance element will really elevate it too. I think there'll be huge interest."

"I do too, and when we know the full story we'll share it," I promise.

"But in the meantime, let's see if we can solve the mystery of the daisy window," Matt decides. "I'd better go. Gina will be sending a search party if I'm gone too long, and I've also rashly promised to read *Harry Potter* out loud to Lowenna. Stephen Fry doesn't cut it apparently: only Dad will do."

The pride in his voice would melt the coldest of hearts. We end the call, agreeing to meet up when he returns to the village. As I slide the phone back into my coat pocket I'm thinking that Matt's a wonderful father – and a wonderful man in general, come to that. I like him a lot. I like the way his hands felt when they covered mine and I like the way he says *we*, because it makes me shiver deep inside. When his eyes hold mine I feel warm all over and...

Hold on! What's happening to me? Do I like Matt as something more than a friend, or is this how all lonely widows feel when they spend time with an attractive man? I wait for the stab of guilt that ought to come from thinking that any man except my husband is attractive, but it doesn't come – and no matter how hard I try to summon him or how much I plead with him to stay with me, neither does Neil.

Just like Daisy Hills, he's vanished without a trace.

CHAPTER 4

CHLOE

"So far it's come to a bit of a dead end," Matt sighs. He looks exhausted. A week of tearing up and down to Exeter to visit his daughter is taking its toll, and I can't imagine that all the long evenings have helped. He's spent so many of them poring over printouts from genealogy sites and copies of records from various other sources. "I've managed to trace Dr Charles Hills and Mrs Marie Hills, but with his medical career and her Oxford education that was relatively simple. We already know that Marie Hills died at 6 Charlotte Villas in 1911 and Dr Hills died in 1937 at the same address. Daisy's brother, Edward Hills, was born there and he died in the same area at a ripe old age, but there's no mention anywhere of his sister. I can only assume Daisy moved away."

It's a raw Saturday before Christmas and Matt and I are in the pub, drinking coffee and thawing out by the wood burner. We've chosen to meet here because the manor house will be absolutely freezing without the fire. We've ordered some cheesy chips and commandeered a table in the window, where Matt's spread out all the research he's managed to do so far as he struggles to piece Daisy's story together. She's proving elusive. After she placed the biscuit tin beneath the floorboards and hid Kit's poems in the wall, Daisy Hills slipped from sight and out of history.

It's as though she never existed and I hate this. Kit loved Daisy. It was the thought of her that kept him writing and gave him hope. If he hadn't shared his poetry with Daisy, the twenty poems the scholars are now so excited about would have turned to pulp in the trench mud. Daisy deserves to be remembered and I'm not the only person to think this way; somebody else felt so strongly that they paid to add the daisy to Kit's window.

Somebody else knew about Daisy and Kit. But who?

In an attempt to find out, I've trawled a few websites myself. It's fascinating if time-consuming stuff and I've gained so much respect for Matt, whose painstaking research highlights my own clumsy and amateurish efforts. After only a couple of hours spent reading, my eyes were sore and gritty. I was searching for anyone linked to that time who might have known about Daisy and Kit. Sue had already shown me Reverend Cutwell's grave, marked by a plain cross starkly silhouetted against the sky (which conveys perfectly his stern personality). Gem had died long before him in the war, of course. I managed to find Nancy Trehunnist, or Nancy Poldeen as she later became. Nancy hadn't travelled far from home and I was pleased to learn that the young girl who'd loved and lost her Gem had eventually married and had four children. I couldn't imagine she would have paid for the alterations to the window, but it was one more avenue to pursue. Nancy's descendants still lived in Rosecraddick and it was odd to think I must have passed them in the street. Maybe I could trace them and ask what they knew? I'd also hunted for Mrs Polmartin, only to discover that she'd died shortly after the Armistice in the flu pandemic of 1918. So that ruled her out. Recalling how she'd wept for her lost son, I hoped she'd found peace. Both women were buried only yards from my front door, and when I'd returned home that day I'd pulled the weeds from their neglected graves and paid my respects for a few quiet moments. Gone but not forgotten. Nothing is ever forgotten.

I couldn't help being moved when I read the records; it felt like catching up with long-lost friends. After all, I knew these people! I saw them wherever I went and I heard the echoes of their voices. I was even sketching them in the places where they'd lived and worked, using Daisy's descriptions to help me. Matt had photocopied the diary for me and I'd read it several times now. The people and events it contained seemed more vivid than my own life. As I'd scanned all the historical records, I'd been hoping desperately to see Daisy's name again, but I'd found nothing to suggest that she'd ever returned to Rosecraddick. Mr Emmet the butler had cropped up and so had Clarence, the Rectory's ancient gardener. Both had outlived their employers, but I shouldn't be surprised by this. Hadn't I seen first-hand how death had no respect for youth? On and on I'd read, but it hadn't made the slightest difference because there were no mentions of Daisy at all.

She'd totally disappeared from Rosecraddick.

"Did her brother have any children?" I ask Matt now. It seems odd to think of little Eddie being a grown-up.

Matt pulls a sheaf of papers towards him, leafing through with a frown until he finds the piece he's looking for.

"He was married in 1930 and he had a daughter, Mary, whose birth was registered in Fulham, but I'm yet to trace her. She probably moved away and married. There was a son too, another Edward, born in 1939, and I'm still looking for him as well. These things take time."

I nod and take a sip of my coffee. "I can totally see that. It's like needles in a haystack."

Matt pulls a face. "If only it was that easy. This feels more like trying to find one grain of sand amongst all the others on the beach. The right clue's there somewhere but we have a mammoth task in front of us first. We'll just have to keep faith that at some point we do come across the information we need."

He sounds so disheartened and, without thinking twice, I lean across the table and squeeze his hand. It's a natural reflex of comfort that takes us both by surprise, but fortunately Matt doesn't seem offended; he squeezes mine in return.

"You've done a great job," I tell him, gently sliding my hand away, even though it was resting there easily. "You've traced Daisy to the hospital where her father worked, so at least we know she did get out to the Western Front. There were thousands of women nursing there, so it's an achievement that you managed to find her."

"That link was relatively easy to make once I'd found where her father was based. And we now know she was in the VAD right until the end of the war." Matt flicks through his notes. "We also know that she contacted the Red Cross several times during the 1920s in her search for Kit. She wrote regularly to the War Graves Commission too. She used the Fulham address for those letters. Although she must have returned home, she never gave up her search."

"Of course she didn't! How could she when there was no proof Kit was dead?" I cry. Several other people in the pub look up from their steak pies. I lower my voice. "There was no grave and no evidence that he was dead, so of course she never gave up."

"He was reported as missing in action," Matt says gently.

"That doesn't necessarily mean he died. You told me yourself that records were sometimes inaccurate back then. The paperwork wasn't always completed, movements of troops were confused, index cards were stuck together—"

He holds his hands up. "OK! I admit it! There could have been a mistake but, and this is the problem, there's no record of Daisy ever finding Kit, is there? He didn't return to Rosecraddick, which means she never found him. That's the tragedy of the whole thing. She wasted all that time and energy hoping she might find him when he was already dead."

"But you don't give up if you love somebody. You love them forever."

"That's how you feel about Neil, isn't it?"

We've never mentioned Neil. He's always there on the periphery – and sometimes he even chips in a word or two, although that's been happening less and less lately – but I never talk about him and Matt's never asked.

I'm the elephant in the room, Neil says from somewhere behind me.

299

Just call me Nelly! Shall I blow my trumpet?

He isn't here, of course, but if he were here, he'd be telling me it's time to be brave.

"I loved Neil," I say simply. "I love him still, Matt. I do and I always will. He was everything to me, just as Kit was to Daisy – but, unlike her, I know beyond all doubt that the man I loved is never coming back. I fought as hard as I could for him but it wasn't enough. No matter what I did I let him down because I couldn't save him."

It still stings. All the prayers and positive thinking and clean eating had counted for nothing in the end, had they? A tear rolls down my cheek and splashes onto the table. It's soon followed by another and another. Oh crap. The floodgates have opened.

"Oh, Chloe, of course you couldn't." At some point our food must have arrived without me noticing. Matt pushes the bowl of chips aside to hold out a napkin. "There's no way you would have let Neil down. You're the bravest and most tenacious person I've ever met, and I know you'd have done everything."

"Brave?" I half laugh and half sob. "Hardly."

"Yes, you are," Matt insists. "You've moved here to a place where you don't know a soul, taken on that mausoleum of a house and made it work. You've made friends and beaten the demons that stopped you painting for so long. You've even managed to stand up to Jill! If that's not brave, then I'm not sure what is."

I hadn't thought of myself as brave. Daisy was brave battling polio and defying convention and later on nursing at the Front, but me? Most of the time I feel like jelly.

"I'm sorry I've upset you," he adds. "I wouldn't have done that for the world."

I dab my eyes with a corner of the napkin. "You haven't."

"Fibber. I've made you cry."

"Cancer taking Neil has made me cry, not you. You make me…"

I pause, lost for words because what does Matt make me feel? Not happy, exactly – but less sad, that's for sure. I look forward to meeting up with him and I enjoy our conversations too. It's just that I feel so confused. If I love Neil still, then how is it that I'm thinking so much about Matt Enys? I flounder, searching for the right words.

"You make me feel real again," I offer. It sounds feeble but it's true. When I'm with Matt I feel that I'm Chloe again. I can paint and talk and think clearly once more. The sadness is still there and I know I'll carry it forever, but it's no longer unbearable. That's because, in some way I can't explain, Matt is taking its weight too.

"You make me feel real too," he whispers, and the way he says this makes my heart turn over. "I've never had what you and Neil or Daisy and Kit shared. I thought I did but it was only an imitation. I realised that fairly soon, even if I didn't want to admit it. I tried my hardest, God knows I did, but I could never be myself and we never really talked. It's not Gina's fault either. We just weren't right for each other."

Neil and I always talked about everything and anything. Even years into our relationship we chatted away and never ran out of words. Sometimes we'd lie in bed, holding hands in the darkness, and talk until the night slipped into day. I know that Daisy and Kit were the same and I suspect Matt and I would be like it too.

That's what terrifies me. Matt Enys comes very close to making me want to try again.

"That's why you ran out on me that evening, isn't it? Because you love Neil and you felt guilty about having dinner with another man?" he says now.

I think I'm going to pass out from the pounding in my ears and the rush of blood to my cheeks. I'd like to look away from his searching grey eyes but I can't because they demand the truth.

They deserve the truth.

"Yes," I say quietly. "It felt as though I was cheating on him."

He sighs. "I'm so sorry if I made you feel that way. That was really insensitive of me. I never meant you to feel uncomfortable."

"I know that, Matt. It wasn't your fault and I'm sorry I ran out on you. That was unforgiveable."

"No it wasn't. I'd forgive you anything, Chloe."

"Because I found Kit's poems?" I try to tease, but there's a strange tension between us now and the laughter withers on my lips.

"No, because of you," he says quietly.

There's a heartbeat's silence. Then Matt grins and the tension melts like grey Cornish skies into blue.

"Maybe I ought to say I'd forgive you *nearly* anything? If you scoff all those chips then I may have to reconsider!"

And then we're chatting easily again and he's dolloping ketchup onto the dish as he helps himself to my chips. If it wasn't for the damp napkin balled in my fist I might have believed I'd imagined the moment. Something's changing between us, something which echoes the journey we're following, and I hardly dare to name it.

But if I did? Then I guess I might say that it feels a little like falling in love.

CHAPTER 5

CHLOE

Even tucked away in Rosecraddick, there's been no escaping the festive season; as the big day draws closer, the village is as busy as it was in the height of the summer season. Holiday cottages that have been shut since September have been aired in readiness for visitors, and the Fisherman's Arms is packed with day trippers enjoying hearty pub lunches after their walks across the cliffs. Even the beach is being visited by brave souls swaddled in scarves and hats and with their feet pushed into colourful wellies. The main street is festooned with bright lights splashing primary colours all the way to the seafront, and fairy lights twinkle from cottage windows and from the front door of the manor house. Now that Sue's turned the Rectory into something that looks like Santa's grotto, I can't avoid Yuletide when I'm at home either.

Neil loved Christmas. A big kid at heart, he spent hours decorating our flat, draping everything in tinsel and playing carols at top volume through his beloved Bose speakers. If I hadn't put my foot down I know he'd have put the tree up as soon as Halloween was over and the outside of the flat would have given the Oxford Street illuminations a run for their money. He'd mull wine in an old jam saucepan we'd liberated from the bowels of my mother's kitchen cupboard and bring home carrier bags bursting with M&S goodies which we'd nibble in the soft glow of the fairy lights. Christmas for me always followed the busiest term at school, filled with parents' evenings and dark commutes. By the time we broke up for the holidays I'd be so exhausted it was all I could do to carry my bag upstairs, so it was Neil who did everything to make it magical. When

I lost him, Christmas lost its magic too.

This year I'm planning to keep myself to myself. My parents, after threatening to visit, are staying put in London – and my sister's decided I'm not about to hurl myself over the cliffs and so has given up nagging me to go to hers. It's going to be peaceful and I intend to let Christmas pass me by completely while I hide away in the attic studio and lose myself in painting.

Since finding Daisy's diary and Kit's poems, something deep inside me has unlocked and I've been painting all day every day, and sometimes late into the night too. As well as the commissioned pieces, I'm drawing the scenes Daisy describes and visiting the places she knew, in order to capture them in my sketchbook. I see the cove and the church and the manor house through her eyes and I even draw parts of the Rectory as I imagine it might have looked then. Maybe I'm hiding from my own reality by slipping into someone else's past. That's what Perky Pippa would probably say, but if it makes life more bearable then where's the harm? I'd far rather hide in Daisy's busy world than stumble about all alone in my empty one.

That sounds melodramatic. I'm not alone. Not really. I have the volunteers at the Manor to chat to, I see Sue most days (although she's pretty busy in the run-up to Christmas) and, when he isn't racing back to Exeter to see the twins, there's Matt too. I've only caught him a couple of times since our lunch because he's flat out with work. At least, I hope that's the reason and not because he feels awkward. Something changed between us that day, and no matter how many chips we ate and how hard we tried to steer the conversation back to Daisy and Kit, it wasn't possible to return to the way we were. On the surface all looks the same, but beneath there are all kinds of strange currents and riptides threatening to pull me under. The question I have to answer is whether or not I want them to.

I'm not ready to decide just yet. To be honest I don't know if I ever will be.

Today I've been painting since sunrise. Time has slid by in the magical way it always does when I'm absorbed in my work; although it feels like minutes since I first picked up a brush, the reality is that hours have passed. As I work I think about Daisy – it's impossible not to now that I know this was her room – and I have a gut feeling that I'm missing something. There's a piece of the puzzle that I'm overlooking, but what is it? At least I'm able to keep hold of her belongings, as it's been confirmed that Mr Sargent definitely doesn't want them, but no matter how many times I go back over everything, the trail is still cold. Daisy has vanished.

"Can't you tell me what happened to you?" I say, but Daisy's long gone and there's no reply. Matt and I are just going to have to carry on sifting through old documents and online databases until we get lucky. At least we have a wealth of information at our fingertips – unlike Daisy, who would have had to write letters and then wait patiently for replies. I can't imagine she'd have found that easy. Knowing her as I feel I do, I'm not surprised she took matters into her own hands and searched for Kit in person.

Leaving my painting, the third in the commissioned series, I shut the door on the attic and wander downstairs. The hall's bristling with tinsel thanks to the Perry family. Even the kitchen hasn't escaped and, as I make a sandwich, I'm treated to a display of flashing fairy lights that Tim's strung above the big window. They certainly look festive. With these, the heat of the range and the addition of a spotty red tablecloth that Sue donated, the room looks cosy and welcoming. All in all, the Rectory's starting to feel more like home. I recall what Matt said about me being brave, but looking back on the woman who arrived in November with no clue about firewood or wood-fired ranges, I wonder whether "stupid" would have been a better adjective.

Having been in the attic for so long, I decide to stretch my legs and enjoy some fresh air. It's a perfect afternoon for a walk across the cliffs and, as I set off along the path Daisy followed all those years ago, I admire Cornwall's bleak beauty. The sea hurls itself furiously against the rocks, boiling like a cauldron, and it's hard to believe that the long summer days of saltwater bathing and sailing will ever return. It's too rough to venture down to the cove, so I continue along the coast path until I reach the war memorial. A young couple dressed in hiking boots and bobble hats are already there studying the names.

"Look how many died," says the girl, pointing a gloved finger. "It's really sad. They're so young."

Her boyfriend nods. "See these, Mel? Gem Pencarrow, Peter Tuckey, Samuel Trehunnist and George Samson. They were only teenagers."

I recall how excited Daisy had said they all were. It was the adventure of a lifetime for these lads – and what a blessing it was that none of them knew just how short that lifetime would turn out to be.

"There were whole families wiped out." The girl cranes her neck to study the names. "Michael Trehunnist, Samuel Trehunnist and William Trehunnist. Three members of the same family. How awful. Do you think that was all of them gone?"

"Maybe," says her boyfriend, but it's clear his mind is on other things as he checks his watch. "Come on, babe, we need to get a move on if we're going to make lunch at the pub. It's bloody freezing. I need some mulled wine to thaw out!"

He reaches for her hand and they turn towards the village, their thoughts now on food. The lost generation of Rosecraddick is forgotten in an instant. Once the two of them have gone, I step forward and study the war memorial again. I've seen it many times before, but something that young couple just said has jolted me.

The names of the two sons and the husband lost to Nancy's poor aunt are on the memorial: Mick, Sammy and Will Trehunnist. Daisy had described how Anne Trehunnist, sick from the grief of losing two sons and a husband, had faded away to a thin shadow of herself. But Anne had another son, didn't she? What became of Dickon? He who signed up first out of everyone in Rosecraddick and boasted about his prowess with a gun? He was her son too. Where's his name on this memorial?

I step back and, shielding my eyes against the sun's glare, scan the names again and again. The bold black text jumps and blurs as though alive but Dickon's name doesn't appear. I even walk around to check the back of the memorial just in case I've missed it, but the back is blank and I'm not mistaken: there's no mention of a Dickon Trehunnist. Swaggering Dickon, who so spitefully relished telling Reverend Cutwell about Daisy and Kit, isn't mentioned here. His name's absent from the roll call of the deceased. That can only mean one thing, surely?

Dickon Trehunnist didn't die in the First World War. He survived.

I sit on the bench and gaze out to sea. This revelation feels like an important part of the puzzle, but I'm not sure why.

"Think, Chloe!" I say impatiently, and the calling gulls seem as though they're mocking me in response. *We know!* they cry. *We know!*

I do too. I just need to sift through the facts. Dickon was badly injured, I remember that much from the diary, and he'd been in hospital somewhere. He was shell-shocked, and just before the séance Mrs Polmartin told Daisy that there were some injuries worse than death – which suggested that Dickon's trauma must have been severe. Kit's poem *Madness*, like Wilfred Owen's *Mental Cases*, paints a harrowing picture of the effects of shell shock. He could have died in hospital, I suppose, but in that case I reckon they'd have put his name on the memorial too.

So, if Dickon did survive, then he could be the missing piece in the jigsaw. Dickon knew about Kit and Daisy when everyone else who'd also known was either dead or had moved away. He could have been the sole surviving person to still possess that knowledge and to hold onto their secret. But a stained-glass window? That makes no sense. Dickon was no fan of either Daisy or Kit. He'd deliberately gone out of his way to cause trouble for them. When

Daisy had visited the Manor, Lady Rivers had even alluded to him spying for her. It seems unlikely that Daisy's spurned beau would have wanted her romance with another man commemorated, or that he'd have shared the story with somebody else who might have done so.

The truth is just a fingertip's reach away but I keep missing it. *Think, Chloe, think. What would Matt do?* I wish I could call him and ask for advice, but Matt's with his family in Exeter and it isn't fair to disturb the precious time he has with the children. I feel awkward too; as I said, something's changed and I need time to process my emotions. As much as I like Matt Enys, and I do like him a great deal, my feelings for him are tinged with sadness and guilt because he isn't, and should never be, Neil.

So, I'm not going to think about feelings right now. Instead, I'll focus all my attention on facts. Matt would surely try to find out what he could about Dickon Trehunnist. I could kick myself for not thinking of this earlier. Maybe I could go online and see what information I can unearth. It's probably easiest to do that at the Rectory on my laptop, so I might as well turn back. My head-clearing stomp across the cliffs will have to wait for another day.

I retrace my steps and I'm just passing St Nonna's when a sudden thought occurs to me. Sue said that the memorial window wasn't installed until the 1920s, and Matt's told me that those who died later on from war-related injuries were often added to the list of the fallen. If Dickon had died just after the war, which sounded entirely possible given what Daisy had heard, then his name could be in the window – a detail that could save me hours of trawling through historical records.

The pretty church is dressed for Christmas. Greenery swathes the windowsills and tops the pews, fat candles burn at the altar, and oranges from an earlier Christingle service fill the air with festive spice. There's a tree and a nativity scene too, and the end of each pew has a jaunty red bow taped to it. Tomorrow's Christmas Eve and Sue will be celebrating midnight Mass. She's invited me to come and I surprised us both by agreeing. I'm actually looking forward to singing the ancient words of the carols and welcoming the arrival of Christmas, and as I walk to the south transept I realise that the bitterness that boiled within me for so long has gone. I still ache for Neil and I know I'll miss him every day for the rest of my life, but the anger's evaporated. Coming here has soothed my heart – and although Neil doesn't appear, I know he's pleased by this.

The memorial window shines brightly with the kiss of winter sunshine. As I stand before it I think of all the men of the village, young and old, who had believed the war would be over by that first Christmas of 1914. Many Christmases have passed since then but the world still weeps for their loss, while conflict and wars continue to rage in the far-flung corners of the earth. We don't learn from history. Matt told me this once, and now I have a greater sense of the waste of this. If we don't take heed of the lessons of the past, then we'll make the same mistakes over and over again. Maybe that's our tragedy?

"That's a long face," remarks Sue, joining me. "I thought only busy vicars and stressed parents looked miserable at Christmas?"

Her hands are full of carol sheets, which she's laying out on the pews in readiness for the evening service, and she does look tired. I guess this is her busiest time of year and Caspar probably has lots of presents that require wrapping too. Then there's the big Christmas dinner she's cooking for all the waifs and strays. Never mind a cassock – Sue ought to dress as Wonder Woman!

"I was thinking about the men who never came home for Christmas," I say.

Sue squeezes my arm. "It's a hard time of year for anyone who's lost a loved one."

I nod. There's no more to say and we contemplate the window quietly. My eyes scan the list of people, skipping through until the surnames beginning with T, where Dickon should be. Once again

Michael, Samuel and William are remembered, but Dickon's absent.

So either he didn't die of war injuries or there was some other reason why he wasn't added. I wonder which?

"You've got that look on your face again," Sue says.

"What look?"

"This one." She screws up her eyes and pokes her tongue out of the corner of her mouth.

"I don't look like that!"

"You so do. Matt does it too. Tim and I call it the Kit and Daisy face. It's very attractive! Not!"

Actually I think I might have seen Matt pull it a few times.

"OK, you may be right," I admit. "Although I wasn't strictly thinking about either Daisy or Kit, but rather somebody they both knew and who I think might have been linked to the daisy in the window."

"Tell me more, Miss Marple," Sue says, looking intrigued. "This story just gets better and better."

"I'm looking for a Dickon Trehunnist, who was the first lad from Rosecraddick to enlist."

I don't mention that he was a nasty piece of work; in fairness to Dickon he was very young and jealous, and I know from experience just how daft teenagers can be. Besides, this is the season of goodwill to all men and, if my hunch is right, Dickon may well have had a change of heart. Who's to say people can't change? I'd bet a great deal of money that fighting in the trenches changed a lot of men.

"Trehunnist, did you say?"

"That's right. I think they were local farmers? His brothers and his father died in the war, and they're mentioned on here and on the clifftop memorial – but there's no sign of Dickon, which means he may have survived. I need to do some more digging."

"Tracing your Dickon should be dead easy," Sue says. "The Trehunnists are very well known in the south-west. You must have seen their showrooms? Trehunnist Autos? Trust Trehunnists?" She starts to sing a catchy little jingle, which peters out when it's obvious I have absolutely no idea what this means. "You don't know what I'm on about, do you? The Trehunnist car dealers?"

"Aren't they farmers?"

"Not unless they're growing cars! Trehunnist Autos is the biggest car dealership around here. I think it's a Mick Trehunnist who runs the company these days, but they're very much family based and one of them is bound to be related to the man you're thinking of. Why don't you give them a call?"

And that easily I find myself sitting in the vestry, my feet singeing courtesy of the fan heater, and with my mobile clamped between my ear and shoulder as I scrabble to grab some paper and a pen from beneath the debris on Sue's desk. I've dialled the flagship Truro showroom and on just the second ring somebody picks up.

"Good afternoon! *Trehunnists! Motors you can trust!* How may I help you?"

This chirpy male voice has been well drilled. My mechanic at home always sounds practically suicidal when I call – which is ironic really, since what he charges is almost enough to send me over the edge.

"Hello," I say, uncertain quite where this call will go. Chances are I'll be fobbed off or put on hold to be tortured by tinny telephone music until I leave them in peace. "I'm wondering if you could help me? My name's Chloe Pencarrow and I'm doing some research into some local history. I'm looking to speak with somebody who might know of a Dickon Trehunnist, who was a young soldier during the First World War?"

I wait to be given the polite brush-off but it doesn't come.

"Dickon? As in Mr Richard Trehunnist, you mean?"

Of course, Dickon was his nickname. There was no Richard mentioned on the war memorial though. I would have noticed.

"That's right, and it would be helpful if that's at all possible," I say gratefully. "I appreciate it's a long shot."

"Not at all, madam. We get asked about Mr Trehunnist all the time. It's some story after all, isn't it? Really inspiring rags-to-riches stuff. He was an incredible man."

He was? I sit up at this, knocking piles of Sue's papers onto the floor. I'll worry about those later.

"You can actually tell me about him?"

"Better than that. You're in luck because we're having a bit of a company party this afternoon and everyone's here. Give me just a moment, madam, and I'll fetch Mrs Roe. She's the person you need to talk to."

There's a clatter as the receiver's placed on a desk, and I can hear the chatter and laughter of a party rise and fall like the tide for a few minutes before there's a click and then an intake of breath.

"Ms Pencarrow?" says a beautifully spoken voice. "I'm Kathy Roe and I believe you want to talk about my Uncle Dickon?"

CHAPTER 6

CHLOE

I drive to Kathy Roe's house the very next morning. I feel a little awkward about intruding on her Christmas Eve, but she was insistent I come over for coffee and mince pies while she told me about her Uncle Dickon.

"He truly was an exceptional man and I can't possibly do him justice over the telephone and with our Christmas party in full swing," she'd told me. "I can also look out some pictures and some information you might find useful. Besides, it sounds as though you may know some parts of his story that I haven't heard either."

I was mindful that the parts of her uncle's past that I knew of weren't the most palatable; nonetheless, I was keen to learn more, so I'd found myself agreeing to meet her at half ten the following day. She lived on Bodmin Moor – hence I set off early, with my phone set to satnav mode and the route already mapped in my head. I had a feeling that this was going to be an important meeting and I didn't want to ruin things by getting lost or running late.

As I drive through narrow lanes sunken between high hedges and roofed with the naked limbs of knotted trees, I brush my fingers across Daisy's diary, which is wrapped in soft fabric and resting on the passenger seat. I hope it brings luck and the answers I'm searching for. I guess I could have brought photocopies of the entries about Dickon, or told Mrs Roe about them, but I felt certain that having the original handwriting in front of us would mean more. When I'd mentioned the diary and Daisy's name, Kathy Roe hadn't sounded at all surprised. Rather, she'd exhaled slowly as though she'd been waiting a long time to hear of these things.

"Daisy Hills," she'd said softly. "Well I never, and after all this time too. Yes, Ms Pencarrow, I think you'd definitely better come over at a time when we can talk properly."

The satnav tells me I'm very nearly at my destination, so I slow the car and bump along a potholed drive, the spine of which is ridged with tufty grass. My little Peugeot does its best, but the moors are rough and I would have been better off in Matt's Land Rover and even better off if Matt had been with me. He's still away visiting his children before Christmas and I find that I miss being able to call him and chat. The Manor's been shut up for the festive period and I'm realising just how much time I've spent there sketching and talking to him.

I miss Matt Enys. Is that allowed?

It's fine, Neil says from the passenger seat, where he's clinging to the door handle as the car bounds over the rough drive. *And it's as it should be. Watch that pothole, Chloe! Jeez! What have you got against the underneath of this car?*

I laugh because Neil always was a dreadful passenger. He used to spend entire journeys telling me when to indicate and where to steer. His guidance wasn't always welcome but I did listen.

So listen to me now, Neil says firmly. *Spend time with Matt. He's a nice guy, OK?*

I nod but I have to focus on guiding the car over the bumps, and by the time I reach the end of the tree-lined drive he's gone. As I stop the car I feel comforted. I know he wasn't really here – I'm not totally mad – but those words are *exactly* what Neil would say. He was all about grabbing life with both hands and living it. I'm seeing him less and less lately but that's fine too. He's in my heart and he's a part of me and I know that, whatever direction life takes, a part of Neil Pencarrow will always come with me.

Winter sunshine dazzles me as I get out of the car. Shading my eyes, I look up at an imposing Georgian house that's three storeys high (four if you count the attic rooms), with a symmetrical arrangement of windows. A central flight of stone steps ascends to a sage front door flanked by potted bay trees in lead planters. The formal gardens laid out to the front are winter bare, but neat and well maintained nevertheless. As I walk to the front door my feet crunch over immaculately raked gravel. I'm impressed by how far Dickon's family have come in just a few generations. Back in 1914, Nancy had complained that Dickon's parents thought they were better than the rest of the Trehunnists; I wonder what her reaction might be today?

The front door swings open before I can even knock. A slender grey-haired lady wearing cream trousers, a flowing oatmeal sweater and silver bangles that chime on her slim arms smiles at me and holds out her hand.

"Mrs Pencarrow! What a pleasure to meet you. Welcome! I'm Kathy Roe."

I shake her hand. The grip is firm and the eyes smiling up at me are as bright blue as they must have been when she was a girl. Nancy and Dickon's eyes, I think with a jolt. Her hair, although faded, must once have been golden like theirs. How incredible to see the past woven through the present like this. Although she must be in her early seventies, Kathy Roe exudes vitality and humour and I like her instantly.

I wonder if she's like Nancy?

"Please, call me Chloe," I say. "Mrs Pencarrow sounds like my mother-in-law!"

Kathy Roe laughs. "In that case, call me Kathy or I'll sound like mine – and, believe me, she was a terror! Now, come in out of the cold, my dear. I hope you didn't have trouble finding the house? I know it's hidden away."

"Not at all," I say. "And it's a gorgeous spot."

"Thank you. I think so too, although I must apologise for the drive. It's due to be repaired in the new year. My late husband liked it this way – he felt it kept unwanted visitors at bay, the antisocial old bugger – but I'm tired of scraping my exhaust and the company will go bankrupt if I keep replacing my cars," she laughs. "Now that he's gone, God rest him, I'm going to tarmac the damn lot and get a sports car! If you can hear a rumbling, that'll be him spinning in his grave!"

I follow Kathy Roe inside, to a hallway laid with black and white tiles. Elegant stairs sweep upwards towards the right, and a cupola above pours sunlight down onto us and makes the baubles on the enormous Christmas tree twinkle. I can smell woodsmoke, polish and the spicy aromas of oranges and cloves, and as I follow Kathy along the corridor my mouth waters at the scent of mince pies.

"I hope you don't mind sitting in the kitchen," Kathy says as she leads me into a room with a cream-coloured Aga and a vast Welsh dresser covered with decorative plates and silver-framed photos of various family members. Mostly they're on ponies or sailing yachts. Seeing me looking, she smiles and adds, "That's my family. There's a lot of us and the whole bunch will gather here tomorrow for Christmas. It's become something of a tradition."

"You're a big family?" I feel a twist of envy because I grew up longing for this lifestyle. I always wanted to have a smiley grandmother who lived in a country house, with a ginger cat dozing in a basket beside the Aga and pots bubbling on the hotplate. I would have loved having a tribe of siblings and cousins to run around with. There'd have been ponies, sailing, beach picnics and autumnal blackberry picking. A semi-detached house in London wasn't quite the same.

"Huge. We breed like rabbits," says Kathy cheerfully. "Or rats, depending on whether or not you like us! Take a seat and I'll make us some tea and, since it's Christmas Eve, I think we can probably allow ourselves a mince pie. Calories don't count between now and New Year, do they?"

I sit down at the kitchen table, which is covered with a red and white spotty cloth and has a poinsettia taking pride of place in the centre.

"You have a beautiful home, Kathy."

"Thank you. It once belonged to my Uncle Dickon and he left it to me." Kathy places a teapot and two cups on the table and then fetches a cake tin filled to bursting with mince pies. Sitting down opposite me, she pours the tea and continues to explain. "I'm a Roe now by marriage but my father was a Trehunnist. He was Dickon's brother. Sugar?"

"No. Thank you."

She slides the cup and saucer across the table and offers me a mince pie. The golden pastry's dusted with icing sugar, and the pies smell so richly of spices and plump fruit that I can't resist. The taste is exquisite.

"I thought all Dickon's brothers were killed at the Front?" I ask, through a mouthful of pastry.

"My father, Robert, was the baby of the family and far too young to fight," Kathy explains. "I won't bore you with the family tree, but Uncle Dickon never married or had any children of his own. I was something of a favourite, I suppose, which is why he left this house to me. Not wholly undeserved, I might add! I worked in the family business all my life – as did my husband, who became a partner."

I'm finding it hard to keep up.

"So the family line didn't end with Dickon?"

"Hardly! I have two brothers and a sister, and there are distant cousins still living in the Rosecraddick area, although they have a different surname. As I said, my dear, rabbits!" Kathy replaces her cup in the saucer and steeples her fingers, giving me a searching look. "However, you haven't come all this way to listen to me rattle on. You wanted to know something specific, didn't you?"

I reach into my bag to pull out the diary. As I lay it out on the table I'm scrabbling for the best way to tell this warm and welcoming lady that the uncle she loved, and who adored her enough to leave her this house, was sly and cruel and a bully. It's going to be harder than I anticipated because of course Dickon didn't stay eighteen and a brash youth. He saw and experienced things that would have changed him forever and he must have become a very different man.

"I found this at Rosecraddick Rectory," I begin, as I open the cover, "It's—"

"Daisy Hills!" One papery-skinned hand flies to Kathy's mouth and she looks up at me, her eyes wide with shock.

"My goodness! This was hers? This was Daisy's?"

"So you've heard of her?"

Kathy's fingertips brush the diary almost reverently. "Oh yes."

I wait for her to say more but a cloud has crossed her face and she pushes the book away.

"Oh dear. I can't imagine that any accounts of Uncle Dickon in here are particularly complimentary. Chloe, dear, I'm afraid some things might be better left unknown. If you were hoping I'd read this you may have had a wasted journey. I know my uncle did Daisy Hills a huge wrong, but he did his best to make amends. Nobody could have tried harder, that I can promise you."

She knows something.

"Mrs Roe – Kathy – I promise I haven't come here to upset you and of course you don't have to read the diary," I say quickly. "I was hoping you might be able to help me understand a few things and maybe shed some light on a puzzle."

Kathy doesn't reply. She looks shaken.

"You've heard of Daisy Hills," I continue, "and you said your uncle did her wrong but made amends. What do you mean by that?"

I don't want to push her but I need to know. The story can't end here. It simply can't.

Kathy picks up a mince pie and crumbles it between her fingers before placing it back on her plate and sighing.

"My dear, Uncle Dickon was hugely private and quite a recluse by the time he died. I don't know the story first-hand, and most of this is family legend and hearsay, but I'll tell you what I can anyway. I think he would have wanted that."

"Thank you," I say.

"Uncle Dickon must have been tall and handsome once like my father, and I know he was the bravest of all the boys in the village because he was the very first to enlist when the First World War began – but when I knew him he was very different. He'd been in hospital for a long time with shell shock, and even all those years on he used to shake and mutter. Sometimes he'd yell out in his sleep when he came to stay. It was enough to curdle the blood, and his mood swings terrified us all. My father said that Uncle Dickon had returned to us physically but that the man he used to be died in the Great War. I guess now we'd call it post-traumatic stress, wouldn't we? Poor man. How he must have suffered."

She pauses and the ginger cat leaps onto her lap. I want to ask more but I know that the story will be told in Kathy Roe's own time, so I bite back the flurry of questions. Kathy strokes the cat absently and there's a faraway look in her eyes.

"As I say, he had dreadfully dark moods and times when he wouldn't speak to anyone. He never said a great deal about his experiences, but my father once tried to explain to me how in the war Uncle Dickon had had to do some truly dreadful things. He carried that burden all his life and as far as I know he never shared it with a soul."

It's a tragic story but I know Dickon wasn't alone in this. My reading and research have taught me more than I ever wanted to know about the horrors of the Great War and the shattered lives washed up in its aftermath.

"He worked hard on his return and he had foresight too. He sold the family farm – I don't think he could have coped physically anyway – and began to invest in automobiles. To cut a long story short, he was very shrewd and he made an absolute fortune."

I think about the stunning house Dickon left to Kathy and the chain of smart car dealerships across the south-west, which is his legacy. I'm impressed.

"So your uncle became very successful and wealthy," I reiterate. "That's a wonderful story, but you said earlier that he'd done Daisy Hills a great wrong? You know about Daisy?"

"Everyone in the family knows about Daisy Hills. She was the love of my uncle's life. It's the stuff of family legend. I don't know what it was he did to her, and," Kathy holds her hands up as though warding away a revelation, "I don't want to know either. It was a long time ago and it was his business, but the guilt of it was like a sickness to my uncle and I don't think he ever forgave himself. It haunted him forever and he said he wished he'd been a better person. He said that the thing he did to her ruined her life. It certainly blighted his."

I think of all the stupid things I did as a teenager. How dreadful to be haunted for your entire life by the actions of wounded teenage pride.

"I really don't think that was true," I tell her gently. "Daisy Hills was in love with another man and your uncle was hurt by that, which made him do something spiteful. If anything ruined her life it was the war coming when it did."

Kathy shrugs. "True or not, Uncle Dickon believed he'd ruined her life. He did his best to make up for whatever it was he'd done. He was a huge philanthropist and he gave vast amounts of money to charities. He also commissioned a big memorial window in St Nonna's Church, to honour the fallen of Rosecraddick. You must have seen it? It's next to the one for that poet which the tourists love to visit."

I sit bolt upright. "Dickon paid for the memorial window?"

"He certainly did – and no expense was spared. He was good friends with the then vicar, I believe, and he even sent for an artisan glazier from London to do the work. He spent a lot of time at St Nonna's and he worshipped there for many years. He was a very devout man, my uncle."

This doesn't sound like the Dickon Daisy knew. *That* Dickon bragged about his conquests, lied, bullied and couldn't wait to go to war. He wasn't exactly Mother Teresa.

"My uncle often said that the church in Rosecraddick was the only place he felt at peace," Kathy muses. "He had a big thing about atonement and redemption. My husband reckoned he should have joined the clergy or become a Catholic."

"Goodness," I say.

"You sound surprised?"

"Yes, I suppose I am. I mean, I know from the diary that he went to church regularly, everyone did, but he doesn't seem…"

I pause because I don't want to offend her by saying that the Dickon who pulled girls, made threats, and who looked forward to going to war hardly epitomised the teachings of Christ.

"He doesn't seem particularly religious from what I've read," I finish, as diplomatically as I can.

Kathy laughs indulgently and reaches across the table to pat my hand.

"Well, of course not! He wouldn't have been back then, dear! It was the war that changed him – and age too. He believed with all his heart that the shell shock was a punishment from God for something he'd done in his youth. He said the only reason he'd been spared death in the trenches was that he had to atone for his sin. I'd always thought this obsession with Daisy Hills might have been part of his illness, but now I'm not so certain. Oh, my! What on earth did he do to that poor girl? He didn't…"

I can't bear to think that her imagination is running away and conjuring all kinds of dreadful possibilities.

"No! Nothing like that! It isn't as awful as you probably think. I'm a secondary school teacher and, believe me, it was pure teenage stuff and very petty. Dickon deliberately caused trouble for Daisy's relationship with Kit Rivers. They were split up by his parents because of it – and then war came and things could never be put right. I think that was what he meant. He must have fixated on her and blamed himself for things that were never his fault."

But Kathy isn't thinking about this. She looks taken aback.

"Daisy Hills was in a relationship with Kit Rivers? As in the Cornish war poet?"

I nod. "Daisy and Kit were seeing each other, and his parents disapproved because she wasn't considered a suitable match. Dickon believed he was in love with Daisy and so he did his best to break them up, which caused no end of trouble. Kit was killed in the war, of course, and Daisy was heartbroken. It's a really sad story."

"Well I never," says Kathy. "Uncle Dickon was very taken with the Kit Rivers window too. He always said he'd helped to mend it and put it right. I never knew quite what that meant. I wonder who broke it?"

There's a rushing in my ears. So it *was* Dickon who paid for the daisy to be placed in Kit's window. It was his way of trying to make amends for his jealousy and his betrayal of Daisy and Kit. He'd brought them together in the only way he could and made sure that their story wasn't lost. Who would have thought it? I really hope the older Dickon found some comfort sitting in the church and looking at it. They'd all been so young when Daisy and Kit had been lovers, the same age as some of the kids I used to teach – and just like my students, Daisy, Kit and Dickon had no idea of what lay ahead. How were they to know that their actions would spread outwards for the rest of their lives like ripples on a pond?

"He meant that he'd broken the two of them up," I say. "That was what he thought, but the reality was that Daisy Hills and Kit Rivers were engaged. They would have been married if they'd had time or if Kit hadn't been lost in action."

"I've never heard that before. Are you sure? Uncle Dickon never mentioned it."

I incline my head towards the diary. "He wouldn't have known because it was all a big secret after he betrayed them. Kit's parents didn't approve of the relationship at all and forbade them to meet. There was talk of disinheritance and beatings and all sorts of unpleasantness. It's all written here. Recently a few more things have come to light about Kit Rivers, and I can promise you that Daisy Hills was definitely his fiancée. She hid a lot more of his poems away too; they've been missing for a century and now at last they've been found."

Kathy Roe shakes her head in wonder. "My goodness. That's so exciting. It sounds as though there's lots more to discover. It's like a puzzle."

"That's exactly it and why I'm here to see you! I'm following clues."

"Uncle Dickon thought he loved Daisy, there's no doubt in my mind, but how much of that love was really warped guilt we'll never know. Maybe I have more clues here for you?" Tipping the cat from her lap, Kathy gets up and walks to the dresser, where there's a big Manila envelope. Picking it up, she returns to the table and slides it over.

"I looked these out for you, Chloe. Uncle Dickon left them for me and I never knew what to do with them until now. Maybe there are more answers here?"

I reach inside and my fingers meet paper. Slowly I draw out a collection of photographs: sepia images of people frozen forever in time. There's a brawny young man in uniform whose confident gaze meets the camera head-on. There are also pictures of a family outside a farmhouse, a group of young soldiers in a dugout and then, finally and unexpectedly, two girls in jaunty boaters and pretty dresses looking as though they're finding it hard to keep still and straight-faced for the camera. One is blonde and looks just like a young Kathy, and the other has a pretty heart-shaped face, a forthright gaze and wild curls that tumble over her shoulders.

It's Daisy! It's really her!

I feel like I'm seeing a dear friend after far too long. My throat tightens.

"I think this was taken on enlistment day?" Kathy says while I struggle for composure. "By all accounts it was like a fair and they all had a marvellous time. The blonde girl is called Nancy; she was some kind of cousin of mine, but I can never remember quite what the relationship is. Once removed, maybe? And the other girl is Daisy Hills. My uncle kept that picture with him his whole life. I think he treasured it above his business, house and just about everything."

The photograph's dog-eared and furred around the edges. A fingerprint has smudged the corner and a splash of water, maybe a tear, has blurred the top – but even so, this decades-old snapshot of two girls forever sixteen and vibrant brings a lump to my throat. They were all so impossibly young. What chance did they stand?

Beneath the pictures is one solitary envelope that's still sealed and addressed to Miss Daisy Hills, care of an Oxford address. The stamp is franked July 1975 but there's a line scored through this, and written in faint blue ink are the words *return to sender – no longer at this address.*

"He traced her?"

"I think he tried to and this was as far as he got. He died shortly after this letter came back. A broken heart was what we said at the time, which sounds dreadfully romantic, doesn't it?"

It doesn't sound romantic at all to me, having thought I was dying of the same thing not so long ago. Now I just think it's terribly sad.

"It was harder to find people then," is all I say.

Kathy sighs. "It was, more's the pity. I think he would have loved to have found Daisy and apologised properly. Now all people seem to do is log onto Facebook and there it all is. It must be exhausting, and painful too if one wishes to forget."

I think of Neil's Facebook page, which I haven't dared look at since he died. I think *painful* is an understatement.

"Yes," I say quietly. "It is."

"You're most welcome to keep the photographs and the letter if you think they may help you."

I have an address for somewhere Daisy might have lived at some point. This more than helps! It's as though she's reappeared again, decades on and with vast echoing gaps, but at least Dickon did get this far. With Matt's help I know we'll catch up with her – and I can't wait to share all this information with him.

"Thank you." I slide the pictures and the letter back into the envelope. My hands are shaking. We have a possible address for Daisy Hills and we know for sure that the window was a clue. We're catching up with her, I know we are!

Matt Enys couldn't have a more perfect Christmas present. As Kathy refills the kettle and urges me to have another mince pie, it's all I can do to remain seated instead of jumping in my car and tearing back to Rosecraddick. I hope Matt's home soon.

I can't wait to see his face when he hears what I've discovered.

CHAPTER 7

CHLOE

I have no idea how I manage to stop myself from calling Matt at once and telling him everything I've found out. It's just as well I'm driving because otherwise I would have been so tempted just to whip out my phone and ring him, Christmas family time or not. Instead, I drive back to Rosecraddick with my thoughts whirling. To have swaggering Dickon recast as a lonely philanthropist who, filled with regrets, did his best to unite Daisy and Kit in the imagery of the stained-glass window takes some adjustment. I can picture him sitting in the church, an elderly and broken figure, asking God for forgiveness and praying that he could find Daisy and make amends. How sad that he spent the rest of his life eaten up by guilt and that his youthful jealousy poisoned his adult life.

So many lives ruined.

Still musing on this, I park outside the manor house and wander into the village to pick up some last-minute bits and pieces to tide me over. The village looks so pretty with the twinkling lights and the decorated shop windows. Everyone around me seems happy and full of excitement that Christmas Day is only one more sleep away. Small children hold their parents' hands and gaze wide-eyed at the toy train in the Post Office window, two giggling teenage girls wearing Santa hats and high heels teeter past trailing tinsel, and the pub door swings open to release a young woman racing out shrieking and chased by a lad armed with mistletoe. When he catches her for a kiss she doesn't put up much of a fight, flinging her arms around his neck and kissing him back as though her life depends on it. I smile to see how loved-up they are, before waiting for the pang of misery that usually follows such sights of affection.

It doesn't come. How strange. Maybe the Christmas atmosphere is rubbing off on me? Or perhaps I don't want to end up as lonely and as filled with regrets as Dickon Trehunnist? As I'm mulling this over, I bowl into the village shop and walk straight into Matt.

"Chloe!" he cries. "This is a nice surprise!"

My pulse is racing at coming across my friend so unexpectedly. Matt's wearing a battered leather jacket with a soft blue scarf that matches his faded jeans. His dark hair falls over his shoulders in glossy waves and his face glows with warmth from the shop. He looks delicious.

"What are you doing here?" I say.

"Err, shopping?" Matt holds up a flimsy carrier bag; through the thin plastic I can see that he's bought a ready meal, some milk and a packet of digestives . "Is that allowed?"

I feel my face heat up.

"I didn't mean you shouldn't be here," I say hastily. "Of course not! It's just that I thought you were in Exeter?"

"I was until about two hours ago, but Gina soon made it clear I was surplus to requirements when her new man rocked up. So here I am again, the Rosecraddick bad penny."

Matt says this with a smile but I'm not fooled. I know how upset he was about not seeing his children on Christmas Day, and it must sting to have another guy stepping into his shoes for the festive season.

"It's fine. Honestly, Chloe, don't look worried," Matt insists. "He seems like an OK person – heaven help him with Gina in that case – and the kids are so hyped up about Santa coming they'll hardly notice I'm gone. I'm more than happy with a microwave meal and some crap telly."

"Sounds like the perfect Christmas Eve." I pick up a wire basket. "Something very similar is on the agenda for me too. I'm just coming in to choose my Christmas dinner from the ready-meal selection."

"Allow me to assist," says Matt. "I am the meal-for-one expert – and there's not much I don't know about oven chips and chicken nuggets either!"

He takes my basket and I gasp as a charge of longing fizzes down my arm and through my torso at his touch, and zaps me straight in the groin. Lord! What is all this?

Luckily Matt doesn't notice me jump. He's far too busy peering into the freezer cabinet.

"May I recommend the chicken poppers or the frozen pizza? I'm proud to say that I can cook both to perfection! In fact, I'd go as far as to say they're my staple diet."

"It's a wonder you don't have scurvy," I scold. "Whatever happened to upping your green vegetable intake?"

"I'm not a fan of veg? Idleness? No point cooking for one? Take your pick."

We peer in and it's a meagre choice because the freezer cabinet has very nearly been emptied by last-minute shoppers.

"It's between frozen chicken tikka masala and madras – or maybe a lasagne. What do you think?" I ask.

"Oh, definitely curry. Log fire, rubbish movie and rice with spice. What more could you want?"

You, I'm shocked to find myself thinking as an image of curling up with Matt by the log burner with his arms around me floods my mind's eye. Thrown by this, I pretend to be fascinated by the range of frozen food and end up selecting several boxes of curry that will probably never make it as far as the range oven – if you can even cook such things in one, of course.

"Madras, wow." Matt peers over my shoulder. "You like hot curries then? I must admit I'm a wimp. It's korma all the way for me."

The madras was a Pavlovian reaction because Neil adored hot curries, the hotter the better, and instinctively I'd selected it. I'm most definitely a mild-curry eater too. Oh dear. I don't quite know what to do now. I can't think straight with Matt this close to me. He smells wonderful, of lime and basil and mandarins. My heartbeat's racing.

What did Kathy put in those mince pies?

Oh! Kathy! For a moment I was so distracted by the strange fluttering in my stomach that I'd almost forgotten about my visit to see her. It's a relief to be back on the firm ground of Kit Rivers and research. That's familiar and safe. Talk about Kit and Daisy, Chloe. Keep it professional.

"Oh! Matt! I was going to call you this evening. I've managed to find out who put the stained-glass daisy in the window and I've got Daisy Hills' last known address too."

Matt looks astonished. "Seriously?"

"Seriously. It's so obvious now that I think about it. It was Dickon Trehunnist all along. He became a very successful car dealer and he had the money and influence to put the memorial window in and tamper with the one for Kit. He was feeling guilty because of causing trouble for Kit and Daisy. His niece told me all about it."

"Trehunnist Autos. Of course." Matt shakes his head. "I can't believe I didn't make the connection before. I guess I'd assumed he died. First rule of being a historian – don't just make assumptions. I always told my undergraduates that in their very first seminars."

"Ah yes, Doctor Matt!"

"No jokes about games of doctors and nurses, please." Matt waggles his eyebrows. "Unless you want to get my hopes up?"

What's that supposed to mean? I study the freezer's contents as an excuse to avert my gaze, and when I look up again Matt's serious once more. His grey eyes have a faraway gleam.

"And an address for Daisy too," he says slowly. "I've only been gone a day and you've found all this lot out. Maybe we should have a job swap and you should be the historian from now on? Although you wouldn't want me painting pictures for you. Window frames and doors are about my limit."

He reaches into my basket and places the boxes back in the

freezer.

"That's my supper!" I protest, although I'm secretly relieved to see the back of the hot curries.

"Not any more. Apart from the fact that it's Christmas Eve and curry for one isn't really the way forward, I think we need a good catch-up." Matt strides ahead of me, swinging my basket and loading it up with an eclectic selection of whatever's left on the shelves.

"Prawns. Curry paste. Rice. Naan bread. Spinach. Potatoes. Wine." He frowns. "What have I forgotten?"

"Kitchen sink?"

"No, you have one of those at the Rectory," Matt quips. "Which is where I'm going to cook you the most amazing curry you've ever eaten in your life and where, in exchange for my culinary genius, you're going to tell me everything you've found out about Dickon Trehunnist."

"I'd tell you anyway! You don't have to cook for me. Besides, I thought you could only cook chicken nuggets? And spinach is definitely a vegetable."

"Doesn't count in a prawn sag aloo," he says dismissively. "Anyway, I didn't say I could *only* cook nuggets. How very dare you! That's just the kids' easy dinner of choice – and I'll have you know that Jamie Oliver is very afraid when he sees me step into the kitchen. Even Ramsay runs sobbing to his mummy. Prepare to be amazed."

Sometime later on this Christmas Eve, I'm seated at the Rectory kitchen table and being amazed while Matt dices, chops and sautés. As he prepares the food I fill him in on what I learned from Kathy Roe and we bounce ideas back and forth. Before long, my mouth's watering at the aromas from the cooking.

"I can't believe it! This looks fabulous. I'm impressed!" I say as he dishes up.

Somehow, and with just a few ingredients, Matt's managed to create something that wouldn't look out of place in Brick Lane.

"O ye of little faith. My mastery of the range cooker always does it

330

for the ladies," he laughs, setting a huge plateful before me and sitting down opposite. "Now, I hope this isn't too mild for you? I made it a little hotter than normal but I'm a wimp, I'm afraid."

I almost confess to my madras madness, but I stop myself in time because I'm still embarrassed. Try as I might to steer things back to the way they usually are, I can't seem to manage it. It's as though we're caught up in a current that's intent on taking us in its own direction.

Do I even want to swim against it? As Matt pours the wine and smiles at me across the table, I realise the answer's a resounding *no*. I glance around the kitchen for Neil, who's usually good for a comment or a piece of wry advice, but he's gone. Maybe Neil's absence *is* his comment?

Matt raises his glass. "To new discoveries."

I have the distinct impression he isn't just talking about our research. We chink glasses and I take a sip. Rich red wine as dark as sin slips down my throat and warmth floods me. At least, I think this is caused by the wine. For a few moments we eat in silence and the flavours in the curry are like a party for my poor taste buds, which have been resigned to toast and bland pasta for months on end.

"So, we now know that Dickon had a bad attack of guilt for his behaviour towards Daisy and Kit and spent the rest of his life wanting to make amends," Matt muses. "Poor guy."

"It seems an over-the-top reaction to me." I've been thinking about this a lot and I can't fathom it. "Why would he feel that way? He didn't owe either of them anything."

"War changed his perspective?" Matt suggests. "Dickon must have witnessed things that altered him, and it makes sense that he felt his shell shock was a punishment for what he'd done to them. You'd look for meaning in a war that bloody senseless, wouldn't you? God seems to have become his reason for it all. Dickon certainly wanted to atone and Kathy told you he spent a great deal of time in church. I don't think we can ever underestimate, or even understand, what the men went through in the trenches."

"I think he put the daisy in the window as a message," I say.

"For Daisy? Or for posterity?"

"Both – but also for himself, as a reminder when he was in St Nonna's. He would never let himself forget his sin. Poor Dickon."

"Aren't people complicated?" sighs Matt, and although we're talking about Kit and Daisy I have a feeling it isn't them he's thinking of. He tears off some naan bread and mops up his curry thoughtfully. "It's sad to think of him becoming an old man who spent his life reliving the past. Life's for living, don't you think?"

"Yes. Yes, I do."

There's a pause and Matt looks as though he's on the brink of saying something more but then thinks better of it.

He clears his throat. "Any more?"

The moment's gone. Maybe I imagined it? I feel oddly deflated.

"A little," I say, forcing my thoughts back to the food. "It's delicious."

"I hate to say I told you so, but…" he winks. "I told you so!"

He fetches the saucepan from the hotplate and ladles more sag aloo onto our plates, and the conversation heads away from the emotional rocks and flows instead to the topic of Daisy's last address. Matt is optimistic about this.

"I know Oxford pretty well. The fact that we know where Daisy was living in the seventies is really helpful. I wonder why she went there?"

"It was where her parents studied," I recall. "Perhaps she wanted to find her roots?"

"It's possible. Maybe some of Daisy's descendants are still in the area? In any case, we're a lot closer to finding her than we were, thanks to you. Not to mention the rediscovered poems, which are the best Christmas present any Kit Rivers fanatic could wish for." He reaches across the table and lays his hand over mine. "You're amazing, Chloe Pencarrow."

I wait for a quip or a clarifying comment, but his expression is serious. Matt isn't playing about now.

"Truly amazing," he says softly, "in every way."

He leans forward and for a moment I think he's going to kiss me. Then his lips brush my forehead and I realise that I'm right, only this is a tender and reverent kiss. A kiss filled with friendship and respect, rather than passion.

It's terrifying how utterly disappointed I am.

Do I want more? Should I want more? I could take the initiative, tip my chin up and press my mouth against his, but something holds me back. Maybe it's the knowledge that, if I do so, something will change between us that can never be put back to how it was. So instead, I smile at him.

"Thank you," I say quietly.

Matt smiles back and it's a smile of such sweetness that I almost crumple there and then and tell him the truth. Because, just like Nancy and Daisy, who sat here long before me, wrapped in daydreams and hugging their secrets close, I think I may be falling in love.

Of course you are, says Neil, from somewhere far, far away. *And so you should be. Happy Christmas, Chloe. And hopefully a happy new year, too.*

And maybe it will be, I think as Matt fills the kettle and chats easily about his plans for Christmas Day, but only when I know for sure I'm ready to be happy. Until then, I'm more than contented with things just as they are.

But without Neil being here, it still doesn't feel right.

CHAPTER 8

CHLOE

I've always thought Oxford is a beautiful city. Even the most poetic descriptions of dreaming spires don't do the place justice, and on a frosty December morning it glitters like a Christmas card. As Matt drives, I crane my neck to gaze up at the ancient buildings built of pale Cotswold limestone and dusted with lichen. Latticed windows wink and sparkle, grey rooftops meet the bright blue sky, and more bicycles than I can count are chained to railings. Even at this early hour there's a scholarly vibe, and I feel certain this is what drew Daisy to the place. She once dreamed of being a writer and I can picture her reading in the Bodleian or cycling along these streets.

"It's lovely, isn't it?" Matt says. He's been giving me a tour, pointing out the landmarks and showing me the college where he taught for a while. His face lights up as he explains the history of the city and the stories behind the famous landmarks. He must have been inspirational in the lecture theatre. Look at how he's captured my interest in war poetry and modern history. Kit Rivers aside, I haven't been able to stop reading and researching. Having been in education for years, I know a gifted teacher when I meet one.

"You must really miss it here," I observe.

"I did at first, terribly actually, but looking back maybe Gina did have a point? My job was becoming my life and it was time for a change. Besides, Cornwall has its compensations."

He smiles at me and I feel my pulse quiver. Since Christmas Eve I've been in a state of delicious anticipation and longing. When I'm not with Matt my thoughts are flying to him and I keep drifting off into daydreams. Nothing's happened apart from that one chaste kiss either; I'm worse than a teenager.

That evening spent in the kitchen was gentle and sweet and filled with promise. If I had acted and felt differently, then maybe it could have led to many things, including heading upstairs together – after all, neither Matt nor I are young and innocent. Nothing of that nature happened though. Instead, we talked and talked until our voices were hoarse and headlights and chatter outside announced that it was time for midnight Mass.

We'd headed to the church, where the ancient words of the service saw in Christmas Day. As the candles flickered on the altar and we sang the carols, I wouldn't have been surprised to see Kit Rivers seated in the front pew with Daisy a few rows behind, her brown eyes gazing adoringly at the back of his golden head while his fingers tenderly traced the daisy etched in the worn wood in front of him. Dickon Trehunnist could have been kneeling down nearby too, his hands folded and his eyes trained on the daisy window as he prayed for absolution. The service flowed by, the past and the present coming together as is so often the way at Christmas, and even Neil and I had our place there somewhere. It was part of a pattern that included us all in its design, and it was only now I was starting to understand this.

How strange, I'd thought as the service had come to an end, that after all my railing against God and religion I'd finally made my peace with it all in a church.

You always were contrary, is what Neil would have said, but he doesn't say it now and I know deep in my heart that I won't be hearing from him anymore. I'll miss him, I'll always miss him, but he knows I have to face the years ahead without him – and I'm certain he wants me to live every second of them.

It was a beautiful night with a full moon silvering the bay, and stars sprinkled across velvety skies. While Matt chatted to Jill, I stepped into the porch and watched my breath rise like smoke.

"I can see you're going to have a very happy Christmas," Sue

335

Perry said. Standing in the doorway to bid Merry Christmas to her flock, she beamed at me. "Oh, don't look so coy, Chloe! I'm a vicar but I'm still a romantic too. I can see the way you two look at one another."

I hadn't been aware that Matt and I were looking at each other in any kind of way. In fact, we'd sat as far apart as the crowded pew would allow.

"And sitting miles apart?" Sue shook her head. "Dead giveaway. Anyway, it's none of my business, except that it's obvious you're made for one another – and now you have the vicar's blessing too! You know where we are if you both want to pop in for food today. Tim's bought half of Asda and if I don't manage to share it I'll never fit into my little black dress!"

It was a kind offer, but in the end I had my low-key painting day and Matt drove to Exeter to see his children for a few hours. Gina had rung him up, saying the twins had been begging to see him, and so he'd been invited to share some of the day with them after all. I was surprised just how much I missed him – and Neil was nowhere to be found. Perhaps my husband was telling me that he wasn't prepared to hang around for any longer? Maybe there were rugby games to watch and rivers to canoe where he was now, and he'd had enough of watching me moping about? Whatever the answer, I felt that he was pleased to see me spending time with Matt.

On Boxing Day, Matt and I met at the Manor, where he pored over various documents and then, unable to resist, started to search online for people named Hills who lived in Oxford. First thing the next day he made calls from the Rectory kitchen while I went to the attic and continued to paint. Three paintings in the series were completed now and I was quietly very pleased with them. Now that I was painting again it was hard to stop – and it felt as if the brush had been in my hand for only a matter of minutes when Matt burst into the studio.

"How do you feel about a road trip to Oxford?"

"Right now?" Having been immersed in my artwork, I felt disorientated. Besides, I was still in my paint-spattered smock, with my hair in a topknot skewered with a brush.

He laughed. "Maybe not right now, but very early tomorrow? I've found Daisy's great-nephew and he's a bit mystified but he says he's happy to talk to us. The only thing is, he's going away skiing in the afternoon – so if we want to meet up it has to be either tomorrow morning or in a week." He pulled a face. "I don't know about you, but I can't wait until he gets back. I'll burst."

"Me too," I agreed. "What did he say?"

"Not a great deal really. He said she was his great-aunt and he never met her but his dad had talked about her. There were some documents he thought he could fish out for us to have a look at. He even thought his parents might have some letters of hers. Can you imagine if they were from Kit?"

"Kit was already missing when she left here, so it's unlikely," I reminded him gently.

Matt sighed. "I know and he never miraculously reappeared either, so Daisy was clearly wrong about him still being alive."

I hate that thought. Daisy had been so certain that Kit was waiting for her somewhere. She'd been adamant that she would know if he was truly lost to her. It's hard to believe or accept that she was wrong.

"Hopefully we'll find out more tomorrow," was all I said, and Matt nodded.

"I hope so too. Can you believe Daisy's great-nephew was only third on that list? Dave Hills? It was so easy I'm starting to think somebody somewhere wants us to follow these clues."

This morning we'd set off in the dark, racing to meet the sunrise and reaching Oxford by 9 a.m. Now we're only streets away from meeting Daisy's great-nephew and I'm suddenly nervous. As much as it feels that I know Daisy, this is still just a story to me – whereas for this Dave Hills she's a family member and this is his family history. I wonder what he'll tell us?

My hand slips into my bag and touches the cloth-wrapped bulk of Daisy's diary as though it's a talisman. *I'll make sure your story's told,* I promise her silently. *I won't let history keep you and Kit apart any longer.*

Dave Hills, the grandson of Daisy's little brother Eddie, lives in a smart terraced house only minutes away from the city centre. It must have been grand once but it's since been divided into flats. When he buzzes us in we have to step over the piles of junk mail strewn in the entrance and brush past a dusty rubber plant standing guard on the landing. His flat's on the top floor and by the time we reach it I'm puffed.

"Sorry about the climb. It's a bugger, especially with shopping," says the man in his mid-thirties who's peering over the banisters as we pant our way upwards. When we finally reach the summit, he holds out his hand. "I'm Dave and you must be Matt and Chloe. Come on in. I'm intrigued about all this."

Dave Hills has a wide smile and cute dimples, warm brown eyes and a mop of deep red hair. If the stairs hadn't already snatched my breath then the sight of Daisy's great-nephew certainly would; from the merry freckled face to the dimples in his cheeks to the mane of curly red hair, it's clear that he's related to the girl in Dickon's picture.

"You look like Daisy!" I exclaim.

"We have a photograph," Matt adds quickly. "There's a strong family resemblance. She also had red hair, I believe."

Dave rolls his eyes. "This ginger hair is a family curse. My sister has it and I know Grandpa did when he was younger, but I never met Daisy so I'll take your word for it. Anyway, we can talk about this in comfort and over coffee. Come on in."

With his front door wedged open with the toe of his trainer and his stomach sucked in as we pass, or so he laughingly tells us, Dave Hills lets us into his hallway. Then he leads us to a small kitchen diner flooded with light and boasting a bird's-eye view of the plane trees below. We sit down at a table and make small talk while Dave throws beans into a grinder and brews rich, dark coffee. It takes a while and I spot the cardboard box for the coffee grinder, set aside at the end of the room.

"Christmas present?" I ask.

"From my mum," he explains as he sets the mugs down in front of us. "I thought I'd try it out on you guys. Hope you don't mind being coffee guinea pigs."

"Are your family nearby?" Matt asks.

"They're in Chipping Norton, so not far. They'd have come over today, but they've shot off to see my sister in Reading. She's just had a baby and they're gaga over him." He takes a sip of coffee. "You do know Chippy's where Aunty Daisy lived at the end of her life?"

"To be honest we don't know all that much about what happened after she left Cornwall," says Matt. "That's why we're here."

"I'm not sure how much help I'll be. I didn't even know Aunty Daisy had lived in Cornwall," Dave remarks. "I know she travelled through France and Belgium a great deal and she nursed in London for a while – but she lived in Cornwall? That's news to me."

"Maybe I can fill in some gaps?" Matt offers. "I think I explained over the telephone that I work for the Kernow Heritage Foundation and we're restoring Rosecraddick Manor, the childhood home of Kit Rivers, the war poet? I'm Dr Enys."

Dave nods. "I Googled you. You used to teach here at Oxford. Modern history, wasn't it? Specialising in the First World War? Very impressive."

Matt flushes. "Probably sounds more impressive than it is."

Dave smiles. "I think you're being a bit modest there. Anyway, I don't know much about that, I'm afraid, and I can't see what any of this has to do with my great-aunt."

I slide the diary out of my bag. The cloth slips away and the leather-bound journal that Daisy was so proud of sits on her great-nephew's table. Without saying a word, I pass it to Dave.

"This is your great-aunt's diary. She lived in Rosecraddick during the First World War and she was engaged to Kit Rivers. He was the love of her life but he was declared missing in action and her story seems to have been lost. I thought I knew everything there was to know about him until this came to light," Matt says.

"Daisy Alice Hills 1914," Dave reads out loud as he opens it. He shakes his head in wonder. "And this was hers? She was engaged to a poet? Are you sure? I've never heard any of this before."

Matt nods. "Totally sure. It's some story and I'm really hoping you may be able to help us piece the rest together."

While Dave flicks through the diary we sip the bitter coffee (he needs a little more practice on that machine) and tell him everything we know about Daisy and Kit. By the time we're talked out, a good hour has passed by and Dave's looking stunned.

"This is absolutely incredible," he says. "You say there were missing poems too that she'd kept safe?"

"That's right," Matt tells him. "Your great-aunt managed to save some of the most important writing of the twentieth century."

"I'm not surprised she hid those away after that old boot burned Kit's letters. What a cow. Poor Aunty Daisy!" Dave's furious on his great-aunt's behalf and I just know that the way his brows knit and his chin juts out are all hers. "Can you believe she never mentioned any of this? I wonder why she didn't publish Kit's poems herself?"

I've been thinking long and hard about this and the only conclusion I can draw is that Daisy had felt the poems belonged to Kit. Maybe she was waiting for him to publish them himself when he returned?

"It's a mystery she took with her," is all I say.

Dave sighs. "Indeed it is. My parents have no idea about any of this and I can't imagine Grandpa did either. She certainly kept a lot of secrets."

Matt swirls his coffee dregs. "There are lots of gaps, that's for sure."

"There are, but I think I can help you fill a few in. Mum's the family-history buff and she knows a few things about Aunty Daisy, although to be honest most of the research she's done was on my great-grandfather, who was a field surgeon in the First World War. We're pretty proud of Charles Hills. My mum's kind of adopted him, I think, even though he's not a blood relation of hers."

"He was Daisy's father," I say.

"That's right. My grandpa, Edward Hills, was a doctor too. And my dad before he retired. My big sister's one too. Just not me. I'm happier with computers. Crap with blood."

Little Eddie became a doctor. Funny to think of Daisy's naughty brother having such a serious job.

"You're a medical family, all right. Daisy was a VAD during the war," Matt says.

Dave looks blank.

"A volunteer nurse," I explain. "Officially she was too young, but we think she might have lied about her age."

"Or maybe your great-grandfather pulled some strings to get her in," Matt suggests. "Anyway, the point is, she certainly played her part in the war effort. After that we lose track of her though. She simply disappears. You're the first lead we've had."

"I really hope I can help." Leaning back in his chair, Dave twirls a red ringlet around his forefinger. "A lot of this is pretty second-hand and cobbled together from what I've been told over the years, but I can tell you that it's a bit of a family legend that Aunty Daisy had her heart broken and never got over it. She never married and she spent her whole life searching for her fiancé, who'd been lost in action in the First World War."

"Kit Rivers," I say, and Dave nods.

"I guess so, but we never knew his name. Now I'm starting to wish I'd asked Grandpa more about it all when he was alive, but to me she was just an old lady I'd never met. She wasn't very interesting."

I feel a sting of indignation. "Daisy was funny and clever and brave!"

"I'm sure she was all those things," Dave says hastily. "Sorry, I didn't mean to sound disparaging. I'm afraid I was just a little boy when Grandpa spoke of her, and her story didn't really interest me. Any pictures I saw of her were an elderly lady who lived all alone."

"So she never married?" Sorrow clutches my heart like a fist.

"No, never. My dad says she carried sadness with her like a heavy backpack because she'd lost her fiancé in the war. I had no idea he was anyone out of the ordinary, though. Hers was a tragic story, but hardly uncommon; I've never really thought to ask about it. So many women lost their men back then, didn't they?"

"They did and lots of them never married because of the war," Matt says. "Entire futures were wiped out and family lives never lived because of the loss of a whole generation. I'm always struck by all those private tragedies."

"Yes, that was definitely the case for Daisy," Dave remarks. "She travelled a lot, Mum says, searching for her fiancé in case he'd lost his memory and was in a hospital somewhere. She did that for years. Then she wrote letters to the Red Cross and the War Graves Commission. She was pretty tireless by all accounts. The story goes that she always believed her fiancé was alive somewhere and she'd sworn she would wait for him forever, so that was exactly what she did."

I will love him every day and until my eyes close for the very last time.

I hear Daisy's words from the journal as clearly as though she were sitting next to me. She had meant it with all her heart. There had only ever been Kit. If there was even a slim chance he might return, of course she would wait for him.

"She had a sad life, didn't she? She had no children or family of her own," Dave continues. "I think she helped out with my dad when he was small, which might explain why she settled in Oxford. Dad was the closest thing to a son she had, and Daisy wanted to be near him when she was older. She owned a small house here for a while too, which she bought with the money her godfather left her and—"

"Her godfather left her money?" I sit up at this. Such generosity doesn't sound like the Reverend Cutwell to me. "Really? Are you sure?"

"According to my dad he left her the lot, so she eventually bought a house in the city and a cottage in Chipping Norton. Grandpa sold them both after she died in the seventies. Dad really wishes he hadn't. They'd be worth a fortune now!"

I'm not interested in discussing the housing market.

"'Where's Daisy buried?" I ask Dave. I want to go there. I need to go there.

"She wasn't buried. She was cremated and she asked for her ashes to be scattered in the sea. I think Grandpa organised it but, again, it was before I was born and he's long gone too. I can ask my dad. He might know. I bet it was where Daisy met Kit, wasn't it?"

I glance at Matt and I know he's thinking the same as me. This must have been at Rosecraddick. Daisy's been there all along, watching and urging me on. Her ashes were scattered in the cove. I just know it. She's been there the whole time.

"I think it must have been," Matt agrees.

Dave checks his watch and sighs. "I'd love to talk more about all this and I know my parents will too, but I really need to get going if I'm to make it to Heathrow. I've got a few bits and pieces here which make more sense to me now, and I'm sure they'll help you. If you take them with you and you manage to figure the rest of it out, then I'd be interested to know more."

He fetches a carrier bag from the worktop. It's full of envelopes.

"It's letters mostly, and a couple of photos," he says as he hands them to Matt. "There's some jewellery too that Mum looked out. You're really welcome to see it but I'd better keep it here just in case..."

The words peter out and Dave's fair skin flushes.

"That's absolutely fine," Matt reassures him. "I wouldn't expect you to part with anything valuable to a stranger."

Dave looks relieved. "It's not that I don't trust you or believe you, and I don't think it's worth much, but it's a family ring."

I lean forward. "A ring? Can I see it?"

"Sure. Help yourself. It's in a box somewhere at the bottom of the bag, amongst all the other stuff."

There must be over fifty letters in the bag Matt's holding, each with just the initials K.R. and a date on the envelope. Every single one is sealed.

"I have no idea what they are," Dave confesses. "Dad said they were with her when she passed away, so they must have been important, but we've never opened them. It didn't feel right. Are they to him, do you think? Kit?"

"I think they must be." Matt's shuffling through the envelopes. "They're all dated on the same day and it looks as though she wrote one a year. One a year for over fifty years."

Dave shakes his head. "Poor Aunty Daisy. To think that she missed this guy for the rest of her life. It's tragic, isn't it? She just couldn't move on."

"She didn't know for certain what had happened to Kit, so she was never able to stop hoping," I say.

"Closure, you mean?"

That's a word Perky Pippa liked to use. At the time I let it all wash over me because I'd been convinced that I was never, ever going to accept that Neil was gone, but now I see she'd been right. All those clichés about time healing were true. I'm not sure if acceptance is the right word because I'll always rail against the unfairness of losing him; still, at least there's no doubt about what happened to Neil. I was there to see it, I arranged the funeral and I said goodbye to the plume of grey that danced across the lake. Daisy never had that; she never knew for sure what became of Kit. Of course she never gave up.

"That's exactly it," I agree.

"It's so strange to think of her as a young woman in love," Dave says quietly. "I never met my great-aunt. I'd love to know more."

"By rights her diary and belongings should go to her family. We can leave everything with you, if you'd like?" Matt offers, but Dave waves his hand.

"No, don't do that. You guys found it all and if you hadn't her story would still be lost. Pass me some photocopies. That way I can share it with my folks. If anything, her diary belongs at this house you told me about, with all the other bits you found. After all, she's part of the Kit Rivers story, isn't she?"

"She *is* the Kit Rivers story. Without Daisy he may not have written as honestly as he did. She didn't just safeguard his work: she inspired him," Matt says. "Your Great-Aunt Daisy's part of the literary heritage of World War One and I promise I'll do everything I can to make sure her story isn't forgotten."

Dave plucks a photo from the bag. "Well, here she is as a girl. Hey! She was beautiful and he was really quite handsome. They look like film stars."

I lean over and study the picture. A young couple stare out at me across the decades. They're in a formal pose, the man in his uniform and the girl looking startlingly modern with her direct gaze, wild curls and pretty dress. The bottom right-hand corner of the picture bears the name of a long-lost photographic studio in Truro and the date, May 1916.

"That's the photo they had taken when they got engaged! Daisy writes about it!"

I may be in an attic flat in the middle of a different city a century later, but it's that long-ago day in Truro I'm seeing, Daisy and Kit arm in arm as they walk along the street to the grand hotel where they celebrated. When Dave passes me the daisy ring I can hardly breathe. It's as sparkly now as it must have been then, and to see it for real is incredible. It's a tangible symbol of a love and a promise that neither death nor time could erase.

I can't quite believe I'm touching the very same ring that Kit Rivers placed on Daisy Hills' finger.

CHAPTER 9

CHLOE

To my beloved Kit – how do I miss you?

I miss you in the early hours of the morning, when we used to meet each other at the cove more asleep than awake, and you would hold me in your arms warm and safe until the sun rose. I miss you at breakfast when I give Reverend Cutwell his paper – read first by me, of course! When I despair a little at the world I miss you making me smile and promising all will be well.

I miss you when I sit in church and your seat in the front pew is empty. I miss you when I walk past Rosecraddick Manor. I always knew you were at the window watching me until I was lost from sight. Now when I walk past I say to myself, 'Don't look back – he isn't there.' But I do look back, and when I see that there's no handkerchief at your tower window my heart breaks all over again.

Small things occur in my day and the thought flashes as always, 'I must tell Kit!', and so I save up the little treasures to share with you in my letters – snippets from a patchwork of observations that I know you will unpick and stitch back into poems. Then I remember there is no Kit to tell, that you are not going to meet me in our cove or leave a poem in the wall. I don't know how to tell you any of this now, my love, because I don't know where you are or how to find you.

When I walk down to the beach I still feel that flutter of excitement as I watch out for you. Sometimes I expect to find you waiting there for me, wearing your jacket with the sleeves rolled up and with the light gilding your hair. The sun shines in my eyes and for a moment my heart lifts because I really do think it's you. But, my darling, you are not there, and I stumble down the path with my eyes blinded by tears.

I miss that funny little whistling sound you made while you drafted poems. You never could whistle properly, my love, but it always reassured me to hear it as I dozed in the sunshine and listened to the waves. Sometimes I hear a small sound from a bird and my heart leaps as I think, 'There's Kit!' and I expect to see you just around the corner. I try to run to you, scrabbling up the cliff path and with gorse scoring my arms, but I never manage to catch up. You are always, always just out of reach.

Where are you, my darling? Where have you hidden?

Oh Kit, I miss sitting beside you on the rocks, your hand always holding mine. Sometimes you held it so tightly that I had to release my fingers for a moment, always to slide them back into yours. I would never let you go now, Kit, I promise. If you come back and take my hand again I will hold on and for the rest of my life.

Yesterday I swam again in the cold water and then I snoozed on the beach as we so often did. As I awoke I stretched out my hand for you to pull me close, as I did so many times, but there was no you.

I miss a thousand little things which have no being in words. Days and nights have passed since they say you left, my love, but I cannot believe that you are gone. How did I not know? How did I not feel it? Why didn't you come to me? If you called to me right now I would fly with you into eternity. Gladly. Willingly. But if that is not to be then how can I drag myself through the weary days?

You cannot be gone, Kit. You cannot have left me. I would know it. I will find you and we shall meet again, someday and somewhere.

xDx

To my beloved Kit,

You used to say to me, 'I will love you all of my life', and you did. You did. You did. And I will love you all of my life too. Then, now and forever.

xDx

To my beloved Kit,

I miss your sense of humour. Always you had me laughing at some foolish thing or other. Anything that happened, you could turn into a funny tale. I hope your men appreciated that, my love? And I hope it carried you through those dark days? Forgive me that I never asked more. They told us that we couldn't write anything that might help the enemy and sometimes you told me things that they censored. How that grieved me, to think that your thoughts and your beautiful imagery may be buried beneath those thick black lines.

Kit, I miss your protectiveness, your kindness – always putting me before yourself. Sometimes we would argue because you always wanted to give me the 'best bit' of everything. Your great generosity. You never wanted to keep things for yourself, only for me. Did you know that I always felt I didn't deserve you, a Rivers from the big house? And me just a doctor's daughter, and one with a limp as well. I couldn't understand what you saw in me, my love, when you were the sun, the moon and the stars. Yet you saw something special and you made me feel so loved and so precious. Our time has been cut so short yet I wouldn't trade a moment. Every second we spent together is worth the years of loneliness ahead and the endless searching. I will never stop looking for you. Never.

xDx

To my beloved Kit,

It gets worse, my love. I'm so lonely without you and I am ashamed to admit that some days I don't feel I want to keep trying.

I promise that I will keep your poems safe and guard them forever. You were right: your father and mother would fear them, but your words paint a vivid picture that must be protected for all time. I promise I will keep them safe until you return for them.

I shudder to think that you were in that sucking mud that you wrote about. The noise of the shelling shrieks through every line of your verse, and your images of men turned to carcasses haunt my dreams until I wake up screaming. It's my old childhood nightmare that I now know was a premonition.

My love, they say they never found you. Where are you now? I cannot believe that you are gone from me. Surely I would feel it? There are men who have seen such sights that they have lost their senses, and others cannot even remember their own names. Are you one of them, my Kit? Are you waiting for me to come and find you, take your hand and lead you back? How can I come and find you? Where did you go?

I have searched and searched and tomorrow I will begin again. I will never stop.

xDx

To my beloved Kit,

Missing you becomes worse as time passes, not better. I'm so lost without you. I miss your letters. I miss your touch, I—

"Please don't read any more, Chloe. I think you've read enough now."

Matt places one hand over mine and with the other he gently slides the letters from my grasp. We're sitting in the car, still parked outside Dave's flat, but I've already opened a few of the envelopes in the hope of finding an answer. There's no way I could have managed to wait until we got back to Cornwall. The letters I've read so far are ones I plucked at random, darting back and forth across the decades, but they're enough to prove that Daisy spent the rest of her life missing Kit and searching for him. She never gave up and she never looked at another man.

And she left his poems hidden, in the faith that he would return for them...

So Matt's right: I don't need to read any more of them to understand Daisy's situation. I look down again and realise that I've been crying. Tears have splashed onto the paper and soaked into the decades-old ink. It's hard not to be moved by Daisy's words, even though she wrote them a lifetime ago. It's poignant too that the rounded handwriting I recognise from her diary matured into neat script and finally began to tremble with old age.

Maybe I shouldn't have read any of the letters, but I hadn't been able to resist. I'd hoped against hope that I might find evidence of some kind of resolution, if not a happy ending exactly. Instead, Daisy's loss is as raw at the end of her life as it was the day Nancy Trehunnist inadvertently broke the news. It's almost too much to bear, to think that Daisy – the bright and vibrant Daisy of the diary, who freewheeled down hills and had strong views on women's suffrage – spent the rest of her days pining for Kit and refusing to give up the hope that he would return to her. It's as though I've tapped a bottomless well of grief that's rushing out of me with such force I hardly know whether it's Daisy and Kit I'm weeping for or Neil and myself. Maybe it doesn't matter? Loss is loss.

"She never gave up on Kit," I choke through my tears. "She kept her promise."

Matt passes his hand over his face and exhales. "All those years of studying history is one thing, but this is different. This is real."

I nod. I've read books and worn poppies and seen films, but until now the war was removed from my own experience and I could be appalled and saddened from a distance. Having read the diary, Daisy and Kit feel like friends and the horror of the First World War has become personal. Their lives and those of their friends in Rosecraddick were changed forever. As soon as I opened the hidden diary, their tale was woven into my own. The biting grief in Daisy's letters is the same emotion that's often found me staring wide-eyed into the darkness or made me cry until I all but pass out with exhaustion. If there had been hope that somewhere Neil was alive and waiting for me to find him, would I have given up? Or would the slim chance that he could have lost his memory or been stranded somewhere, maimed and unable to reach me, have sustained me for decades?

I know the answer to this of course, and my heart bleeds for

351

Daisy. I would never have believed it before now, but having that small flicker of hope is even worse than the finality of death.

"Oh, Matt! She never found him. All those years of searching and all those years alone. What a terrible, terrible waste."

Matt doesn't reply. Instead, he leans across to the passenger seat, pulls me into his arms and holds me while I cry. I bury my face in the soft wool of his sweater and breathe in the comforting smell of him, mingled with the scent of his fabric conditioner, until my heartbeat slows and my sobs abate. Then he wipes my tears away with his thumb and drops a tender kiss onto the crown of my head.

"What a waste of all that love and potential," he says eventually. "I can't imagine for a moment that Kit would have wanted Daisy to mourn him for the rest of her life."

I think of the Kit I've grown to know from his poetry and from the diary, and I'm convinced Matt's right. The young man who once held Daisy close and told her that she was free to love again should he not return would have wanted her to be happy. Kit Rivers loved Daisy and true love isn't selfish.

"Of course he wouldn't," I agree. "But the thing is, Matt, Daisy never knew for certain that he was dead. There was never a body or any evidence. All she knew was that he was missing in action. It wasn't conclusive."

Matt sighs. "I think it was, Chloe. Imagine the carnage at the Front when shells exploded. Many soldiers were never identified."

"But she was so convinced he was alive, wasn't she? It's hard to believe she was wrong all along." I shake my head. "It sounds crazy, but Daisy *knew* he wasn't dead. She said she would have felt it here."

I press the heel of my hand against my breastbone as I say this. How can I describe the dull ache deep inside that's always present when I think about losing Neil? There aren't any words for it, but I know Daisy would have felt it too if Kit had been killed in action.

"Denial?" Matt suggests.

"It was more than that. She knew in her heart that Kit was alive, and that was what sustained her. It doesn't make sense otherwise, Matt. Daisy wasn't stupid! She was bright and educated but I think she was realistic too. She must have had the strongest conviction he was alive. She and Kit were soulmates."

"Were you and your husband soulmates?"

Matt's question takes me by surprise.

"Sorry. That was unforgivably rude. You don't need to answer that. It's none of my business. I wasn't meaning to compare..."

The words fade awkwardly and he looks away.

Matt Enys has become my friend and my confidant, and somehow slipped under my defences and into my heart. I half expect Neil to lean over from the back seat and challenge me to say something, but he's increasingly reticent lately so it seems I'm on my own.

Except I'm not on my own anymore. I'm here with Matt.

It's time to talk about my past, otherwise I could end up searching for something that's eternally out of my reach. Neil isn't coming back, and I need to accept that. Our lives pass in the blink of an eye, don't they? Daisy's sad story doesn't have to be mine. It's time I stopped being afraid of the past and instead allowed it to become a springboard to the future.

"It's OK, Matt," I say softly. "I'm happy to talk about Neil. I'd like to tell you about him."

I reach for Matt's hand and weave my fingers through his, savouring the comfort such a simple touch brings and the sweet relief that follows when his hand squeezes mine. As we sit here with our hands linked, I think about the invisible bond that's growing between us – something that's so much more than a physical connection. It's slow and steady and I trust it. It doesn't have the urgency and the fire Daisy and Kit shared, and it doesn't have the history Neil and I had, but that doesn't make it any less valid or precious. Love can come in many guises. And I know now that I'm in love with Matt Enys. It's gentle and tender and has crept up on me, but it's love all the same.

"Neil was my best friend," I begin. "We started dating at school as

353

teenagers and we grew up together. He knew me better than anyone and I knew him inside out too, but soulmates?" I frown as I think about this. "I'm not sure that was how you'd describe us! We argued and we were opposites in many ways. Sometimes I could have throttled him, and he probably felt the same way, but I loved him with all my heart and I know he loved me too. I couldn't imagine being without him. He was part of me, if that makes sense, and when he died something of me died too. Nobody will ever share those memories with me again or recall the silly sayings or all the daft stuff we got up to in our teens. When I lost him, it felt as though I lost myself too."

Matt's fingers tighten. "You sound like soulmates to me."

"Neil would tell you off and say you were being sentimental using an expression like that! He wasn't very good at being romantic. Putting the loo seat down was his idea of romance."

He laughs. "No woman will ever understand just what a big deal that is. It's actually very romantic! But seriously, I know it's not a macho way to think but I do believe in love and in soulmates. Just don't tell the fishermen in the pub that, OK?"

"It's our secret, Romeo!" I tease. "Besides, I bet they're all secretly very romantic when they're at home. Neil did his best, but red roses and slushy words weren't his thing. He was more of a practical person. Too practical at times. Soulmates and the concept of fate wouldn't really feature in his way of seeing the world."

I pause here. Matt doesn't need to know about the neatly made will, the clothes and the shoes all sorted out for me, the list of instructions regarding bills and pensions. Neither does he need to know how Neil told me over and over again that I had a whole life to lead and that he expected – no, demanded – that I lived every minute of it.

"I want you to marry again and I want you to have children and a wonderful life," he'd ordered me just days before he slipped away. His face was thin, the cheeks sunken, but his eyes had burned with the same determination that had persuaded me to go out with him all those years ago and that had ground even the formidable Moira down. "I mean it, Chloe. I don't want you wasting years mourning. If you do, then I swear to God I'll come back and haunt your ass until you get back out there again. I need to know you'll be happy. I *need* that, Chloe! I need it! Otherwise it's all a waste. Love has no limits and it shouldn't be buried. If you don't carry on then what's this been about? If you love me then you'll love again. That's what I want you to do! Can't you see why it's so important?"

I couldn't, and I hadn't honoured what he'd wanted. How could I when I'd missed Neil so much that even opening my eyes in the morning was too much of an effort? I'd been so angry with him too, for saying such awful things. How could he even think of me being with another man? Didn't he care? Didn't he love me?

Only now, sitting in this old Land Rover, with my hand in Matt's and with Daisy Hills' heartbreaking letters scattered on my lap like fallen leaves, do I truly know that it was *because* he loved me so much that Neil said these things. My future happiness was his legacy: he was the one who'd shown me that love was possible and wonderful and the reason for it all. Neil didn't want both of us to stop living when one of us died. Rather, he'd loved me so much that he wanted me to find happiness; he'd given me the hope that it could be found again.

Matt's waiting for me to speak. He doesn't harry me or seek to fill the silence. His index finger skims my hand and then he raises it to his mouth, brushing my palm with his lips and gently folding my fingers over it as though sealing the kiss for me to find later. All the time his eyes hold mine and I see such tenderness and understanding there that my heart swells.

"None of this means Neil didn't love me," I conclude softly. "I think love comes in many different forms and I believe we can love more than once in our lifetime too. Maybe Daisy would have found that out if she'd known for sure about Kit. Perhaps she could have

355

been happy with Dickon, even? He spent his life alone because he never got over the wrong he felt he'd done her."

"So many wasted lives," Matt says. "Gem, Kit, Daisy, Dickon and goodness knows how many others."

I glance at the carrier bag filled with Daisy's letters. Over fifty years of missing Kit and hoping to find him. It's not a tale unique to her either: I can imagine that countless other heartbroken young women did exactly the same. Maybe some were lucky and did find their men, either recovering in a sanatorium or resting beneath a simple marker of white Portland stone. Those kinds of stories would have sustained Daisy in her search, just as much as her conviction that Kit was still alive. I wonder though, did her belief that he was alive fade with the years? It was such a driving force to begin with.

"The road can fork at any point. There are so many possibilities, aren't there, and so many 'what ifs'," I say to Matt.

In answer he lets go of my hand and cups my face, his head close to mine and his lips just a kiss away.

"And what if I said I'm in love with you?" Matt asks. "What if I tell you that you're in my every thought? What would you do then?"

His questions shimmer in the air like a heat haze. I see the road ahead of me split and I know that whichever path I choose now will lead me in a very different direction.

If Matt said he loved me, what would I do? My breath catches and possibilities ripple like wheat in the wind because I know the answer. I reach out and touch his cheek.

"I would do this," I say, leaning forwards and brushing his mouth with mine. "And then I would say that I'm in love with you too, Matt Enys. That's what I would do."

Matt rests his forehead against mine.

"I think that sounds like the perfect course of action," he whispers.

Then he kisses me, deeply and as though he never wants to let me go, and I wind my arms around his neck, melting into his kiss and losing myself in his touch. There's no more need for words. I know that wherever this fork in the road takes us we'll find our way there together.

CHAPTER 10

CHLOE

Time is a strange creature. When Neil died it hung as heavy as wet woollens on a line. I would lie on my bed and wonder how I would make it to the end of the day. To think beyond that was to peer into a void too terrifying to contemplate. My life without Neil yawned wide open before me, empty and unrecognisable, and I had no idea how I would ever manage to negotiate it. Somehow, though, the days became weeks and then months, until I woke up one morning and I realised that almost three years had passed.

Rosecraddick is full of contradictions. In some ways it's a timeless place. Restless waves race up the same beach where Daisy and Kit met, and the same bells ring in the same church tower. The seasons melt into one another as the farmers and fishermen work to the ancient rhythm of the land and the tides. Yet in other ways change comes faster than I ever expect. Once my first Christmas at Rosecraddick had passed, it was a mere blink of an eye before the snowdrops shoved their way through the frosty earth and primroses speckled the verges. Daisies as pretty as their namesake now foam on the banks and nod in the sea breezes, and I wonder whether Dickon planted these as a bittersweet memorial to the girl he felt he'd wronged so badly.

As Easter approaches, the biting winter chill of the Rectory is fast becoming a memory. I find myself opening the windows and filling the old house with fresh salty air that lifts the rugs and blows the curtains, so that the place feels as though it's breathing. I fill jugs with gaudy yellow daffodils, which I carry up to the attic and paint. I even throw caution to the wind and turn off the cast-iron radiators. Most nights now Matt is here to keep me warm, and there's nothing nicer than snuggling up under the covers together and listening to the waves break in the cove.

So, spring is coming and life is returning in a way I suspect is metaphorical as well as literal. When Matt and I drove back from Oxford with Daisy's letters and the faded photos, I made a conscious decision that it was time for a new beginning. The fork in my path was very clear to me and there was a choice to be made. I could follow Daisy's example and focus on the past, dedicate myself to it and become a breathing memorial to grief, or I could do what my husband had asked of me and start living again.

As Matt had driven us both home, I'd rested my hand on his knee – and when we'd eventually arrived at the Rectory, the violet shadows stretching across the lawn and the ancient cedar tree black against the sky, I'd taken his hand and led him up the stairs to my bedroom.

"Are you sure?" Matt had whispered as we'd paused outside the door. "Is this what you want?"

In answer, I'd reached up and pulled his head down to mine and kissed him. It was a kiss that told him just how badly I wanted him to stay. There had been no need to say any more. I'd opened the door and we'd held each other close until dawn's paintbrush had streaked the sky gold and pink and a new day had arrived. Maybe even a new world? I'd curled against him and listened to his gentle breathing, and I knew I was moored in a safe and calm harbour.

We're taking things slowly. I'm still raw with grief at times and although I never see Neil anymore he's never far from my thoughts. Sometimes I need to be alone to think about him and reflect on how much my life has changed. These are the times when I climb the stairs to the attic and paint myself into a trance, finding peace in the strokes of my brush and the swirl of colours on canvas. Moira has nothing to worry about with the commission because the pictures almost paint themselves. While I work I slip back into Kit and Daisy's era, seeing the manor house through their eyes as I recreate the long-lost world of England before the Great War. This has to be some of my best work and I know that if Neil were here he would tell me so. I will always miss him, but when I think of him now I feel so thankful for the years we did share and the memories that still make me smile. Daisy and Kit never had the luxury of time. It's funny how their story has made me see my own anew and even reroute the direction it was heading in.

Matt works hard at Rosecraddick Manor and when he isn't there he has the children to think of. They come to stay at the small converted barn he rents outside the village and I've started to spend time with them. Initially we risk tentative weekend lunches and walks to the beach, before we do more together. The children are curious at first, but as the weeks pass the novelty of my presence wears off and we fall into a comfortable pattern of spending the weekends as a foursome watching films and cooking dinner at Matt's place before I return to the Rectory. It's a little coy maybe but there's no hurry. Life, I've come to realise, will pass at the right pace; there's no need to race or stress. When the twins lean into me as we watch a film together on the sofa, my heart melts and I know for certain it isn't just their father I'm falling for. With Matt Enys and the children, things as simple as buying groceries or baking a cake become joys, and I wake up now with excitement about the day ahead.

I never thought the day would come when I would say this, but Perky Pippa was right all along: time really is a healer – if you let grief do its work. I wish with all my heart that Daisy Hills had discovered this.

Life in the Rectory has changed too. Matt and I often cook dinner together on Mrs Polmartin's old range. His contributions are big curries, while I experiment with the fresh produce I find at the local farmers' market or make lasagne so hot it scalds our tongues. We found an old sofa on Freecycle and placed it in the sitting room so that we could curl up and watch the flames dance in the wood burner while we talked late into the night. We talk a great deal, Matt and I, and we never run out of things to say. He tells me about his marriage break-up and his sadness at being apart from the children so often, and in turn I talk about losing Neil and recount funny stories about our teenage years. It no longer hurts to remember these anecdotes and I often find myself laughing. Sometimes I even sense Neil in the shadows, smiling and shaking his head with embarrassment at some of his daft antics.

The house is still far too big for one person and filled with echoes of the past, but imagining Daisy being here and picturing Nancy sneaking a kiss from Gem in the scullery makes me feel less alone. These people from the past are old friends and we live alongside one another very companionably. Matt has made me a copy of the diary and I reread parts of it from time to time, but it's painful to equate the lively and determined Daisy who bursts from those pages with the elderly woman who'd spent her entire life searching for a lost love. Sometimes I go into the church and look at the window badged with Dickon's clumsy attempt at atonement and try to make sense of it all, but I always fail. There's something I haven't grasped, I'm sure of it: the final piece of the jigsaw's still missing. Love doesn't just end or give up. Daisy never did. And the thing is, she was convinced that Kit was alive. What if she was right? What if he hadn't died in action at all? But surely that's impossible?

Oh! It's so frustrating not to know! Stained-glass Kit, with his eyes raised to heaven and with angels escorting him into the clouds, is still keeping something back. But what?

"Maybe we'll never know?" Sue Perry said one time when she came across me squinting up at the window. "Perhaps some things are meant to remain a mystery. What if Daisy had found Kit and he'd been so shell-shocked that he didn't even recognise her? Maybe ignorance is bliss?"

"She would have been overjoyed to see him no matter what," I insisted. Daisy had loved Kit unconditionally. Broken or whole, she wouldn't have changed her feelings for him. No matter what Daisy might have discovered at the end of her search, she would never have walked away until she'd known for certain that she'd exhausted every avenue.

While I've been focused on my painting, Matt's continued to work on the manor house and to help his colleagues with further research into Kit's poetry. The Lost Poems, as the documents from the wall have come to be known, have caused considerable excitement in the literary world. Interest in Rosecraddick Manor is building too, just as Matt had hoped. Several national papers have run features on Kit, and a BBC crew's keen to film a documentary. Although the Manor's still closed, Matt tells me that he's asked at least twice a day by visitors whether they can come in and look around.

"I think the love story's really captured people's imagination and added a whole new dimension to things. Hopefully we'll have a lot of visitors," he tells me. "This place may well pay for itself after all, which will take a huge amount of pressure off the Kernow Heritage Foundation."

It's so good to see the strain fall away from his face when he says this. The worry of the finances and the future of the house have weighed heavily on Matt, more heavily than I ever realised, and I send Daisy a silent *thank you* for helping to lift the burden. Matt's right: Kit and Daisy's story will draw people in. I just wish that the ending to it wasn't so abrupt. I can't shake off the feeling that there's more.

When I'm not painting I still volunteer at the Manor, although when I do come over Jill's so cold towards me I'm in danger of getting frostbite. She once caught Matt kissing me hello and gave me such a disapproving look I thought she was going to put us both in detention. Sue and Tim, on the other hand, are thrilled we're together, and Matt and I are now regular visitors to the New Rectory for pizza nights. I'm putting down roots in this Cornish village that my husband was so fond of, and it feels right. Loving Matt hasn't lessened my love for Neil; if anything, falling in love again has reaffirmed what I felt for my husband. I was so adored by Neil that I know that love, when found, is worth holding onto. The more you give, the more there is.

I know that Daisy Hills felt exactly the same way.

As the days become lighter and the holidaymakers return to the village, the manor house finally comes together. The rooms have all been cleared and are undergoing their last renovations before the house can be dressed and arranged. The icing on the cake will be the tour up through the Manor to Kit's tower, where an exhibition about his poetry and World War One will be set up. At some point there'll be a room dedicated to Daisy too. The Kernow Heritage Foundation is currently in talks with the Hills family regarding this, and Matt is very excited.

In addition, Trehunnist Autos is sponsoring a multimedia experience that'll take visitors back in time to Cornwall during the Great War. A team of builders has just started on the project by taking down the plasterboard in the rooms above the solar and the entrance hall. Matt's convinced that Kit's family would have slept in these rooms, and he's hopeful that some of the original features will have survived beneath all the later adaptations. The coach house and stables have already been converted to a tea room where Jill and her trusty volunteers will serve lunches and cream teas, so there'll be an extra stream of revenue from that. Matt's quietly optimistic that with the heightened interest in the newly discovered poems, the documentary and the added romance of Kit and Daisy's love story, Rosecraddick Manor will be the Kernow Heritage Foundation's greatest success story.

The Manor's big opening is planned for the Easter weekend and the village is buzzing with excitement. If I'm a little sad to be sharing Daisy and Kit with everyone else, then I do my best to keep this selfish emotion to myself. Daisy would want Kit's poetry to be shared and I know she'd be thrilled to see him receive the recognition he deserved. But as for her own part in his story? She never breathed a word about it when she was alive and I hope that by including her we haven't disrespected her wishes. She wanted to be a writer though. Through the diary she did tell a story, so I like to think she'd be pleased. Her unsent letters have been returned to the Hills family for safekeeping, but they've kindly loaned the Kernow Heritage Foundation her engagement ring and have insisted that her diary should remain at the manor house with all her precious treasures. Daisy stays close to Kit this way, which feels right.

The week before Easter brings mild weather to Cornwall. Light breezes make the sleepy daffodils nod and unseasonal sunshine sends holidaymakers to the beach. With my completed paintings carefully packaged and waiting to be couriered to Moira, I find myself at a loose end. Rather than starting something new, I decide to walk to Rosecraddick Manor and catch up with Matt. It's a beautiful day and I'm going to help the volunteers working in the gardens. I might not have the greenest of fingers but my weed-pulling skills might come in useful. Besides, after weeks of being cooped up painting, I'm looking forward to some fresh air.

"Hello, stranger!" Matt says, looking up from his laptop with a smile when I find him in his office. The sun slants through the diamond-paned window and his dark hair is glossy in the light. My heart lifts at just the sight of him. "I take it the paintings are all packed up and ready to go?"

I nod. "All finished and done. Can you believe it, Matt? I really thought I'd never paint again."

"I never had any doubt you'd do it. You're the most talented, determined and sexy woman in the south-west."

I put my hands on my hips and give him an outraged look. "Just the south-west?"

"Err, I mean the entire world? If not the universe? Will that do?"

"You're off the hook," I say.

Matt abandons his work to pull me into his arms and kiss me. I kiss him back, delighting in the sensation of his arms around me and the pure joy of the embrace. Desire curls in my belly and I marvel at how just a kiss can fill me with darts of longing.

"Yes, definitely the most beautiful, talented and sexy artist in the universe!" he affirms when we break apart.

I'm about to reply when a loud throat-clearing interrupts us. Dale, the foreman of the building team, is standing in the doorway looking awkward.

"Sorry to interrupt, Matt, but there's something you need to come and have a look at."

"Your timing's awful, Dale," Matt groans. "Please tell me it isn't dry rot or deathwatch beetle?"

"No, nothing like that. It's a building issue."

"Can it wait until tomorrow? The Project Manager will be back then. I'm not much use to you, I'm afraid. Not unless you want a history lesson."

"You might want to give him a call, mate?" The foreman suggests. "The thing is, Callum got a bit carried away with the wrecking bar when he was taking the plasterboard off..."

"Something tells me I'm not going to like the next part of this story," Matt says, wincing. "You're going to tell me there's a bloody great hole in the wainscot underneath the plasterboard, aren't you? As in, the wainscot that needs to be preserved?"

"Afraid so, boss. We've been rushing to try and get it all finished by next week and Callum was a bit overenthusiastic. Anyway, it's not just *that*. There's something else."

"There's more?"

"Yeah, there's more – but don't look so worried. We haven't trashed anything else. We've found something really odd and it doesn't make sense to us, but it might do to you lot. Come on."

Intrigued, Matt and I follow Dale upstairs and through the rooms above the entrance hall, until we reach the final chamber directly over the room where Lady Rivers burned Daisy's letters. Without the featureless plasterboard in place, the original panelling is laid bare. At the far end of it, a fireplace has been revealed. Sure enough, there's a big hole in the panelling on the right-hand side and I see Matt flinch.

"We knew a fireplace would be there because it connects to the flue below," he begins, but Dale interrupts him.

"It's not the chimney I'm showing you. Well, not exactly. It's this. Look." The builder pulls his phone from his jeans pocket, turns on the torch and directs the bright beam into Callum's handiwork. "This part isn't connected to the room behind, although it ought to be. See? There's no light coming through from that room. It's totally hollow. It looks to me like there's a tiny room next to the chimney breast but behind the panelling. Weird, huh?"

"No, not weird at all. Absolutely brilliant!"

"Brilliant?" Dale echoes. "Can I have that in writing before Kernow Heritage Foundation sues my company for damaging priceless panelling?"

"I don't think they'll do that. You've found something very exciting. This is a priest hole!" Matt's buzzing with this discovery. "I thought there might have been at least one at some point, given what we know about the family who lived here in Elizabethan times. I never could figure out how the tower room would have worked as one, though – it's far too visible. They must have been using this little cubbyhole instead. What a great find!" He turns to me. "Come and have a look, Chloe. It's fascinating."

I step forwards and peer in while Dale shines the light. The smell of dust and age hits me and as my eyes adjust I make out a small room barely big enough to sit in – and something on the floor, which looks like a book.

"There's something in the far corner," I say, puzzled.

Matt peers over my shoulder. "You're right. What on earth is it? Hey, Dale! Can we get the rest of that plasterboard off right now, but maybe with a little less enthusiasm?"

"Do you need to call someone to check it's OK before I get going?" Dale says, poised for action. "Like I said, mate, I don't want to be sued."

"The Foundation wants the plasterboard removed in any case, and you're nearly there anyway," Matt replies. "I'll check in with the Project Manager first though."

He pulls out his mobile and, after a brief conversation, gives Dale the thumbs up. "It's all good. Go steady and let's see what's there."

Dale nods. "No probs. Give us ten minutes and we'll be clear."

While the builders set to work we stand back and watch. Matt takes my hand and I feel him trembling.

"This is incredible," he says. "I wonder what's inside?"

As the plasterboard falls away I shiver. What else is lurking in the dark? The remains of a long-dead priest, starved to death while trying to hold out on those who hunted him? Are his bones bleached with age and pearly in the gloom? Part of me wants to run into the bright spring sunshine. Another part is transfixed by the slow striptease of the old house as she reveals her secrets.

Finally, the last chunk of plasterboard is prised away to reveal the dusty wainscot. Matt stands beside the fireplace, passing his hand over the old panelling and frowning.

"These priest holes were carefully concealed, but perhaps for this one there's a place on the panelling that will release a catch, if you know where to press. It's worth a try, anyway."

He presses his palms against the wainscot. His fingers reach high and low until there's a loud click. One panel swings back and a hole gapes open. All I can see are blackness and cobwebs. I step away, repelled by the musty stench and the darkness, but Matt has no such reservations and squeezes inside as best he can, stooping and turning sideways to cram his tall frame into such a small space. Seconds later, he reverses out again clutching a cracked leather document folio. It's dusty and cobwebby but, even so, there's no mistaking the embossed initials.

C.R.

Matt and I lock eyes. We both know what this means, even if we don't quite understand it.

C.R. Christopher Rivers. Kit.

"Shall I open it?" Matt asks me. There's uncertainty in his voice. "I think there are documents inside and I'm pretty certain they're his."

My thoughts are swirling. If Kit hid anything in such a secret place it's because he wanted to make sure it was safe. But safe from whom? His mother? The servants? People who had no right to look at it? People like us? Or did he use the priest hole in the hope that at some point it would be discovered? Is there something in here we need to know? More poems maybe? Or a childhood diary?

I imagine Daisy leaning over my shoulder. The jigsaw is nearing completion.

"Open it," I whisper.

It's time for Kit to speak. He's been waiting to do so for a very, very long time.

CHAPTER 11

KIT, 1916

It was strange how he'd once been able to think so clearly, to distil images into just a few sharp words or contain outrage inside the twist of a metaphor. In battle he'd been decisive and fast, his brain never fogged by fear or mired by confusion. In love, too, he had chosen once and never deviated. His mind had been a blade and his thoughts slices of clarity. But that was a different time and a different world. Now, when he needed so badly to write, the words wouldn't come. No vocabulary existed to describe what had happened to him or to pretty up the grotesque he had become.

Fragments of ideas whirled and danced in a storm that never stilled or settled. He found himself in the laudanum-heavy hinterland between sleep and wakefulness, where wind blew rain against the glass, footsteps scraped across boards and hushed voices tightened with concern. He floated on these sounds a while before spiralling back into the deep place inside, where soft arms held him and warm lips brushed his. He tried to call her name and beg her to stay, but the explosion had shattered language as well as limbs and nothing remained but gurgling.

Daisy.

Her name had been his charm. It was the amulet he'd worn into every battle and each gut-churning patrol. It had kept him safe for so long. When his men had wept or, broken by the horror, fallen senseless to the ground, it was only Daisy who'd kept him from buckling. He would have given away his inheritance in a heartbeat to keep hold of his greatest treasure: a faded photograph blurred by the caress of fingertips, and fraying where it had been folded. He couldn't have lived through it all without bringing her to the forefront of his mind. Only the determined tilt of her chin and the clear gaze that stared out from the picture could dredge his courage up from the deepest place. In the insanity of this conflict, this Hades of mud and wire and confusion, it was her he fought for. The politics were meaningless now, the enemy as confused and as afraid as him. From what Kit saw of the miserable prisoners they took, they were just like his own men, except for their languages being different. The dreams of fighting for Shakespeare and Keats and an Albion seeped in the golden haze of nostalgia were long over. Kit simply fought to stay alive and to return to Daisy. She was everything.

When he snatched a few moments to write, it was poetry that spewed from his heart and the lines he scrawled were for her. There was no holding back; to do so would have been an insult to her intellect. Instead, Kit penned savage imagery that would doubtless sicken and appal her. He was determined, as was she, that there would be no gulf of understanding to bridge when he returned. There would be no need to explain or to pretend it had been a jolly boys' jape. She would have seen the Front through his eyes and shared the horror.

He often pictured her walking along the cliffs with the salt wind snatching her hat and turning her skirts into sails. She'd turn onto the sharp steep path and climb down to their cove, where she'd open the letters and pore over the stanzas. He visualised her biting her bottom lip, and those curls of damson and fire falling into her eyes and then being pushed impatiently away. The image of her sitting on the rocks reading his poetry was so vivid that he would be jolted to find himself in a narrow bunk rather than at her side.

Kit had kept alive for her. He lived for Daisy's letters, with their news of a world once familiar but now as remote from his own reality as anything written by Homer or Sophocles. The anecdotes about Mrs Polmartin trying to catch chickens made him smile and the description of the storms that chased across the bay transported him back to those long-lost days of boating and swimming. They seemed like fairy tales now. Kit's world had become one of gunfire and death and eyes gritty with lack of sleep, but Daisy was his lifeline back to another time. Her letters and love would lead him back. Kit swore he would return to Rosecraddick. He wasn't going to die here in the alien mud. He would go home to Cornwall and one day lie beneath the soil there, but it wouldn't end here. It couldn't. He would do anything, *anything*, to leave this place alive. He was going home. He was.

The gods had heard Kit and granted his wish, but how they must have laughed. Like Tithonus granted immortality but not youth, he had been gifted life shrouded in a living death. Kit had little memory of that last day at the Front. It was like any other, with the long hours of waiting, the cold and the rain and the sudden flurry of activity when the orders came. His legs dead from inactivity, Kit staggered from the outpost trench to the main trench, a route he'd taken a hundred times before, when a shell exploded and launched him into the air like a surprised khaki-coloured bird in full flight. Kit knew he must have lost consciousness, and he certainly owed his life to whichever men had risked theirs to drag his mangled body back to safety, but after this there were just echoing chambers of emptiness. Even his dreams had been blank. When he eventually awoke in the hospital, he wanted nothing more than to sink back into them – or, more fitting still, sink into that restful mud where in centuries to come a farmer might plough up his bleached bones. Anything was better than a half life. A half-remembered line of poetry drifted through his memory.

Oh happy men that have the power to die.

They had taken him home to Rosecraddick Manor. He'd known this because the smell of the salty air and the cries of the gulls had seeped into his dreams. Nightmarish scenes of rotting flesh and bloated corpses, blackened and familiar as he passed them on routine patrol, were smudged by images of rolling waves and inland seas of rippling wheat, wooded hills and warm brown eyes. Voices and movements, light and shade. And then the bowel-loosening realisation that all he once was and all he'd once hoped for had been blasted away.

Dr Parsons was here at times. Emmet the butler too. Shame and embarrassment were soon forgotten and, although they never spoke, Kit felt the other man's pity; it hurt even more than the wounds. Reverend Cutwell sometimes came to pray, but Kit turned his face to the wall. Hadn't God turned His face away from Kit and all the men at the Front? Prayers were meaningless. There was no God. Or at least, not the loving forgiving kind. Mars and Pan and Odin were real now, and they had taken from him all they wanted.

Kit's face was bandaged and his eyes were closed beneath the linen, but he learned to identify his visitors by the way they entered his room: the awkward clearing of his father's throat and the tap of his stick over the boards, or his mother's scent, the cloying violets summoning a flood of childhood memories and uncurling weakness deep in the pit of his belly. Although she couldn't hold his hand, he sensed her sitting beside him. He heard her cry, and beneath his bandages damp crescents bloomed as Kit wept too. Everything had changed. All was dust.

Drifting on the opium-laced tide, Kit sometimes overheard hushed conversations he was never meant to hear. His father gruff and disappointed; better to have a dead hero son than this maimed shell. The doctor, concerned and wanting to send Kit to London to a specialist hospital. His mother, adamant that he would stay at home with them. Emmet said nothing but Kit knew from the gentleness of his touch, as tender as any woman's, that he alone understood the depth of Kit's despair. Kit had called for Daisy in his nightmares, but when he was awake he shuddered at the thought of her seeing him so reduced and without coherent speech. If she ever heard him try to call her name, nothing would keep his Daisy away – and what good could come from two lives being shattered?

This room, the furthest from the family quarters and above the solar, was his world now. Nobody was to know he was here. His father was revolted by his son's injuries and ashamed to hear him making mangled sounds and sobbing with nightmares. This wasn't the stuff of *jolly japes* and *giving the Huns a good thrashing*. This was something that the Colonel didn't – couldn't – understand. Real soldiers didn't wake up screaming or shake with nerves. They came home in flag-festooned coffins or with crutches and medals. They were heroes and to be paraded as such, sons to be proud of. The pieces of Kit that had returned couldn't be slotted back into any pattern his father might recognise. The Colonel's only answer was to hide his broken son away. Kit understood and he didn't blame the old man. He was damaged inside and out. A ghost of his old self. Better if he had died that day.

Sometimes as he lay in silence Kit thought maybe he had died after all. Words had left him and snatches of verse ebbed and flowed through his mind. The days slipped into weeks and months. Emmet changed his dressings and spoon-fed him small sips of soup and gruel that made him splutter and puke. He might walk again, Dr Parsons thought, and some of his sight was coming back too. In time a man could learn to live without an arm, but the damage to his face could never be undone. There were no mirrors in his room but Kit didn't need them to know that the reflection wouldn't be pretty. It was surprising how indiscreet people became when they thought you were unconscious.

He was a creature doomed to live in the shadows. He could never expect Daisy to love him like this, and neither would he want her to. His beautiful girl deserved more and Kit would never expect her to keep her promise to marry him. Far better that Daisy Hills believed he had died in action; perhaps then she could find happiness with another man. It was a thought that pained him intensely, but she was made for love and passion and deserved more than a life sentence as his nursemaid. Kit wanted his Daisy to be happy.

There was nothing ahead for him now but a gaping void. The emptiness terrified him more than his injuries. He was learning to stop himself from thinking about Daisy, knowing that if he kept the memories locked deep inside he might just be able to keep control. If he gave into them, he would tumble into a dark place from where there would be no returning. Kit's soul belonged with hers and wrenching it away when he longed for her so much was a second living death.

In his sickroom, hidden away from the life of the house, it was hard to know how much time had elapsed. A few months, Kit thought, although he wasn't sure. Some days passed in a blur of pain and others dragged so slowly they were little deaths in themselves. On one occasion his mother sat by the bed and took his hand in hers, and coughed out desperate, angry tears and a mangled confession about burning letters. His letters to Daisy, Kit had realised. Daisy must have come to find him, and been closer to doing so than she would ever know, and his mother had shooed her away like a cockroach. His brave Daisy. How much courage must it have taken for her to come here, knowing how his parents felt about her?

"I was afraid, Kit. She was so determined and so adamant you were still alive," his mother had pleaded. "God forgive me, but I was cruel to be kind. I only wanted her to go away and to leave us in peace. It was the best thing for everyone."

His mother was right but Kit had wept into his pillow that night as he'd thought of Daisy scrabbling in the fireplace, the heat searing her hands as she tried to save his letters. His mother hadn't said as much, but he knew this was what Daisy would have done. Then she would have walked away with her head held high, as dignified as any duchess his parents might have hoped for him to wed. Kit knew that Daisy had gone away, because Reverend Cutwell had mentioned it, but he hadn't wanted to hear any more. Like the past, his future with Daisy was a foreign land; it was one he would never see again. It was best to put her from his mind.

Little by little he had started to walk about the room. When not plagued by headaches, he could read for a while – and often he stood in the window gazing over the gardens. Yet he was careful to avoid being noticed, even by the servants. Accordingly, Kit kept to the shadows. Once he was strong enough to walk greater distances unaided, he ventured about the house, albeit only at night. With a wide-brimmed hat pulled low over his injuries and a bandage to conceal the worst of the damage, he was almost amused at this new incarnation of himself as a gothic creature – Quasimodo maybe, or perhaps Frankenstein's creature, created not by science but by war?

He couldn't compose poetry anymore and he had set Daisy free, but something in Kit couldn't rest. Maybe it was the writer in him or maybe it was the ego screaming that he shouldn't be forgotten; whatever the reason, he felt compelled to record his empty days. For whom, he did not know. For himself perhaps, as a kind of solace.

On his late-night wanderings Kit collected the things he needed, piece by piece, and stored them in his room. The brief excursions exhausted him for days afterwards, but once he had what he needed there would be no reason to leave again – or at least, not of his own accord.

Paper. Ink. A pen. His leather portfolio from school. Laudanum pilfered from his mother's still room. These were prizes he would secrete away until the time was right to use them.

He knew of a perfect hiding place, too. In the old wainscot by the fireplace was the long-forgotten priest hole. Kit had discovered it by chance as a boy and hidden there for hours while his nanny hunted everywhere for him. The tiny room had been musty and dry and cramped, even for a small boy. He'd shivered to think of a grown man crouched there, holding his breath and clutching his prayer beads in his shaking fingers as the house had been searched. Still, it was ideal for his purposes now. Kit's left hand, maimed and clumsy, had fumbled with the mechanism and something close to delight had filled him to see that the door worked as well now as it had in his childhood. Thanks to the ingenuity of its craftsman (Nicholas Owen, he presumed), Kit was able to secrete the stolen items away and nobody would ever be the wiser.

With these things in his possession Kit knew what he had to do. He would have to do his best to write with his left hand. The first attempts were shaky and childish and he hurled them onto the fire in a fit of frustration. Days passed. Chest infections burned and chilled him without mercy, while nightmares held him in an iron grip. By the time he was ready to try again the leaves had fallen from the trees and the fields were scalped. Even the year was fading away. It was fitting.

Kit knew he had to focus; he couldn't allow himself to drift on the tide. Each day that he turned his head away from the spoons of broth Emmet fed him was a day he became weaker. Before long there were whispers of tubes and force-feeding. Dr Parsons visited and the vicar too. Kit would have to act soon.

It was a drab December night when Kit finally knew he was ready. The wind hurled rain against the windows and puffed its icy breath beneath the door. Carpets lifted in the hallways and Kit's candle flickered. He retrieved his items from the priest hole, hauled himself to the table and spread out the paper. Then he exhaled slowly and allowed himself to think about Daisy. This time he wouldn't slam the doors on his memory or close his ears to the pleas of his heart. What harm could it do for this one final night? She would be the last thought he would ever have and her name would be the last mangled sound he would utter.

Unbidden, an image of Daisy laughing up at him came to Kit. She was so vivid that for a moment she was real again and he was whole and able to hold her close, smell the honeyed warmth of her skin and feel her soft curves pressed against his chest. He shut his eyes but the vision departed as swiftly as it had come, drifting away from him like dandelion seeds in the summer breeze. Others followed: a flash of slim thigh kicking through blue water, a glint of red curls, hands linked, a boat rocking gently in a hidden cove...

Tears dripped onto the paper. Kit dashed them away with the back of his left hand, then picked up the pen so that his heart could speak for one last time. He hadn't intended to write to Daisy – she would never see this letter, would never know that he had come home as he had promised – but in these last and darkest hours there was nobody else he wanted to tell his story to. She was the only one who mattered.

My darling Daisy…

The script was clumsy and his hand lagged behind the racing of his thoughts, but he no longer cared. The moon rose and the sky was dusted with stars as Kit began his letter; when he'd finished it, the stars had hidden away and the first larks were calling.

Time was running out.

Kit felt strangely relieved as he folded the paper and pressed it against his lips. Maybe there was something to be said for confession after all? Others who had hidden away in this room must have known this, and the sense of comradeship soothed him.

Kit tucked the letter into the portfolio, then placed this tenderly on the floor of the priest hole. It seemed fitting that his last confession of love should hide there, away from prying eyes. Then he clicked the door shut and darkness swallowed his letter for who knew how long? Maybe forever? It no longer mattered. Writing it was the part that had counted, Kit realised. It was an unburdening of the soul. Wasn't that what his best poems had really been about?

He wondered whether Daisy would keep his poems a secret or whether she would share them. He would never know, of course, but Kit trusted her with the innermost workings of his mind just as much as he'd trusted her with his heart. Daisy would always do what was right; her integrity was one of the things he loved so much about her.

It was also why he had to make this final choice for them both.

The sun was rising now and the sky beyond was peachy with promise. Morning was coming for some, but for him an eternal night would follow. Kit was gladdened by the thought of rest because he was so, so tired. He was tired of being sick. Tired of pain. Tired of needing Emmet for the most basic of functions. Tired of hiding from windows and reflective surfaces. Tired of dreams that left him shaking and cold with sweat. And most of all he was tired of longing for the woman he knew he had to let go.

Kit picked up the bottle of laudanum and raised it in a toast. No nectar could be sweeter.

"To you, Daisy." The words rose from the depths of his soul; they were the clearest sounds Kit had spoken for months. "Be happy, my love."

As he drank deeply and the room began to blur, Kit's last thoughts were filled with flame-red curls, laughing brown eyes and butter-soft kisses. He drifted away on the waves, just as a mermaid girl had once drifted into his heart, and when they found him shortly afterwards, it seemed as though his poor damaged lips were smiling.

CHAPTER 12

CHLOE

Matt and I stand in the window, the letter laid out on the crumbling wooden sill. I'm struggling to make sense of everything because there's been too much too fast: a torrent of new facts sweeping away what I thought I once understood and leaving behind the detritus and silt of a new realisation.

Kit Rivers wasn't lost in action at all but had been terribly, catastrophically injured. His wounds had been life-changing and, to his mind, too awful to inflict on the woman he loved.

I stare at the letter. The spidery writing is shimmering and blurring and I'm in danger of falling apart right here in this dusty room. Grief scoops out my chest. I know it makes no sense because Kit died a century ago and Daisy's long gone too, but the emotion that flows with the ink is as raw now as it was on the night Kit Rivers sat down to write his last words. Although nothing has changed in this room – the builders are still hacking away at plasterboard while the radio plays in the background – everything is altered. The passing of time hasn't soothed anything: Kit's suicide is devastating.

Kit was angry as he wrote, frantic to pour his words out onto the paper before the dawn and exhaustion caught up with him. The writing judders at times, and the pen spat inky tears onto the paper and gouged out sections as he rammed the nib against the page. There's a lifetime of love, regret and longing here. On these pages are the same commitment to tell the truth that scalds through his poetry: an honesty that meets horror face on and never flinches. It's awful to know that moments after he scrawled his name at the foot of the page Kit had shut his letter away, not knowing whether it would ever be found, and reached for the laudanum. He was determined to set Daisy free in the only way he believed possible. As my fingers brush the paper I shiver, knowing that the last hand to touch it was Kit's own.

"You were wrong, Kit," I murmur. "She didn't want to be set free. Daisy wanted to be with you and she wouldn't have cared how injured you were, because she loved you."

Daisy's instincts had been right all along: her heart, her loyal and true heart, hadn't misled her. Kit Rivers had survived. He had lived and while she'd searched far and wide for him he had been only steps away. What an awful, tragic truth. Worse still, his decision hadn't set her free at all. For as long as Daisy lacked answers, she would continue to seek him. Unknowingly, Kit had bound her to him as tightly in death as he had in life.

"Christ," Matt groans. "Poor man. What a mess. What a bloody, tragic mess."

Horror stalks around the edges of Matt's words. He can't speak of it outright and I understand. It's easier to allude to what happened to Kit than to meet it head on.

"He was here all along. That was why Daisy was never able to feel that he'd died in France and why the records were so vague. I can't bear it, Matt. It's so cruel," I whisper.

"They must have brought him home secretly, while pretending he died in action," Matt says. "Colonel Rivers was still influential within the regiment so it wouldn't have been impossible to arrange, especially in the confusion of battle. There were fewer servants at the Manor too, so less eyes to see what was happening. I'd imagine it would have been relatively simple to have said it was the Colonel who was incapacitated, especially since he'd already been unwell."

"I don't understand it. Kit was injured but he was still alive! Why did they feel they had to lie? He was still a hero, even if he was so badly hurt."

Matt spreads his hands hopelessly. "It was a different time. There wasn't the understanding of these things that there is now. Bear in mind that this was the first time that a war had been fought like this. Those kind of injuries had never been seen before and there was no precedent. There are countless stories of young men who were so dreadfully altered that their wives and sweethearts rejected them – and many more turned to drink or took their own lives. They were ashamed of what they had become."

"But that's awful!"

"Awful yes, but true. For some a return to civilian life was almost impossible. Their injuries were so frightening to behold, so dreadfully conspicuous, that they were socially marginalised and even referred to themselves as 'broken gargoyles'. Thanks to medical advances and the work of men like Daisy's father in field hospitals, they survived shrapnel wounds and other injuries – but piecing shattered lives together was often far harder."

He's slipping into lecturer mode, but I know Matt Enys well enough to appreciate that for him this can be a means of coping. Losing himself in his work is just another way of bearing grief. Some of us run away. Others spend a lifetime searching and some, like the one my heart is breaking for, can only see the darkest of answers.

"I've never heard about this before."

"No, I'm not surprised. It wasn't commonly spoken about then or wholly understood. Plastic surgery was only in its infancy, although there were specialist hospitals. Some men wore special masks to hide missing jaws or noses or mouths; some never spoke again and many had to have specialist nursing and feeding for the rest of their lives."

"That's what Mr Emmet was doing for Kit?"

Matt nods. "I think so. He'd been the Colonel's batman and I imagine he would have been stoic when it came to battle injuries. He was also fiercely loyal to the family and wouldn't have breathed a word to anyone. The other servants probably wouldn't have been allowed in the vicinity, so they'd have assumed it was the Colonel who was unwell."

"When Daisy visited the Manor, Nancy's sister told her that the Colonel was behaving oddly and had shut himself away," I recall. "Only it wasn't him at all, was it? It was Kit. And they had so few servants left at that point anyway that there weren't enough people to think too much of it. Oh! It's horrible to think Kit was shut away in the shadows so close to Daisy. I know she wouldn't have cared what he looked like as long as he was alive! She loved him!"

"But don't you see? This wasn't just about love – or rather, not in the sense that we've come to understand it. It wasn't about the injuries either, or at least not in the obvious way that we might assume. Kit knew his parents didn't approve of Daisy and that they'd never have allowed him to marry her. Defying them meant having to get a job to support both himself and Daisy, and then, hopefully, their children. That was what Kit had had in mind, if you remember. But with his injuries, those plans were scuppered. How could he take care of Daisy and provide for her? How could he find work? He was dependent on his parents now."

"Daisy would have worked! She would have provided for them both!" Tears of frustration spring into my eyes. "Why did Kit deny her the chance? Why was he so selfish?"

"Do you really think that of him? He was a proud young man, Chloe. Women didn't even have the vote, although the tide was starting to turn, and Kit would have had certain ideas about what was expected of him as a husband. He wouldn't have wanted to be a burden on his wife and he wouldn't want to see Daisy struggle. Kit believed he couldn't deny her the future she deserved. He thought he was setting her free. He was ill too and traumatised. Shut away from everyone, and with no counselling available, is it any wonder he became desperate?"

I'm silent because I know Matt's right. It's too easy to see Kit with my twenty-first-century eyes, but he was from a different era. I also know from what Daisy wrote in her diary just how highly principled he was and how adamant he'd been that he would forge a career that would keep her and the family they hoped to have. Could he have denied her the life they had imagined? Could he have let her go without or live a life of hardship?

Kit Rivers couldn't. No matter how much he'd longed for Daisy, he loved her too much for that – just as Neil had loved me too much to want me to be alone mourning him for the rest of my days.

A tear rolls down my cheek and splashes onto the dusty floor, and my heart aches for Kit's misplaced courage. Unable to burden Daisy, and knowing that his elderly parents would struggle to care for him, he'd taken the only choice he believed remained.

But he was wrong. So terribly, terribly wrong. There was so much still to live for. Kit's death was a waste of love and life and talent. Worse, in taking his life, Kit had taken Daisy's future away – the last thing he would have wanted. Nowadays there would be all kinds of help and support available for him but, as Matt says, the early twentieth century was a very different time. Suddenly I feel thankful for Perky Pippa.

"So Kit overdosed." I'm not asking, but Matt nods anyway.

"Laudanum."

"I've heard of that. Isn't it the stuff all the romantic poets were off their heads on?"

"That's right. It seems crazy now, but it was a popular drug in the nineteenth century and pretty much prescribed for anything from menstrual pain to settling babies. It was better regulated by the early twentieth century, but I imagine Lady Rivers would have been stockpiling it for years, and with the local doctor in on Kit's secret it wouldn't have been difficult to come by. I bet they had gallons of it at the Manor."

Secrets. Secrets. I turn to Matt as sudden understanding dawns. "Reverend Cutwell knew Kit was alive! That's why he left everything to Daisy. He felt guilty for lying to her about Kit."

"When Kit died the Reverend would have felt a whole lot worse," Matt says grimly. "So many secrets taken to the grave. The loyal servant who never spoke a word. The doctor bound by the Hippocratic oath and the vicar who could only tell God. When the Colonel died there was only Lady Rivers left, and of course she would never breathe a word. No wonder the poor woman nearly went out of her mind with grief. She must have blamed herself for sending Daisy away when Daisy was the only person left who could have given Kit hope and something to live for."

I've wanted to hate Lady Rivers for what she did that day. It was cruel and spiteful but fear does strange things to people. Even Daisy, shocked and distressed, had written that Kit's mother looked frightened. A cornered vixen, she'd snarled and threatened in order to guard her cub.

"She was trying to protect Kit the only way she could, but she got it wrong, didn't she? Daisy would still have loved Kit and he would have had something worth living for."

"No wonder she spent a fortune on his window and published any poems she could find. She must have felt she had a lot to make up for," Matt says. "I wonder where they buried Kit in the end?"

"The churchyard?" I suggest.

"Maybe. I guess we'll never know without Reverend Cutwell to tell us."

While the builders carry on around us, ripping away the centuries and oblivious to the impact of their discovery, Matt and I look out of the window, across the courtyard and to the rosemary garden planted by Lady Rivers – a grieving mother who would spend the rest of her days tortured by the knowledge that she'd turned away the only person who could have kept her son alive. That garden where she spent so much time during her last years must have been her only solace.

A rosemary garden for remembrance.

Suddenly I feel as though I'm trying to clutch smoke in my hands: there's something there, something real and tangible, and if I can only catch it and hold on I think I'll know the answer to Matt's sad question.

The garden…

The garden!

I grab Matt's hand. "I think I know where Kit is!"

He doesn't question me, and without saying another word I lead him through the manor house and out through the gardens. Wood pigeons' calls tremble in the air and the sun feels warm on my skin, but I don't pause to enjoy these things; instead, I tug Matt across the lawn and through the door in the wall that leads to Lady Rivers' rosemary garden. We brush against the plants and the air's heavy with scent. Memories bloom just as the original designer intended, until we arrive at the centre where the seat invites reflection. I've walked this path a hundred times before but I never realised until now what I was looking at. I can't believe we missed it. Kit Rivers has been hiding in plain sight all along.

Captain Christopher 'Kit' Rivers

Beloved Son

1896–1916

'Their name liveth for evermore'

"This isn't a memorial, Matt. It's Kit's grave."

Matt's holding my hand so tightly that it hurts. He's shaking.

"I think you're absolutely right. He was here all the time. He was always here. Poor Daisy; he wasn't far from her and he wasn't far from us."

As we stand in the garden, bathed in the spring sunshine, my heart aches for Daisy Hills, whose lifelong search for Kit led her everywhere but back to the starting place. Sometimes the thing we long for the most is where we least expect it to be, there all along and simply waiting for us to recognise it. I know that Neil, if he were here, would agree. When Matt pulls me into his arms and rests his chin on my head, I close my eyes and allow the peace of the garden to wash over me. This sense of coming home isn't just about Kit.

"We found him for you, Daisy," I tell her quietly and from the depths of my heart. "Wherever you are now, I really hope you know that."

And when the soft breeze whispers back to me through the rosemary fronds, I feel certain that she does.

EPILOGUE

CHLOE

Frost sparkles on the path and rimes the shivering rosemary bushes. Amidst them a poppy wreath lies on the memorial stone, shockingly scarlet against the pale marble. The day is bitingly cold and nips at my face as I walk through the silent garden, my gloved hand held tightly in Matt's. Above us the sky is a blue dome where gulls soar and freedom beckons, the freedom that Kit and Gem and Dickon and millions of other young men fought for, and for which they paid the ultimate price.

Impossible to think that World War One ended all those decades ago today. At 11 a.m. on the eleventh day of the eleventh month, the people of Rosecraddick gathered at the war memorial on the cliffs to lay wreaths and pay respects to the fallen men of the village. Their faces may be unknown to us now, but their names live on and we will never allow them to be forgotten or their stories to fade with the years. After we observed the silence, Matt read Kit's poem *God Hid His Face* and the powerful words punched the air and the gut alike, just as Kit had always intended. His writing, and that of all the other soldier poets of the Great War, will make sure that we never forget. Whether we understand or learn from the mistakes of the past is another matter. Kit's verse warns the reader over and over again of the ultimate cost of failing to do so.

As we remembered the dead, I glanced across the bay and watched the waves hurling themselves onto the hidden coves where Daisy and Kit once swam and picnicked and made love. Sometimes I think I see them out of the corner of my eye or hear the swish of skirts or the sound of laughter. Daisy and Kit are always out of reach yet never far away. I'll turn to catch them, but no matter how fast I spin on my heel I'm never quick enough. They're already gone, running through the churchyard to the cliff path or tearing away in a big motorcar, scarves blowing in the wind and rounding the corner in the lane so fast that all I catch is a blue blur.

The memorial stone in the walled garden was lifted and the remains of a young man was discovered beneath. The body was sent away for a forensic examination, but Matt and I hadn't needed to wait for the test results to confirm that this was Kit Rivers. I stayed away when the tent was erected and the white-suited figures arrived, but Matt was there and he saw the medals still pinned to scraps of khaki and the remains of once golden hair. The forensic report noted that there'd been catastrophic damage to the skull and right arm, but we'd already known this from Kit's letter and none of it came as a surprise.

At this point the story had been picked up by the national and international media. There was a surge of interest in both Kit's poetry and the ill-starred romance with Daisy, on a scale that would have seemed impossible just a few months earlier. His tragic death provoked sympathy and raised questions about the treatment of war veterans that were as poignant now as they had been then. I think Kit would have been proud that his story is making a difference.

The opening of Rosecraddick Manor attracted huge numbers of visitors, as did the airing of the BBC documentary. Shortly afterwards, a major publisher bid a significant amount for the Lost Poems. The Kit Rivers Society which, sure enough, had been willed the rights to his work by Eunice Rivers-Elliott all those years ago, suddenly found itself in possession of more money than it could ever have imagined. Not only that, but more funding became available for the manor house. Already, plans are in place for a bigger tea room and an extended Great War exhibition. Matt's even been approached by a Hollywood film director keen to use the story. Daisy and Kit's romance has gripped the public's imagination and there can be no doubt in anyone's mind that she was his muse and the great love of his life. Daisy Hills is no longer lost in history's labyrinth, and her search for Kit is over.

The Lost Poems have received much critical acclaim. Perhaps eventually Kit Rivers will even be spoken about in the same breath as Owen and Sassoon and Brooke. Yet he's far more than this to me – he's as real as I am or as Matt is. He's not just a gifted poet and a visionary: he's the young man who drove fast, loved to sail and fretted over his troubled relationship with his father. He's the boy who wandered the lanes and cliffs, and fell in love with the red-haired girl who floated in the sea in her shift like a mermaid come to life. That Kit, the real Kit, needed to be laid to rest at home. When there was talk about Poets' Corner, Matt argued passionately against it. Kit belonged at Rosecraddick, he said. This was where he was born and it was the place he loved and where he'd chosen to die. There was simply nowhere else he ought to be. He belonged in Cornwall.

Christopher "Kit" Rivers was finally laid to rest on a late August day once the crowds of visitors had left and Rosecraddick Manor's gates had closed. There were only a few of us present: the Hills family, Kathy Roe and some of the key members of the Kit Rivers Society, and Sue Perry took the simple service. As she intoned the familiar words, I twined my fingers with Matt's and let my mind wander away from graves and death to scenes from Daisy's diary. Happy memories of swimming and hiding out in hay barns on rainy days, of making promises, of kisses as soft as butterflies' wings, and of the golden glow of a long-lost summer.

I thought about Daisy and Kit and how they'd known a love that was stronger than war and time and even death itself. My journey with Matt was just starting out, but I was certain we also knew that depth of feeling – and hopeful that the years would be kind and allow us to tell a story of our very own. Once Sue had finished her part, I stepped up to the grave and dropped the lock of hair Daisy had so treasured onto the small oak box that held Kit's remains. Following that, the Hills family released the sparkling daisy ring into the darkness.

"It seems right," Dave's father had explained afterwards, looking rather embarrassed. "I know lots of people will think we're crazy burying a diamond ring, but it feels that it should be there. My aunt was a funny old stick, set in her ways and very determined, but she loved that poor young man right until the minute she closed her eyes. Her engagement ring belongs with him. That way, a part of her will be there too. I think she would have liked that."

Matt had nodded. "I'm certain she would."

So now, on the eleventh day of November, all these decades after the so-called "war to end all wars" was over, Matt and I stand by Kit's grave and quietly think about the lives that were given so freely. Not just the lives of the boys either, but those of their wives and sweethearts and mothers whose worlds also changed forever. There were so many sacrifices and so many lost stories, so many broken hearts and shattered lives, that it's impossible to count them all, and so many events that were beyond the control of this lost generation. By remembering Daisy and Kit, perhaps we can go some way towards honouring them all – and maybe we can learn something too? I can only hope so; that way their sacrifices weren't in vain.

So Daisy and Kit's tale is told. All those years ago, Daisy's ashes were scattered in the bay by her brother and she floated amid the sea spray and the cry of the gulls until Kit was finally able to join her. They're together now and they're free. I can't explain how I know this; it's simply a certainty that resonates deep within me. It's the same knowledge that tells me that Neil, my much loved and forever missed husband, is at peace too – and it's the same conviction that says Matt and I were also destined to be together. Love has no limits. Love isn't bound by time. And, ultimately, love is why we are all here today and why we carry on.

So today, as Matt and I pause in the centre of the rosemary garden, our breath forming white plumes in the icy air, I think about how Daisy and Kit managed to fit a lifetime of love into the few months they were granted. Their story will go on to touch so many lives.

I hope they're finally at peace.

Then Matt inhales sharply.

"Chloe! Do you see that? Is it real?"

I follow his gaze and gasp. Lying on the marble is a solitary daisy, as fresh as though it's just been picked from a summer meadow. A finger of sunlight creeps across the garden, parting the rosemary fronds and lighting upon the little white flower.

I turn to Matt. I see a smile in his eyes, which I know he must see reflected in mine, because here is the answer I've been searching for. This is what Neil was trying to tell me all those months ago.

Nothing is ever forgotten because love never ends.

I take Matt's hand in mine.

"It's love," I say softly, "and there's nothing more real in all the world. Love goes on forever."

THE END

Dear Reader,

I really hope you've enjoyed this book. It's a novel that's very important to me, as it's a fictionalised homage to my Great-Aunt Ella's own tragic love story. Her fiancé, Arthur Sidney Bacon, was lost in action in 1917 and Ella spent the rest of her life searching for him and wondering what happened to him. Her loss, one that was sadly not unique, is the inspiration for Daisy and Kit's story. The author's notes below explain this in far more detail. This book is written for Ella and Arthur. To unite them here after one hundred years apart means a great deal.

I spent a lot of time researching the lives of young men and women during the First World War and I feel humbled by their bravery and sacrifice. There are so many stories, from those of the young men who fought in conditions of unimaginable horror, to the women who nursed them at the Front, to those who stayed behind to 'keep the home fires burning'. Each story is full of courage and paints a picture of a generation who sacrificed everything so that future generations might enjoy the privilege of peace. Wilfred Owen's *Anthem for Doomed Youth* at the start of the book sums up some of the horrors and appalling losses suffered. I would like to thank the Wilfred Owen Association for granting me permission to reproduce the poem here.

As always, if you enjoyed this book please leave a review on Amazon, Goodreads or any other sites or pages that are relevant. I would also really appreciate it if you could tell other readers about *The Letter* so that my great-aunt and her fiancé's story, and indeed the stories of all those brave people who inspired the book, live on in Daisy and Kit.

x Ruth x

NOTES FROM THE AUTHOR

The inspiration for *The Letter*

This wasn't a novel I expected to write. I was set to begin my next Polwenna Bay book (and I was looking forward to it) but one of the strange things about being an author is that books never do what they are supposed to and they all have their own timings.

My parents were having a clear-out and my mother came across some old family documents, a tin and some pictures. Among these were faded sepia photographs of my great-aunt, Ella Hills, and her fiancé, Arthur Sidney Bacon. I was struck by how young they both were and by how modern they looked. I remembered Aunty Ella as a rather austere and, to my small child's eyes, scary old lady. She lived alone and had never married. My granny had once told me how Ella's entire life had been spent hoping her fiancé might return from the war. I didn't understand back then what this meant but now I learned that Arthur had been declared missing in action during World War One. Like so many soldiers, his body was never found and there was no funeral held for him or grave to visit (hence Wilfred Owen's *Anthem for Doomed Youth* at the start of the novel). Ella had no solid proof that her fiancé had died and no closure. He was last seen in hand-to-hand combat at the Battle of Cambrai on 30th November 1917.

Ella refused to believe that Arthur was dead and hoped that he may have been in hospital, suffering from memory loss or shell shock. Perhaps he had even been so dreadfully wounded that he didn't want her to know he was still alive? She spent years searching for him in France and Belgium, always hoping that she would find him in a hospital or sanatorium. She wrote endless letters to the Red

Cross and never gave up hope. She even enlisted the help of her Member of Parliament. She left no stone unturned.

My great-aunt never married or had a family of her own. She never loved another man and, like so many of her generation, the life Ella should have led was ended on the battlefield. I was really moved by her unwavering belief that Arthur was still alive. My great-aunt's tenacity and loyalty were incredible and the future that was stolen from her was another tragedy of war. She is the inspiration for Daisy.

Like Daisy, my Great-Aunt Ella enjoyed writing. Some letters and notes in her Bible are all that remain of this pursuit. A 1914 Princess Mary tin, some medals and some faded pictures of her fiancé in uniform were all she had left of Arthur. I have correspondence from the Commonwealth War Graves Commission which states where Arthur's memorial is in northern France, but no other details of him survive. Theirs is a lost history and a bleak example of futures destroyed by conflict – a tragedy that was repeated millions and millions of times across Europe.

Ella never wrote a novel or told her story, and I felt that I needed to do this for her before her story was lost. My granny has passed away and my mother and my uncle are the only people left who know the details. Ella left no property or diaries, and much of what I know about her has been gleaned from stories my grandmother told me and what my mother remembers. The character of Daisy Hills shares many of my great-aunt's characteristics as well as her surname. Like Ella, Daisy Hills is determined, educated and independent.

I couldn't find out much about Arthur Sidney Bacon. He seems to have slipped from history, but he must have been very special to have held Ella's heart for an entire lifetime. I had little more to go on than a faded picture of a handsome boy in uniform and my imagination. He served with the 10th Battalion King's Royal Rifle Corps and died when he was only twenty-five, during the Battle of Cambrai. His name is carved on the Cambrai Memorial in the Louverval Military Cemetery in France. His body was never recovered.

At this point I was also reading Siegfried Sassoon's memoirs and Wilfred Owen's poems. I began to imagine Kit as the heir to a big country estate. He is privileged like Sassoon; like Owen he dreams of being a poet and, like Arthur Bacon, he has a sweetheart he loves dearly. At odds with his traditional father and longing to write, Kit already has issues with family and class expectations. The social differences between Kit and Daisy are intended to add to the tension and the romance. These also explain why their relationship is kept a secret and their story remains unknown.

Why I chose the title *The Letter*

I wrote this book before I thought about a title. To call it after Daisy would give the first third of the novel away. I considered calling it *The Window* but this title didn't excite me. It was only once I had finished the book that I realised the hidden letter in the priest hole is the key to the whole story. It also proves that Daisy was right all along: Kit wasn't dead but less than a mile away from her. In the context of the early twentieth century, Kit truly believes he is doing the right thing for Daisy. Tragically, he underestimates her and the consequences. The letter is the only point where we hear Kit's voice and it is the final piece in the puzzle, which reunites the young lovers.

Why I didn't write Kit's poems

I would never presume I could write poetry that would do justice to the horrific experiences young men like Kit, Gem and Dickon witnessed – and I felt very strongly that Kit's poetic voice had to be authentic.

As I undertook research for the book, I read the poems and memoirs of Siegfried Sassoon, the poems of Rupert Brooke and, of course, the poems of Wilfred Owen. I had studied Owen as an undergraduate and taught his work countless times at GCSE and A level. Approaching his writing with this story in mind, I was staggered by the power and immediacy of the language. He truly does convey the 'pity of war'. Like Owen, Kit Rivers refines his poetic voice in the crucible of action and slaughter. I have chosen to leave the reader to imagine Kit's verse and have hinted at poems by First World War poets which contain similar sentiments and subject matter.

Why does Daisy vanish in the third part of the story?

Daisy slips away from our sight. In contrast to the vibrant girl we grow fond of, who defies class and convention to see Kit and who has the courage of her convictions to search for him, the Great-Aunty Daisy that Dave Hills talks about is a shadowy figure. We don't learn much more about her life other than that she became a nurse and searched extensively for Kit. She never married or became a writer but, like so many other women of her generation, lived a quiet and rather lonely life. Daisy's later years echo my Great-Aunt Ella's. The future she dreamed of was extinguished by the coming of war. Not all stories have exciting or happy endings. Chloe is upset when Dave doesn't seem interested in his great-aunt, but to him Daisy was a distant and rather forbidding old lady, just as my Great-Aunt Ella was to me. Chloe and the reader have got to know the real Daisy through the medium of her diary and we see her very differently. Daisy is symbolic of a lost generation. She doesn't die in action but quietly fades away as the years pass. Of course, she has a whole life and career we never know much about, but she chooses to have her ashes scattered at the place where she met Kit and fell in love. Her entire life is spent missing him.

Why Daisy didn't return for her diary or the poems

Daisy is a pragmatic young woman. Once she leaves Cornwall the search for Kit is her focus. She knows his poems are safe and she has his picture, the engagement ring and her memories to sustain her. By the time the war is over and she has returned to England, her godfather has died. A new vicar would have been appointed to the living of Rosecraddick. Daisy knows Kit isn't in Cornwall, so there's no need for her to return there. She's convinced he's still alive and she will not rest until she finds him. She doesn't seek to publish the hidden poems because she believes these belong to Kit. She is the guardian of the poetry and Daisy never feels she has the right to place them in the public domain.

397

Why the present frames the past in *The Letter*

I didn't set out to write a historical novel and I don't view *The Letter* in this way. Rather, it is a story that includes a journey into the past in order to help the heroine, Chloe Pencarrow, come to terms with her present. I wove details from both periods into each narrative, as I wanted the reader to feel that the past is never far away from our present. When we meet Gem Pencarrow we see aspects of his descendant Neil Pencarrow reflected in him, and we remember that Gem's name is written in the memorial window. Gem's future, like Kit's, is already sealed.

When I finished writing Daisy's section of the book I felt a real sense of loss. I shared Chloe's anger that she had become little more than a barely remembered maiden aunt. My Great-Aunt Ella was once as vibrant and as passionate and as determined as Daisy Hills, and writing the book helped me to see her this way. She is somebody I admire very much.

Chloe's interest in the past becomes her means of healing and the start of a new life with Matt, continuing the idea that past and present are hand in hand rather than linear.

Where the book is set

I live in beautiful Cornwall and I am exceedingly lucky to be surrounded by fantastic scenery. From the dramatic coastlines, to secret coves, to rolling countryside – it's all here. This is also a county where the veil between the past and the present feels very thin. I live near the River Fowey and it gives me shivers to know that Daphne du Maurier walked past my house. Like me, she would have sailed her boat along this creek and out to sea. It's a timeless place.

Rosecraddick is my own blend of Talland Bay and Fowey, a seaside town on the Cornish coast where there are plenty of hidden coves and beaches for young lovers to meet. Talland Church overlooks the sweep of Talland Bay and is the inspiration for St Nonna's. The war memorial can be found on the cliff path halfway between Talland and Polperro. It's impressive and there's a real sense of timelessness and peace as the waves roll towards the shore. The names carved on the cross are still borne by local people and friends of mine. It's truly sobering to see how many families lost members. Some, like the Trehunnists in the story, lost every male over the age of eighteen.

Military action

I never intended *The Letter* to be a war story. It's a novel about loss and love and the tenacity of the human spirit in the face of what seems like a hopeless cause. The First World War is the catalyst that divides Daisy and Kit, just as it divided Ella and Arthur, and the narrative is concerned with the impact of this rather than with the battles and events at the Front. My interest is centred on the microcosm of the everyday tragedies of lives shattered by the conflict – the Ellas, Anne Trehunnists, Dickons and Mrs Polmartins – rather than the horrors of trench warfare. There are many authors who write powerfully about the action and the trenches, but it was not my aim to take my readers to the Front but rather to concentrate on the private battles fought at home. I have deliberately left out details of battles and offensives.

Sympathy for Dickon

As I researched the novel and immersed myself in the world of the early twentieth century, one of the things I realised was that the main characters are very young – the age of the students that I (and Chloe) taught in secondary school. Dickon is eighteen and, like most eighteen-year-old boys, he is filled with confidence and feels invincible. Good-looking, relatively wealthy, and strong, he's used to being admired and would have been considered a good catch for any young woman in Rosecraddick. When Daisy turns him down he is shocked as well as hurt. Dickon's spiteful behaviour is a symptom of his immaturity and has consequences he could never have imagined. Dickon is another character whose life is destroyed by the war. He suffers from shell shock and when he returns from action he is utterly changed. We learn that he is consumed with guilt and believes God punished him for his past behaviour. Dickon spends the rest of his life atoning for this. His clumsy attempt to join Daisy and Kit through the daisy in the window is how Chloe begins to explore their story – so, ultimately, he does reunite them. Dickon ended his days a different man to the brash boy Daisy knew, and my feelings for him are sympathetic rather than judgemental. His lesson is a very hard one.

Premonitions and the supernatural

The story is filled with a sense of foreboding. Daisy's childhood nightmare foreshadows the events that take place later in her life. The séance that Daisy attends is symptomatic of the growing fascination with the occult at this time as the bereaved sought to make sense of their losses and find comfort. Mrs Polmartin's longing to contact her son and Nancy's desire to reach Gem are understandable – although whether or not one believes in spirits coming through is a matter of personal opinion. Daisy certainly doesn't, but when Kit doesn't speak it is an affirmation of some kind that he is still alive.

For Chloe Pencarrow, it's a comfort to be surrounded by the world of 1914 and a welcome distraction from her own grief. Her interest in Kit and Daisy becomes a means of healing for her. She speaks a lot to Neil and sees him about the place too, more at the start of the novel than at the end. Is he a ghost or does she imagine him? We know Chloe has had a breakdown and comes to Cornwall to recover and paint. Does Neil vanish because he was only a figment of her imagination and she no longer hallucinates or needs the idea of his presence as she recovers? Or is it only when she begins to live again that Neil can slip away, at peace in the knowledge that the woman he loves is happy? These are questions for the reader to answer.

Ruth Saberton

SIGN UP FOR MY NEWSLETTER TO FIND OUT ABOUT FUTURE BOOKS AS SOON AS THEY'RE RELEASED!

You might also enjoy my other books:

Runaway Summer: Polwenna Bay 1
A Time for Living: Polwenna Bay 2
Winter Wishes: Polwenna Bay 3
Treasure of the Heart: Polwenna Bay 4
Recipe for Love: Polwenna Bay 5

Magic in the Mist: Polwenna Bay novella
Cornwall for Christmas: Polwenna Bay novella

Rock My World
The Season for Second Chances
The Island Legacy
Escape for the Summer
Escape for Christmas
Hobb's Cottage
Weight Till Christmas
The Wedding Countdown
Dead Romantic

Katy Carter Wants a Hero
Katy Carter Keeps a Secret
Ellie Andrews Has Second Thoughts
Amber Scott is Starting Over

402

Writing as Jessica Fox

The One That Got Away
Eastern Promise
Hard to Get
Unlucky in Love
Always the Bride

Writing as Holly Cavendish

Looking for Fireworks
Writing as Georgie Carter

The Perfect Christmas

ABOUT THE AUTHOR

Ruth Saberton is the bestselling author of Katy Carter Wants a Hero and Escape for the Summer. She also writes upmarket commercial fiction under the pen names Jessica Fox, Georgie Carter and Holly Cavendish.

Born in London, Ruth now lives in beautiful Cornwall. She has travelled to many places and recently returned from living in the Caribbean but nothing compares to the rugged beauty of the Cornish coast. Ruth loves to chat with readers so please do visit her Facebook author page and follow her on Twitter.

Twitter: @ruthsaberton
Facebook: Ruth Saberton/author
www.ruthsaberton.com

Made in the USA
Middletown, DE
20 October 2020